THE LAST GIFT

THE LAST GIFT

God Stones Book 5

OTTO SCHAFER

Sound Eye Press

Copyright © 2023 by Otto Schafer

All rights reserved.

No part of this book may be reproduced in any form or by any electronic or mechanical means, including information storage and retrieval systems, without written permission from the author, except for the use of brief quotations in a book review.

All characters and events in this publication are fictitious and any resemblance to real persons, living or dead, is purely coincidental.

Published in 2023

ISBN 979-8-9860760-3-4 (hardback)
ISBN 979-8-9860760-2-7 (paperback)
ISBN 979-8-9860760-4-1 (ebook)

Cover design by Damonza
Editing by The Blue Garret

Sound Eye Press
www.ottoschafer.com

For Kristen.
Your feedback often drove me to shake my fist in the air and curse, but after many deep breaths, I always buckled down and worked your suggested revisions. Words cannot express how much I appreciate you and all that you've taught me about writing. Thank you for the past five years of dedicated work editing this project, and cheers to a future filled with many more stories desperately in need of your help!
Oh, and could you please help me edit this dedication?
—Otto

Contents

Part I
THE FIRST WAR

1. A Brand-New View	3
2. We Continue Forward	7
3. First Contact	14
4. The Voice	20
5. The Chase	25
6. Pull Back	32
7. A Grave Mistake	39
8. Born Anew	46
9. The Name on the Wind	52
10. Battle at the Wall	60
11. The Second Question	71
12. Fallen	79
13. A Face in the Crowd	89
14. The Seer	99
15. Spin the Bottle	112
16. Lady of the Lake	117
17. Night Slayer	132
18. The Deal	144
19. Nyana	151
20. The Brightest Glow	162
21. Soup to Nuts	168
22. Fish Fingers and Fire	179
23. Ice Ember	188
24. The Queen of Sky	200
25. Mist Storm	211
26. Soul and Ellis	229
27. Love Ember	240
28. A Promise Kept	246
29. A Sister's Secret	251

30. The Dark Narrow	257
31. Fistfighting Fire	273
32. Kilug	282
33. You Could Be the Hero	298
34. Only Skin Deep	305
35. Dragon Runes	317
36. The Offering	329
37. The Mazewood	336
38. What Good Are Gods?	348
39. Cloud	357
40. King Deep	365
41. The Chase	372

Part II
THE PROMISE AND THE SACRIFICE

42. The Failure of James Paul	381
43. The Sentence	387
44. No Escape	395
45. Not a Single Chair	398
46. Step Up	405
47. A Restless Night	421
48. Fragile Alliances	436
49. Onward to Osonian	444
50. Nightmares and Dragons	463
51. Please, Please, Please!	471
52. The Sea Goddess	475
53. Karelian Coffee	480
54. Bring Down the Wall	490
55. The Confession	495
56. Fatal Error	501
57. Chain, Bone, and Scales	506
58. Behind the Wall	510
59. The Golden Staff	519
60. No Way Out	529
61. Lead from the Front	535
62. Stand Witness	542
63. Purple Rain	551

64. Mercy	558
65. Now Is Our Moment!	565
66. The Irony of His Fate	568
67. The Lowest Class	572
68. The Wish	578
69. Road Trip	588
70. So Long	594
71. Reunited	603
72. The Walk	621
Epilogue: Turek	630
Acknowledgments	641
About the Author	643
Sign Up to Read More	645

PART I

THE FIRST WAR

1

A Brand-New View

God Stones – Moon Ring 1
The Portal, Karelia

Garrett and his sages darted through the portal from Earth to Karelia. As they stepped into another world, Pando's voice echoed in his mind. *Do not forget your promise, Garrett Turek. Six months from this day. Fail me, and humanity dies!*

Behind him, the portal snapped shut, blinking out and leaving them assaulted by cold air and the smells of sweaty nephilbock and the coppery tang of spilt blood.

A heavy weight pressed upon Garrett's chest. What had he done? The door to Earth was gone, and he'd left the Keepers of the Light behind. Six months. Six months to find a magical item that would allow the trees of Earth to remain unbound. If they failed Pando, the queen of trees would order everyone on the planet to be slaughtered, including the Keepers, Bre's dad and brother, and Garrett's mom. He felt like he was going to be sick, and the smell wasn't helping.

Breanne's hand squeezed his own. Pulling him back to

the moment. Damnit, focus, he told himself. Apep was dead, Jack had the Sound Eye, and Gabi was here somewhere and in danger. He swallowed dryly, sharing a silent look with Bre that said so much. Garrett met her eyes with determination and nodded. Everything they had was gone – everything but the tasks before them and each another. The first tasks were to get their bearings and find Gabi. She and the small dragon had come through the portal before them, charging after Jack's big three-headed dragon.

In the distant sky, a dragon swooped low and roared. Flames shot downward, vanishing into a valley Garrett couldn't see from his current position.

"We should move," Paul said, eyes sharp as he swept his pistol left, then right.

Breanne nodded, her eyes darting around the strange place. "We need to find Gabi."

Still clasping Breanne's hand in his, Garrett stepped forward. A breeze kicked up, whipping snow past them in a cyclone of purple flakes. The horrible stench of battle was replaced with the familiar smell only a crisp snowfall leaves behind. He drew in a welcome breath as the strange-colored flakes flecked his cheeks.

They were standing on a stone floor, like the temple roof back on Earth, though this one was dusted with snow. Above him, stone spires tilted in to meet in the middle, forming a polyhedron, but there were no walls. It was like standing inside the massive skeleton of a pyramid. Ornate symbols were etched into the stone of each spire, similar to the dragon runes on his arms, chest, and back. Pulling his eyes from the apex above, he walked forward to where the stone met the edge of a grassy hill that sloped down away from the open pyramid. The others followed cautiously.

Garrett's eyes widened as the view from the top of the hill revealed a long, open valley full of giants and elves battling with sword and shield, while dragons crowded the sky above, flying in seemingly random patterns. The valley was flanked on both sides by an overstuffed forest so thick with foliage he couldn't tell where one tree ended and another began. The otherworldly canopies seemed to tangle, giving the valley borders the appearance of massive hedgerows.

Something beyond the dragons, high in the distant clouds, caught Garrett's eye. He tipped his head back to consider the strangeness of what he now realized was not one but many peculiar-colored moons peeking between a scattering of purple clouds. They had to be moons because across the sky two suns shown distinctly different from one another, casting rays of both yellow and white light onto the battlefield below.

"Look," Lenny said, pulling at Garrett's attention.

"There are so many, you guys! Thousands. Let's not go down there!" David said, his voice cracking with terror.

"The elves must have had their army already on the battlefield. It's like they were expecting an attack," Paul said.

Lenny pointed. "Not at the battle! The other side of the valley! The wall between the mountains. And what the hell is that sticking up from behind it? Is that a… a tree?"

Governess stepped alongside him. "The tree! Could it be Goddess Druesha?" she asked in awe.

Garrett squinted. What must have been a few miles into the distance beyond the battle, a grey wall rose from the valley floor high into the sky, taller than any wall Garrett could have imagined. On both sides, the structure met colossal mountains, nearly matching them in height. How was it possible anyone could have built such a thing? But more amazing was the massive canopy of a tree visible rising above, and yet some distance beyond the wall. How could a tree stand taller than a mountain? That couldn't be right. A tree couldn't be that… that big. It was impossible, wasn't it?

"Someone please tell me what I'm looking at?" Garrett asked.

"It looks like a wall alright!" David answered.

But Garrett wasn't talking about the wall.

Lenny shook his head. "I thought those were some kind of strange mountains, but it's definitely a tree. There's something else, though. What are those blobs hanging from its branches?"

"Those aren't blobs, guys," Pete said, his eyes narrowed and crackling with Sentheye. Super-vision, the result of his exposure to the God Stones back in Petersburg – back when they'd all thought their heads were going to pop. "Those look like cities hanging from the branches!"

"Cities hanging from a tree?" Breanne asked, but her eyes weren't focused there. She was scanning the area around them, searching for Gabi. "Where the hell could she have gone?"

From over a rise to his left came the sound of snapping jaws, growling, and a pained roar.

"Oh, that didn't sound good!" David said.

Gabi's voice filled Garrett's mind. *I'm sorry, Zerri, but Azazel killed my family!*

2

We Continue Forward

God Stones – Moon Ring 1
The Creators' Mountain, Karelia

"You liar!" Ereshkigal shouted, ripping her hand away from Turek's, breaking the physical connection and with it the rules they had all agreed upon. Sit in the circle, maintain their physical connection, and – above all else – do not interfere. Before Ereshkigal's outburst, following the rules was exactly what they had been doing.

From the Great Hall located in the heart of the Creators' Mountain, the seven creators had been peering through the pool of Sentheye they encircled. This was their window to the world below, and through it the creators observed the portal open between Karelia and Earth. With bated breath they'd watched as the great dökkálfar king of Osonian stepped through onto Earth and, with the help of Breanne Moore, beheaded Apep. It was this very action that set off Ereshkigal, creator of the dökkálfar. In the chaotic moments following Apep's death, thousands of nephilbock and dragons filled the valley between Osonian's Great Wall and the portal on the hill. The battlefield below became instantly engorged with conflict and spilt blood. Perhaps most concerning, Jack Nightshade now held the God Stones connected in their most powerful form: the Sound Eye.

Turek looked down at his empty hand, dread filling him.

The radiant creator, Ereshkigal, shimmered with angry Sentheye as she floated up from her seated position. For Turek and his brethren, their true form was a shape very much like a human or dökkálfar, or for that matter, a fairy, gnome, dwarf, and countless other species. Two legs, two arms, a torso, and a head. Their physical bodies, though, were not of flesh and bone but Sentheye itself – the source of creation. Beneath Ereshkigal, the pool of Sentheye dissolved into an unadorned floor that looked as if it were hewn from gemstones. Though beautiful, it was now void of the magical window. However, this was not what filled Turek with dread. With the physical connection of the circle broken, there would be no way to ensure Turek's brethren, the other creators, would not choose to be in two places at once. Thus, there would be no way to know if they were obeying the rules agreed upon or interfering with their favorites.

"There was no deceit on my part, Eresh!" Turek pleaded, holding out his hands.

"He's right, sister! There is no way Turek could have known ye boyo Apep was going to lose his head! We were all physically connected!" said Durin, the creator of dwarves.

Rán, mother of the sea and creator of her favorite, the mermaid, shot daggers at Durin. "No, it is our sister who is right. Apep is dead!" She turned her icy glare to Turek. "And now your human possesses the Sound Eye! Yet you expect us to believe this is not some clever orchestration? You play us for fools, Turek! And you, brother Durin – you may play the fool, but I refuse!" She released her hands from the others'.

"I've already told you – Jack is not mine. He is something else now," Turek said, his eyes flashing to Typhon.

Aurgy, the creator of the nephilbock, spoke from his light form, which now was no bigger than the others' forms, but still his voice filled the Great Hall oceans deep. "I'll tell you what he is. He's an abomination. I agree with our sisters. We will not be taken for fools!"

The creator of trees, Druesha, spoke next. "Treachery on your part, despite the innocence you portray. Even if it isn't so, brother Turek, how can you expect us to remain idle? How? We must cleanse this mess before it gets out of hand."

"How is one boy, human or dragon, any worse than one dökkálfar bent on revenge?" Turek asked, his hands radiating the light of Sentheye as he held them palms out. "I thought we were past this. I thought we would sit and see. This is the promise you made to me. I know the Great Mother is at work in our favorites, but this is the only way I can show you that she not only watches but is very much influencing our creations. You all agreed! You agreed to see my proof! Besides, do you really think I would have made it so this boy, Jack, blood bonded to a dragon with three heads, acquired the single most powerful item in the universe? Great Mother, to what end?"

Ereshkigal hovered above the floor. Her and the others' inner light reflected off the massive stone columns supporting the hollowed-out mountain top. Nearby, a crystal stream flowed quietly through the center of the hall, capturing their light in its prisms. The Sentheye-born light refracted and reflected in ever-changing patterns brought on by both the creators' movements and mood. "Oh, I think it is much worse. A dökkálfar would know better than to attack Metsavana," Ereshkigal said.

At these words, the Great Hall fell quiet. Metsavana was not only the greatest tree in Karelia, he also maintained the balance of the natural world. Should harm come to Metsavana, everything the gods had created would come undone.

"Jack Nightshade has not harmed the great father tree. Which reminds me, brothers and sisters, why were the dökkálfar allowed to wall in the great city upon my departure? This was to be the one place where all were welcome to trade and make offerings to Metsavana. You shut the world out, Eresh? As if the Forest Father was for yours alone?"

"We won Osonian fairly, Turek. You and yours fled. You hold no judgment over what we've done in your cowardly absence," Eresh snapped.

Aurgy looked at Typhon. "Neither dragon nor giant have ever been welcome at the father tree."

"Perhaps this is because yours are always eating the others," Rán snorted.

"Our focus must be the Sound Eye," Ereshkigal said, her patience clearly ebbing.

"Jack only holds the Sound Eye. It doesn't mean he knows how to use it," Turek countered.

"I've heard enough," Typhon, creator of dragons, said.

Turek sighed. Typhon, the most influential of the seven creators. This was unfortunate, as Typhon's next words would surely sway his brethren. Thinking back, Turek couldn't think of a time when Typhon had ever agreed with him. Now it seemed this whole thing would be over before it truly started. All of this – the prophecy, the death of so many good people, the great wrong never to be made right – all for naught. Turek let out a long, sad sigh.

"Typhon, finally, a voice of reason," Ereshkigal said.

All eyes burned with anticipation as a pregnant silence fell over the creators.

"Turek is right," Typhon said evenly.

Turek couldn't believe it, but there was no guile in

Typhon's words. He meant them! Typhon, of all his brethren, was going to keep the agreement.

The hall erupted, everyone talking over everyone else.

Finally, it was Ereshkigal's voice that rose above all the others. "Silence!" she shouted, pointing a contemptuous finger at Typhon. "Go on then, brother. Tell us of your change of heart. How will this benefit your cause, oh great Typhon, for surely there is much in it for you!"

Typhon's mouth parted in a smile, showing only more Sentheye where teeth should have been. "If the boy has promised himself to the dragons and bound himself to this three-headed creature in blood, and clearly he has, then he no longer belongs to Turek – he belongs to me. And since you all agreed, like fools, to stay idle and view Turek's *evidence*, we shall let this play out."

Ereshkigal looked as though she wanted to smite him.

"Oh, come now, sister – you wouldn't be complaining if one of yours held the Sound Eye," Typhon mused.

Ah, and there it is, Turek thought. He should have guessed – Typhon was practically drooling at the thought that his favorites could possess all the stones. With that kind of power, he could unify Karelia under one rule, his favorites' rule. Turek didn't want to imagine a world where dragons ruled all.

Yet he wasn't so sure Typhon had it right. Jack, whatever he was, didn't belong to any of them. Jack belonged to himself. Turek didn't worry so much about Typhon and his greed, but he worried about what Jack was becoming. He worried about the darkness growing inside him. Sentheye would feed on darkness as much as light, hate as much as love. The Great Mother created Sentheye in a balance of both.

"Oh, how convenient for you, Typhon!" Druesha accused.

"The fact is, we agreed," Typhon said. "Besides, I truly do not believe Turek staged this. The Sound Eye could just as easily have fallen into anyone's hands. The dökkálfar king, a dragon, or what about your favorite, Aurgy, King Ogliosh? Druesha, for Great Mother's sake, you had Pando within reach, plus another tree in human form standing atop the temple! They were all right there! No. We continue forward. And further, if you are interfering, it stops now!"

The Great Hall fell silent once more.

Turek smiled, knowing Typhon's support would ensure his brethren fell in line, albeit reluctantly. But none were holding hands, and his brother was right – they were almost certainly interfering at this very moment. He knew he was, even if only by way of a whisper on the wind. But then, all was fair. Disconnected physically from the others, a creator could be in two places at once. Thus, while physically here, his brethren could still meddle below. A physical connection was the only way to be sure they were all fully present in this single place. Turek would not be naïve to what the others were doing. Without the connection, they would all be sticking their noses in even now, especially Typhon, despite the clever ruse.

"Shall we return to the circle, then?" Turek asked, holding out his hands.

With a sudden and startling burst of Sentheye, Turek's suspicion was confirmed. Light tore from Typhon's torso and head, flashing across the bejeweled floor. The being of Sentheye separated, momentarily losing shape.

The others drew back, their shock filling the Great Hall.

Typhon drew himself back to form, but he was kneeling now, as if he'd collapsed under a great weight. He pushed himself up, anger flushing his face in a red, hot wave.

"What did you do, Typhon?" Ereshkigal asked.

Typhon, seething, said nothing.

"He did what we were all doing. He interfered," Turek said, appraising his brother. He narrowed his eyes. "But you meddled with Jack, didn't you?"

Typhon's lip curled.

Turek took the look as affirmation. "Well, judging from that little display, it wasn't well received. Was it, Typhon?"

"Great Mother, he can do that? Did it… hurt?" Rán asked in wonder.

"Don't be ridiculous! I am fine!" Typhon snapped.

Clearly, his brother was more embarrassed than harmed.

"This changes every—"

"This changes nothing! I was overzealous is all. I said I am fine!"

"Then let us get back to it. Much is happening," Turek said.

Hesitant nods made their way around the circle. One by one, they sat and joined hands, the pool of Sentheye reappearing in the center. Once again, the creators were fully present in the Great Hall, sharing a vision of a battle unfolding near the portal.

Turek closed his eyes. *Great Mother, please show them as you have shown me.*

3

First Contact

God Stones – Moon Ring 1
The Battlefield, outside of Osonian

Gabi gasped as the Sound Eye materialized atop Jack's head.

The curly-haired boy's sinister smile fell into a sneer as his words reverberated in Gabi's mind. *Your mother's murderer… is sitting on your back!*

Gabi pushed Jack's words away as she fought to press her will into the mind of Cerberus, compelling the three-headed dragon to eat itself. "Te odio, Cerberus! El Tule was good! He was so good, and you burned him! You burned him to death!" she screamed.

Cerberus roared, his heads snapping at each other with saliva-drenched teeth, clacking and biting. "She's in my head! She's… twisting my… my…"

"He's lying – isn't he, Gabi? Please, tell me," Zerri begged.

"Go on, you little shitstain, tell her what you did! Tell her how you killed her mother with a rock from a slingshot! Tell her how her mother choked and gagged before she blew into tiny pieces! And while you're at it, tell her the whole of it. Tell her how I tried to stop you! I tried, Zerri. I tried to get to her. Hell, I practically killed myself jumping off the pyramid when she ran away after... after destroying your mom!" Jack shouted.

Tears overflowed Gabi's eyes and spilled down her cheeks.

"It's true, isn't it? You killed my mother, Gabi?" Zerri asked.

"I'm sorry, Zerri, but Azazel killed my family. She—"

"The Queen of Queens was my mother. My mother! She was everything!" Zerri shouted, shaking her scales and throwing Gabi from her back onto the strange-colored snow.

Gabi's focus over Cerberus slipped away, but she didn't care. Pushing herself up onto the palms of her hands, she pleaded, "Please, Zerri, I'm sorry I lied to you, but I'm not sorry for what—"

"Silence! How could I have ever let you sit upon me? You used me! You used mind control to cloud my judgment! You are no friend to me!" the young dragon said, turning on her.

"Kill her, Zerri!" Jack urged.

But Zerri only stood there, unmoving, her mouth agape.

"I said kill her!" Jack shouted again.

Gabi held her hand in front of her face as if it could somehow protect her from the fire to come. But the flame never came.

Gabi stared up, blinking in confusion, expecting to be dead. Then she heard a voice.

"Gabi! Get out of there!" Garrett shouted.

Gabi spun to find Garrett and the others descending the hill. Garrett, his face strained, held his hand out before him.

"Kill her, Cerb! I'll deal with them!" Jack said, raising his own hands.

Cerberus roared.

Gabi's eyes went wide. "No!" she shouted, grabbing Cerberus's mind and with it his will. The dragon's three heads twisted and shook as the creature fought for control of itself.

Governess screamed words of power.

Gnarled vines erupted from the snowy grass, tangling around Cerberus's feet, legs, and wings. The vines constricted like a hundred Burmese pythons, then pulled taut to anchor the beast to the Earth.

Jack said, "We can end this here and now, Garrett! Fight me like a man! You and me, one-on-one!"

"Call off your dogs, Jack, and let's finish this!" Garrett answered, but Gabi knew he hadn't let go of time – Zerri was statue still.

Jack was up to something. Gabi could feel it! He was surrounding them with sickness. He was drawing power into himself in some kind of measured way. The Sound Eye! It must be. She shouted in mind speak, *Bre! He's doing something! Don't... trust him!* She could barely hold control over the big dragon's will. Any second, the beast would break her hold and kill her.

Come on, Gabi! Breanne urged. *Garrett, Jack's lying – don't trust him!*

"Garrett! I don't feel so good," David said.

Gabi pushed herself onto her feet and began to circle toward her friends.

Paul grabbed his stomach and coughed vomit into the purple snow.

Suddenly, the ground shook as three giants crested the hill in a full-on run.

"Oh, that doesn't look good," Pete said, backpedaling.

"Oh, thank god for you, Pete!" Lenny shouted, turning to run. "If not for your incredible insight, I would have stood here wondering if giants running toward me were a good thing or a bad thing!"

But worse than the giants were what the three nephilbock were running from. Gabi gaped at the group of dark elves riding on curious-looking horse things. Some elves had swords held high, gleaming in the shine of the planet's strange suns. Others rode without holding on, with their long bows fully drawn.

As the group of dökkálfar descended the hill, they loosed arrows into one of the three nephilbock. The giant fell forward, sliding on his belly toward Gabi and Cerberus.

Cerberus strained and flexed, the roots that bound him snapping one by one. And like the roots, so too snapped the strands of Gabi's mind control over the massive creature. She was on the precipice of losing him.

Might I suggest we run, young lord? Governess asked in mind speak. The question was for Garrett, but they all heard it.

Then she heard David shout, "Run, Gabi!"

Zerri! Zerri, if you can hear me... I'm sorry! And she meant it. She was sorry – sorry for lying, sorry for how badly this betrayal hurt her heart, and sorry for ever caring for this dragon in the first place. But despite it all, she did care, and she hated it. But sorry for killing the murderer of her mother and father... no. That she would never be sorry for.

The dead giant pushed up dirt and snow as it plowed forward on a collision course with her and Cerberus. She waited as long as she could... and then she ran.

Cerberus roared, snapping free of the vines as the dead giant collided with the three-headed dragon.

Gabi expected flames at her back, but they never came. When she stole a glance back, she saw Garrett only now releasing Zerri. "Go! Go! Go!" he shouted, waving his hands as he hurried toward her.

They ran together now, bringing up the rear of the group as more than a dozen dökkálfar descended upon Jack,

Cerberus, Zerri, and the two remaining giants in a clash of steel and screams.

As she and Garrett followed the others into a thicket of taller grass along the edge of the field, Gabi glanced back one last time.

Another giant had fallen, but so had every dökkálfar.

"Hurry, Gabi! Go!" Garrett urged.

David was directly in front of her now. The mustached boy reached back and took her hand in his, leading her into the tall reeds. "Come on, guys!"

The wide blades stretched high above their heads as they pushed deep into the tall grass until finally, after a few meters, they broke from the thicket onto a worn dirt trail. To their left, the narrow path vanished around a corner. To their right, the trail stretched on for some distance before disappearing as well.

"Which way?" Pete asked.

Before anyone could answer, a young girl, maybe Bre and Garrett's age, appeared from around the corner, her eyes wide in terror. In one hand, the girl held a spear, cocked over her shoulder. Gabi recognized the device holding the thin spear as an atlatl from her archeology studies. This deadly spear-throwing device was the precursor to the bow and arrow. But there was something even more familiar about the olive-skinned girl. She wore a sleeveless earth-tone tunic and loincloth. Affixed to her feet were sandals secured with leather straps. Lean with muscle but thicker in the thighs, the girl instantly reminded Gabi of the Tarahumara runners: natives of the Copper Canyons of Mexico and some of the best long-distance runners in the world... well, not this world, Earth. That felt weird to think about. But even weirder was this strange girl, clearly different from Gabi's Tarahumara natives, but in some ways the same. What was she doing here?

Gabi knew one thing for sure, and if Garrett and Lenny

were paying attention, they probably knew it too. Just like the Tarahumara, this girl, standing before them like a frightened hen, was a runner.

She's going to run! Gabi shouted in mind speak.

And just like that, the girl turned and ran.

"Wait!" Garrett shouted, darting around Pete and David, with Lenny right on his heels. Everyone ran then, turning the corner to find that the trail straightened. The girl quickly opened up some distance before vanishing onto a side trail.

Garrett and Lenny pulled ahead of Gabi and the others, quickly vanishing around the same corner.

Somewhere behind them, a dragon roared and warriors screamed from the battlefield. But the sounds of battle were growing faint now as Gabi and the others ran farther into the maze of tall grass. When Gabi made the corner, she saw the girl again, standing at an intersection.

"Wait! Please!" Garrett shouted again. "We won't hurt you!"

Can you slow her? Lenny asked in mind speak.

I could snare her, young lord, Governess suggested.

No. Don't. I don't think we want to start out that way, Breanne said.

The girl stood with the atlatl cocked back, ready to launch the spear. With her free hand, she pointed at them, shouting words Gabi couldn't understand.

Beside her, David's face lit with recognition as his astonished voice filled Gabi's mind. *Bre! She knows your name!*

4

The Voice

God Stones – Moon Ring 1
The Battlefield, outside of Osonian

By the time Jack spun to see what was coming, a giant riddled with arrows collided with Cerberus in a tangle of dragon heads, talons, legs, and arms. With a swiftness no horse on Earth could achieve, the group of at least a dozen dökkálfar descended upon Jack, Cerb, and Zerri.

Jack's fist tightened knuckle-white as he watched Garrett and the others run toward a thicket of tall grass. *You can't run forever, Garrett,* Jack thought as he spun away, redirecting the dark Sentheye to the dökkálfar closest to him. Three of the elves fell from their horse things, landing hard in the snow-coated prairie grass, where they began writhing and puking blood.

Zerri, if you want to live, you fight with us now!

The elves were pointing at him and speaking words he couldn't understand. One of the dökkálfar shouted above the others as Sentheye swirled around the elf's hands like he'd seen when Apep prepared to cast. Jack realized they were pointing less at him and more at what he wore atop his head – the Sound Eye.

Jack grimaced, clenching his jaw. "You want a fight, asshole? Well, bring it on!" Jack raised his own hands, thinking about how Apep had used the black Sentheye to form a shield to protect himself. The Sentheye seemed to understand his will as it followed his thoughts, swirling from his hands around his body in a black ribbon.

The dark elf sneered from atop his big-ass horse thing, flexing his fingers forward and shouting magic words.

Jack's heart raced, but he stood his ground – ground that seemed to thaw and change under his feet, suddenly sucking them into it like quicksand.

But then, with a startling flash of dragon breath, the loudmouthed elf and a couple of his buddies burst into flames! Even their horse things caught fire.

Cerb! Jack thought, looking to his left, but Cerb was only getting to his feet. *Zerri?* The small dragon closed her smoking mouth and leapt forward into flight.

Jack frowned in confusion, reflexively lifting his hands to defend himself from the smaller dragon. Movement from the corner of his eye filled his peripheral vision. Jack reeled, tugging at his mud-stuck feet as the flaming horse things ran directly at him.

Jack gasped, jerking his feet in a panic.

But it was Zerri who got to him first. The force of the small dragon hitting him nearly stole his breath as she wrapped him in her talons. Zerri's forward momentum yanked his feet free of his boots and sent them both sprawling across the snowy ground.

Jack rolled, his face driven into the snow. He got a mouth full of the purple crap, but it didn't taste or feel any different from Earth snow. As he pushed himself to his feet, Cerberus roared. A gout of flame washed over the remaining dökkálfar.

A quiet fell over the area, as Zerri, Cerberus, and the one remaining giant stood, gathering themselves. The whole place smelled like burnt flesh, and a smoky haze covered the low-lying area like a blanket of fog.

The giant, one of Ogliosh's original seven nephilbock, stood with his big bulbous eye staring at the ground. This one was Eroch, or maybe Mesog. Jack got the two confused. Both had the same build, thinner than the others. What the hell was he staring at? With sudden horror, Jack's hands went to his head. The Sound Eye! It had fallen off when Zerri shoved him out of the way. Jack ran sock-footed through the snow, placing himself between the enormous giant and the spot it was staring at, but he couldn't see the Sound Eye! It must have fallen into the grass. Jack spun on the giant. "Don't even think about it!" he shouted up at the one-eyed monster.

The giant looked at Jack, then the dragons, which were now closing in on both sides.

"Don't look at them! Look at me!" Jack said in perfect nephilbock. Holding out his hands, he looked from one side to the other. "Cerberus, Zerri, don't attack! We just saved your ass, you big idiot," Jack shouted up at the giant. "If you even think about taking one more step, it will be me and only me who kicks your ass."

The giant, seeming to consider his options, gazed toward the grass again, showed his teeth, and then turned back the way he'd come from – back toward the battlefield.

The ground shook as the giant bounded back toward the fray. Behind him, Jack found Cerberus and Zerri circling each other. Jesus Christ, already! *Stop! Don't kill her, Cerb!* he said telepathically.

The Last Gift

Do not be so sure he could! Zerri hissed.

Cerberus's three mouths stretched open and roared, but he obeyed and didn't burn the little dragon.

Oh, he could, Jack answered, searching the thick grass for the Sound Eye. *Now stay put, both of you!* The last thing he needed was his dragon stepping on the damn thing. The Sound Eye was close. He could feel it.

No. I don't think so, Zerri said.

No, you don't think so what? You think you could take Cerberus the Mighty? Jack chuckled, still searching the weeds.

No… I'm talking to… wait. Don't you hear him? Zerri asked.

Hear who? Jack asked.

No. No, I won't be silent.

Jack stopped and looked up, then around the area. *Who are you talking to, Zerri?*

Yes. Yes, I see it. It's right there.

Zerri? Jack tried again.

He wants me to claim it on behalf of my dragons. To claim it as the Queen of Queens.

Cerberus, be ready! Jack said, spinning in a circle. *Zerri, answer me! Who are you talking to?*

But he is blood bound to the dragons! And if you really are Typhon, then is he not your son too?

Typhon? Typhon, my father, speaks to you?! Cerberus asked in disbelief.

Frantically, Jack searched. He could feel the Sound Eye right in front of him! It had to be here! Dropping to his hands and knees, he swung his arms desperately through the grass. Why couldn't he see it?

Typhon is blinding you to the Sound Eye. Only I can see it, Zerri said, dipping her head low and pushing her muzzle into the snowy grass. When she lifted her head, she had the Sound Eye pinched between her teeth.

No. No! No! No! Jack shouted, lifting his hands and drawing in a deep breath, sucking in all the shadow, all the darkness, and all the disease. *You won't take it from me!*

5

The Chase

God Stones – Moon Ring 1
The edge of the Shadow Forest

The smell of smoke and sound of crackling reeds signaled to Breanne they had narrowly escaped dragon fire as they'd fled from Cerberus, Zerri, and Jack. High above, the clouds parted to reveal two suns sagging low in the sky, one almost eclipsing the other in what felt like a late afternoon. Of course, Breanne could only go by feel as the foreign sky told her nothing about the time of day. On the dirt path ahead, the strange girl with the atlatl stood less than twenty yards away, shouting and pointing directly at Breanne.

"David, you understand her?" Breanne asked.

"Yeah, of course! Can't you? I mean, sure, she has a bit of an accent… but not that thick," David answered.

Lenny pointed at David's cargo pants. "No, but your head is, you dipshit. You have the Eyra of Tunga in your pocket!"

"Oh, that's right!" David blushed, pulling the small medallion from his cargo pants pocket and tossing it to Breanne.

The shouting girl's words slowed and twisted and soon what sounded like, "Yume! Yume er et une! Bran Mur! Et Une Het kume ti soe uets!" stretched and bent into, "You! You are the one! Breanne Moore! The one who has come to save us!"

Breanne gasped. "How do you know my name?" she asked in the girl's language as she tossed the Eyra of Tunga to Paul, who listened for a moment and handed the medallion to Pete.

"The wind whispered to me! It told me to come this way. It told me you would be here! And here you are!" the girl said, still holding the atlatl threateningly.

Switching to mind speak, Pete passed the medallion to Garrett and asked, *Hey, you think it could have been Turek?*

What else could it be? Maybe Turek's helping us! Garrett said hopefully.

Governess's eyes followed the medallion with interest. *If you can understand the little flesh sack...*

Pete shot Governess a frown.

Ahem, my apologies. If you understand the little human, then perhaps it is time you share the Eyra of Tunga device with me, young lord?

I thought you understood all languages. Garrett handed the medallion to Lenny.

The languages I have learned are vast – however, they are Earthly in origin. This is not a language I am familiar with. Given a few hours of careful listening to a conversation, I could easily decipher the dialect, but I am sure we should move farther from the battle, lest we find ourselves discovered. Also, would it not be wise to simply kill the little flesh sa... human? She is pointing a weapon at us.

As the group conferred in mind speak, the girl looked at them with a curious urgency.

No! We don't want you to kill her! Breanne said.

How unfortunate.

Governess, your jokes are getting better, Lenny quipped.

I assure you, Lennard Wade, I do not jest. Governess reached for the Eyra of Tunga, plucking it from Lenny's hand like ripe fruit from the vine.

The girl was speaking rapidly now. "You must follow me away from here, Breanne Moore. My people are waiting for you!"

"Waiting for me? They know we are here?" she asked.

"No, but still, they wait!"

Not sure I like this, sis, Paul said, giving Breanne an uneasy look.

David reached for the medallion, but Governess stretched her arm high above his head.

Hey, lady! What are you trying to pull? Give it back! David protested.

Ah, ah, ah, grubby boy. Governess winked, handing the Eyra of Tunga to Breanne.

Oh, she's messing with you, bro! I dare say, I like this side of you, Gov. Lenny laughed, but his laughter was cut short when somewhere behind them dragon fire flashed, reeds crackled, and creatures screamed.

David paled, looking back over his shoulder. *Well, we can't stay here!*

Breanne knew David well enough to know the boy was about to have a full-on panic attack. *Garrett? David's right. We can't. I think we should follow her,* Breanne said, nodding toward the girl, who looked like she was about to give up on them and flee.

Garrett nodded. "Take us to your leader."

Pete's hand went to his face.

Oh, no you didn't! Lenny laughed. *Douche canoe!*

Prince Lennard Wade. I am not familiar with the term douche canoe, though I am familiar with the two English words separately. However, I do not see the relation between a douche and a canoe. To my vast knowledge, one has nothing to do with the other. Additionally, I find the young lord's request to be quite apt. Would we not want—

Oh, for the love of god, Gov, Lenny said, slapping his hands against his thighs in exasperation.

Guys! Breanne pointed. The girl with the atlatl turned and ran. Breanne followed with Garrett and the others in tow. The narrow passage between the tall grass was only wide enough for them to chase single file, and Breanne wasn't the fastest, especially when carrying a backpack and wearing a sheathed sword on one hip, a handgun on the other.

For several minutes they ran, trying to keep up with the girl through a maze of trails. Eventually Breanne realized that if the girl had wanted to lose them, she would have. She wasn't ditching them – she was guiding them. Soon they had made so many turns Breanne couldn't tell which way they had come from. Then she heard voices arguing.

"This way!" a thin voice said.

"How can you be sure?" asked another, deeper voice.

"Believe what you want, but I'm telling you I had a vision! Goddess Ereshkigal spoke to me!" the thin voice said.

A third, skeptical, voice chimed in. "You expect us to believe the goddess spoke to you, Vidry—"

"Wait! Did you hear that? Over there!" the thin voice said.

Reeds crashed behind them, forcing Breanne to run faster still. So fast, she felt like she might be sick. Finally, they broke from the maze of tall grass onto a border of shorter grass separating the thicket from a long row of trees.

In front of her stood a forest unlike anything she had seen before. Each tree appeared uniformly placed. Beyond the first few rows, shadow swallowed the forest in darkness. But from what she could see, not only were the trees spaced evenly, but also they had canopies at the same height. The bright yellow, burnt orange, red, pink, and blue foliage – the variation in color reminded her of fall in the Midwest – tangled into one another, making it impossible to tell which foliage belonged to which tree. It was a solid wall of leaves supported by geometric tree trunks. Breanne glanced up as she ran. The tree canopies stretched so high she could see small clouds vanishing into the forest as they moved across the sky.

Behind them, three elves riding the horse-like creatures broke from the grass. One of them shouted something.

"Run for the forest!" the girl shouted.

A ball of purple light appeared in one rider's hands.

Breanne didn't understand how in the world they were going to outrun these things, but she followed the girl toward the edge of the wood.

David's shouts filled her mind. *Oh god. Oh god. Oh god!*

As soon as she and the others broke the plane of shadow, the girl juked left between a row of trees, then she switched, cutting hard right between two more of the evenly spaced trees. The tree trunks themselves were as big around as large oak trees back home.

Breanne squinted, straining but failing to keep sight of the girl in the darkness under the dense forest canopy.

Finally, the girl shouted, "Here!" and vanished behind one of the large trees.

Breanne and the others cut between the rows of trees, desperately trying to keep up with the runner girl. When she disappeared behind the tree, Breanne wondered how in the hell they were all supposed to hide behind that one tree. It was big alright, but not big enough to hide eight of them. Besides, the elves could surely see them! After all, Lenny and Janis had both been able to see in the dark.

They're coming! Pete shouted.

As Breanne prepared to step behind the tree, she glanced back the way they had come. The dark elves were on foot now, running with swords drawn. For whatever reason, they must have dismounted their creatures before they entered the wood. The elf with the ball of strange light drew back like he was about to pitch a fastball.

"Come, Breanne Moore!" the girl urged.

She followed the girl, almost getting barreled over by Lenny and Garrett as they came around the trunk and slid to a stop.

"What are we doing?" Lenny asked, falling into a fighting stance. "Is there a ladder or something?"

David and the others appeared beside them, panting. "Guys! They're gaining!" David shouted.

The girl placed her hand on the tree and spoke what Breanne was sure was a word of power.

The tree trunk moved. Wood grains stretched as a jagged crack glowed moonlight silver in the deep fissures between the tree's gnarled plates of bark.

At first, Breanne thought the tree was changing into something else, like Governess shape-shifting, but then she realized it wasn't changing, it was opening. Like curtains, the long zigzagging crack spread wider and wider.

"This way, Breanne Moore!" the girl said, stepping inside the tree and vanishing into the internal darkness.

She hesitated.

Go, Bre! Paul urged.

Time to climb, she thought, knowing the strange opening must lead up into the massive canopy above. She stepped forward into the darkness. The floor vanished from beneath her and she dropped.

Breanne screamed.

6

Pull Back

God Stones – Moon Ring 1
The Battlefield, outside of Osonian

"Zerri! Give me the Sound Eye!" Jack shouted with fingers splayed.

"And what of me, Jack? Tell me, why shouldn't I take it for myself – for my dragons? Can you imagine what I could be? Imagine it, Jack. Imagine how all of Karelia would bend the knee to the Queen of Queens with the crown of power!"

"Zerri, your mother made me dragon! And it was me who told you the truth! Now you're going to turn traitor. Well, you'll have to kill me and Cerberus. Because that's what it's going to take to keep it!"

Zerri stared daggers at Jack. "No, Jack, I only have to kill one of you, then the other dies."

Cerberus let out a guttural growl as he dipped his heads low, ready to lunge in.

Jack could feel this about to break bad and quick. He needed to think fast. Stalling for time, he said, "So that's the way it's going to be?"

Zerri didn't respond.

Hadn't Azazel said something to Apep once? Something like the power not belonging... Shit, what was it?

Should I kill her, Jack? Cerberus asked telepathically, all three of his mouths stretching open.

Jack waved him off, remembering Azazel's words and repeating them. "Just because you hold the God Stones doesn't make their power yours, Zerri! I feel their power filling me too, and I will kill you! But look, it doesn't have to be that way. We can work together. Think about it. Even if you somehow kill us, how will you free the enslaved dragons from the elves? Do you think the hordes will follow you without us? Do you think they will believe you are the daughter of Azazel? What about the other dragon queens on this planet? Will they just hand you the title of Queen of Queens?" He could see it – the doubt in her eyes. "And what about the nephilbock? You think they will just follow you when you can't even get your own hordes to follow?"

Cerberus hissed and roared.

Zerri hissed back.

Jack held out his hand, waving Cerberus off again. "Join me, Zerri. I can make sure the dragons go free. I can unite the Earth-born nephilbock under my rule, and you can claim your throne standing alongside the son of Typhon, after having freed your people! Can you imagine that? Can you imagine how powerful you can be with us at your side?"

"You sound so sure of yourself, human!"

Jack held out his hand, palm up. "Oh, Zerri, I am certain. And don't you see me? What I really am? No. No, you couldn't, because if you did, you'd know I'm no human."

Zerri stared at Jack for a long moment.

"Our dragons are straying, the nephilbock are dying. You need to decide now! Do you want to be a queen and save your people?" Jack shouted, pointing back toward the battle.

"Know this, Jack Nightshade. I already know you will betray me. You will betray us all. But in doing so, you will destroy yourself. That is a truth you can't run from."

No. He was smarter than Apep, smarter than Azazel. Let her underestimate him, just like they all had. Jack nodded toward his hand. "Well? Come on then. We're out of time."

Zerri dropped the Sound Eye.

Jack snatched it from the air, smiled, and placed it back atop his head.

"Now can I kill her?" Cerberus asked.

Zerri drew back like a giant cat, her back arching. She hissed again.

"No, Cerberus. I am going to keep my word to our new Queen of Queens." Jack climbed atop Cerberus's tail and ran up onto his back, seating himself where the dragon's three massive necks joined. Jack knew this little dragon girl was important and, under his leadership, he could use her to rule this whole damn world.

Apep had it wrong, Danny. But where he failed, I'm gonna get it right. I want Garrett dead too, and I promise I'll make him pay, but payback takes patience. That's what Apep got wrong. He got in too big a hurry, Danny. Then, as if Danny were there sitting right next to him, he heard his brother say, *Yeah, but it doesn't hurt to make it hard for the little bastards either.* Jack grinned to himself. *You're sure right about that, Danny.*

To Cerberus, he said, *Cerb, order four or five dragons to burn that thicket Garrett and those little shitstains ran off into. Now let's climb the hill. I need to see what we're dealing with.*

As Cerb walked up the hill, an unfamiliar voice filled Jack's mind, accompanied by a pressure similar to the first time he was exposed to the God Stones.

If you betray my people, I will see you suffer unimaginable pain, the voice said.

Somehow, Jack knew instantly who this voice belonged to. *Now you want to talk to me, Typhon? Now I'm worthy of your attention?* Jack answered through the crushing pain. It felt like this asshole was biting down on his brain.

Heed these words, hu—

Jack cut him off. *Let me tell you something, dickhead. The way I figure it, the only reason for a god to make threats is if he's scared. So I figure you must be crapping your pants right now, or why bother?*

You dare—

Oh, I dare! Now, how about you come on down here and do something about it? Jack said, hesitating as he wondered if this Typhon might actually appear. But when he didn't, Jack drew in the power of the Sound Eye as he shoved back against the pain and the voice in his mind. *No? Didn't think so! Now get out of my head!*

Jack? Are you okay? Cerberus asked.

You didn't hear that?

Hear what?

The pain was gone and so was Typhon. *Never mind. Yeah, I'm fine, Cerb. Hell, I'm better than fine!*

In the valley beyond the hill, the battlefield was a bloodbath of nephilbock and armored elves atop their giant horse things, which Jack now realized could fight on their own. The large creatures were biting off whole hunks of nephilbock flesh as the elves hacked with their swords. From his quick assessment, the elves were losing, but only just. They were being driven slowly backward toward the towering stone wall.

Let's get in the air! I want a closer look at that wall!

Cautiously they flew close enough so Jack could see that, atop the wall, elves stood behind big crossbow-looking things, and next to them stood a figure in a golden robe. A wizard, Jack guessed, and tipped his head to the sky. His dragons were flying chaotically, and more than half were missing. *Dammit.* Of the ones still trying to fight, occasionally one would dip low to breathe fire, but in doing so it would kill as many nephilbock as elves. Then the crossbows would fire, and from the few attempts Jack observed, only one of his dragons escaped the long metal spikes launched from atop the wall.

Behind the elves' ground forces, full-grown dragons appeared from steel gates set into the wall. The wall itself must have been over a mile long in each direction. Jack counted the slave dragons: twenty in total. Ten on each side of the main gate. The elves had chained the dragons around the neck. He frowned when he realized the chains were being slowly let out like fishing line on a reel. The slave dragons were being allowed to spread out and slowly flank the battle on both sides.

It's a trap, Cerb. The elves aren't retreating because they're losing. They're drawing the nephilbock in and surrounding them!

What's the plan, Jack?

Jack searched the battle until he found Ogliosh. The giant was still alive and way down in the thick of it, but as Jack appraised him, the giant stopped fighting, seemingly coming to the same conclusion Jack had. Ogliosh turned toward the forest and ran.

Jack looked across a sky speckled with his horde flying this way and that. *Get us back to the portal, Cerb.* He reached into the minds of all of his visible dragons. *Jack's horde! Pull back and rally near the portal.*

Zerri said, *The nephilbock will be slaughtered if you abandon them now. I don't see how this helps us free our enslaved.*

The Last Gift

Zerri, I'm going to show you why you need us. Jack smiled, his red eyes still fixed on the battle as he searched. Truthfully, he could give two shits about Ogliosh. Helreginn, king of the half-breed nephilbock, was down there, and he had to find him. As he searched for the smaller king, it was the giant with the tennis shoe necklace still full of feet that led him to Helreginn.

There! Jack pointed, as Cerberus settled onto the ground next to Zerri. *Send the fastest dragon we have, Cerb. I need Helreginn brought here now!*

I am the fastest dragon you have, Jack, Zerri said, matter-of-factly.

You! Cerberus scoffed, laughing hardily.

Jack said, *Don't be crazy! You'll be vulnerable to spikes and who knows what else if you go down there. Plus, they have at least one wizard on the wall. I saw him with my own eyes. No. I'm not risking my Queen of Queens.*

I outflew Cerberus the Mighty, didn't I? Zerri stated.

Cerberus's laughter cut off.

Zerri stepped forward and flexed her wings. *If you send another, you may sacrifice a dozen before one succeeds, Jack. You may even run out of time before the elves spring their trap. If you want this done and done quickly, send me. I won't fail.*

A plan was taking shape in Jack's mind. To rule over all dragons, Earth-born and Karelian, aligning with Zerri, the rightful Queen of Queens, seemed the shortest path. Allowing her this task would either build her legend or see her dead. The question he needed to ask himself was, did it matter? Could he still do this if she got herself killed? The answer seemed obvious. Of course he could.

Zerri, succeed in this and they will sing songs about you.

Zerri leapt from the ground, wings pumping.

Why did we not retrieve Helreginn ourselves, Taker?

Cerberus asked. *You could easily disease the elves atop the wall, and then we could focus on freeing our dragons and making those elf bastards pay!*

You may be right, brother, but I'm not ready to win yet. First, we need something from Helreginn.

What do we need from the puny nephilbock?

Jack smiled coldly. *His allegiance.*

7

A Grave Mistake

God Stones – Moon Ring 1
The Shadow Forest

Garrett leapt into the trunk of the tree behind Breanne and dropped, falling through darkness so absolute, he felt momentarily weightless. Below him, Bre's scream ended with a guttural *umph*. Garrett tensed reflexively, landing hard on his ass against a steep slope. Letting out his own cry, he continued downward, sliding recklessly on a smooth… something. Whatever it was, it was moving as if alive – as if he were sliding down a giant serpent's back as it slithered beneath him.

Above him, he heard the shouts of the others as they landed and slid. Gabi and Lenny for sure, then maybe a high-pitched scream from David. Far below him, Garrett could see a dim light growing. He braced himself, not knowing what to expect. A moment later, he dropped again, but this time the ground came fast as he rolled through loose dirt, a cloud of dust erupting all around him. He tried to stand, and he'd barely gotten to his feet when someone's hands grabbed him and pulled.

"Look out!" Breanne said, as Gabi fell from the chute above him.

Garrett fell back, twisting and grabbing for purchase. Both of them fell, Breanne landing hard atop him, her chest pressed against his and her cheek touching his face. "You, okay?" she asked, her breath warming his ear.

"Hoooooly shit!" Lenny shouted.

Gabi dove clear as Lenny landed in the space she had just occupied, gracefully cartwheeling and springing up and onto his feet. He turned, raising an eyebrow as he shook his head. "Really, you two? This couldn't wait?" he asked, pulling off his pack to inspect his guitar.

Breanne pushed herself up onto her palms as David spilled onto the floor and rolled like a hot dog to make way for the next to drop from the chute.

"Lenny! We weren't—" she started.

"Weren't about to make out?" Lenny cut in with a chuckle as he resecured his guitar.

David smirked. *Really, Bre. Now?*

Garrett's face flushed as he realized that David had asked in mind speak and that the fact he could hear him meant David wasn't only talking to Bre. The whole freaking world could hear. Paul could hear.

Yet despite the jabs, Garrett couldn't help noticing how perfect Bre looked in the soft turquoise light. This thought was immediately followed by the realization that he could see. He looked past her, curious about where they were and where the odd light was coming from. Glancing around the small space, he expected to find candles or maybe a torch or something, but he quickly realized the soft glow wasn't coming from one distinct source of light but from everywhere – from the walls themselves.

"Well, whatever you two are doing, Paul is close behind." Lenny nodded toward the chute.

Breanne smiled shyly and rolled off Garrett and onto the ground.

Paul appeared next, landing on his feet in a squat, like some kind of superhero. He looked at them, then at Bre. An eyebrow went up. "What did I miss?" he asked.

"Nothing! Better move, Paul," she said as the others dropped from the ceiling.

Paul rolled as Governess and Pete piled onto the floor, one after the other.

Across the room, Garrett looked to the girl in the sandals with the atlatl, who stood with her head cocked to one side, watching them curiously.

"Are we safe from the elves?" Garrett asked.

"Elves?" the girl asked, as if tasting the word.

"Those blue guys with pointed ears!" David said, standing and brushing himself off. "The ones on the horse things that were chasing us! What if they follow us down here? Wherever the hell here is!"

"I know what an elf is. But you needn't fear. They cannot follow us down here," the girl said.

"How can you be so sure?" Pete asked.

The girl pointed.

The chute that had brought them to this place extended from the ceiling. The small portion poking out looked like a tube-slide at a water park, only this tube was made of wood, with smaller roots growing all over the outside. As they watched, the tube wilted back, shrinking and twisting closed. Soon the tube was gone, and all that remained were thick tree roots. "The elves hold no sway over the trees of Shadow Forest."

"So, we're safe?" David asked.

"You are safe," the girl said.

"What's your name?" Breanne asked.

"Tell," the girl said.

"Tell? That's a weird name," David said.

"And what is your name?" she asked.

"David."

"David," Tell repeated, her brow crinkling. "They must have an abundance of food where you come from, David."

"Hey! Now, listen here!" David said, raising his voice.

Tell stepped back, lifting her spear without bothering with the atlatl.

From the dirt walls of the small space, the light changed from blue-green to an angry orange-red as the tree roots twisted and thrashed.

"David, I meant you no offence. It is good to be so plump. You must be held in high regard to be allowed so much food. Even our so-called king may be thinner than you." Tell chuckled.

"Oh, I think you and I are going to get along just fine, Tell!" Lenny said, smiling.

The thrashing tree roots calmed and the strange light returned to an eerie turquoise. Garrett now realized the light was coming from clumps of glowing moss, reminding him of the Spanish moss that hung from the oak tree called Angel back on Earth – if it were radioactive.

"You are controlling the trees?" Governess asked.

"No. I am controlling nothing. But the trees will not tolerate any action taken against my kind. Not from outsiders."

Young lord, I think it is time my brethren learn of my presence, Governess said, her feet changing and rooting to the floor.

Wait, Larrea! Pete shouted.

Governess's roots sank deep into the floor and for a second, she froze perfectly still.

Lenny pulled a face. "Larrea? Larrea! Seriously, Pete? Is that your pet name for her, Larrea?" he teased.

"That's her actual name, you dick! Well, one of them! She likes it when I call her that," Pete said, moving close to the tree woman, his face creased with concern.

Governess's eyes sprang open, and she screamed out in a pained cry.

Pete reeled back, startled at first, then lunged forward. "Larrea! What's wrong?"

Governess's human form fell away as the dirt erupted below her, purging her from the ground and throwing her across the small chamber and into the wall.

"No!" Pete shouted, running to her. "What the hell did you do?" he shouted at Tell.

"That was not my doing. What in the name of Karelia is she?"

"She is a tree! Well, a shrub, to be more specific!" Pete shouted, placing his hands on her limbs. "David... David, fix her! Heal her!"

"I don't... I don't think I can heal a tree, Pete. I'm... I'm sorry," David said.

"Well, dammit! For the love of god, you better try! She's more than a tree, she's one of us, and she's my friend," Pete said, emotion choking his words.

David knelt and put his hands on the shrub woman's tiny trunk.

Garrett and the others knelt too. It felt so odd to see the fiery red-haired woman reduced to her true form. She looked like a dried-out shrub, ripped from someone's front yard and left alongside the road for the yard waste truck to pick up.

David's glow flooded the small chamber of turquoise moss in a shine as if from a yellow sun.

"You are a mage! A healer!" Tell said in awe.

But David's shine was short-lived, and it didn't flow into

Governess, instead dissipating like smoke from a cigarette. Slowly, the light in the dirt chamber faded to turquoise once more.

"It's not working," David said.

"Try again!" Pete shouted angrily.

"Pete, I'm not even tired or dizzy – nothing. It isn't working."

"What did you do?" Pete shouted, spinning and taking Tell by surprise. The girl dropped the atlatl and spear to the dirt floor as Pete charged forward, backing her into the root-tangled wall.

"Pete, stop!" Garrett shouted.

From the wall, roots changed shape, twisting together in a thick braid. The braided root, looking not unlike an arm, stretched out, grabbing Pete around the throat and lifting.

Lenny launched forward, throwing himself onto the root arm, trying to pull it down so Pete could get his feet and hopefully draw a breath, but the root didn't drop a single inch under Lenny's weight.

"Let him go!" Paul growled, springing into action, grabbing the root in one hand and rearing back with the other, his fist clenched for a swing.

Everyone went into motion, watching in horror as Pete flailed for breath. But Garrett caught something else, and his eyes went to Tell.

The girl stood with her eyes closed, mumbling words of power.

Paul, wait – don't! Garrett shouted. *Guys, stop – don't attack!*

Suddenly, the root lowered, setting Pete back on the ground. A moment later he was free – gasping for breath, but free.

"You *are* controlling them," Garrett said.

"No," Tell said, her voice full of irritation as she picked up her spear and atlatl.

"But I saw you talking to them. And you spoke to the tree above too, just before it opened."

Tell looked away, focusing her attention on Breanne. "I control nothing, Breanne. But the trees will protect me. So please tell your subjects not to attack me, or next time I may not be able to help. Despite what magic you may possess, down here the trees rule."

"They are not my subjects," Breanne said. "They are my friends, and the trees have done something to Governess. Why would they hurt her? She is a tree creature like them."

"Hmm. This creature of yours is something else, but it isn't like them. It was a grave mistake to attempt a psychic connection," Tell said. "Now please, come. My people aren't far."

"Wait! What's that even mean? Can you help her?" Pete begged.

"No. I am sorry," Tell said, appraising the shrub. "I think your friend is dead."

8

Born Anew

God Stones – Moon Ring 1
The Battlefield, outside of Osonian

Zerri flew across the battlefield, wings pumping and eyes watering. No. Not watering, crying. She had held it together in front of Jack and Cerberus, but inside, she felt gutted. A wretched sob broke from deep in her chest – from her soul. Each sob was followed by another and another. She was losing it. How? How had a human girl done this to her? She had known Gabi for all of one day, but she had felt closer to her than any dragon she had ever known. Gabi had felt like more than a friend – she was a sister. Was! Now she knew the truth! It had all been a lie!

Helreginn was right below her now. All Zerri needed to do was snatch him from the battle and race back to Jack.

As she dove, she heard the first arrow whiz past her face, its fletching practically brushing her snout. Part of her wished it would have killed her right then and there, ending her heartache.

From atop the wall, rows of dökkálfar drew back their bows.

The small grey dragon spun, threading the needle between half a dozen more arrows, each narrowly missing her, but the barrage forced her to abandon her attempt to grab the giant king. Pulling up into another spin, she banked hard, wings pumping with all she had. Zerri screamed as she flew across the field. She screamed until the scream became a roar and the roar became a torrent of fire. Now it was the dökkálfar who screamed. She might have killed a giant or several, but she didn't care. This was a release of anguish – of brokenness.

More arrows flew, but this time three other juveniles were the target as they flew within range of the wall. Seeing her chance, Zerri blinked back her tears and launched herself upward, surging up above the battle and into the Karelian sky, out of reach of the elves – out of reach of it all. She stopped then, relaxing her wings and easing into a moment of weightlessness. For a split second, gravity did not exist. And in that suspension of time, the tears clung to her cheeks – frozen and ice cold – and she wished she *would* just die. Could this frozen moment be death? And if so, couldn't this weightlessness be her eternity? Could she stay in this place where the world had no pull over her, and where her stupidity in letting a human girl break her heart didn't matter? Could this nothingness be the answer to her unbearable heartache?

High above a wisp of clouds, Zerri tipped backward, gravity yanking her from her desperate thoughts, and she fell.

She would let herself fall and continue falling straight down into the Karelian ground – into the end. On the other side of it – maybe nothing, or maybe her mother would be there waiting to embrace her.

Zerri fell faster still, refusing to open her wings.

And if her mother was there, waiting on the other side, what would she say? Would she be happy to see her? No. She knew her mother would not be happy. "Why?" her mother would ask. "Why have you come here and not avenged me? Why have you, the Queen of Queens, chosen the coward's path?" Then she would turn her back, and Zerri's heart would be crushed in death as it was in life.

Down she plummeted, punching a hole through a low-hanging cloud of smoke. As the ground came into focus, she saw for the first time the elder dragons in chains. The slaves her mother had promised to free. These chained elder dragons were the very reason her mother had made the deal with Apep and agreed to go to Earth in the first place – to align with the dökkálfar prince and, in return, guarantee the release of all enslaved dragons.

The tears on her cheeks melted as her anguish turned hot, igniting in her chest like dragon fire. A new rage boiled inside Zerri. No. She would not die, not until she freed every enslaved dragon on Karelia and had her revenge on her mother's murderer!

The ground seemed to race up to meet her, eager to receive the Queen of Queens. But on this day, the ground would be disappointed.

Zerri opened her wings, swooping so low to the ground that elves and giants alike dove to their bellies. With talons stretched open like an eagle preparing to snatch a fish from the water, Zerri seized Helreginn from behind. Her talons clenched the giant's upper arms as he staggered forward from the force. For a moment, Zerri thought the weight of the nephilbock would send her crashing into the fray.

Helreginn's feet slid along the ground as he struggled to get free. "Hold still!" Zerri shouted as they both surged forward.

Helreginn shouted something back, but she couldn't

understand his strange tongue and realized he probably couldn't understand hers either. She flexed her wings, pumping them with all she had. Thank the gods this giant was smaller than most, or there'd be no way she could pull this off. But she needed the giant king to stop fighting her! His flailing was making this nearly impossible. What would he understand? "Jack!" she shouted. "Helreginn! Jack!"

The giant stopped struggling. The two lifted off the ground, but not high enough to clear a charging dökkálfar riding some strange beast with a sword held to strike. As Helreginn collided with the elf, he kicked it in the face, sending it flying backward from atop the creature it rode.

Zerri pumped her wings again, pulling herself and the king safely above the battle below. *Yes!* she cheered, new purpose filling her. She would show them. She would claim her place in the world and make her mother—

Zerri's breath hitched with a sudden sting of pain. Something was wrong. For a moment she feared Helreginn had stabbed her, and she nearly let go of the nephilbock. Craning her neck to see, she found the horror of a long metal shaft with a triangle-shaped tip protruding from her chest. Her eyes went wide with panic, her breaths coming short. Twisting her neck in the other direction, she found a metal shaft with three fletches protruded from this side too. This was no arrow from a bow – this was a dragon slayer.

Blood surged up the back of Zerri's throat as darkness filled her peripheral vision. *Oh, Mother. I'm sorry!* She tried to keep her wings pumping, but she couldn't feel them anymore. Ahead, she saw Cerberus and Jack standing on the hill watching her – watching her die!

Jack's voice found her. *Come on, Zerri! A little farther! Don't you fail me!*

Zerri felt herself dropping, and when the ground was close, darkness claimed her.

The moments following were a blur between the gaps of unconsciousness.

Jack standing over her.

Helreginn shouting at Jack.

Jack shouting back.

She couldn't breathe.

Cerberus talking, but not to her.

"Jack, perhaps you could heal this little one if you find her valuable."

"I've never tried healing someone else, Cerb. I may kill her."

"She's going to die anyway."

"Yes. Okay, have a half a dozen of those elves taken alive and brought here. Wait! Make it an even dozen."

She blacked out again, and the next time she opened her eyes, Jack was speaking. "Well, I can't do anything with that giant-ass arrow sticking out of her chest. Pull it out, Cerb."

Zerri heard a horrendous scream. It sounded like some poor soul was being slowly murdered. A second later, the pain told her the scream was her own. What followed was a violent crunching of bone and tearing of scale-covered flesh. It felt as if her insides were being pulled out.

The last thing Zerri heard before merciful darkness drew her into a dreamless sleep was the clang of metal falling onto stone.

When she next opened her eyes, Zerri had no way of knowing how much time had passed. She couldn't move, save for shivers from the cold chills racking her body. Her breath came fast and gargled, and the pain... oh, the pain.

Taking in her surroundings, she noticed that Helreginn was gone. Instead, several juvenile dragons stood watching her. Kneeling before the juveniles were a dozen elves.

The Last Gift

"Better hurry, she's bleeding out," Cerb said from somewhere.

A fuzzy image of Jack with his arms out and palms up filled Zerri's vision. All around her, dökkálfar screamed until their screams faded into moans, then to silence.

Jack's arms shook, then his whole body, as if about to explode. He staggered forward, slapping his palms against the scales of her chest.

Lightning surged through her, electric and hot, but the pain was different. This pain was giving her... giving her life! More than life! It poured into her chest, and it kept pouring – filling her lungs, filling her soul. Zerri gasped in a deep breath – a breath that would have been impossible to take in only a moment ago. Her eyes went wide and clear and she saw! Really saw! She saw what she was and what she would become.

Jack roared and dropped to one knee, then both, still pouring it on as he screamed.

Zerri roared too. But the roar wasn't her own, couldn't be her own! It was deep and different. She was different. This was not the pained cry of a dying dragon; this was the roar of a queen being born.

Jack's hands finally pulled free of her scales, and the little human fell onto his back.

Zerri rolled onto her belly and then stood.

Around her lay the smoking husks of a dozen dead dökkálfar. Around her, too, stood dozens of juvenile dragons, eyes wide in silent awe of what they had just watched unfold before them. What they had witnessed was more than healing – it was a rebirth.

Zerri looked down at herself anew, spread her wings for all to see, and smiled.

9

The Name on the Wind

God Stones – Moon Ring 1
The Shadow Forest

"No!" Pete shouted, dropping to his knees. He cradled Governess in his arms and lifted her from the floor. "She can't be dead! Are you sure?"

Tell raised an eyebrow. "Your friend appears to be withered, dried out, and her roots are clearly damaged. To me, she looks dead. I am not an expert in this, but my mother is. Please come now. We are not safe here for very long."

"Wait, I thought you said the dökkálfar won't come here?" Breanne asked.

"No, they can't, but it isn't them I'm worried about. It's humans," Tell said, picking up her spear and turning toward a wall that seemed to go nowhere. She placed her hand on a root, spoke the same words she had spoken above, and the roots changed.

"Hold on a second," Paul said. "We thought you were… well, human. Are you something else?"

"What?" Tell asked over her shoulder. "Of course I am

human. Don't I look human? Now please, this way." The roots twisted and moved, the dirt creating a nook that also seemed to go nowhere, but with every step Tell took, the space opened deeper and stairs formed, leading her up.

Breanne and the others shared uneasy glances, but they were trapped in a room below the ground with only one way out, leaving them with little choice but to follow. *We have to go.*

Garrett nodded, kneeling next to Pete. "Pete. We have to go."

"I'm not leaving her!" Pete shouted.

"Of course not. Do you want me to carry her?" Garrett asked.

"No. I'll do it. Just help me get her strapped to my pack."

While Garrett and Lenny secured the now-scraggly shrub to Pete's backpack, Bre pulled David to the side and addressed him in mind speak. *Here,* she said, extending the small medallion to David. *I think I speak dökkálfar now too.*

Seriously, how? he asked, carefully stuffing the medallion back into his cargo pocket and giving it a pat.

When the elves were chasing us, they were talking, and I understood them.

What did they say?

She squinted, replaying what she'd heard in her mind, something about a vision, and the name Ereshkigal. What had he said? *You expect us to believe a goddess spoke to you?* What did that mean?

Bre?

"Come. This way," Tell said.

They were just yelling, you know... don't let them get away, she said, not wanting to lie but not wanting to get into this – not when she didn't even understand what she'd heard. *Come on. Let's go.*

With a silent nod, they fell in behind Tell.

The hike was long and winding. The tunnel was always opening just ahead of them and closing off just behind. The tree roots seemed to manipulate the dirt to create the strange glowing tunnel. Mostly they climbed upward, but sometimes they hiked on even ground through the turquoise light before ascending once more. From what Breanne could tell, they were always heading up and never down.

Finally, after some time of silence, Breanne asked, "Tell, you said we weren't safe from other humans. Can you tell us what you meant?"

"It will be best if my mother explains this to you when we get home." The girl stopped and turned to face her. "Breanne, your name was whispered on the wind. As I'm sure you already know, you are very important to my people. But I must ask you. Are all of your remaining companions human? The creature who tried to speak to the forest was quite the surprise. If you have more among you who are not what they appear, it would be best if you told me now."

Breanne's mind reeled. She had no idea why she would be important to this girl's people. Garrett being important would make sense, but her? Also, what about Lenny? How was she supposed to answer?

As if reading her hesitation, Lenny spoke to her in mind speak. *Do not tell her what I am. I'm pretty sure they hate elves.*

Yeah, I agree, Bre. Those elves back there were not chasing us to make friends, David said.

Her mind filled with everyone's voices at once, all agreeing they should tell this girl as little as possible. Except Gabi. Gabi was quiet, and she had said little of anything since they got here. Something was wrong, but that would have to wait. *Okay!* she agreed.

"Why do you not answer, Breanne?" Tell asked.

Borrowing a move from Tell's own playbook, Breanne said, "Oh, well, we look human, don't we?" It was all she could think of without outright lying. And something told her lying wasn't a good way to start. So, instead, she decided not to tell the truth... exactly.

Tell smiled. "I guess that is fair. But your tree-like creature looked human too – until it didn't."

"Well, none of us are like her," Breanne answered truthfully.

"Very good. Let us continue then. We will arrive soon."

On they walked through the narrow, ever-changing tunnel. It was cool, but it wasn't cold, not like it had been above in the strange snow. It was also dry, and Breanne felt the thickness of dirt in her mouth, stirred up from the constantly changing structure of the tunnel forming as they walked.

Tell glanced back. "It seems we've pulled slightly ahead of the others," she said in a low voice. "May I ask you a personal question, Breanne?"

"Um, sure," she answered curiously.

"Are the men who travel with you your admirers?"

"What? Admirers?" she asked, unsure exactly how Tell was using the term. "I'm only seventeen years old," she said.

"What does that mean, years?" Tell asked.

"You don't have years?"

"No," Tell said evenly.

"Well, where I come from, we measure time by the travel of our planet around the sun. We call a trip around the sun a year, and a single day, twenty-four hours, is measured based on our planet's rotation. How do you measure time?"

"Ah, your day is like our moon ring, but we just say ring. For your hours we have shades, though there are more than twenty-four of them in a ring or what you called day. And what you called a year, I think must be like our moon cycle, or four hundred and fifty moon rings. We have seven moons, each belonging to one of the seven gods. We are currently in Turek's cycle as his is closest to our planet."

Breanne had a dozen questions, but as she opened her mouth to speak, Tell cut in.

"But enough of these mundane things. Let's talk of these men you travel with. If you are seventeen of these years, by the gods, you should have many admirers. Have you called any of them to your flower room? They are all so attractive. None of them would last long without being called here. Even the little hairy one."

Breanne blinked. "Flower room?"

"Tell me about the one I heard called Lenny?"

Breanne looked at Tell anew. The girl's body was hard and toned. Her loincloth didn't cover much, nor did her tunic, which ended just below her breasts. Wasn't she cold? Her black hair was long and braided in one long plait, adorned with beads, that stretched down her back. She may have been a little older than Bre, nineteen or maybe twenty. One thing was for sure: Tell was beautiful.

"Hey, are we getting close?" David called from behind. "I need water or I'm going to die."

"Some of your men seem a bit on the weak side," Tell whispered, then shouted back, "Just a little farther."

"No, it's just that it's been an incredibly long day for my people, and we have traveled very far," Breanne said, trying not to sound defensive.

"Of course, Breanne. I meant no disrespect. We are here," she said, stepping through the opening at the end of the shifting corridor.

Emerging from the trunk of a tree, they were once again in the Shadow Forest, but ahead, she could see a brighter area where the trees thinned. As they drew closer, she heard voices and could smell a cook fire.

Oh my god! You guys smell that? Someone's cooking meat! David said, his voice full of longing.

Breanne's stomach growled, yet despite her own desperate hunger, she couldn't help feeling apprehensive. With no vision of what the next few minutes might hold, she would have to rely on her gut and right now, her gut was telling her that something was off.

Stepping from the underbrush, they soon found themselves on a trail. Ahead, a small village of structures made from stacked stone topped with thatch roofs sat against a rocky outcrop rising into a steep mountain backdrop.

The image was breathtaking, but the village itself was underwhelming. Breanne wasn't sure what she'd expected other than… more. Was this really it?

"Come, you must meet my mother and the others," Tell said.

"The others?" Lenny asked.

Tell cocked her head and smiled.

Breanne realized now the smile was flirtatious.

Tell reached for Lenny's hand. "Come on!" she shouted, breaking into a run.

Lenny bolted after her, and the rest of them followed.

As they entered the village, the first thing Breanne noticed were three men sitting around a cook fire near the center of the camp. A few more men milled about. One was tossing handfuls of feed into a pen of birds that looked similar to chickens; they stood on two legs and had wings, but they had ears like lop-eared rabbits and, instead of feathers, they had brown fur that looked as soft as chinchilla. Two other men were stacking stone from a wooden cart onto a short rock wall. As they approached, all the men stopped and stared, bowing low as Tell passed.

Breanne noticed Tell did not bow back but only nodded to each. From their earlier conversation, Breanne expected the town to be full of women. "Tell, where are the women?"

Tell scrunched her face. "Why would you think them here?" she asked over her shoulder. Not waiting for an answer, she gestured them forward again. "Come, we are almost there."

They continued into the small village until they reached a long wooden building constructed on a foundation of stacked stone. All the wood used in the structure appeared to be from fallen trees, and the building was covered in a roof of thatch.

"They are waiting for you in here," Tell said, climbing a set of stone stairs. On either side of the door stood two muscular female guards dressed similarly to Tell and with black hair braided down their backs. Both held spears in hand. Unlike Tell, these women wore red bands tied around their upper arms just above their biceps and had matching red stripes down their nose and each cheek.

As Tell climbed the steps, the two women bowed. But Breanne noticed they did not bow as low as the men had, and this time Tell returned the gesture.

She is someone important, Pete said, in mind speak.

It was the first time he'd spoken since Governess went down. Breanne was glad to hear his voice. *You're right, Pete. And those men back there doing the village chores… Are you thinking what I'm thinking?*

The women appraised the others dubiously, but when their eyes settled on Breanne, they bowed low.

Breanne bowed back, trying to match the depth of their bow like Tell had.

Matriarchal? Pete asked.

Yep.

One woman turned and rapped a pattern on the door.

Um, Bre? I actually don't know what that means, David said, sounding embarrassed.

It's okay. It means—

The door swung open.

"Come. My mother is waiting!"

Inside the dimly lit structure, Breanne craned her neck to see past Tell. Dozens upon dozens of women, sitting on top of pelts, were gathered around a fire burning inside a ring of stacked stone. Others sat or lay upon deep sleeping shelves, also covered with layers of pelts, that lined the walls.

The chamber was deadly silent save for the crackling fire. Breanne could feel the room's eyes on Tell and the strangers that accompanied her.

Tell leaned her spear against the wall and stepped forward. "Mother, did you hear the wind today?"

A woman at the far end of the longhouse stood slowly, as if being careful not to upset the fragile calm of the room. Carefully, she walked between the seated women. As she drew closer, Breanne saw that she looked like an older version of Tell, maybe in her thirties. She wore a nearly transparent silk wrap, sparsely covering her chest and pelvis. Scars on her shoulders, arms, and stomach looked patterned, maybe tribal, but a few others, one on her left shoulder and one down her left side, looked different… unintentional.

The woman lifted her chin and spoke. "We all heard the wind today, my child. Turek has finally spoken! Now tell us, who are these strangers?"

Tell stepped to the side and pointed at Breanne. "This *is* Breanne Moore! Just as the wind said. She is really here, Mother! She has come to lead us in battle against King Deep and take back the queendom of Sky!"

10

Battle at the Wall

God Stones – Moon Ring 1
The Portal, outside of Osonian

Atop the hill where the hollow pyramid stood, Jack stared up through fuzzy eyes and forced himself to his feet. Even he knew better than to show weakness in front of those he led. Steadying himself, he tried not to sway as he blinked away the blurred image of an unfamiliar dragon standing before him.

Cerb's chest rumbled as he laughed. "By the belly of Typhon! Look at what you've created, Jack!"

Jack blinked again… and he did look. Before him stood a full-sized female dragon. Each dragon scale looked like black glass traced in thin, blood-red lines. The dragon's horns, and she had many, were all pointing back like thick locks of hair. She stretched open her wings, each spiked on the tips with hooked horns. But it was her eyes that found Jack, not red eyes but white – bright like two stars.

Zerri? he asked.

The dragon folded her wings and spoke. *I am Zerri, the Queen of Queens.*

Her voice was strange too. Just as nothing in Zerri's appearance remained of the small grey dragon, nothing of Zerri's old voice remained either. Now she sounded otherworldly. She sounded a lot like Azazel had.

Cerb laughed again. "Taker! Look at what you have done! Think of it, you could do this with all of our hordes! Think how powerful our army would be!"

Jack looked down at his hands. Something was wrong. They were shaking and throbbing. He turned his palms down, looked at his fingernails and froze, his heart pounding. They were turning black. Not the flesh around his fingernails, but the flesh beneath them. Almost as if he had painted them. This was a sign. *Apep,* he thought. Not me. No way. Not me!

"No, Cerb. I've seen where this leads, and I won't be making the mistakes Apep made," he said, keeping his attention on Zerri. "Just remember who saved you, Zerri." He took a step closer to her. "Better still, remember who made you."

Zerri dipped her head and hissed. "And you remember who made *you*, Jack the Taker." She withdrew her head to stand tall once more. "Now what of the slave dragons, Jack? I brought you your giant. What now?"

Jack smiled. "Helreginn has pledged the allegiance of all of his nephilbock. I've already ordered our hordes to form up here at the portal so that we can attack in full force. But don't take my word for it. Turn around and see for yourself, my Queen of Queens!"

He watched as the magnificent dragon turned to the battlefield below. The nephilbock were pressing forward, pushing the elves back toward the wall. From Jack's vantage point overlooking the battle, it seemed obvious that the nephilbock were being led into a trap as elven warriors slowly fell back toward the wall's main gate, allowing the enslaved dragons to flank the giants as they surged forward. But the elves didn't know what Jack knew. All around the portal, the hordes were gathering en masse, filling the hillside like an overgrown flock of geese, preparing to launch in full force.

As the enslaved dragons below reached the end of their chains, and the elves prepared to spring their trap, Jack gave the order. *Jack's hordes, fly directly at the chains and the elves controlling the dragons. Burn the chains and kill the dragon masters first! Cut them off from retreat! We can't let them get back to the wall! Succeed, and you will all have full bellies on this day!*

Jack ran up the back of Cerb. *Cerb, see those bastards on top of the wall? Let's light them up!*

There was a slight hesitation in the hordes, as if they were waiting for something else.

You heard Taker, Zerri shouted. *Now hear your queen! I order you, one and all – to the fight!*

Well, that was annoying. But he let it go. Instead, Jack held up a fist and shouted in the minds of every dragon. *Well! What are you waiting for? To the fight!*

Cerberus flapped his wings, echoing the war cry, *To the fight!*

Thousands of dragon voices erupted in Jack's mind. *To the fight!*

Like a flock of birds spooked from a field, the dragons lifted from the ground and raced toward the battlefield.

Below, the nephilbock lifted their weapons high and surged forward.

Across the field, a horn blew.

That must be their signal, Cerb! The elf bastards are springing the trap! Get to the wall! Zerri, we'll go right, you take the left. Let's light 'em up!

Cerb flew hard for the top of the wall and Jack held on with all he had. The cold wind bit brutally against his cheeks. But thankfully he had his leather jacket and besides, there'd be dragon fire to warm him soon enough.

This was what it was all about – flying your dragon to war! Shitloads of fire and burning elves! "Yeah!" Jack yelled, letting go with one hand just long enough to punch a fist in the air.

As fast as Cerb carried him up into a sky hanging low with clouds, his speed was nothing compared to the streak of black and red that blew past them in a blur.

Don't be long, boys! Zerri shouted.

Holy shit, Cerb! If Zerri was fast before, she's light speed now!

She's okay, Taker. But I could fly faster if not for fear I'd lose you, Cerb said with annoyance.

Jack wanted to call the big bastard's shit talk for what it was, but a small part of him worried Cerb might actually throw him from his back if he really could go faster.

When Jack didn't respond, Cerb asked, *You doubt me, brother?*

Jack didn't bite. *Look out!*

From atop the wall came a ball of fire sailing in their direction. Cerb banked and the flaming ball blew past, dropping into the nephilbock army below.

One measly fireball! Ha, is that the best you got? Jack taunted.

Below them, Jack could barely make out the elves finishing their hasty retreat toward the gate. Now safely behind a half circle of evenly spaced elder dragons, the dökkálfar were protected and the nephilbock were sitting ducks.

They had to act now. *Jack's horde! Dive behind the dragons! Kill the dragon masters and free the slaves! Do it now!*

Hundreds of dragons dove.

Arrows launched into the air, from both atop the wall and through slots in the stone at various heights. But no number of arrows could stop this many dragons, especially when dragon scales deflected most of them. Sure, dozens of dragons fell, crashing into the battlefield below, but it was insignificant. Jack had the overwhelming numbers.

From the far end, the top of the wall exploded in dragon fire as Zerri released a torrent of dragon flame into the bowmen, killing dozens of dökkálfar.

Yeah! Jack shouted. *Fire, Cerb!*

Cerberus the Mighty did fire, and from all three heads. Three streams of black-and-orange dragon fire raced down the wall that separated them from Osonian. Elves screamed, falling hundreds of feet, flailing limbs set afire before they collided with the ground far below.

Jack laughed. *That's what you get!*

From somewhere behind the wall came another ball of flame, then another. It started with a few, then quickly became a dozen flaming balls, then suddenly, the sky was full of fireballs. Thick dark smoke trailed the balls of flame, filling the sky with dense black soot. Far below, nephilbock were crushed, sometimes several at once.

Sometimes the fireballs stuck fast to the ground, digging in, but if the angle was right, they rolled like giant flaming bowling balls, taking out dozens of giants and leaving a path of fire. As the sky blackened, the dragons lost visibility, unable to see and thus unable to dodge.

The hordes came alive with voices.

I'm blind!

My eyes are burning!

I'm choking! Who could breathe this?

Dammit! Jack said, trying to see what was happening on the ground. *Listen to me! Cerb and I will handle this. You all need to fly low. Smoke rises. We can't stop until the slaves are free! Follow your orders! Kill the dragon masters and free our dragons!*

Below, an enslaved elder dragon let loose a roar and a blast of flame.

The screams of burning nephilbock and juvenile dragons reached Jack and Cerb all the way up near the top of the wall. A moment later, a wave of heat washed up from below.

Shit! Jack shouted, slamming a fist down on Cerb's scales. *The slavers are forcing the enslaved dragons to burn our army!*

Stay calm, Jack. Our hordes will free the dragons.

Jack frowned. *Well, they better do it quick! And Jesus H. Christ, Cerb! What the hell are those fireballs?*

From the smell, I would guess burning tar. From the damage they're inflicting, they must be boulders.

Jack choked, pulling the collar of his T-shirt up over his nose. *Tar-dipped boulders! I think it's time we show these elves what a severe case of bubble guts feels like. Then we'll see how effective they are when they're doubled over and shitting their pants!*

Cerb hesitated. *Jack, we don't know what else they might have on the other side of that wall, and with the low clouds and all this smoke... Perhaps we'd be wise not to cross over until we've freed the slaves?*

Jack shook his head. *We don't need to cross over, Cerb. Just pass by the wall close enough for me to touch it and I'll pour life-sucking disease into each and every one of those bastards! Then we'll be able to blast that wall into pieces!*

Cerberus roared, dropped, and pivoted.

For Jack, it felt as if he were on a roller coaster at Six Flags and he'd just tipped over the hill for the big drop. As his stomach lurched into his throat, his arms tensed, forcing him to renew his grip on Cerb's horns.

Jack shouted as sudden vertigo forced him to slam his eyes shut. *Cerb! Jesus Christ! I said get close, not run into it!* For a moment, he was sure Cerb was going to sideswipe the stone wall.

Close enough?

Jack forced his eyes open, glancing to his right.

If you are going to do it, best do it now! Cerb laughed.

Jack did not laugh.

What? You wanted to be close enough to touch it!

Dick! Jack shouted, knowing that at the speed Cerb was flying, touching that wall would rip the flesh from his hand. Jack quickly concentrated just as he had back in Petersburg when he'd reached for the Sentheye and sent disease through the door in Undertown. Reaching out with disease, he probed through the stone wall.

Reaching and reaching when… what the?

Something was wrong – horribly wrong.

Cerb, do you feel that? Jack asked, but before Cerb could respond, Jack's right arm began to burn. He looked at the back of his hand. It was swelling, and large boils were forming. His throat felt suddenly tight, and his head ached. What the shit? This wasn't right. He was being diseased. Someone was diseasing him. His mind flashed to the image of the dark elf in the golden robe standing atop the wall.

"Cerb! Get away from the wall!" he shouted aloud. His voice was slurred by his fast-swelling tongue, but he had no choice. His head was splitting, and he couldn't think clearly enough to use telepathy.

Down they dropped through plumes of ash and smoke, a hundred feet, then two. Below, the battle raged. Elder dragon fire and the smell of burning flesh filled the battlefield.

We have only freed two of the slaves! a familiar voice shouted into his mind. *The slavers are fireproof! They will not burn. And worse, when we get too close, they take over your mind!*

Jack's blinding headache faded as Cerb navigated away from the wall and closer to the battleground. Although his head felt better, his mouth, throat, and the whole right side of his body stung as if burned. He tried to use telepathy again. *Ahi! Is that you?*

It is I, Ahi answered.

Jack had thought the last of Azazel's elder dragons were dead. Where in the hell had he been? More importantly, was Ahi going to be a problem? If so, it was one he didn't need, not now.

As if sensing his concern, Ahi replied to the unanswered question. *What are your orders, Taker?*

Jack opened his mind to the hordes. *Listen to me, all of you! We can't get close enough to stop the fireballs! They're using some powerful wizards or something. Focus on laying down cover for Helreginn and the nephilbock. They'll have to take the slavers down. Then once we free the slaves, we withdraw!*

You don't want to press the wall? Try to take the city? Ahi asked.

The slaves are our priority. Once we free the last of them, we need to regroup.

He's right, Ahi, another familiar voice answered. *There is too much power within the wall. The slaves are all that matter.*

Understood, my queen. Lord Taker, Ahi answered, *I will personally see we make a way for the nephilbock.*

Zerri! Jack said, sounding more relieved than he meant to.

I'm fine... Lord Taker, Zerri said, amusement in her voice. *You better go fetch your giant. I will assist Ahi in protecting the nephilbock.*

Lord Taker? He could get used to that. *Cerb, find Helreginn. We have to get him on the same page, or he and his army are screwed.*

Cerb let out a strange grunt and then said, *I'll find him.*

What was that?

Arrow.

Arrow? You're hit? Jack asked, panic filling him.

Ha! Cerb laughed.

Why are you laughing?

I am Cerberus the Mighty! I have been struck by twenty-three arrows in this battle and none have pierced my scales!

Relieved, Jack laughed nervously. *Twenty-three arrows, Cerb? And you're okay?*

I am fine, but you are not. You need to heal, Jack.

After we find Helreginn, Jack said, pointing. *Look! Right there at the front! Let's see if you can pull this off as smoothly as Zerri did earlier!*

I see him, but I do not believe he will be happy to see us. Hold on!

Jack looked down to find Helreginn standing on blood-soaked ground, fighting alongside tennis shoe necklace guy and another giant that looked like a bigger, younger version of the king. Blue-skinned elves lay dead all around their feet. Cerb was right. The king wasn't going to be thrilled about getting pulled from the fight again. They were at the front of the battle, pushing back a group of dökkálfar. Apparently, the dökkálfar had sent reinforcements from behind the wall to hold the line and keep the nephilbock inside the half circle of dragons. Between the rain of fireballs and the slave dragons closing in, thousands of nephilbock were about to be toast.

Cerb, I don't want to be this close to the wall for any longer than we have to be. Get him and get out.

Cerb dropped low, breathing a gout of fire into the dökkálfar as he pulled Helreginn from the battlefield. The elves dropped low into formation as they interlocked their shields to form a deflective wall. The fire from Cerb did only minor damage, but it gave him and Jack the time they needed.

Jack glimpsed tennis shoe necklace guy looking on with horror as they stole away his king for the second time in the last hour.

Below Cerb, Helreginn's voice shouted up angrily, "Why? Why have you pulled me from the battle yet again? We have nearly pushed them to the gates! A little closer and their sky fire will pass over us! Why, Jack?"

Jack ignored him. Not that he didn't want to answer, he simply couldn't find the energy to yell, and his head was spinning again.

Cerb descended to a safe place behind the battle.

Jack slid down Cerb's side and nearly toppled when he landed, only then realizing he couldn't bear weight on his right side. He grimaced and looked up at the king.

"Take me back!" Helreginn ordered, looking down at Jack, then back toward the battle. "My warriors need me!"

"I will take you back. I will take you right now, but you need to focus everything on killing the slavers," Jack said evenly.

"And surrender our push to the gate? Why? Your dragons are supposed to be taking care of this!"

"We can't kill them—they're fireproof, and they're using some kind of mind control on my dragons, turning them against each other when they get too close," Jack said, grimacing as a sudden shock of pain cramped his gut.

"They may be fireproof, but their heads will split like any other dökkálfar."

Jack forced a smile. "Good. Abandon the gate and rush the enslaved dragons, but don't attack them. Instead, overwhelm them and go straight for the slavers while we provide you cover from the air. Then, after they are free, get your people out."

"Get out! Why? Why not push on to the gate and take the city?" the giant asked, so angry he was spitting now.

Jack blinked. Not at the spittle, but at the overwhelming sensation he might pass out. "The dökkálfar have powerful magic in the wall, and at least one of them can disease like me," he managed.

"You have powerful magic atop your head! Do you not understand war? In war, the victorious take everything. We could have an entire city to do with as we please."

Jack, swaying on his feet, stared up at the king. "No. Circle back to the portal. We will… will meet back there."

The king opened his mouth to speak again, revealing his menacing double row of shark-like teeth, but stopped short, pulling his mouth closed once more. The king frowned and looked at Jack anew. "You are injured? Is this the magic from the wall?"

Jack stood a little straighter, trying not to show his weakness to the giant, but he knew it was too late for that. "I'll be fine. But you will lose your army if you try to breach that gate. We need to regroup. Besides, once we free the dragons, you will have earned your alliance with me, King. There is no reason we have to push forward now. We need to be smart. We need to do this right."

The giant king looked down and nodded. "Quickly, take me back."

Jack nodded in return. "I need you to do something for me first."

"What is it?"

Jack's vision blurred as he tried to blink the fuzziness away and focus on Helreginn once more. "Lift me onto my dragon."

11

The Second Question

God Stones – Moon Ring 1
The Shadow Forest

As Tell stepped to the side and pointed at Breanne, the room exploded in cheers, all the women shouting at once. The eruption was so loud, Garrett had to squint against the outburst of joy.

"Turek has spoken from the wind!" said one woman.
"Breanne Moore has finally come!" said another.
Still another shouted, "She will lead us in battle!"
Around the room, the shouts continued.
"Finally, the so-called king will pay for his treason!"
"We will show the men back to the true way!"
All the women were now on their feet cheering.

What's happening? Lenny asked in mind speak, voicing Garrett's own confusion.

Slowly, the longhouse calmed back to quiet as the women noticed their leader holding up a hand for silence. She lifted her other hand and then lowered both. The women bowed and lowered themselves back to seated positions, ensuring there was no obstruction between their leader's line of sight and Breanne.

The leader stared with intense eyes, her gaze fixed on Breanne as if in silent judgment.

You guys, what the hell did we just walk into? Breanne asked.

Garrett wasn't sure, but as he shared uneasy glances with the others, he noticed it was David who looked like he was champing at the bit to blurt something he shouldn't. *David? What?*

David sighed. *Well, it's just, why would Turek speak Breanne's name and not yours, if you're supposed to be the chosen one? Shouldn't we tell them you're the descendant of Turek?*

No! Garrett answered quickly. *Don't say anything about me. If Turek really is behind this, he's doing it for a reason.*

Roger that, Paul agreed.

Roger what? David asked.

Don't you get it, kid? Do you think these women would follow Garrett? Not a chance, Paul said.

Pete shrugged to adjust the weight of his pack. No doubt it was heavy with Governess strapped to it. *Paul's right. This is a matriarchal society, just as Breanne and I suspected.*

David shook his head. *Well. That seems just… well, no offense, Breanne, but that seems crazy. That would never fly on Earth. And if – correction, when – we figure this whole thing out and we bring the Keepers back here, they're going to have to get used to a different way of doing things, or we may have to make our own whole new—*

Pete pinched the bridge of his nose. *David, please shut up. You have no idea what you're talking about and you're getting way ahead of yourself.*

Well, shit, Pete! You don't have to be—

Breanne interjected, cutting him off again. *Pete's right.*

David frowned.

Sorry, Breanne continued, *not that you should shut up, but that you don't have any idea what you're talking about. There are plenty of examples of matriarchal societies both in Earth's history and in present-day societies. Women have been leading throughout history, David, and they are still leading today.*

Well, Lenny said, crossing his arms and shooting David a sour look, *I think Pete was right on the other part too. You should just shut the shit up, David.*

Listen, however you are going to play this, Breanne, Pete said, his voice cracking even in mind speak, *please hurry. We have to see if they can help Governess.*

"This is interesting," the leader said.

Garrett realized the women were no longer looking at their leader. They were watching them.

"What's interesting?" Breanne asked.

The leader raised an eyebrow. "You speak our language as if you were born speaking it."

"But that isn't what you found interesting, because I had yet to speak," Breanne said confidently.

"Indeed," the woman said, the corner of her mouth hinting at a knowing smile. "I was referencing the magic you are using to talk among yourselves."

David's panicked voice filled Garrett's mind. *Shit, she knows! What if she heard everything we said? What if she can hear me right now?*

Then maybe you should shut that hairy freaking face of yours like I told you! Lenny said.

"You can hear us?" Breanne asked aloud.

"No. But we are not blind. The short, well-fed one talks with his hands." The leader pointed at David. "He was literally just doing it."

David's eyes went wide, and he balled his fist. "Listen,

lady!" he said, raising a hand to point as he stepped forward toward the group. "I won't have you talking to me like—"

Five women sprang to their feet from the floor of the longhouse without even using their hands as five spears lifted, simultaneously coming to rest an inch from David's face.

David reeled back and nearly fell. "Holy... come on! Please? Don't! Sorry!" he rambled, slamming his eyes shut and waving his hands.

David, so help me god! Lenny started.

Everyone except Gabi get behind me, Breanne ordered. *Gabi, step in front of the guys and stand with me. David, go to the back of the group.*

Smart, Bre, Garrett said, seeing where this was going.

And no one except for Gabi or I speak out loud unless you are asked a question, or I give you permission.

They all nodded as onlookers cocked sideways glances at their strange, wordless gestures.

Breanne turned toward the leader. "How may I address you?"

"Please call me Key. And I must apologize for our rudeness." She waved the spear-wielding women off. "We are the women of Shadow Forest, but once we belonged to the queendom of Sky."

"And you were their queen?" Breanne asked.

"My mother is still *our* queen," Tell said.

Key smiled. "You flatter me, daughter, but the truth is as long as King Deep sits on the throne of Sky, there is no queen, only unbalance, chaos, and brutality." She looked at Breanne curiously. "Besides, if you are who you say you are, then—"

The door burst open, and a woman stumbled across the threshold. Garrett recognized her as one of the two who had been guarding the door outside.

"Gateman has escaped," she cried out, her face strained.

Garrett noticed her eyebrow trickling blood. Someone had attacked her.

"Mother, should we send after him?" Tell urged.

"No. Forget him. He has gone to warn Deep. We have four rings, five at most," Key said, her own face showing concern. "We've known for some time there was a spy among us. I have had my suspicions about Gateman. Perhaps I should have acted on them sooner, but what's done is done."

"The men we saw outside, they're your prisoners then?" Breanne asked.

"What? Gods no. We are good to our men. They are not prisoners to us. The men you see here could have all revolted during the uprising but are here because they choose to be here with us. Not only have they chosen our way, but they also wish to return to the way it was."

Key nodded to the bleeding woman. "Go. Have Tindleman see to that eye."

The woman bowed and retreated backward out of the longhouse, closing the door behind her.

"Now forgive us our manners. You all must be thirsty, hungry, and cold. Come away from the door and sit by the fire. Our men will serve you."

Next to Garrett, David rubbed his hands together.

Three men Garrett hadn't even noticed among the women stood and moved to the edge of the fire while another retrieved a waterskin and started forward. The men by the fire began skewering strips of meat onto long metal prongs that reminded Garrett of marshmallow roasting sticks. As soon as the meat touched the flame, it sizzled and smoked, the smell wafting past his nose.

Holy heck, yes! David blurted, but thankfully only in mind speak.

The man with the waterskin stepped forward.

David licked his lips.

Key held up her hand.

The man paused.

"First, there is one small matter I must attend to before I can extend my most gracious hospitality," she said, leveling her eyes at Breanne.

Great, what now? Garrett wondered.

"Please, go on," Breanne said.

"You are speaking to your companions using magic. Who is to say you have not tricked the wind with this same magic? Who is to say you are who you say you are? I do not mean to disrespect you, but you do see my dilemma, don't you?"

Oh, come on! David shouted into Garrett's mind. *Does this mean we aren't getting any food?* he complained, raising his hands and slapping them down dramatically against his thighs.

Lenny glared at David with a look Garrett had rarely witnessed from the even-keeled boy. *I am going to kick you in the balls so freaking hard they're going to land in your stomach. And I promise as those little nuts roll around in the bottom of your belly, swelling to the size of baseballs, the last thing you will be thinking about is food! Now shut the hell up!*

Well, that was unnecessarily graphic! David said, crossing his arms.

Lenny's jaw worked as he shook his head.

Garrett feared where this was going and quickly nudged Lenny in the ribs with his elbow, giving him a "knock it off" look.

"Even now I see your companions are talking to each other, no doubt planning some clever strategy? Oh, don't worry, Breanne Moore, I cannot hear them. Whatever they conspire to, I only see the looks of intense conversation, especially in the round one's flurry of hand movements."

Yeah, if only she knew this conversation is about as clever as a bag of rocks, Paul said, giving both Lenny and David the stink eye. *Now both of you, stow it.*

Holding Key's gaze, Bre seemed to ignore all the distractions. "How do I show you I am who I say I am?"

Key nodded. "Yes. Indeed, how? I will tell you. Simply answer two questions correctly, Breanne Moore, and I will know that you are truly the one and that the wind was truly Turek and not some trick of magic. But be warned – if this is a trick, some clever put-on by King Deep, the consequences will be dire."

I don't know if this is a good idea, sis, Paul said.

It's fine, you guys, Breanne said.

How can you be sure? Garrett asked.

Breanne nodded. *Because whether you believe it was the wind, Turek, or something else, someone spoke my name to these people. And it wasn't us.* Then out loud she said, "Please, proceed with your questions, Lady Key," and bowed her head slightly.

"Our species hold relatively brief lives compared to dragons, elves, and giants. In fact, our lives are shorter by nature than many of Karelia's inhabitants," Key said. As she stepped around the fire pit, women scooted back, opening a path for their queen. As Key drew within reach of Bre, Garrett noticed the other women tense uneasily.

"What we have – have always had – is a robust written language. For moon cycles untold, our kind has kept records. When our god, Turek, left this world with those she could quickly gather, she wrote an entry into our scroll. It said, 'When the time comes, another will foreshadow the promise of my return and lead a group back to Karelia – back home.'"

A woman? Turek had never appeared to Garrett as a woman. He was about to use mind speak to say as much when he that realized Turek, whatever he was, could probably appear as anything he – or they – wanted.

Key stepped even closer, right in front of them now. Patterned scars on her otherwise dark-brown skin reflected in the firelight. Behind her, all the women climbed to their feet, spears in hand.

Garrett felt his armpits sweating.

"Very few have seen this scroll, and none of them have been men – certainly not this so-called king of Sky!" she said, glancing at Garrett and the other guys before leveling her eyes on Bre once more. "In the scroll, written in Turek's own hand, she states the leader of this group will have a special ability, a magical gift only she possesses."

"A magical gift?" Breanne repeated.

Key nodded. "Tell me, Breanne Moore, she whose name was spoken on the wind, what is your magical gift?"

Breanne! Wait! Let's think about this, Paul said. *For starters, you have the ability to use telepathy.*

Lenny cut in. *But we all have that ability, Paul.*

Lenny's right, Garrett said. *But Bre's the only one who can teleport, and she's the only one who can see the future.*

So, which one should she say? David asked.

I don't know, sis, maybe you can ask her to—

"I can see the future," Breanne said evenly.

Key stared at her for what felt to Garrett like a full year as the room held a collective breath. Finally, she said, "Yes. Yes, Breanne," her eyes wide with wonder.

The room erupted in cheers.

Key raised her hand for silence once more. "You must now answer the second question. Tell me, seer – what future do you see for us?"

12

Fallen

God Stones – Moon Ring 1
The Battlefield, outside of Osonian

When the dragon talons finally released King Helreginn, he dropped from high above his warriors, landing hard in the slop of war. The unintelligible shouts of dökkálfar filled the evening battlefield. Late evening, he thought. Though it was hard to say with two suns watching from an unfamiliar sky, both obscured by a shower of fireballs and black smoke. But the day had been long, and it felt like it must be evening. Would darkness come soon? Did darkness even exist in a world with two suns?

The king raised his sword, made of Shard Mountain steel, and pushed his way forward through the blood, smoke, and death, shouting, "Out of the way! Let your king pass!"

Through the smoky haze, a massive giant swung a war hammer at a charging dökkálfar. The single blow erased the elf's head from existence. The elf's body tumbled from its horse-like creature, but the creature charged forward, riderless, teeth bared to bite. Snatching hold of the beast in a clenched fist, a giant warrior snapped its neck.

The horse thing collapsed lifelessly to the ground.

If not for the strange tangle of human foot coverings strung around the nephilbock warrior's neck, Helreginn would have thought the massive High Guard to be King Ogliosh himself. But this giant of a nephilbock was not Ogliosh. And what of Ogliosh? Gone, along with the other full-blooded nephilbock. Whether dead or fled, it hardly mattered now.

"Zebrog!" Helreginn shouted, knowing that his favorite son, Gato, would be close.

The big nephilbock turned, revealing a face covered in dökkálfar blood. "My king! You have returned to us! We thought you lost!"

"I cannot be lost! But hear me, High Guard."

Others who could hear turned from the battle to listen.

Gato, hearing his father's voice, pushed his way over. "My king! You're safe?"

"We have a new mission, and we must act now. The chained dragons are slowly squeezing us into a trap."

"But the dragons were supposed—"

Helreginn grabbed his son by his chest plate and yanked him forward as a flaming boulder fell from the sky. The boulder missed Gato but slammed another to the ground; gore and flaming tar splashed around them.

Burning tar covered the back of Gato's arm. He knelt, shoving his arm into the blood-soaked mud, extinguishing the fire with a hiss.

The wounded nephilbock lay pinned, screaming out, his legs crushed and burning.

Zebrog raised his war hammer.

"No!" Helreginn said, stepping over to the pinned

warrior. "You have done well, my child. You have made your king proud. Your fight is over!" Helreginn drove his own sword down through the nephilbock's chest and twisted it with a grunt.

The warrior went still as the king withdrew the blade and turned back to the others. "Listen to me. The sky dragons cannot kill the slavers. The burden lies with us! We must split the field. Zebrog, take half of the nephilbock and charge past the dragons. Once we kill the slavers, the dragons' minds will be freed, and they will not attack us."

"And if they attack us before?" Zebrog asked.

"If the dragons breathe fire before the slavers are dead, then we are dead." He could see the look on the nephilbock faces gathered round. His warriors were brave, but even they knew they couldn't outrun dragon fire. "Look at me, warriors of Agartha. Have I not done as I promised? Have I not brought you back to your true homeland? Trust in these words. The enslaved dragons will not breathe fire until the dökkálfar warriors positioned in front of them fall back. Speed will be the key! The bulk of the dökkálfar have their forces at the wall protecting the gate. They expect us to push forward until they spring their trap!" The king motioned at the flanks. "This leaves the dökkálfar forces on the flanks thin, and if not for the enslaved dragons, the battlefield's flanks would be weak." Helreginn looked up, meeting his High Guard's eyes. "Unexpected, overwhelming force, Zebrog! This is the only way. We will charge them like angry buffalo!"

"Yes, my king! And may the gods smile upon us!" Zebrog said.

At Zebrog's words, sudden outrage flushed Helreginn's face, but to his men it must have looked like battle rage, for they too bared angry teeth. In truth, this new anger shocked him. And for a second, he almost felt ashamed, but no, why should he? He hadn't lied. He hadn't abandoned his people. Anger swelled again. The gods were false! Pseudo gods! Imposters! The king quickly pushed these emotions from his mind. To lose focus on the task before them was to fail when his nephilbock needed him most. These new revelations would be dealt with. But now was not the time. Helreginn nodded. "May the gods smile upon us, Zebrog!" he answered, slapping the shoulder of his biggest warrior. Turning to Gato, he continued, "My son, we will take the other half of our forces and charge the opposite side! Now, shout the orders! We go on my count!"

Another fireball hissed past, followed by a shower of arrows. Helreginn looked up with only enough time to respond reflexively, dipping his head back down to take the arrow directly to the forehead. The arrow sliced his skin to the bone before deflecting off his thick skull. Blood filled his eyes. Just another battle scar in the making. "On me! Surge forward now!"

The mass of nephilbock shoved forward as if launching a renewed attempt on the gate.

As they pushed, King Helreginn shouted full out, "Three! Two! One! Turn and charge!"

The field split, starting in the center and flowing like a wave crossing the Blood Sea of Agartha, as they charged the dragons.

The dragons roared, but just as the wise king had predicted, the enslaved dragons couldn't breathe flame until the rows of dökkálfar moved from the line of fire.

Unintelligible dökkálfar shouting came from the direction of the gate. For a moment, Helreginn worried the elves might rush onto the field, filling the split and attacking them from the rear.

But when the attack never came, the king stole a glance back and found the sky dragons plunging down from above

The Last Gift

by the dozens. The small dragons doused fire into the charging elves. The elves should have been running, fleeing the fire to come, but they did not flee. Instead, they met the fire head on, forming an interlocking shield dome around themselves.

From the wall, a fresh wave of steel bolts and flaming stone dropped from above, even more than before. Dragons fell from the sky one after another. Most smashed into the ground, but occasionally a dying dragon would collide with the elven warriors, killing those not fast enough to move.

The strange creature, Jack, may have been sacrificing many of his dragons, but just as he had promised, the dragons were providing cover. The bulk of the dökkálfar army was being held safely at bay.

Helreginn pushed on, having nearly crossed the field when he heard swords clash as elves and giants screamed the cries of battle.

"Father! We are close! Look, the stupid elves aren't pulling back! We will crush them!" Gato shouted.

A sick feeling filled the nephilbock king's stomach. The elves weren't pulling back their warriors on the flanks even though their force was too thin to stop his wave of nephilbock. Another thought crossed the king's mind, and he felt sicker still. *In war, sacrifice the few for many.* "Do not stop! Push through and press for the slavers!"

"Father, what is it?" Gato said, keeping pace with his father as he pushed forward through the muck.

The king pointed ahead. "The slavers are going to sacrifice their own warriors to kill us."

"They would kill their own?" Gato questioned.

The answer came as all thirteen enslaved dragons around the battlefield roared in unison.

"Gato!" Helreginn shouted over the roar. "Quickly, find cover!"

When the flames came, Helreginn couldn't have been in a worse place: Standing opposite a crowd of dökkálfar, staring up at a giant, red-scaled slave dragon as it exhaled fire. The mighty king of the nephilbock could see the dragon's tongue shake as the flames ignited. There was no escape for him.

"Gato!" Helreginn shouted, but his son was gone, lost in the chaos. In front of him, three dökkálfar lunged forward, their strange swooping eyes stretched wide. The king could see it in the blue devils' eyes. They knew this was their end. They knew, and still they raised weapon and shield. *Shield!* Helreginn thought, remembering how the elves near the gate had formed up, locking their long shields together and deflecting the sky dragons' flames.

Behind the elves, the flames came forward in a roiling ball of hellfire.

Helreginn dropped his sword, grabbing two of the three dökkálfar, one by the chest plate and the other by the arm. He bashed them together, snatching their shields as they collapsed.

The mighty king dropped into the mud, slamming the shields together in front of himself. Flames came hot and fast, deflecting around the shields. The heat burnt his shoulders and outer thighs, but the area behind the shields stayed cool, as did the shields themselves. Beyond, hundreds of screams were swallowed in flame. How many had he just lost? Gato?

When the dragon fire dissipated, the king rose from behind the shields, picked up his sword and charged forward, battle rage swelling inside him. "Kill them!" he screamed.

Nothing save the burnt bodies of nephilbock and dökkálfar stood between Helreginn and the slavers who'd just killed his people. Helreginn fixed his ire on a silver-robed dökkálfar with panicked eyes as shouts of "Kill them all!"

answered back. Despite his tunnel vision, the king knew he was not alone.

The robed elf was pointing at him and shouting strange words. *Sagely words,* he thought. Words of power. To the king's left, the dragon, large as any he'd ever seen, groaned, turning its attention to Helreginn.

Helreginn realized he would not close the distance in time.

The elf knew it too, his expression of fear twisting into a confident smile as he continued to chant.

The dragon's head swung around to show exposed teeth.

The king stopped, reared back, and threw his sword with the might only a nephilbock could summon.

The sword did not spin. Instead, the Shard Mountain steel – strong, light, and perfectly balanced – flew like a trident thrown from the hand of a god!

The dökkálfar sage barely had time for his eyes to widen before the blade punched through his chest all the way to the hilt. The elf lifted from the ground, the weapon continuing to carry him back several strides.

The king spun to face the massive dragon's head, its jaw stretched open and teeth bared to bite. Weaponless, Helreginn extended his hands in a desperate attempt to grab the beast's open jaws.

The dragon's head leveled, meeting Helreginn eye to eye.

The king met the dragon's eyes and watched as they narrowed in confusion.

The king lowered his hands.

The dragon closed its mouth.

Looking past the dragon's eyes, Helreginn's own eyes followed the chain drooping low from the dragon's neck. The thick steel links connected to a collar clasped around the dragon's neck.

The dragon watched the nephilbock assess the chain, and

though no words passed between them, none were required to understand what came next. The dragon lowered its head and looked away, exposing its neck and with it the collar.

With both hands, Helreginn grasped a large steel pin holding the collar together. The implement of imprisonment was simple enough to understand. The king turned the pin, lifted, then turned again, repeating the process until he was able to remove the pin. The collar opened and clanked heavily to the ground.

The dragon stood up tall and roared. But there was something in the roar. Rage, yes, but more than rage. The dragon flapped its wings and lifted from the ground. Helreginn wondered how long it had been since the beast had flown. The thought was short-lived as he turned back to the field. Other enslaved dragons were flying up into the smoke-filled sky. They had done it. Not all were free, not yet, but they would be soon enough.

Now where was Gato? he wondered, scanning the field. He could think of no better way to celebrate their imminent victory than with his favorite son. Perhaps the gods were truly smiling upon him. Not the false gods of Ogliosh and his ilk, but the real gods! Perhaps in this world he would finally meet his true god!

Helreginn retrieved his sword from the dead slaver and looked toward the next dragon, a magnificent silver beast. This must be the direction Gato had gone, but the crowd of nephilbock were too far away for him to tell if his son was among them.

With a great flap of wings, the silver dragon lifted from the ground to the cheers of his people. The king smiled. Another dragon freed. Excited to join the others and find Gato, the king turned to run when something caught his attention from the corner of his eye.

Scattered across the field were dead juvenile dragons,

dead dökkálfar, and nephilbock alike. But what caught Helreginn's attention was something out of place. Among the dead was one of his High Guard. Even though the nephilbock lay facedown, Helreginn could identify him as High Guard by the kraki armor back plate. He also knew every one of his one hundred High Guard by name. Each had been hand-selected by himself with the help of the leader of his High Guard, Gato.

To see a dead High Guard pained him greatly, and he owed it to Gato to see who this nephilbock warrior was. They would celebrate him, honoring him in death.

The king approached, navigating over the burnt dead until he finally reached the fallen High Guard warrior. The nephilbock was badly burnt, and the king bent down to roll him over.

The warrior's front was burnt worse than his back. Pride swelled inside the king. This High Guard had faced the dragon fire head on, refusing to turn away.

The name of every High Guard warrior was etched inside their kraki chest plate. The purpose was twofold. As a member of the High Guard, you were responsible for caring for your armor – and armor created from the bones of a kraki was priceless. But the etched identification was also intended for this very purpose, in the event a body could not be identified.

Unclasping the breastplate, the king folded over the black bones. The kraki armor had survived the dragon fire, but it had not stopped the heat transference like the dökkálfar shields had. The skin beneath the plate had boiled. He ran his fingers over the bone plate, feeling for the etching.

Several strides away, a boulder slammed to the ground. They hadn't stopped falling, but this one had been too close. The king looked back down at the breastplate, rubbing away the burnt skin and ash from the inscription. G... A... T... O.

The king's throat constricted as a sob threatened to escape his throat. "No," he rasped. "No! Not my son!" Helreginn collapsed onto his knees, and he bent, falling forward over Gato's burnt corpse. "Not you, Gato!"

13

A Face in the Crowd

God Stones – Moon Ring 1
The Battlefield, outside of Osonian

Somehow, despite the fever and moments of blacking out, Jack held on to Cerberus, refusing to fall off. Time passed, though he was unsure how much he'd lost. Through the fog of his mind, he could hear Cerb shouting orders.

Everyone, pull back! The nephilbock freed the last of the slave dragons! The mission is complete! Return to the portal with as many dökkálfar prisoners as you can capture! Those of you who fail to find live prisoners should return with the dead! Do not return to the portal empty-handed!

Cerb, Jack moaned, *what are... what are you doing?*
You are dying. I'm saving our lives, brother.
I'm okay.

One of Cerb's heads twisted around to look at him. *No. You're burning up. I can feel the heat of your body through my scales. You need to heal. The horde will bring prisoners for you to use to get well, and the rest they will feed on! Now just hold on, Jack, we're landing.*

Lifting his heads as he dropped, Cerb's wings opened to catch the air.

Jack's eyes rolled back as the whoomph, whoomph, whoomph of the dragon's massive wings slowly flapping drowned out all other sounds. The only comfort Jack felt was Cerberus's cool scales against his face. This was odd, considering dragons weren't like lizards. Their scales weren't cool, they were warm – sometimes even hot.

The flapping stopped.

"What's wrong with him?" Zerri asked in a tone that wasn't concern.

"Elven wizard magic. Taker was diseased. He needs to heal," Cerb said, one of his long necks twisting around to look Jack in the face. "Get up, Jack. Heal yourself!"

Jack forced his spinning head to lift from Cerb's scales. When he did, something awful happened. The skin on that side of his face peeled away. "Ah! Shit!" he shouted, squeezing his eyes shut.

When he finally forced his eyes back open, he heard the collective gasp before he saw the source. They were back at the portal – at the edge of the pyramid of leaning pillars. Standing inside on the stone floor was what must have been over two hundred dökkálfar. Surrounding the elves in every direction were dragons feasting on the dead.

Cerberus walked toward the crowd. "Take them, Jack! Heal yourself!"

All the dragons stopped eating and watched in anticipation of Jack the Taker preparing to take. Come to think of it, his dragons had never seen him heal. Let them stare. This would be a good lesson for them to see firsthand. The dökkálfar stared too, confused, maybe even a little frightened, but they held themselves bravely.

From the crowd came a commotion as one elf pressed itself forward through the crowd. It was a male wrapped in a filthy grey cloak. He was speaking. No, shouting. Shouting and pointing. Pointing at Jack.

Jack forced himself to swallow, and it felt like swallowing crushed glass – like his throat was bleeding.

The elf looked back at the crowd and motioned at Jack again. He was trying to rally them to charge forward and attack him! What an idiot!

The elf shrugged off his cloak to reveal a golden robe. The area was lit in purple light as the elf's hand glowed with purple Sentheye.

Son of a bitch! The glowing hand? Was this a slaver or maybe the bastard who had diseased him? As Jack reached forward with Sentheye of his own, he realized he had no idea the power this mage possessed.

With a sudden scream, four juvenile dragons launched themselves forward, attacking Cerberus and Zerri.

Jack's reflexes failed him as he swiped for Cerb's horn but missed, falling off the dragon and landing on the ground with enough force to push the air from his lungs. He rolled over, shoving his hands into the muddy, piss-soaked grass, and pushed himself onto his hands and knees, gasping for air. *That mother of a... where did he go?* Jack searched, panicked, but found the dökkálfar still standing exactly where he had been.

The elf shouted something else and smiled.

Jack's mind went foggy, like he'd just fallen into a dream. A voice from nowhere yet all around him said, *Give the Sound Eye to your master and all will be forgiven.*

Right. Of course, Jack thought, why hadn't he thought of this before? Jack reached up and lifted the Sound Eye from his head. *Yes, master. Here, please, take this and forgive me.*

The golden-robed elf stepped forward and looked down, reaching.

Cerberus shook off two smaller dragons and roared, fire spilling from his left mouth.

Jack stumbled back, shielding his eyes from the flame as it consumed the dökkálfar.

The fire burned hot, and all creatures in the vicinity backed away. The pain of the heat against Jack's diseased and blistered skin ripped him from the dream-like state. Leather jacket smoking, he scrambled farther back, watching the elf burn. But the elf did not die. Instead, he stepped from the flames. He was fine! Shit, even his robe was fine.

Jack sneered and shouted at the elf, "You want to go, asshole?"

The elf held out splayed fingers glowing with purple Sentheye.

Jack's stomach turned. He raised a hand of his own. Black Sentheye streamed a thick ribbon of death, wrapping the dökkálfar over and over, from head to toe like a giant snake, until nothing of the elf could be seen. "You don't know me! You don't know what I am!"

Jack closed his red eyes and drew in deep.

The elf tried to resist, shouting some words. Jack felt his power, but it was no match for him, no match for the power he could draw directly from the Sound Eye. Deeper and deeper, Jack pulled, fresh breath filling his lungs with stolen life. In it went, soothing his throat and healing his head.

Behind the black cloud, the elvish prisoners screamed.

Jack swallowed, and it hurt, but it hurt less. Back on his feet, he stepped forward, pain shooting up his right leg, but less pain. The cloud of black Sentheye dissipated and a hollow husk dropped onto the ground, covered by the stained golden robe. The elves gasped and went silent.

Freed from the now-dead elf's mind control, the four juvenile dragons cowered at the feet of their Queen of Queens and Cerberus the Mighty, groveling for forgiveness.

The Last Gift

"Silence your tongues!" Zerri ordered, and the four dragons obeyed.

A large dragon drifted down from above, landed, and bowed to Zerri, then Cerberus and Jack.

"Oh my, what did I miss?" Ahi asked, eyeing the golden robe as his wings folded into place.

Jack took another painful step toward the elves. In response, the crowd pushed back deeper into the hollow pyramid, scrambling over each other, no doubt trying to get away from the monster who'd just devoured their most powerful wizard. Jack smiled. "Hold that thought, Ahi."

Jack's crown flashed through a spectrum of color, finally settling on the color of his own soul. The area around the portal dimmed as he sent forth the black Sentheye, randomly taking the life of first one elf and then another – then the next and the next. And when he was done, five more elves lay dead.

"Jack! How do you feel?" Cerb asked.

"I feel like a million bucks," Jack said, bending and pulling loose the golden robe to examine what was left of the dead slaver. Beneath his robe, he'd worn a tightly knitted sweater. It felt soft yet strong, and it also had a hood. *I think I'll keep this,* he thought, grabbing the sweater by the collar and tugging it off the corpse. The light husk lifted and flopped back down on its back as the garment came free. Jack shook out the sweater as he examined the dead dökkálfar's skin, which was still intact. Tossing the sweater aside, Jack lifted the arms, but he saw no markings. The skin was dry and cracked, but it was otherwise clear.

"What are you searching for?" Ahi asked.

"Answers, Ahi. Answers," Jack said, cocking his head to the side. A single black line crossed over the top of the slaver's shoulder, ending at his collarbone. Jack wedged the toe of his boot under the torso of the dead dökkálfar and flipped him over. The mysterious line zigzagged diagonally across the dead elf's back, ending on his hip. But it wasn't a single line. There were others too, crossing each other strangely, some red, some black. Jack didn't need to know what it said, if it even said anything. Their existence was all the answer he required.

These symbols were how the dökkálfar slavers resisted fire. The symbols were also why Garrett didn't burn back on Earth. Garrett could slow time too. Was that because of these same lines? No. If that were the case, these slavers would have been slowing his dragons in battle. He'd also never seen Garrett control any of his dragons. Not that he knew of, anyway. But he'd felt sick too. Garrett couldn't do that. So what? Was this one something more? Was he a slaver and a wizard? He must have been. And if so, were there more?

Zerri switched to telepathy. *The runes are how they control us, Jack, and why the dökkálfar wouldn't burn.*

Intense frustration surged through Jack. *Garrett Turek has these same markings on his arms. So, you're saying he can control our dragons' minds?*

If I may, my queen? Ahi asked.

Zerri nodded.

No, Jack. Our kind have no memory of a human having ever become dragon marked.

Jack frowned. *Dragon marked?*

Yes. It requires a special set of circumstances. One which could be dangerous to discuss here.

But we're using telepathy, Ahi.

The silver dragon nodded. *Indeed. But, my lord, powerful magic exists all around us. We should never speak of how to become dragon marked outside our own queendom. I will explain if you command me, but I respectfully implore you to forgo this discussion until we are sure it is safe.*

Respectfully implore? Shit sakes, here we go with the fancy talk, Jack thought. *No, keep the how to yourself for now, Ahi. What of the sickness? I felt it on the wall and then here from this one.*

Ahi's forked tongue flicked in and out. *As I said, magic exists all around us. The dökkálfar have always been known for their wizardry. Apep himself was a powerful mage, and he was not dragon marked. Perhaps this one was both.*

Jack poked at the husk with the toe of his boot. *Well, he ain't shit now. Besides, I'm more interested in what this means for Garrett, and it sounds like you really don't know for sure, do you?*

Ahi dipped his head, bowing slightly. *I apologize, my lord – I only know what the stories tell us.*

We live in strange times, Jack Nightshade, Zerri said, stepping down on a nephilbock carcass with her front foot as she pulled loose a thick strip of meat from the dead giant's upper thigh. She chomped and swallowed. *Gabi can control the minds of several at once and, to my knowledge, she isn't even dragon marked. I cannot say if this Garrett Turek can control the minds of dragons, but I have seen no indication he is capable thus far. Although...* Zerri trailed off, ripping at another piece of nephilbock flesh.

Although what? Jack asked.

It would behoove us to kill Gabi. The sooner the better. She already has the power to control us, and there is a debt due to me.

The girl was dangerous, to be sure. Perhaps, if he could convince Zerri to forgive the girl, he could manipulate Gabi into joining him. It was a long shot, but maybe. *Jack's horde! Finish filling your bellies quickly. Round up the slaves, and the rest of you gather the dead.* Then, focusing his telepathy on Zerri, Cerberus, and Ahi, he continued. *I must find out if*

Helreginn lives and, if not, I'll need to know who's in charge now.

That's what I wanted to tell you, my lord, Ahi said. *Helreginn is heading this way with his army.*

Good, Jack said, nodding approvingly.

Perhaps, but he is carrying a dead nephilbock in his arms, Ahi said.

So they're probably bringing as much food as they can carry. Speaking of food, he was starving and despite the fact he was no longer fully human, he still couldn't bring himself to eat raw flesh.

My lord, only the king himself is carrying the dead. I think it may be his fallen son.

Oh. Well, shit. How far out?

He is approaching the base of the hill, Ahi said.

Do you want us to halt his passage? Cerb asked. *He may blame you for the losses he's taken and the death of his son.*

No, Jack said, clicking idly at a fingernail with his thumb. *How many of his army remain?*

I would estimate ten to twelve thousand, my lord.

Despite the dragons' help, Helreginn had lost nearly fifteen thousand since showing up in the Amazon. *And us?* Jack asked.

Three thousand strong, Ahi answered quickly.

Only three thousand. They had lost so many! Yet Ahi was proving useful as hell. The elder dragon had the history and the numbers at his command, and he probably knew his way around this world, which made him incredibly useful. Plus, he kept calling him *my lord*, which was the respect Jack deserved.

Cerb laughed. *We have the air, and you have the Sound Eye, Taker. We can defeat them easily. With our slaves freed and Apep dead, there is no reason to maintain this alliance.*

Still picking at the nail on his index finger, Jack looked

down at his hands to find all his fingernails blackened. Frowning, he lifted his hands toward his face. Half his fingernails were missing. He gave one of the remaining nails a light tug and it pulled away. *What the...?*

You're losing it, kid, a voice said.

Danny? Is that you?

Sure, it's me alright.

You see me, Danny? You see what I can do?

Oh yeah, I see you, little brother.

Cerb's voice boomed, drowning out Danny. *Jack! Do you hear me? We could end them now while they are battle worn and half-starved. Fresh meat. More than we could hope to consume.*

Jack ignored Cerb, listening for his brother's voice again. *Danny? Danny!* But the voice was gone. He looked down at his hands again. Shit! He was losing it, wasn't he? He looked back at Ahi, Zerri, and Cerb. Then to the dozens of dragons surrounding the prisoners. His hands were like Apep's, and he knew the crazy elf had been talking to the voices in his head too! Was he really becoming like Apep? He spun in a circle. They were all watching him. Shit, shit, shit! Jack looked back at the prisoners and there, among the cowering and afraid, a female elf stared back defiantly. Why wasn't she afraid? He wanted to scream at her, to disease her and rip the life from her soul. *No, you idiot. Don't use the Sentheye, no matter what. No matter how any of them look at you. No matter what Helreginn wants. Even if he wants war.* Jack could not tap into the power of Sentheye. Not now – not until he allowed himself to recover from using too much already.

He looked again for the female in the crowd, but she was gone. She'd been right there only a second ago, a wicked smile plastered across her stupid blue face.

Taker! What's wrong with you? Cerb begged. *Helreginn's*

army is near the crest of the hill. Our hordes are allowing them to pass unobstructed. Now is the time! Do you hear me, brother? Do we fight?

14

The Seer

God Stones – Moon Ring 1
The Shadow Forest

"Tell you what future I see?" Breanne asked.

"Yes. If you are truly a seer, you will tell us our future," Key said, holding out her arms and looking to her people.

The group of women nodded, murmuring words of encouragement.

Paul's voice filled her mind. *Sis, you better tell her it doesn't work like that.*

"If I told you the future, you'd have no way of knowing if I were telling the truth," Breanne said.

Oh, yeah, that's good, Bre, Garrett said.

Yeah, or just make something up, David said.

That's a dumbass idea, Pete said flatly. He continued, with more urgency, *Well, whatever you're going to say, we need to do something! Governess needs us.*

They were all speaking in her mind now, and she couldn't think. *Pete, I know, but guys, please, be quiet.*

Key folded her hands at her waist. "Breanne Moore, you claim you are not of this world, let alone these lands. The scroll of Turek tells us she took her people to another world, and that her chosen would return in a great number, yet you are only six."

Seven, Pete corrected, but he didn't say it aloud.

"I want to believe you, Breanne. I want to believe you have come here to deliver us from the darkness and back to our rightful place in the land of Sky. But you have brought no army, and you are resistant to telling us our future. I fear trickery is afoot. I fear magic is at play. Do you understand, Breanne? These are troubling times, and we cling to but a thread of hope. A thread King Deep knows to be thin. He would stop at nothing to see us wiped from the land for good."

The women were all standing, spears in hand. And like a light switch, the excitement of a prophesied woman come to rescue her people changed to tension thick enough to choke on.

Breanne's pulse quickened.

Guys, this is bad! David said, his voice pitching high in her mind.

"Now I will ask you again, whoever you are, produce an army I can see, or show me a future I can believe!"

As Key's voice rose, the room of women shouted, "Ki-ya!" in harmony, drawing up their spears.

But Bre no longer saw Key, or the spears, or the women of the longhouse. And as her eyes clouded over to pure white, she found herself outside the village gate, staring down the trail leading into the forest and back the way they had come. In the distance, people moved through the trees, slowly, deliberately. As they drew closer, she realized these weren't people; they were elves. They were tall and muscular like Apep, but these elves wore uniforms, grey trimmed in gold, and they all held swords in one hand and tall shields in the other.

Quickly, Breanne counted – two, four, six, eight, ten. There, two more from the shadows, twelve, fourteen, sixteen, twenty!

The vision faded.

Breanne blinked, the white cloud clearing from her eyes.

Key was closer to her now, staring into her eyes with hands raised, commanding silence in the room.

"Well, now, that was something, but is it something I can believe?" Key asked skeptically.

Bre? What the shit? Are you okay? Garrett asked, his face full of concern.

"This town is about to be invaded by twenty elves," Breanne breathed in a low, almost hesitant tone.

"Elves?" Key asked, her eyebrows knitting together.

Tell's eyes went wide. "Dökkálfar! Here?"

The room erupted in commotion.

Key's expression changed to one of concern. "Are you sure of this? What did you see exactly?"

"I'm not sure when, exactly, but I saw them, at least twenty, coming from the woods."

"So, if you are telling the truth, then you *are* her. The seer, come home to lead your people." Then her eyebrows rose thoughtfully. "Tell me, what was the light like in your vision?"

Breanne narrowed her eyes, trying to remember. "It was strange. Not dark, but close. Sunset maybe."

"Sun sit? I am not familiar with the term. When both suns sleep, it becomes ebon night under the canopy of Shadow Forest – far too dark to see. But we have several shades before ebon night is upon us."

"Well, it was darker than when we arrived, but not too dark to see," Breanne said.

Tell shook her head. "But if this vision is true, it may not even be this moon ring. Could it not be any ring in the future? And besides, I traveled underground. The elves could not have followed."

"My visions usually come true sooner rather than later, and my gut tells me this one is coming soon," Breanne said confidently.

Key nodded. "Well, if your description is accurate and they come before the suns sleep, then we still have time to prepare, but we should make haste," Key said.

"Wait! I'm sorry. Wait! Please," Pete burst out.

Key narrowed her eyes.

"I'm sorry, but we can't go anywhere until you help our friend."

Pete, let me handle this, Breanne said in mind speak.

I'm sorry, Bre, but I'm not going anywhere until we help her! Pete said, crossing his arms.

He's right, Lenny said.

I agree. We have to try, Garrett said.

The others nodded, except Gabi, who seemed to be somewhere else altogether. Bre wanted to check in on the girl and find out what the hell had happened with her and the little dragon she'd been riding, but it would have to wait. And of course, whether her vision of an attack came sooner or later, Governess couldn't wait. *I know, of course. All I am trying to say is this society works differently than ours. We need to respect this.*

"Breanne Moore. What is this help your man speaks of? What friend?" Key asked.

Breanne motioned to Pete, as if giving him permission.

Pete came forward and shrugged off his pack, and with it, the large shrub attached. "Her name is Governess Larrea. She is a shape-shifting tree from Earth."

Key knelt next to the shrub. "Shape-shifting, you say? Intriguing. What is wrong with her?"

Tell knelt down next to her mother. "We were being chased by the elf. I made the offering to the forest to ensure they could not follow us, and the forest opened a way for us. Once below the forest this... this Governess decided she needed to speak to the forest. She rooted to the ground and a moment later the forest rejected her, purging her from the ground and changing her to her true form – killing her, I think."

At some signal Breanne must have missed, a bronze-skinned man wearing a brown-and-black tunic fashioned from the hide of some unfamiliar animal went into motion. A strip of the same material was belted around his narrow waist, reminding Breanne of ancient Egyptian attire. He was tall and muscular with long salt-and-pepper hair braided back. The man picked up the waterskin he'd almost offered earlier and stepped forward, extending it toward her. Breanne nodded gratefully, accepting the skin. She pulled a long drink. Water had never tasted better than in that very moment. She passed the skin back to Gabi, knowing that would be expected before the men drank.

Key reached into the dry shrub, pinching one of Governess's twigs before snapping it with a twist.

Pete winced.

Key looked up at Breanne. "My people call me Key, but that is not my full name. My full name is Keyhold. Do you know why I was given this name?"

"No, Lady Key, I do not," Breanne said, still trying to respond like she would expect a confident leader to sound.

Key examined the twig closely. "Because I am said to hold the key to this forest. But what it really means is that I have an understanding with the forest, an unspoken agreement – a secret alliance. This is an alliance neither King Deep nor his men hold. Nor do the elves, the dwarves, the nephilbock, nor any other creature. Despite what this friend is or is not, she holds no alliance with the forest and as such had no business rooting to the ground without permission. She is lucky the forest didn't destroy her."

"So, she is alive!" Pete blurted.

Key looked up at Pete and paused, clearly surprised by his outburst, but she nodded. "Yes. Though just barely. The shrub is dying, and I can't save her."

"What?" Pete shouted.

The women stiffened to attention, dozens of hands adjusting grips on spears.

Pete, seriously. I know this is hard, but let Bre do the talking, Garrett urged.

"Forgive him," Breanne said. "Governess is dear to him and a friend to us all. Is there nothing you can do?"

Key's eyes shifted back to Breanne. "I didn't say that." The woman looked over at the man who'd handed Bre the waterskin. "Shine, we need a container filled with dirt. We must get this one's roots covered. Water too, but only lightly."

"Yes, my lady, it will be done," Shine said, nodding to another man, who bowed and vanished out the door.

"I'm afraid this is all I can do for now. But after we see to your vision, I will explain how my alliance with the forest may provide you the knowledge you need to save this very... very strange friend of yours. That is assuming we aren't all killed first."

Pete stepped forward like he hadn't even heard that last bit. "But she'll be okay? I mean until?"

Key stood and smiled. "What is your name?"

"Pete."

"You love her, don't you, Pete?"

Pete flushed and then nodded. "I care about her. I care

about her a lot. Yes. Yes, I think so."

"Oh, you love her indeed. Your eyes are full of it." Key smiled. "Listen to me. Your friend will live for a while. After we deal with this threat, I will show you how she may be saved. But there are no guarantees. It will be up to the forest if they wish to forgive her, and it will be up to you to convince them to do so."

"What does that mean?" Pete asked.

Key stood and brushed her hands together. "For now, your friend will be tended to, and as for us," she said, looking at Breanne, "we've more pressing matters to attend. We can't help your friend if we are all dead. Now, let the women talk," Key said, dismissing Pete with a flourish of her hand.

Pete nodded reluctantly, stepping back behind Breanne.

"Breanne, will you order your companions to help my men?" Key asked.

"Of course, we will help," she said.

Key turned back toward her people. "Men of Sky, gather the children along with two ring's provisions and take shelter in the caves just as we practiced. We will come to you when it is safe."

"Wait, they aren't coming to help fight?" Breanne asked.

Key laughed. "No. The men are far better suited for the heavy lifting. They will gather the children and transport provisions to the caves. Best to let the women handle the fighting."

Shine frowned.

Key smiled sympathetically. "Don't look at me like that."

Shine stepped very close to Key, his nose nearly touching hers. "You know I worry, my love. Just please be safe. The elves are cunning." The man leaned in and placed a kiss on Key's lips.

Key closed her eyes. When the kiss ended, she opened her eyes and smiled. "You underestimate my cunning."

Breanne could see the shock on the faces of Garrett and the others, especially David, who she was now convinced was sexist. She almost wanted to laugh. But she had to remember that she'd had the luxury of having her father, the renowned archeologist Dr. Charles Moore, educate her about both historic and present-day civilizations, including matriarchal societies. The fact was, historically, many societies had placed women at the helm, charged with leading their people in all aspects of society. She noticed that Shine was quite worried about Key, yet he knew his duty was getting the other men and children to safety. God, what she would have once given to study these people. What her father would have given.

Obviously, things weren't all roses if many of the men had revolted, electing to follow this King Deep guy. She hoped Key would understand her situation was different. "Key, my men fight with me. I think you may find their talents useful in battle."

Key laughed. "How strange, Breanne Moore. But I see this must be true by the strange weapons they carry. Very well, I respect your wish to include them, but they should stay out of the way of my warriors. King Deep could never defeat us in battle with his men if not for the fact he had so damn many of them. Men are much larger, slower, and clumsier than us. They truly are better suited for farming, building, and lifting heavy things when heavy things need lifting."

Hey, now, hold on a second! David's voice projected through Breanne's mind. And for a split second she thought he was about to protest Key's opinion that men should stay in their place, but following David's eyes, she quickly realized the kid's focus was somewhere else altogether. What fixed David's attention was the activity around the fire, where the men hurried to pull the meats from their skewers and wrap them in some form of leaf.

Why are they packing up the food? We haven't gotten to eat anything!

A man with a wooden vessel tossed water on the coals. Another separated provisions, stacking some of the leaf-wrapped meats and water jugs in the corner, presumably to be left behind for Key and her warriors.

Quiet, kid. You're fine, Paul said.

"What's the plan?" Breanne asked.

Key smiled. "They will think they have the element of surprise. Once they enter our village, they will drop formation, spreading out as they search the huts. If they find nothing in the huts, they will assume we are all gathered here and converge on the longhouse, but they won't get that far."

"Excuse me!" David said, speaking out loud now and pointing. "Can that guy not put that meat away? We haven't eaten in forever."

Paul shook his head.

Key stopped speaking and assessed David with an unamused look.

Lenny slapped David on the back of the head. *Dude! What is wrong with you?* he asked in mind speak.

"Hey, dick!" David blurted.

"Enough!" Breanne said, using her best directive voice. And it must have been pretty good because David's mouth slapped shut like a Venus flytrap and Lenny straightened. "You will eat once we've assured the safety of the village and not a moment sooner."

That's crap! David said in mind speak.

"Please, Key, forgive the hairy-faced one's rudeness," she said, shooting daggers at David. "Is your plan to wait for them to come here, then?" she asked, quickly changing the subject back to the issue at hand.

"No. We will divide, placing small groups in each of the men's huts. Compared to the elves, we are small. We should do well against them in an enclosed space. Maybe we can defeat them with the element of surprise," Key said, nodding to the women.

Maybe we should all run instead? David said, resorting back to mind speak as he rummaged through his pack, producing what looked like a slightly smashed Twinkie.

Moving quickly past them, the spear-wielding women filed out the door of the longhouse.

Lenny's eyebrows knitted together. *You still have food stashed in there?*

But before he could answer, Garrett went in on him. *You've had food from that snack truck back in Illinois all this time and didn't tell us!*

Technically Missouri, David said, stuffing the treat in his mouth.

I bet the little fur-lipped pack rat has been sneaking it all this time! Talking about he's starving! Lenny said.

Oh, you dick, you better have more! Pete said.

What? Yeah, I got more! But these are the only ones on the entire planet, so don't get all pissed at me because you didn't think to fill your pack!

Breanne shook her head, following Key toward the door.

Behind her, she heard Paul say, *Shut up and move out!*

Outside her mind, Key interrupted. "You think my strategy is ill advised?"

"No. But no strategy is certain, good lady," Breanne said.

"Fine. Order your men to hide behind the longhouse and to attack only if the elves get past the huts."

"Perfect," Breanne answered, turning toward the group and switching to mind speak. *Gabi, do you think you can use mind control on the elves?* When Gabi didn't answer, Breanne narrowed her eyes, studying the girl. Gabi seemed distracted, staring off into space. *Gabi? Are you okay?*

Qué? I mean, yes. No. Not really. I messed up, Bre. I messed up bad, the small girl said, her voice quiet and sad.

I want you to tell me what happened. I want to hear everything. But right now, maybe it's best if you go hide.

Key's women were splitting up, filling the small huts.

No! No, I won't go hide. I will be here with you. What do you want me to do?

Bre pressed her lips tight, unsure. "Key, where do you want me?"

"We will stay here and hide behind the trees." She pointed to an area of dense woodland not far from the longhouse. "The elf in charge will not go into the houses. Instead, he will come up the street as his forces split off. You said twenty?"

"Twenty is what I saw, but—"

"Twenty should be easily manageable since we outnumber them ten times over," Key said, then moved off the street to take cover behind a tree.

Okay, Breanne said and turned back to Gabi, *when the elves get close, use your mind control and keep your distance.* Looking around, she pointed. *There. Let's hide behind that tree.*

Breanne pulled her nine mil from her holster and racked the slide.

Garrett stepped forward and leaned in close. "I won't take my eyes off you, and when they get here, I'll come running," he said, his breath washing over her ear. She'd missed hearing him talk out loud. He kissed her then, and she wasn't expecting it. It was only on the cheek, but she felt her face flush and her stomach tickle.

Garrett smiled nervously and gestured back toward the longhouse. "We'll be right over here."

∼

As everyone settled into place, silence filled the village. Not even a whisper could be heard despite the dozens of huts loaded with weapon-wielding warriors. Breanne knelt next to Gabi, who gazed out over the road with tear-stained eyes. Dusk was strange in this world, but maybe that was to be expected when light shone from two suns, one white and one yellow. It reminded her of a few rare occasions back on Earth where the setting sun sank next to a full moon come early, only these were strangely different.

Gabi? Tell me what happened.

The younger girl seemed hesitant at first, but once she began, it poured out. She started all the way back at the moment when she was snatched from the cenote by Mivras. But what was that... like two days ago? Jesus, she'd been through so much. They all had. And they were about to go through even more. Breanne rubbed her itchy eyes, a good sign she had passed well beyond sleepy.

Don't you see, Bre? I tricked Azazel's daughter into helping me. I made her believe I was her friend. She trusted me. Now... The girl trailed off, tears tracing the trails laid by an earlier stream of sorrow.

Breanne started to say something when David's voice filled her mind.

I'm sorry, Gabi, the boy said, his own words choked with emotion. *But you did what you had to do. You would have died if you hadn't.*

Breanne hadn't realized until that very moment, but she could feel it now. Gabi hadn't been telling only her the story. She'd been telling them all.

Don't you get it, David? I killed her mother. I did the same thing to her that was done to me but even worse, María Purísima. Forgive me! I lied to her and made her believe I was her friend.

Breanne grabbed her and pulled her into a hug. Gabi's

tears came so hard she threatened to give them away.

Gabi, you are a good person, and David is right. You did what you had to do. We will get through this, and when we do, we will figure out what to do next, okay?

Thanks, Bre, Gabi said, wiping her eyes on her shirtsleeves.

Breanne peeked around the tree. Down the narrow dirt street, the small huts were cast in ever-deepening shadow as if they were being absorbed in the woodland itself. This was it. Now or... or not today. But she was sure it was today – it had to be. But what if she got it wrong? What if she really had been seeing something from another day somewhere in the future? No, she thought. Why would she have the vision in that exact moment only to look untrustworthy to Key and her people? No, it had to be today. It had to be now. *Guys, they're coming. I can feel it.*

You have a sensory power too? David asked.

What? No... I'm just saying... hold on. Something is happening.

Across the narrow road, Key abandoned her place of cover and ran toward her. "What's wrong?" Breanne whispered to Key.

"When you had your vision, did you actually see the elves enter the village?" the older woman asked in an urgent whisper, her hazel eyes boring into Breanne's own.

Breanne shook her head. "Oh, well, no. No. I guess I didn't. I only saw them sneaking toward the village from the woods. Why? What is it?"

Key glanced back over her shoulder, then past Breanne, her expression turning grave.

Breanne followed her eyes this way and that. "Oh, no. You don't think..."

Key grimaced. "Breanne Moore, it seems we are surrounded."

15

Spin the Bottle

God Stones – Moon Ring 1
The Creators' Mountain, Karelia

Turek waggled a finger. "You led the dökkálfar directly to the village! Very clever, Eresh. Very clever indeed." He shook his head as if he respected the maneuver, but in truth, he was terrified. *Why? Why do I feel such overwhelming fear?* A wave of shame followed the thought. The Great Mother had thoroughly instilled in her children the full spectrum of emotions. Nevertheless, he should have more control over himself and more faith in his god.

"Oh, come now, you think you are the only one who can speak on the wind?" Ereshkigal asked, smiling.

"Sneaky, but not surprising," Typhon said, feigning disapproval.

"Oh, please! After that little outburst when you attempted to convince the one called… oh, what is his name?"

"Jack, but you know that, sister," Aurgelmir said.

Ereshkigal waved her hand flippantly, letting go of

Typhon's. "Yes. After your folly in trying to convince Jack to give you the Sound Eye, you've no room to lecture me, dear brother. And besides, why shouldn't we interfere? We are the gods of our favorites, after all." She turned to Turek and smiled. "Suppose you are right, Turek, and our Great Mother is not only watching but manipulating events. Why does our interference matter? We should all be doing what is in the best interest of our favorites."

"I'm afraid I cannot agree with our sister," Druesha said. "We've set the course and too much has already happened."

"Well, I'm afraid I do agree," Rán said. "Why not intervene and bring this to a speedy end?"

"Speedy? Interference will only hasten us to war, resulting in catastrophic consequences. Therefore, I do not agree," Aurgelmir said.

"Nor do I," Durin said.

"I agree with Ereshkigal – intervene and end this," Typhon said.

All eyes fell to Turek.

Ereshkigal leaned into the circle. "Well, brother, how much do you really believe Great Mother watches?

"It isn't a lack of faith, Eresh."

"If not faith, then what?" Rán asked.

"It's as Aurgy said. If we open Karelia up to our interference, we will soon be at war with each other. If we allow ourselves to go to war, then surely all the work of creation will be lost. It is because of this I cannot agree," Turek said.

Ereshkigal's chest glowed brighter. "You didn't seem to care about Karelia when we feared this flood of Earth-born dragons and nephilbock would upset the balance!"

"And how many nephilbock and dragons have already been killed by the dökkálfar in the first wave of the attack?" Turek didn't wait for an answer. "I told you this would take care of itself. A mortal war is far different than a war of the creators."

"This is getting us nowhere," Typhon said. "Some of us feel equal help from each would be fair."

"Yet some of us – the majority, I might add – do not," Aurgelmir said.

Rán's soothing voice filled the hall. "Brethren, please. May I propose a compromise?"

All eyes turned to the creator of water-born creatures.

Turek nodded. "Go on."

"I propose we periodically break the connection to allow us to... well, to do what we can."

"What do you mean 'periodically'?" Ereshkigal asked.

"I don't know, perhaps once a moon ring – but only for a short time," Rán said, becoming increasingly excited by her idea.

"Yes, this could work," Durin mused.

"It's better than an all-out war, I suppose," Druesha said.

"No. I'm afraid I still cannot agree," Turek said.

"For Great Mother's sake, such trepidation! Tell me, what calamities do you fear now, brother?" Typhon asked with great annoyance.

"You answered my question with your own."

Typhon crossed his arms. "Riddles – is this the game now, Turek? Riddles?"

Turek nodded slowly. "I will agree to allow us time to break away – time to help our chosen – but not all at once. For without rules and structure, I fear the calamities will be great indeed. Instead, I propose we randomly choose just one of us at a time to interfere for a short period."

Durin crossed his swirling arms of Sentheye, which now matched Typhon's own. "How can we possibly make a truly random selection?"

The Last Gift

"Easily. On Earth, they play a game called spin the bottle."

"Spin the what?" Rán asked.

"The bottle," Turek answered.

"What is a... bottle?" Druesha asked.

"It's a vessel," Durin said.

"And you spin it to what end?" Ereshkigal asked.

"Never mind, we don't have one, anyway. But what I do have is this," Turek said, removing a dagger from his waistband. He reached forward and placed the dagger in the center of the circle.

"Well, that's... unimpressive," Typhon said, and he wasn't wrong. The knife was plain in every way, from the wooden handle to the narrow, double-edged steel blade.

Durin laughed. "What is the purpose of this mortal instrument, Turek? Did you plan to stab someone?"

"Please, don't stab me with something so unfashionably ugly," Ereshkigal snorted.

"No one is getting poked with it. The idea is to spin it," Turek said, motioning with a flourish. "Typhon, if you please."

Typhon reached into the circle.

"Wait!" Turek said, waving him off.

"What? You said spin the knife!"

"Yes, I did, of course. However, let me be clear. Do not use the Sentheye to manipulate the spin. That goes for all of us."

Typhon shrugged and flicked the handle of the knife with a glowing finger.

The creators leaned in as they watched the small wooden-handled dagger spin.

Turek watched too, detecting no Sentheye as he prayed silently. *Let it be your will, Great Mother.*

Finally, the dagger slowed to a stop.

Rán gasped. "Oh, I win!" She clapped, then stopped abruptly. "What did I win?"

"You shall be the first to be given leave. You may go below and influence for one moon ring. When you return, we will spin the knife again and see who goes next," Turek explained, smiling with satisfaction.

"Hold on! What does this prove, Turek? Would you have us believe this little game of chance is somehow the result of the Great Mother's will?" Ereshkigal asked.

In truth, he'd no idea. But what he believed was that everything happened for a reason, and a gut feeling compelled him not to allow open season on interference from the creators.

"Do it ten more times. If it lands on Rán each time, then maybe I'll believe there is something to this," Aurgelmir said.

"I'm not saying this is the Great Mother. What I am saying is this is fair. Now let's allow this to play out, and the next moon ring we all have another chance to be chosen," Turek urged.

Druesha scowled. "Well, Rán, do make the most of your time below."

"Yes, and remember, dear sister, influence only. You are not to fight the other's battles," Ereshkigal warned.

Typhon shook his head. "I am unsure what mischief you could get up to, sister, since there is no ocean close to the fight and no measurable risk to your favorites. At least not yet."

"Oh, dear brethren, I've no intentions of fighting your favorites. But I would fancy a little mischief!" Rán giggled naughtily.

Durin snorted, "Oh, well, this should be good."

16

Lady of the Lake

God Stones – Moon Ring 1
The Battlefield, outside of Osonian

Cerb's gruff voice spoke aloud. "Do you not hear me, Taker? The nephilbock are approaching. Give the word, and the dragons shall feast upon their flesh!"

Absently, Jack noticed Zerri step closer, but his focus was elsewhere. He wanted to find the girl in the crowd – and he wanted to hear Danny's voice again, despite what it meant.

"Look at him, Cerberus! He's behaving like Apep. Precisely as my mother had warned would happen to the dökkálfar, the Sound Eye is destroying Jack's mind."

Finding himself once more, Jack glared up at the Queen of Queens. "Don't get your hopes up, Zerri. I'm sharp as a whip!"

"And isn't that what Apep said?" she countered.

Jack reeled, feeling his fist double up. If he could reach her face, he'd take a swing. "I told you I'm—"

"Fine. Yes. I heard you the first time," Zerri interjected. "Jack, for your own good, listen to me. I'm not telling you this for any reason other than to state an obvious truth. If you want to remain sane, you must remove the Sound Eye from your head and disassemble it back into the seven God Stones. The stones in their true form are powerful. But connected, they serve only one purpose, and that purpose is to open a portal. Combined, the power is too much for any one being."

He knew she wasn't lying to him. This was not some clever trick. So why then did removing the Sound Eye feel like an awful mistake? Like the moment he took them apart, Typhon would show up and kick his ass. He looked at his hands again. They were shaking... shaking like Apep's, dammit!

"You know I'm right, and still you will not listen," Zerri said.

Jack nodded, no longer mad. "You're right. If I continue to use the Sentheye like I just did, I'm going to lose my shit. Maybe I'll lose it anyway. Hell, maybe I've already lost it. But no. No, I don't think I've gone crazy quite yet."

"So, you will not remove it then?" Zerri asked knowingly.

"No. I won't, but I'm not Apep."

"Really? Tell me then, Jack, what's the difference?"

Jack turned to Cerb. "The difference is that my brother is a dragon, and he is the other half of me. And he" – Jack thrust a black-tipped thumb toward Cerb – "has my permission to rip the Sound Eye from my skull if I start to act crazy."

"Start?" Zerri asked.

"Oh, you got jokes. If I start to act crazier than normal. There, are we all happy?"

"Happy? No, Jack, I am not happy, and I won't be happy until this world knows who I am and that my mother, the Queen of Queens, has been avenged. However, I am satisfied. After all, it's your sanity at stake, not mine."

Jack shifted uncomfortably. "Well, that's why I have you, Cerb."

Cerb's tongues flicked out randomly from each of his three teeth-filled mouths. "I too am satisfied. But understand, brother, at the first sign you're losing control, I will take it away without hesitation."

Jack collected the wizard elf's ivory-handled knife and sweater. He pulled the sweater on, lifted the hood, and replaced his black leather jacket.

"I remember, near the end, Apep wore a hood too."

"Shut up, Cerb."

"As you wish, brother." Cerb nodded his big-ass heads toward the valley. "Now what of the nephilbock? Shall we eat them?"

"No, Cerb. Let me handle Helreginn," Jack said, turning to walk toward the crest of the portal mound.

Jack gazed down the hill at Helreginn. Ahi was right; the giant was carrying a body. Even after a battle of such great losses, thousands of giants remained, stretching all the way down the sloped hill and deep into the battlefield. But even there, they were safe. No longer did burning boulders fall or arrows fly. The elves had retreated behind their wall, no doubt waiting to see what came next. Part of Jack wanted to go, push through the wall, crush the now dragon-less elves. But another part, the newer part, knew now wasn't the time. He'd freed the dragon slaves, and once he found the Karelian dragons, Zerri and Cerb would take their place on the thrones, and he would be god to the king and queen of dragons. A dragon god. That was badass. Jack the dragon god.

Helreginn approached and laid a dead giant at Jack's feet.

"King Helreginn," Jack said, tipping his head up at the giant. The giant was a bloody mess, though most of the gore wasn't his own. Elf blood was a different color from the red of nephilbock and human blood, and what splashed

Helreginn from head to toe looked mostly to be the purple blood of the elves.

Helreginn bowed slightly.

"You did real good. You pushed through, and because of your efforts, the enslaved dragons are freed and there are enough dead for all yours to fill their bellies."

"I lost thousands in this battle. I lost my son, Gato," Helreginn said, pointing down at the dead giant.

Jack nodded. "I lost my brother, Danny. I know this is hard."

"Hard? No. This is not hard. This is battle. This is war. My son died an honorable death. He faced the dragon fire, knowing he was about to die. He did not turn away."

Jack glanced down at the badly burnt corpse and nodded slowly, then looked back up at Helreginn. "We will honor your son, Gato, for his bravery in the face of certain death." *That sounded pretty damn good,* Jack thought, feeling impressed with himself.

"Good. This honors Helreginn and his people."

"So, what is the ritual for honoring your son, great king?"

"There is but one honor for a fallen prince that will be acceptable to his king," Helreginn said, reaching and placing a hand on the hilt of his sword.

Jack's hackles raised. Was this dick going to try and kill him to avenge his son? Without even thinking, he reached for the Sentheye, ready to send it forward.

Helreginn drew the sword.

Jack! Cerb warned telepathically as he emitted a deep growl.

Jack raised a hand, staying his dragons. *Wait!*

Helreginn raised the sword to the sky and shouted, "We must avenge my son and every fallen nephilbock!" He dropped to one knee and drove the sword blade into the ground in front of Jack.

Even plunged into the ground, the sword was nearly as tall as Jack.

"We must take the city! We must destroy the dökkálfar once and for all!" Helreginn lowered his voice so only Jack and those close could hear. "Like you said, Taker, the nephilbock have freed the dragon slaves. You will bring honor to my son by helping us have our revenge. The city behind the wall must fall! This is the future of my people. The city behind the wall will be our new kingdom! Help us, and you will have a powerful alliance. This is a strange world. Continuing our alliance will provide assurances for both our kind," said the king, one hand still on the hilt of his sword as he leaned across his dead son's body. "What say you, Taker? Will you help us take the city?"

Jack knew this wasn't the kind of question you answered no to. To say no meant they would all fight to the death here and now. Jack wasn't afraid to fight the giant king, but it would mean the destruction of an army he could align with, plus whatever dragon losses he'd suffer in the fight. That seemed like a stupid play. On the other hand, how many would he lose by taking the city? He made his decision.

"Yes. We will help you take the city, great king. But you must rest your army. There is plenty of food here among the dead. In the meantime, there is more I must do."

"What more?" Helreginn asked.

"I must find the dragons of this world and help them understand who is in charge. But we will return. And when we do, we will be ready to fight. Until then, make camp here, eat, and rest. You've earned it."

Helreginn made a noise that sounded something between a curious consideration and a growl. "How long before you return?"

Considering he had no idea where he was going, he had

no way of knowing when he would return. "Ahi, how far to the dragon lands?"

"Two moon rings' flight, Lord Taker. If we conclude our business quickly, we could be back in five to six."

"Moon rings?" Jack asked.

"Yes. Similar to a day on Earth, but nearly twice as long."

"Okay, so we'll be back within a week," Jack said, turning back to the king.

"Week?" Helreginn asked.

"Before the suns rise a seventh time. And I expect your army to be rested and prepared for battle when we get back."

Helreginn stood. "Upon your return, we shall be ready!" he shouted and pounded a fist into his chest plate. Behind him, thousands followed suit, filling the valley below with thunder.

"Grab the dökkálfar slaves. They're coming with us," Jack ordered.

Juvenile dragons lifted from the ground and rushed forward, snatching up the screaming elves one after another.

Helreginn's eyes narrowed. "You are taking the prisoners?"

"Yes, I am. These are mine, King. The battlefield is littered with dead. We've left yours plenty to eat." Turning his back to the king, Jack ran up Cerb's tail and onto his back, finding his grip on Cerb's horns. "You have nearly a week to get rested and ready, King, and then you'll have your city. I advise you to keep your distance until then and don't be starting no shit with the dökkálfar."

Helreginn bowed his head slightly.

Cerb flapped his wings, while around him dragons yanked the last of the dökkálfar into the air. Talons clutched the elves harshly as they cried out into the night. Jack thought back to his first flight from Petersburg all the way to Central America in the clutches of an elder dragon named Goch. He remembered what it felt like to have the bastard's talons wrapped around him so tight he could barely breathe, but that had been nothing compared to the constant fear that Goch would let go, dropping him to his death. Jack smiled at the memory of tricking the big bastard, killing him, and creating Cerb with the power he'd drawn from the ancient dragon. Jack glanced at an elf soldier dangling face down and yelling at the top of his lungs. *Well, good,* he thought. *Let the bastards scream.*

Now in flight, Jack switched to telepathy. *Ahi, where is this dragon land located?*

Beyond the misting sands of the Nightshade Desert lie the Mountains of Twelve. There you will find the land of the dragon, Ahi answered.

Nightshade Desert? Well, would you look at that. He already had a desert named after him. Oh, he was going to like this world just fine. *And do you remember the way?* he asked.

Of course I remember, Lord Taker. Karelia is, and has always been, my home. But be warned, the journey will be hard on the prisoners and possibly you as well.

How many times must I say this? I'm no ordinary human, not anymore.

I... I understand, Lord Taker, of course, but the misting sands rise into the sky. It is hard for dragons to breathe, but dökkálfar and hu... Ahi paused, reconsidering. *Forgive me. Whatever you are, you will have even more trouble breathing.*

Can't we simply fly over? Jack asked.

No, we would have to fly so high there would be no air to breathe, and we would all die.

We'll go around, Zerri said.

My queen, if we go around, we will have to cross an

ocean. *The trip will add several moon rings and...* Ahi hesitated.

And? Jack asked.

And I'm not sure I could find my way, Ahi admitted.

Talking all that smack about this is my home, always been my home, and now he only knows one way? Jack decided not to give Ahi the mess of shit he felt like giving him. Truth was, if Jack's prisoners died, it would be inconvenient. For shit's sake, he had plans, and while their deaths wouldn't ruin them, it would change them. He sighed. *Fly steady, Cerb,* he said, letting go long enough to pull the hood of his new sweater farther over his head, zip his leather jacket, and pop his collar. It was getting colder as they flew high out over a mountainous forest range toward a desert he hoped would be warmer.

Soon the elves quieted, or the wind swallowed their screams. Either way, this new silence allowed his mind to wander. And for some reason, the image of that elf chick he'd seen staring at him from the crowd wouldn't leave his thoughts.

Hours drifted by. Jack dozed in and out of sleep. His stomach growled. When he next opened his eyes, the night had greyed, soon dissolving into an odd morning as the first of Karelia's two suns shone through the darkness. It didn't seem to rise, exactly – it looked more like its light sort of turned up as if on a dimmer switch. Weird.

Jack yawned, his mind going back to the elf woman like a song stuck in his head. The look of defiance she'd given him wouldn't leave his mind. He was going to need a woman, or maybe more than one, but he'd be damned if he would settle for one of these blue-skinned elves. This woman had looked at him very strangely – unafraid, sure, but more. She looked at him like she knew something he didn't, and he didn't like that. He didn't like that at all. What did she know? He needed to find her, assuming she lived through the flight through these misting sands.

Perhaps we should stop at the edge of the desert to allow the prisoners to rest before we fly through this mist? Cerb suggested. *It will give you a chance to find her.*

Cerb, how do you know about her? Jack asked in disbelief.

You were thinking out loud.

Of course, Apep had told him to be careful with his thoughts. He'd even had Ogliosh work with him on keeping the door to his mind closed when he didn't want others to read his thoughts or intercept his telepathy. But Jack hadn't been guarding himself around Cerb. Why would he?

Look ahead, we have reached the end of the mountains.

Jack leaned forward to get a look between Cerb's heads. The mountains had become foothills that led to sand dunes. But before the sand, a large lake sat nestled among the green foliage of the foothills. A low roar pulled his attention far ahead to the desert. What he saw widened his eyes and twisted his face. *Ahi, what am I looking at?*

A mist storm, my lord.

Jack shook his head. *Shit. That looks like a solid wall of sand.*

Ahi hesitated, then said, *Not solid. As I mentioned before, we can penetrate the mist, but some of our weaker juveniles will most surely die before we reach the other side.*

Can we wait for it to pass? Zerri asked.

Perhaps, but these storms can last for hours or for whole moon rings. There is simply no way of knowing.

A shimmer from the ground caught Jack's eye – they were nearing the lake now. *Horde, there's a lake below. Land there and we'll drink and eat. If the storm hasn't passed by the time we're ready, we're going in anyway.*

The small lake was full of the clearest water Jack had ever

seen, nothing like the muddy water of the Sangamon River back home. Only a few feet out, the shore dropped steeply, plummeting what must have been a hundred feet.

Jack pulled off his clothes down to his underwear and waded out onto the shelf. He stared down at the bottom of the lake, where unfamiliar fish swam. Blue, yellow, green, and red, and all colors in between. The fish, strange in shape, darted, bounced, and swam at all depths of the impossibly clear water. Looking down, vertigo gripped Jack, and he felt for a moment as if he could fall. Reaching into the water, he cupped a handful, then paused. With all the exotic fish, he worried the water must be saltwater and probably undrinkable.

"Ahi? Is this water safe to drink?"

Ahi stomped forward, his massive talons churning up sand as he crossed the shore and stuck his snout in the water. "The water is pure, my lord – better than anything you will find on Earth."

"Let the slaves come forward and drink," Jack said.

Down shore, the dragons released the dökkálfar onto the beach.

Jack turned back to the open water and slurped from his cupped hands. He drank in thirsty gulps until he finally leaned down to plunge his entire face into the water, drinking until his stomach bulged. Staying on the shallow shelf, Jack sat down, washing off and feeling refreshed. Water had never had this effect on him before. He felt more than refreshed; he felt renewed. Jack stood again and spun around, his back to the water. Dragons lined the shore as far as he could see. Elves stood in the shallow water, drinking their fill. He thought of the woman again. Before they moved into the storm, he needed to find her.

From behind him, water splashed the back of his head.

Jack ducked, twisting around, his feet tangling as he fell

forward. His head and shoulders dipped below the water as he scrambled to get his feet under him. Jolting upright, he pawed the water from his eyes.

A woman's voice giggled. "I didn't know a little splash could have an effect on such a mighty human boy."

Jack's hands quickly went from his eyes to his head, relieved to find the Sound Eye still in its place. Setting his eyes on the source of the giggles, he found a woman with milky white skin and long black hair. She was treading water only a few feet away, just beyond the shelf. Only the woman's head was visible above the water, but standing above her from his position on the shelf, he could see she was part fish from the waist down.

Jack swallowed. "Who are you?"

The gorgeous woman giggled again. "I know who you are – Jack," she said, not bothering to answer his question.

"How do you know who I am?" Jack asked, narrowing his eyes.

"Everyone knows who you are." The woman smiled, but Jack wasn't looking at her smile. "See something you like?" she asked, splashing him with water again.

Jack wiped his face. "I'm going to ask you one more time. What are you?"

"Only one time, then?"

"What?"

"You didn't ask what I am. You asked who I am."

"Whatever," Jack shot back.

"Look below me, Jack. What do you see?"

"I already saw – you're part fish."

"Not at me, below me. You do understand the difference, yes?"

Jack sneered, but he looked. Below the woman, thousands of fish gathered. Rather than swimming randomly, they now moved in schools gathering directly beneath her. "You're controlling them?"

"Indeed."

"You're Rán, the one who created the fish? The mother of Hafgufa, the kraken?"

"Ah, now you surprise me. You know of my daughter? The first of my Earthen creations. I left her on Earth to rule the oceans."

Jack thought of disease, of sickness, of hate, and he felt the Sentheye answer, drawing down into his skull – into his mind. "I know of her."

The woman narrowed her eyes, her face drawing into a sneer. "Look, Jack! As deep as eyes so red can pierce, I bid you look!"

Below, the fish scattered, exploding outward in all directions, leaving a hole of clear water visible all the way to the lake floor. But it wasn't the lake floor Jack saw. A shadow stirred there. Smooth, black skin moved, slick like oil, passing across the floor. Passing and passing, long and massive.

"Do you see, boy who holds that which does not belong to him? This is but a single lake. Yet I command all the water-born creatures of this world. Do you understand? There is more water on this planet than there is land, and I command it all! Do you comprehend what I am offering you?"

Jack nodded slowly, unable to take his eyes off the creature as it continued to pass below them. "I understand. You want what I have. Just like Typhon."

"Join with me. In the end, you will lead your dragons and you will keep your God Stone and the humans' stone as well. Perhaps even the nephilbock's. Can you imagine how powerful you will be with three God Stones, Jack?" The woman smiled, her eyes teasing at him playfully.

"Actually, I can imagine myself with all of them because I *have* all of them."

"Don't be a fool! Do you think we are going to let you keep them all, Jack? I am offering you a way to have power and keep it!" Rán said, her playfulness falling away as her visage hardened.

Jack readied himself. "I killed Hafgufa before I even had the God Stones. Truthfully, it wasn't even that hard. If that punk Typhon would have shown himself, I would have killed him too. Now, if you want to live, I suggest you swim your stinky ass back to wherever you came from. And when you get there, tell your friends the next one who tries to take this crown from me is the first one of you to die!"

Rán stared daggers at him. "Your dragons are drinking from my lake. I could kill them all before a single one could lift their snout."

"Then do it!" Jack growled between clenched teeth.

"It is true what they say. Hate not only lives within you, it fills you. The Sentheye you draw upon is born of the darkness. Jack Nightshade is incapable of touching the light. Look at you. Even now, the darkness is consuming you," Rán said, her eyes shifting to the shoreline, then back to Jack. "I will leave you now, Jack Nightshade. I see no need to concern myself with you further."

The woman had looked at his army with disgust, and he didn't much care for it. Another fancy talker. *Why not just kill her, little brother? She is separated from her other gods and sitting right there. This is a tiny lake compared to an ocean. Take her now!*

No way, Danny. Look at her. She's scared. They know they can't stop me!

All the more reason to act now!

Jack nodded toward the lake. "Well, if we're done, then you better leave before I change my mind."

"Change your mind?" Rán asked.

"Change my mind and kill you like I did your daughter."

Rán's eyes flashed murder, but somehow she stayed in control. "You are treading in dangerous waters, little creature."

"I'm going to let you live, Rán, but only because I want you to take a message back to your buddies," Jack said, looking down, watching the shadow below continue to drift past. Whatever was down there was unbelievably big.

"I see. I offer you the water-born armies of Karelia and you insult me, threaten me, and beg me to be your messenger?"

What the shit was she talking about? "Look, I don't beg nothing. I'm telling you to go back and tell the others that the next one of you who tries to strike a deal with me will be the first one I kill."

Rán paused, staring at Jack for a long, uncomfortable moment. "You really believe you can do it, don't you?"

"I know I can," Jack said with a grin.

"I will leave you with this, Jack Nightshade. When you first saw me, your feet became twisted, and you fell."

"So what?" Jack interjected quickly, feeling embarrassed. "You think because I tripped you can win a fight—"

Rán waved him off. "You fell, and you scrambled in the water, fearing the Sound Eye had fallen from your head, lost in the water. But it had not."

Instinctively, Jack reached up to touch the crown, even though he knew it was there. He could feel it and the power it held without the need to touch it. Confused, he stared at Rán.

"Oh, stupid boy, you still don't understand, do you?" Rán asked, taking on an expression of pity. "The Sound Eye did not fall simply because it cannot fall."

Jack's eyes went wide as his hands groped at the crown.

Fingers folding desperately over the top of the crown, he gripped the interlocked stones and pulled. "Ah!" he shouted aloud, realizing with horror that the Sound Eye was clinging to his skin like a leech. No, not like a leech! Like a tick, with a thousand teeth burrowing deep into his flesh. Apep! Apep had ripped the crown of stone from his own scalp when it came time to open the portal. A memory of purple blood spilling down Apep's face as he tore the Sound Eye free of his own flesh flashed through Jack's mind. Jack spun, pulling harder and shouting louder.

Behind him, Rán laughed.

Jack pulled and pulled, but it was like trying to pull off his own head. He couldn't do it. Spinning back to face the sea goddess, he shouted, "How do I get this thing off!" But Rán was gone.

17

Night Slayer

God Stones – Moon Ring 1
The Shadow Forest

Garrett peeked out from behind the longhouse, frowning as Key abandoned her position behind the tree and ran to Breanne.

What's happening? Garrett asked in mind speak.

We're surrounded, Breanne answered.

Garrett turned, looking over his shoulder toward the edge of the woods. He didn't see anything. *Len, do you see anything in the darkness?*

Oh shit, bro!

I'll take that as a yes, Pete said, narrowing his eyes. *I can't see in the dark even when I zoom in.*

Garrett couldn't stand it anymore. *Guys, wait here,* he said, taking off across the open area. He slid like a runner crossing home plate and nearly collided with Key.

Key raised her spear, narrowing her eyes at Garrett. "What are you doing? Your queen asked you to stay behind the longhouse, did she not?"

"Listen, I know, and I promise I totally respect you and your warriors, but we can use the Sentheye," Garrett said, gambling that this woman would know what that statement meant.

Key's eyes widened from annoyance to astonishment. "Sentheye? You can touch the power of the gods?"

Garrett nodded. "Not just me. All of us have some ability. Please, Lady Key, let us help now! I beg you."

"Guys!" David yelled.

Garrett turned to find David pointing at the sky. From the darkness, arrows lit the night, raining down like fireworks at the Menard County Fair.

"The huts! Get out!" Key shouted.

The arrows struck the huts that lined both sides of the dirt street, igniting their thatch roofs like a match to a pile of dry leaves. The women came pouring out of the huts, forced to gather in the village's center street. Smoke billowed from the roofs as the flames grew, brightening the area. In seconds, dozens of fires burned out of control.

From between the burning huts dökkálfar appeared, rushing forward through the smoke.

Guys! It's time to fight, Garrett ordered in mind speak.

Roger that! Paul replied, leading the others from behind the longhouse at the far end of the road.

A group of dökkálfar filed into the dirt street, cutting Garrett and Bre off from the other sages, while still more poured into the street from the other direction. Dressed in what appeared to be lightweight chain armor, the elvish warriors advanced toward Garrett, Breanne, and the women of Sky, swords and war hammers held high.

They should have looked back.

Garrett watched as Paul charged down the smoky street, firelight illuminating a landscape of bad intentions. The elves with their own ill motives were focused on the women and never saw Paul coming as he dipped his shoulder low, charging them from behind. Not slowing, he smashed into the back of an elf. It didn't matter that the warrior was much taller – seven feet if he was an inch, thicker, and armor clad. The elf's feet came up off the ground, sending him careening forward like a bowling ball into the others.

Shouts filled the street as swords and spears clashed. More elves poured into the road, charging the women.

Garrett stepped out from behind the tree and focused on a group of eight, slowing them before they collided with the women.

"You froze them!" Key shouted, as she ran forward and killed the first one with a spear strike under the chin. The woman moved with incredible speed and efficiency through the rest of the eight elves, fatally striking one after the other in a flurry of efficient spins and twists, as if performing a deadly interpretive dance.

Garrett let go of time, and all eight elves collapsed into heaps of death. A sick feeling filled his stomach. Eight deaths because of him, but what was the alternative? Let the women be ambushed?

When he looked back, Paul and the others had finished dealing with the elves at that end of the street and were rushing forward past Garrett and Bre into the group of women still fighting in the street.

Key stole a backward glance at Garrett, nodded, and flashed a blood-smeared smile. Then the leader of Sky vanished into the smoke-filled street to join her people in battle. With his own backward glance, Garrett realized they could all flee now if they wanted to. The way behind them was clear. But Key's smile told him there would be no withdrawal. Clearly retreat wasn't in these women's vocabulary.

David was the last to reach Garrett. *Wait! Stay back,*

David. Your work will start soon enough, but you can't heal others if you're hurt.

Are you kidding? I was just heading for cover behind that fence! David said, pointing with the staff Lenny had given him.

Garrett nodded. *Right. Just be careful,* he said, running forward.

Breanne ran next to him, one hand holding her shirt over her mouth as she coughed, the nine mil held in her other hand pointed down at the ground. The huts were engulfed now, heat pressing in, threatening to singe the hair off his head.

From the smoke, a woman's voice shouted, but she was speaking some different language. She was speaking dökkálfar. *You guys hear that?*

It's one of them! She's giving orders! David shouted.

Of course, David could understand. He was holding the Eyra of Tunga.

What is she saying, kid? Paul shouted into their heads.

Kill them all! Take no prisoners! Breanne answered for him. That's right, Garrett remembered. Bre understood elvish too.

Garrett and Bre reached the group of women in the center of the street as the elves closed in around them. The sound of metal on spear, the breaking of wood, intermixed with the screams of war echoed down the street. Bre's gun cracked out a shot, followed by another, then another.

A dökkálfar dropped still to the ground.

Lenny ran toward a tall soldier, stepping once onto the elf's bent knee as he lunged forward, then again on his hip. Twisting gracefully, Lenny was suddenly behind the dökkálfar, clenching the elf in a choke hold.

The elf flailed for Lenny as if he had a feral cat clinging to his back.

Garrett turned away, his attention drawn by an attacker swinging a sword. He raised his own sword, blocking the powerful strike just in time. The force pushed him back, but he didn't fight it. Instead, he stepped back into a fighting stance, allowing himself to slide on the balls of his feet.

The dökkálfar sneered, its eyes narrowed.

Long ago, Mr. B had taught Garrett that the eyes of any man were usually the first tell in battle. As he looked into the sneering elf's eyes, he could hear Mr. B's voice coming back to him. *Learn to read your enemy's eyes, and you will know his intentions as soon as he knows them himself.*

The dökkálfar lunged, thrusting his sword forward with blinding speed.

Garrett dropped, wind from the elf's blade blowing through his short hair, only narrowly missing his head. He gasped reflexively, driving his own sword up into the elf's stomach.

Confusion gripped the blue face of the creature as his eyes searched Garrett's. The dökkálfar's mouth worked wordlessly open and closed like a fish out of water pulling for air. His sword, becoming too heavy to hold, fell from his hand as his strange eyes grew distant. Slowly the elf blinked and wetness spilled down his cheeks.

Garrett's eyes grew bigger and bigger. Around him, the battle seemed suddenly distant and quiet.

Finally, the elf's mouth fell open and stayed, his gaze shifting down to Garrett's sword.

Garrett swallowed, set his jaw, and yanked back on the sword, ripping it free.

The elf fell back and moved no more.

Emotion threatened to overwhelm Garrett, but there was no time to process what had just happened. The sound of war came rushing in, along with two more elves. The first elf said something to the second.

The other, a taller elf, spun two war hammers and reared back for a swing while his shorter companion lunged in with his sword.

Garrett grabbed time, slowing them both to a near stop.

Clack! Clack! Clack! Clack!

Jumping at the gunshots, Garrett lost his grip on time, both elves falling toward him as he spun away. Momentum carried them forward, their legs buckling as they sprawled out onto the ground. Behind them, Bre stood with her feet shoulder width apart, her pistol smoking.

Around him, both women and elves screamed, backpedaling away from them. Garrett frowned, not understanding at first, and then it dawned on him they were fleeing from the report of gunshots. They had never seen a gun, let alone heard a gunshot. To them, it must have seemed like some strange magic.

"Thanks," Garrett breathed, squinting through the smoke-filled street. *Lenny!* He shouted in mind speak, not able to see which way his friends had gone.

Over here! At the other end of the street! Hurry! Lenny's voice called back.

The huts were fully consumed now, their roofs collapsing in upon themselves, one after the other. As those around them found their courage, battle erupted again and their path forward closed.

"This way!" Garrett shouted. Grabbing Bre by the hand, he ran down the street, dodging the utter chaos of elven swords and shields as they collided with the spears of the women of Sky. Half a dozen steps into the fray, Breanne fired her nine at an elf sitting atop a woman, pinning her to the ground.

Six more strides and an elf reached from the smoke to snatch at Bre as they passed. Garrett severed the elf's hand at the wrist.

Nearing the end of the street, a dökkálfar outright attacked them. The back of the elf's bony hand struck Garrett across his face.

"Garrett!" Breanne shouted.

Light flashed through his head, and then the ground came crashing into his face. He hadn't even realized he'd hit the ground until he was lying on it. Garrett pushed himself up, squinting through one eye as the war hammer swung toward his head. He reached for time, but pain racked his skull, blocking his ability to focus.

Clack! Clack!

The hammer fell from the elf's hand, and when he collapsed, there was Bre. How many times was this girl going to save his ass?

Thanks. I owe you... again.

She smiled – actually smiled. *I'm starting to lose count, you know.*

It's twice. Twice, Bre. I can still catch up. He smiled back.

Twice... oh, maybe twice today?

Lenny's strained voice filled his mind. *Little help... here, Garrett!*

Lenny! Garrett ran past the burning huts, Breanne close behind, breaking free of the smoke and the battle.

Lenny stood on the path they'd arrived on, just outside the village. He was holding his jaw, circling a female dökkálfar with a sword. The woman was clad in silver-and-gold armor, flourishing her sword as she circled. Four other soldiers accompanied the woman and were slowly closing in. But as Garrett and Bre approached, the woman waved off her men, pointed at Lenny, and yelled something.

What did she say? Garrett asked.

She said, "This one is mine. Kill the others!" Breanne answered.

The four soldiers turned on them.

Breanne fired three rounds into a fast-approaching elf, but then Garrett heard the dreadful sound of an empty chamber's click.

The wounded elf raised his sword to swing, but Garrett was there, sweeping the elf's legs out from underneath him. The elf fell back as Garrett completed the spin and kicked him in the head.

Garrett turned back to face the three others, his sword drawn as he reached for time, but the three remaining elves tossed their weapons to the ground and raised their hands in surrender. Their eyes were fixed on Breanne's gun.

Behind Garrett, cheers sounded from the street as the women of Sky began appearing through the smoke. David appeared with them, an injured woman's arms wrapped over his shoulder as she staggered along. On the other side stood Gabi, doing her best to help David carry the woman. Paul and Pete appeared too, both splashed in dark-blue blood but looking otherwise uninjured.

Several women circled around Lenny and the female dökkálfar, while others seized and executed the three surrendering soldiers.

Eyes widening at the sight of her men being killed, the armored elf made a gesture with her hand and shouted something. Narrowing her eyes, she looked at Lenny and pointed her sword.

Key was there now. "Breanne Moore, this dökkálfar has challenged your male to a fight to the death. I suggest you allow us to dispatch her before she kills your male."

Lenny, Garrett, what do I do? Do I let them help? asked Breanne.

Lenny didn't take his eyes off the woman. *David, throw me the Eyra of Tunga.*

David stepped forward and tossed the medallion to Lenny, who snatched it out of the air.

Lenny, what are you doing? Garrett asked.

"Easy, babe, this doesn't have to go down like this," Lenny said, but he was still speaking English.

The elven woman cocked her head as if trying to understand the strange words. She spoke then, but Garrett couldn't understand. *What did she say, Bre?*

"Go on, have your dogs do your dirty work, coward. There is no honor among humans," Breanne said.

Now it was Lenny who tilted his head, listening. Then, when he spoke next, he spoke dökkálfar.

Oh shit! David said.

What? Garrett asked. *Dammit. Am I the only one who can't speak dökkálfar now?*

No, Paul said.

Me either, Pete said. *Well, David, what did he say?*

He said, "I'm no coward. I accept your challenge."

Lenny! Don't do it! Garrett said.

The woman dropped her shield and drove her sword into the ground.

Lenny looked over and tossed the medallion to Garrett. In mind speak he said, *Let me do this, Garrett. She is obviously important. I need to show honor here.*

"It appears your human just accepted a battle challenge laid down by the leader of the Osonian Army," Key said.

"Leader of the Osonian Army?" Breanne repeated.

"That is General Saria Liavaris, the Night Slayer. They say she alone is responsible for the siege of Thunder Keep. The dwarven trade routes still haven't recovered. The loss of Thunder Keep severely damaged their economy, not to mention it was the last move to seal out the rest of the world from Osonian. Your male has erred greatly. What I don't understand is why? This seems completely unnecessary."

Lenny! This girl's badass. You need to be careful! Garrett said, looking at the elf woman anew. Her armor, though flashy, was worn on the knees and elbows in a way that told Garrett she had thrown a lot of strikes from both. The elf's hair, raven black and long, was braided back out of the way. But what confirmed the elf woman was an experienced warrior was the way she moved. If he'd seen nothing else, her fluidity in stance and movement would have been enough.

I got this, Lenny thought back, throwing a roundhouse kick at Saria's face.

Saria sidestepped and punched Lenny in the side.

Lenny bent and covered his side with his hand.

With Lenny's hands down, Saria stepped in and short jabbed him in the nose.

"Ah! Dammit!" Lenny shouted as he backpedaled.

"Key, what happens if she wins?" Breanne asked.

Key sneered at the elf woman. "Whether she wins or loses makes no difference. She dies either way. Why fight her at all?"

"But… well, I suppose he's doing this for honor," Breanne said.

"Ah, I see. Well, he is a man. He must be fighting for your honor, and he will die for it. And then she will die anyway, and you will have lost a healthy male. The fact that the king sent her must mean he knows you are here. Now, I must attend to my people. Some are dead, others are badly wounded." Key turned to another woman, watching as the two opponents sized each other up again. "Push, when this is over, kill her."

The woman, apparently named Push, stood erect and nodded. "Yes, my lady."

Lenny wiped blood from his nose, then countered with a barrage of punches and kicks.

The attack had little effect as the taller elvish woman either dodged or blocked.

This chick is like fighting Mr. B! Lenny shouted in mind speak.

Saria threw a kick that missed, but as her foot landed on the ground, she connected with a straight punch to Lenny's cheekbone.

The boy reeled back, throwing a hand to his already bleeding face.

That's three unanswered strikes, kid! Get it together! Paul commanded.

Not helpful! Lenny answered.

Come on, Lenny! I know you can take her, David cheered.

Saria smiled, sliding one foot back as she raised her sword. "You are disappointingly slow. It's a shame. I would have liked for my last battle in this life to have been a worthy one."

Lenny's jaw flexed as he rolled up onto his toes.

Focus, Len! You got this! Garrett urged.

Saria delivered a front snap kick as Lenny jumped.

Airborne, he stepped on Saria's extended leg and launched himself up even higher, driving his knee into her face. The knee connected with a crack. Saria fell back, releasing an audible exhalation as she landed hard on her back.

Lenny landed and walked over to the gasping woman. "I think we're even, babe. What do you say we call this a draw?" he said, extending a hand.

Saria spat at his hand, rolled back onto her palms, and launched herself up onto her feet. "I have never seen a human do that."

"Who said I'm human?" Lenny said.

Did you just tell her you aren't human? Garrett asked in mind speak.

Easy, kid. These ladies don't know what you are, and I

don't think they will care much for finding out the truth, Paul warned.

"Enough of this." Saria dove, rolled, and ripped her sword from the ground. She spun and struck down at Lenny's face.

Lenny stretched both arms out in front of his face and slapped his hands together on both sides of the dökkálfar blade, stopping it inches from his face.

Saria's eyes went wide. "Impossible."

Still holding the blade between his palms, Lenny stepped back, pulling Saria off balance, and kicked her in the gut so hard her feet lifted from the ground. The elvish warrior landed hard on her stomach. With a groan, she pushed her head up as if she were doing a push-up.

Lenny flipped the sword in the air, caught it by the hilt, drew back, and swung toward Saria's raised head.

18

The Deal

God Stones – Moon Ring 1
The Shadow Forest

Everyone watching, including Breanne, gasped as the sword sliced the air toward Saria's neck.

The blade stopped against the woman's skin. She froze, staring up at Lenny.

No one exhaled.

Lenny stared down at her.

"Well, what are you waiting for?" Saria asked, looking up at Lenny impassively.

Lenny tossed the sword onto the ground.

"What's he doing?" Push protested. "There is no victory until one or the other has died! I respectfully ask you to order your man to finish this or order me to finish her myself!" Push was a thick-built woman with bone shards piercing her ears and cheeks. She had rows of scars down the outsides of both arms and intricate scarification across her exposed stomach. She looked as though someone had splashed her with a jar of dark-blue ink, the result of drying dökkálfar blood.

I'm not going to kill her, Garrett, Lenny said.

Len, if you got some plan you aren't sharing, now's the time. Garrett walked over to stand next to his friend.

Push stomped forward then. Breanne quickly matched the woman stride for stride.

"What is the meaning of this, Breanne Moore?" Push asked as she drew to a stop next to Garrett. Looking down upon the still-prone Saria, the hulking woman raised her spear.

"Hold," Breanne ordered with a raised hand. She turned toward Push and lifted her chin. "The future I have shared has come to pass. Therefore, I must be who I claim to be. Now please, leave us to handle this and help Key attend to your wounded. David is a special healer. He will assist you," she said, nodding back toward David.

The woman stared for a long moment, first at Saria, then shifting her gaze back to Breanne. Push bowed her head slightly and turned back to her people with a flourish. "Show me you're worth your salt, healer!"

Okay, Lenny. What the hell are we doing? Breanne asked in mind speak.

Something I have to do, Bre, he answered, as he knelt next to Saria.

"What is this?" the dökkálfar asked. "You dare disrespect me by refusing me a warrior's death? You dare—"

"If you shut up and listen, you might get out of this alive," Lenny said quietly.

Saria sat up and looked up at Lenny. "If you allow me to live, I will return to my king and report your location. After which, I will bring the whole might of the Osonian army down upon you. Even if you flee, I will hunt you to the ends of Karelia, across the shifting sands of the Nightshade Desert, if that's what it takes to see you die!"

"I'm starting to think you're kind of into me," Lenny said with a smile.

Lenny, dammit, what are we doing? Garrett asked.

Lenny's smile vanished as he addressed Garrett and the others in mind speak. *Guys, don't you get it? Dagrun was my father. She would likely have known him, and she knows the king.*

And your point? Garrett asked.

The point is, I need to know what she knows! I need to know if my grandfather knows about me.

Len… this might be a terrible idea, Breanne tried.

Pete stepped forward. *Listen to her, Lenny, she might be—*

"Do you know Syldan?" Lenny blurted.

Annnnd too late, Pete finished.

"How dare you speak his name! How dare you speak our language at all!"

"So, you know him?"

"Of course I know him. He was my teacher."

"That's funny, he was kind of my teacher too and my coach and, turns out, also my—"

Len-ny, careful, man, Garrett urged, glancing back over his shoulder.

Lenny knelt closer to Saria, lowering his voice to a whisper. "And my father."

Saria's eyes looked as though they might bulge out of her head. "You liar!" she breathed and spat at the ground. "You dare disgrace Prince Syldan Loravaris, heir to the throne of Osonian!"

"And where is he, Saria?" Lenny asked.

The elf woman's strange eyes only stared daggers at Lenny.

"I'll tell you where. He went away to Earth, my home planet, to find the God Stones, but time passes different there and he got stuck. Eventually, he fell in love with a human woman, and she had a son. I am that son, Saria."

"No! You cannot be. He would never. And you don't look—"

"Dökkálfar?" Lenny finished. "No, not yet. But Coach said I will change. And you saw what I did. You called it impossible. Maybe it would be – for a human."

Saria narrowed her eyes, peering deeply into Lenny's.

Somehow, maybe instinctually, Lenny seemed to know what she was looking for. Lenny's jaw tightened, and Breanne knew he was focusing. As his focus seemed to intensify, purple light crackled like lightning through his eyes.

Saria cocked her head curiously. "I don't know what you are, but you are something different, to be sure. You called him 'Coach.' Why?" she asked.

"Oh, um, that's just what we called him. Coach Dagrun."

"Dagrun? He called himself Dagrun?" Saria asked, sounding more convinced.

"Yes."

"Prince Syldan is a dragon master. The greatest ever born. He could control two dragons simultaneously, the first in our history to do so. Until he left for his mission, he was the leader of the dragon slave masters. Dagrun means 'The Dragon' in the old tongue. Where is he?"

"Apep killed him back on Earth."

Saria looked as though she'd been struck across the face. Tears spilled down her blue cheeks. Lenny's news of Syldan's death seemed to suck the life out of her. Finally, she said, "Why do you tell me all this? Even if this isn't some clever ruse, what good is it?"

"This is no ruse, Saria. I want you to live, and I want you to take a message back to King Loravaris. Tell him his grandson is here. Tell him he is my grandfather."

Saria started laughing. "You fool. Even if you are – even

if you had proof, King Loravaris will kill you for the abomination you are!" The woman pushed herself to her feet.

Lenny stood with her, his face becoming a rare visage of seriousness.

Saria went on: "What do you think? Do you think he will welcome a half human home with open arms? Did you think he would cheer for your arrival? Perhaps announce you as the heir to the kingdom? You're a fool! He won't believe a word, and then he will kill you for your blasphemy!"

Lenny reached behind his back and pulled the folded notebook from his waistband. "I can prove every word. This was Syldan's personal journal. It's his story of his time on Earth, but also the story of the gods and how his own beliefs changed. Saria, it isn't for me or for you to decide how my grandfather feels once he's read this. But if you want to live today, I need your word you will deliver this notebook into the hands of the king. That is the price for being allowed to live. What do you say?"

Lenny? Pal, you know Key isn't going to let her go, right? Garrett asked in mind speak.

Lenny, his eyes fixed on Saria, didn't answer.

Breanne saw something in the woman's face – in her eyes.

The dökkálfar stared down at Lenny for a long moment before she finally nodded sharply. "I do not know what you are. But you are not the son of Syldan. Nevertheless, I give you my word. I will deliver this diary to my king, but be warned, the next time we meet, I will kill you. I will kill your companions. And I will see to it every woman of Sky dies by the blade of the dökkálfar. When I'm finished here, I will move on to the so-called King of Sky, and I will destroy him. Every human that remains, I will force into slavery until there are no humans roaming free upon these lands. Do you understand?" Saria did not wait for an answer. "This is my calling now. Ereshkigal has spoken to me. She sent me here to kill you. I failed today, but she protects me. The fact that I will live to return to my king is proof my goddess is not done with me."

"You could just say 'thanks,'" Lenny said.

Saria narrowed her eyes, her lip curling into a hateful sneer.

"Geesh. Never mind. Here, take it," Lenny said, handing her Coach's journal.

Kid, I think we have a problem, Paul said, nodding back toward a crowd of both healthy and wounded women walking toward them. The stocky woman Breanne had sent away was pointing, flanked by Key and Tell, both looking very unhappy.

David, you are supposed to be wowing them with the golden glow, Lenny projected.

Yeah, well, I was about to, but then Push told Key that Lenny won't kill Saria and they sent me away. So, yeah. Incoming, and they're not happy.

How in the hell are we supposed to set her free now? Garrett asked.

Lenny glanced back at Gabi. *Gabi, maybe you can use mind control on Key and—*

And you can forget that! I'm never doing it again… ever! Gabi said, crossing her arms.

Sheesh. Okay. Pete, can you use your nerd vision to create a distraction? Knock over a tree or something?

Nerd vision? Attack a tree, here? After what happened to Governess? Seriously?

While all this conversation took place in mind speak, Saria stared at them, likely thinking they were just standing there doing nothing. "The others are approaching, and they appear fixed for an execution. If you have a plan to free me, you had better hurry," the dökkálfar said, glaring at Lenny. "You do have a plan, don't you?"

"I'm working on it. Just hold your horses and I'll—"

Saria kicked Lenny in the face.

"Auaghh!" Lenny shouted, his head snapping back as his hand went reflexively to his quickly swelling face.

Before anyone could react, Saria turned and bolted.

"Stop her!" Key shouted, running forward past Garrett.

Saria disappeared into the shadows as spears launched from atlatls gave chase.

"Slow her like you did the others!" Key said, motioning to Garrett.

"She's out of my reach, and besides, I can't slow what I can't see!"

"I'll get her!" Tell shouted, flashing past the group, her own atlatl raised.

"Wait! Damn fool girl!" Key shouted after her.

But Tell did not wait. With her atlatl raised, she ran, and in a few bounding strides she vanished into the same shadows Saria had.

"No one can outrun my daughter in the Shadow Forest." Key said, but there was no pride in the statement, only worry. "She *will* catch her. I could send a hundred women after her and none would get to her in time – not now. Damn that girl!" Key said, her fists clenched at her sides. "Still, we must try. Push, take the fastest four and go! Go now!" Key turned to Breanne. "Breanne Moore, I have many questions. First, why did you send my guard away? Second, how was your male able to defeat her? And finally, how did this happen? How was she able to escape with you and your people standing right here?"

Before Breanne could open her mouth to answer, an awful scream broke from the forest.

"Tell!" her mother screamed.

19

Nyana

God Stones – Moon Ring 2
A lake at the edge of the Nightshade Desert

Jack wrestled with the Sound Eye crown, pulling until the pain around his head was too great to bear. Finally, he calmed himself down and brought his breathing under control. *Cerb!*

What is it, Jack?

Where are you? He spun in a circle, looking for the big three-headed dragon, but he couldn't see him.

I'm here!

Jack spun around again, still seeing the other dragons lounging in the sun and dökkálfar wading along the shore, but no Cerb.

Suddenly, water exploded into the sky just behind him. Jack tried to spin, to prepare to defend himself, but a wave of water struck him, knocking him backward into the lake.

Scrambling, Jack pulled the Sentheye to him as he planted his feet and stood. In front of him, something exploded into the air. A flash of fear streaked across Jack's mind like the black shadow from deep below the surface. That bitch, Rán, must have sent the monster to kill him after all!

Ha! Ha! Haaaa! Cerberus roared with hysterical laughter. *You should see the look on your face, brother!*

Cerb? You son of a bitch! Jack shouted, slapping the water with a palm.

High above, Cerb circled, laughing and flapping his wings.

Jack turned away, wading toward the shore. He'd had enough of water for one day.

Taker, Cerb called, still laughing, *don't be so sore!*

Jack ignored him, doing his best to shake off the water before pulling on his jeans over his damp legs.

Come now! You called for me. What is it? the big dragon asked, settling onto the shore in front of him. Cerb was just close enough to the water's edge for it to lap over his taloned feet.

Jack, still frowning, still pissed at being embarrassed, and still wanting to get the hell out of the water, changed direction and waded up past Cerberus.

Oh, for the gods' sake, brother, what is it? Surely you aren't this mad over my startling you?

What the dumb bastard didn't know was that a goddess had just threatened him, and if that weren't enough, this damned crown had bored itself into his head! He wanted help, dammit! But now he didn't feel like telling him at all. He wanted Danny! Or even his… his dad. Well, he'd killed his dad, so that wasn't going to happen. Jack stopped and closed his eyes, drawing in a deep breath. Memories of Petersburg flooded his mind: time spent with his brother along the shores of the Sangamon River, time with friends, fishing and exploring tunnels. Petersburg was gone – burned to the ground – burned at his orders.

Jack, I don't know what is wrong with you. Whatever it is, you can tell me.

No. No, he didn't want to talk about it – none of it, not about Rán, or the Sound Eye affixed to his freaking skull. Not now... not anymore.

I wanted to tell you, brother. The dökkálfar girl you were looking for – I think I found her. She's at the far end of a group down shore. Let me take you to her. Perhaps you'll feel better.

Jack lifted his head and opened his eyes. That's what he needed. He needed to get his mind off of these current issues and, more importantly, off the past. There was nothing there for him. A voice spoke to him then, soft as a whisper. *You don't live there, brother. Leave it back there. Your future is here.*

Danny?

Don't you give up this power, little bro. You make me proud. Kill them all, Jack. Rule the shit out of this world and kill them all!

I will! I promise, Danny! You hear me? I promise!

The whisper was gone. But it didn't matter. Brief as it was, it was just what Jack needed. Those feelings, or whatever they were, it was better to keep them buried deep below a mountain of ash – just like Petersburg.

Jack spun back toward his dragon, let out a breath, and nodded. *Yes, Cerb, take me to this girl.*

~

As he slid down Cerb's scales and back onto the beach, the crowd of dökkálfar retreated as far from Jack as they could. Though there really was nowhere to go. The land beyond the lake's beach was sandy and barren save for sparse weeds and strange-shaped cacti. Along the edge of the beach, away from the water, dragons sunned themselves, resting up for the journey ahead.

For every step Jack took, the frightened elves took a step back, their eyes downturned as they parted to allow a superior being to pass unobstructed. This felt good – it felt like this was the way it was meant to be.

Near the back of the crowd, Jack found the girl. She was wearing baggy pants and a top that didn't fit. Her clothes looked homemade. Most the elves didn't dress this way. Almost all had fancy silks beneath expensive-looking armor trimmed in gold and silver. But not this girl. What was she even doing among these captured soldiers? He could tell that, beneath her clothing, she had a nice figure and, despite her weird blue skin, her face was attractive too. Jack noticed something else. The defiant stare was gone. This woman looked scared now.

"You," he said, pointing, "come here."

Everyone backed away from the girl, leaving her to stand and face Jack alone. Her eyes grew wide, but she didn't move.

"I said come here, girl."

Jack, she can't understand your language, Cerb said.

Oh shit, that's right. Well, how am I supposed to communicate with her?

Cerb bent his neck and twisted one of his heads to meet Jack's eyes. *Though I strongly urge you not to do this, as you need to rest your mind from the Sentheye, you could use a small amount to open her mind to yours and learn her language.*

Thanks to Ogliosh, Jack already spoke nephilbock and thanks to Azazel, he also spoke dragon. But if he were going to learn dökkálfar, he was going to have to do the one thing he'd told himself not to do. He was going to have to use Sentheye. Damn.

He pointed at the girl again and motioned her forward.

She understood the gesture, reluctantly walking toward him.

Slowly, Jack reached up with both hands. She wasn't very tall for an elf, only a few inches taller than himself. He wondered if that was because she was younger than the others.

The girl flinched.

"I won't hurt you," he whispered. Jack placed a hand on each side of the girl's face.

She recoiled, squeezing her eyes shut and twisting her neck to try to get away.

"Shhh. I promise it's okay," he said, closing his eyes and concentrating on her mind. The door Ogliosh had taught him to close existed in all minds. Jack found hers and forced it open. "That's it," he whispered, feeling the Sentheye surge through his mind. His brain began to suddenly ache and burn, but it tapered off, becoming steady and bearable. After a moment, he could feel the magic had finished its work. He let go of the girl's face.

She opened her eyes, looking confused.

"My name is Jack. What's your name?"

The girl gasped. "You speak dökkálfar?"

"I do now. Now tell me, what's your name, girl?"

"Nyana," she answered.

"Nyana." Jack repeated. "Walk with me, Nyana." The words left his mouth before he realized they were the same words Apep would have said. In fact, the old dökkálfar had said those very words to Jack many times. He turned his gaze down the shore. "This way."

They walked away from the other dökkálfar. Dragons still lined the outer shore, but this was close enough to alone. Out of earshot, anyway. "Tell me, Nyana, why did you look at me the way you did back at the portal?"

"The portal? Ah, you mean the sacred monument?"

"Sure, whatever. Why did you look at me as though you wanted to kill me?"

"I think all the dökkálfar want to kill you," she said, but there was no bite to her words.

Jack wasn't sure why, but he wanted to impress this girl. "You make me curious, Nyana. You're not telling me something. Now, I want to know why you looked at me differently than the others. I could force you to tell me, but I promise it will be very unpleasant. So please, don't make me do that." He was happy with his word choices. That kind of grammar might have even made Apep proud.

Nyana stared at the ground as they walked. But Jack couldn't take his eyes off the sky. The suns were shining warmly, with the morning well under way.

"That wasn't me," she said.

Jack stopped and pulled his attention to her. Her eyes were baby blue, reminding him of the color of glaciers he'd seen on the Discovery Channel. "What's that supposed to mean?"

"It means what you saw wasn't me."

"Nyana, I'm not known for my patience. Explain yourself. If it wasn't you I saw, then who was it? Do you have a twin?"

"You saw me, but the look was not my own. The goddess Ereshkigal came to me." Nyana shook her head, frustrated in her explanation. "Not *to* me so much as she became me."

"She possessed you," Jack offered.

"Possessed? Yes, I suppose this is a better way to say it. She took me over and spoke to me as well. She wanted to get to you, but she said she had little time. So instead, she gave me a message to give to you."

"Go on," Jack urged, feeling anger build within him.

"She told me to tell you that the gods are arguing and all seven vie for the God Stones. You, Jack, hold all the power.

However, you are but one being and you are not a god. This much power will destroy you, and then you will have nothing. You will lose it all, Jack. Even yourself."

"And let me guess, she wants to help me?"

"No, my goddess does not care about you, nor does she care about the fate of humans or dragons. She cares about dökkálfar."

"You realize this isn't helping your cause. Because as you probably know, I am both dragon and human," Jack said, the rising anger flaring, his eyes bright red.

"Of course she knows. I am not telling you this to anger you."

"What does she want?" he asked through a clenched jaw.

"I think she wants to make a deal with you, Jack."

Another one. First Typhon, then Rán, and now this Ereshkigal.

"My goddess is good, Jack. She may forgive you for what you have done. If you give her what she wants, she may even protect you."

It was all Jack could do not to disease Nyana and watch her fall dead right here on the spot. But killing her wouldn't get back at the gods. Besides, there was something about her. He wasn't ready to kill her – not yet. "Nyana, what are you doing here?" he asked.

"You captured me, remember?" she said, allowing the slightest hint of a smile to play at her lips.

Jack smiled then. "Fair enough. Let me try again. Why were you captured? You are clearly not a warrior. Shouldn't you have been behind the wall?"

"I am a simple servant. When the attack came, I was out running an errand and couldn't make it back to the wall in time. I tried to hide, and it mostly worked until the end. I thought it was over and came out from hiding. The nephilbock captured me before I could flee."

"A simple servant in the wrong place at the wrong time?"

The girl nodded.

Still, there was something strange about her. "Why do you think the goddess Ereshkigal picked you to deliver this message?"

"I cannot say why the gods do what they do, but Ereshkigal said she would come back to me when the time was right. She said I should be close to you so she may talk to you herself."

Oh, these gods were desperate for what he had. Typhon came first, through Zerri, then directly into his own mind, while the goddess Rán appeared to him in the water – in the flesh, no less. Now this goddess Ereshkigal appeared through the mortal body of another. He wasn't sure if any of this was important or not, but it seemed these so-called gods could come to him in many forms. He'd have to do his best to stay alert.

"Will you allow me to live, Jack?" the girl asked.

The truth was, the thought of a god showing up didn't scare him. Jack had yet to come across a creature he and Cerb couldn't kill. Garrett might be the exception, but only for now and only because the coward kept getting away.

"As long as you behave and do what I tell you, I see no reason to kill you."

Concern creased the girl's face. Jack wasn't sure what he'd said. Then it suddenly clicked. She was worried he'd force her to bed. Rather than put her at ease, he smiled. "Good. We have an understanding then?"

Hesitantly, Nyana nodded.

"Can I ask you something, Jack?"

Jack stopped, realizing they'd neared the end of the beach. Ahead, the flat sand rose into a steep dune. "Ask," he said.

"The Sound Eye. It appears affixed to your head. Are you unable to remove it?"

What a strange question from someone with so little power. He would have thought she'd be afraid to ask such a thing, but there it was. His greatest fear spoken aloud from the lips of a girl he'd known for only minutes – a peasant girl.

Danny's voice whispered to him then: *She isn't what she pretends to be, little bro. You'd be best to have your fun and kill her.*

Rather than answering her question, he asked, "Why would I want to take it off?"

"Legends say the power of the God Stones united is too much for any one being to hold."

"Yet here I am, holding it," Jack countered quickly. Maybe Danny was right. This creature would do for now, but eventually, he might need to dispose of her. He'd keep her around for a while to see if this goddess showed up. Maybe then he could kill her while the goddess was in her body. First things first. If he was going to keep her around, he needed to be sure she knew her boundaries. "Now, you were told by this goddess of yours to stay close to me until she returned. I will allow it, but you need to obey me and watch your mouth."

"Watch my mouth?" Nyana asked. "What is watching my mouth?"

Dammit, Apep would have said something smarter. Jack tried to remember, then settled for, "Just pay attention to how you speak to me. Questioning me and my decisions is a good way to get hurt. Understand?"

Nyana frowned. "I did not mean to offend you."

"Just don't ask me about the Sound Eye, the God Stones, or Sentheye – ever. Got it?"

"I understand," Nyana said, looking down at the ground.

"Good. I think it's time we go."

"Can I ask you another question?"

Jack stopped, faced her head on, and tensed his jaw. "I hope you will be more careful this time."

Nyana's eyes flared wide in surprise. She swallowed and nodded. "Of course. I… I promise not to discuss what you have forbade." She paused, then seemed to reconsider.

"Well, go on then. Now I want to know. What is it?"

"You plan to pass through the mist storm?" Nyana asked, turning her attention across the lake.

Far beyond the water, across miles of rolling dunes, a wall of air so thick it looked like an actual wall of dark stone blocked their path to the Mountains of Twelve. "Yes, that's the plan."

"We will all die then," Nyana said evenly.

"Do you or your people know another way, Nyana?"

"Yes, but it is long and many of us would likely die."

Jack didn't have time for anything longer. The nephilbock expected him back to take the city. "How much longer?"

"Hard to say. There are stories of my people crossing through the storms. But more stories tell of disorientation and death. There is the story of how Apep was banished by his father into the misting sands and somehow found his way out."

"Unless you know how, these stories don't help much," Jack said.

"No. I only know they hugged the coast and crossed on foot at the ground level, not in the air. That's why it would take longer."

"Well, I don't have time for that."

Nyana's face fell. "Then I fear we are doomed."

Jack really didn't want them to die in the mist storm. Not because he gave two shits about any of them. Sure, the girl might be fun to keep around, but these dökkálfar still breathed only to serve one purpose. He wanted them to die

The Last Gift

as sacrifices to the dragons he was on his way to go see. Die, become food, or become slaves – it didn't matter. The point was, they were to be offerings. A show of his power and his defeat of the elven army.

They were nearly back to the group of dökkálfar he had taken Nyana from when he realized there was only one solution to this and, as usual, it was up to him to solve. "You won't die in the mist storm, Nyana, nor will your people. But I expect you, a peasant no less, to be grateful for what a powerful being like me is about to do for you and yours."

"What will you do?" she asked.

Jack smiled, knowing how bad of an idea this was, and then said, "I'll do what I always do – save the goddamned day."

20

The Brightest Glow

God Stones – Moon Ring 2
The Shadow Forest

Another scream sounded from the forest as Garrett and Lenny matched each other stride for stride. Even with his cross-country training, Garrett couldn't match pace with Key, who was easily a half dozen strides ahead.

David! Hurry! I have a feeling you're going to be needed! Garrett said.

Running... as fast as... as I can! David answered in mind speak. Strangely, the kid sounded just as out of breath as he would have sounded if he were shouting the words aloud.

The path Key was following took a sharp turn into a stand of trees, and she vanished into the dense, shadowed forest.

Garrett shared an uneasy glance with Lenny. *Lead the way, Len,* Garrett said, knowing his friend could see better in the dark than he could.

Lenny nodded, taking the lead. Once inside the denser part of the forest, Garrett could see just well enough not to run into a tree, but having Lenny right in front of him certainly helped. It was night now, with moons full and shining for what little good they did. He imagined this part of the forest was dark even in the brightest part of the day. The tangled tree canopy was not far above them, blocking out most of the moons' light. *Do you see her?* he asked.

There, Lenny answered, pointing ahead.

When they reached Key, she was squatting with her back to them, still and quiet. As Garrett approached, craning his neck to see what she saw, a sick feeling filled his stomach.

Tell lay prone on her left side. The girl's own spear was lodged in the right side of her chest.

"Oh god, no. Is she…" Garrett began, but the rattle of blood-filled lungs answered before Key could.

"She is alive, but barely," Key managed. "This isn't something that…" Reaching down and taking her daughter's hand, she finished her thought in a quiet whisper. "This is a fatal wound."

"Maybe not," Garrett said quietly. "Our healer may be able to—"

"Healer? No healer can fix this. Even those who can touch the Sentheye could not heal a wound of this magnitude," Key said bitterly, as though the very idea angered her for daring to give her hope.

Lenny called for the others in mind speak. *Hurry, guys! Come straight in and just keep coming until you see us! And, Mr. Mustache, we need you here like yesterday, bro.*

I'm… I'm in the woods now!

Breanne, Pete, and Paul, along with several of the women of Sky, crowded around Tell, whose breathing was becoming shallower by the second.

Finally, David staggered up, wet with sweat and looking like he might yak from the run.

David, it's time to get that glow, Garrett said.

David dropped to his knees, gasping for breath and shaking his head.

"What?" Garrett asked aloud.

"We have a problem. I can't heal her with this spear sticking through her."

"Okay, so pull it out," Lenny said.

"Um, you pull it out. I don't pull things out. That isn't what I do," David said.

"I will pull the spear from my daughter's chest," Key said. "But... I fear she will not live through it."

Paul leaned in, studying the girl and the quickly forming pool of blood beneath her. "Key's right. I served as a flight medic in the army. I'm telling you now, you pull that shaft out of her chest and she is going to be gone in a handful of breaths, max."

"If my daughter dies, I promise you all here and now, we will go to war with the dökkálfar. Even if it means we all die, we will have vengeance for my daughter!"

"Please, Key. All is not lost, not yet," Breanne said.

"I have an idea," Garrett said.

"Better tell us quickly – we're losing her," Paul said, holding the girl's wrist.

"On my count, rip that spear out of her. I'll slow time for her, And David, you pour it on."

"I'm to trust my daughter's life to your men, Breanne Moore?" asked Key. "The same men who let Saria escape?"

"This is not the time, Key. Let my... my men do what they do. Let them save her," Breanne said. "Now please, all of you, step back and give them room."

Reluctantly, the crowd backed away.

Garrett looked at David. "You ready, David?"

"I think so."

"David, I won't be able to hold her in time for very long

and remember, I can't stop time. I can only slow it. So be quick," Garrett said.

Switching to mind speak, Lenny added, *Yeah, you got this, David. It isn't like the future of two races depends on you saving this chick's life or anything.*

You know, Lenny, you're a real—

Please, you guys! Can we do this? Garrett asked.

David closed his eyes.

"Okay, now, David, don't touch her. If you do, I think I might slow you too. Just pour it on like you did before, okay?"

David nodded.

"Ready then?" Garrett asked.

David nodded again.

"Hang on," Paul said. "I'm going to break the spear off behind her and pull it out the front, so it doesn't do any more damage coming out. Is that okay, Lady Key?"

Key nodded.

"Okay, and um, sorry, but you need to let go of her hand," Garrett said, giving Key a consoling smile.

Reluctantly, Key let go of her daughter's hand and stepped back, tears spilling down the hardened woman's cheeks.

Paul reached behind Tell, gripped the spear, and snapped it. The crack sounded like a bone breaking, and the crowd flinched.

Garrett nodded to Paul, who placed his left hand on one of Tell's shoulders and grasped the spear with his right as Garrett simultaneously grabbed for time.

With a slight nod, Garrett gave the signal, and Paul pulled. The spear slid out, accompanied by a rush of frothy blood that changed in an instant to a dark-red gush. Those watching gasped. The sight of it told Garrett something very important had been damaged in Tell's chest.

Once Paul was clear, Garrett triggered time, and the gasps distorted and fell away.

As if a miniature sun was rising from the forest floor, the entire area filled with golden light

Garrett held time in his grip like an unruly python. Slow now... slow... even slower. He had time right behind the neck, but it twisted in his hands as he willed it to be still. *Stop, damn you! Stop altogether, why don't you?*

Time didn't stop, not completely. Tell drew a breath – a breath that Garrett somehow knew was her last. But all he had to do was hold her here. So that's what he did. He held her there for all he had. One second. Two seconds. Three seconds. The shine from David poured in brighter and brighter. Thick Sentheye streamed like golden syrup from David's outstretched hand and into Tell's chest.

But once the magic hit Tell, it slowed too. Her chest glowed brighter and brighter. With sudden dread, Garrett realized the Sentheye couldn't heal her any faster than the time she was being held in. What would happen if he continued to hold her here and David continued to pour it on? Would it be too much? *Oh god!*

Garrett let go of time.

Sound rushed back to him. Voices were shouting.

"What's happening to my daughter?" Key yelled.

"What kind of magic is this?" another yelled.

"Just wait!" Breanne shouted back.

Tell, released from time, exhaled a long hard breath, but she didn't draw in another.

Sentheye pulsed all around the wound.

Paul lifted the girl's wrist, feeling for a pulse. Pressing his lip into a tight line, he shook his head. "I'm going to try CPR," he said, but Garrett could tell he wasn't hopeful.

"Wait, Paul," Breanne said, pointing.

David's golden glow stopped pulsing and stayed steady

for a long moment that felt to Garrett like hours. "David, any idea what it means?"

David looked over at Garrett and opened his mouth to speak, but rather than words, he puked up what looked like frothy Twinkie.

"Ew, David!" Breanne said, pulling a face.

David's eyes rolled back in his head, and he tipped over, falling onto his side.

I thought we were past this, Lenny said.

Gabi knelt next to David, untwisting his arm and repositioning his head.

Yeah, well, I never saw him pour it on like that, Pete said.

Everyone watched the light in Tell's chest as if this single source of illumination held all the secrets of the universe. Garrett thought maybe that was true. He watched as the light faded. When the light was dim enough to see Tell's skin, Paul tore away a piece of his own shirt and wiped the thick blood from the wound, revealing a white scar of three intersecting lines matching the shape of the metal-tipped spear point.

"Her wound is closed, but she's still not breathing."

"Pulse?" Breanne asked.

Paul shook his head. "Nothing at her wrist." He moved his hand to her neck. "Wait… I think—"

Tell's eyes popped open, and she gasped.

21

Soup to Nuts

God Stones – Moon Ring 2
The Shadow Forest

Key threw herself onto her daughter, embracing her. "Bless Turek, I thought you were lost!" she cried, pulling Tell to her chest.

Tell frowned, staring at everyone with apparent confusion. "Mother, I am fine, but how am I here? I think I was… I was somewhere else."

"Somewhere else? What are you saying?" Key asked as Breanne and the others crowded in close.

"Someone spoke to me. She said I would be fine. Then she said I have much to do in this life, Mother. She said change is coming and I should wake up so that I may do my part."

"Turek? She spoke to you again?"

She shook her head. "The voice seemed different from when I heard her speak on the wind. But yes, it must have been." Tell pushed herself up to a sitting position.

"Careful, go slow – you lost so much blood," Paul said.

You think it was really Turek speaking to her? Breanne asked the others in mind speak.

Hard to say. He spoke to her before, right? Pete offered.

Tell smiled up at Paul. "Thank you. But I feel fine – better than fine. I feel different." And with that, she stood. The other women came forward, hugging Tell and giving words of encouragement.

Did she say "different"? Lenny asked in mind speak. *What the heck did you and David do to her, Garrett?*

Garrett shook his head. *Don't look at me. I didn't do anything but slow her down.*

Breanne thought about it. *I don't know. I've never seen David do so much for so long, and with you slowing everything. Well, it was a long time for the healing power—*

Sentheye, Garrett corrected.

Right, Sentheye. Hey, how did you learn that's what it's called, anyway? Breanne asked. *When you mentioned it to Key, she knew what it was.*

The first night I fought Apep in the pyramid, I heard the word whispered in my mind. The night I lost you, he said, his face slipping.

Breanne smiled, wishing she could kiss him. *You never lost me.*

Garrett smiled back, and the two held each other's gaze.

"Breanne Moore," Key called, breaking the momentary trance each held over the other. "What your healer did was astounding. I've seen nothing like this. Even the most powerful healer in the kingdom of Sky could not have done what your David has done for my daughter." Key stood smiling down at David.

Breanne followed the woman's delighted gaze over to David, who lay on his side, snoring, mouth half-open, with a string of drool pooling onto a leaf. "Yes. He is… quite gifted."

"Breanne, I have many wounded. As we speak, they are being transported back to the longhouse. It is the only structure that didn't burn. Can your David be roused?"

She wasn't sure, but she didn't think so. "I think he has spent a lot of Sentheye and will need to rest before he can heal again. But Paul can help make them comfortable until David wakes."

"I understand, but I pray to Turek he doesn't sleep long. Some of my warriors are severely injured, and it will only be a matter of time before Saria brings a larger force back to finish us off." Key gestured to the rest of the gathered warriors. "Come, everyone, back to the longhouse. We have some time. We can rest and eat." Key raised an eyebrow toward Bre. "And in the meantime, you can explain to me how this happened – how your man defeated the leader of the dökkálfar army."

"Well, Lenny is quite the warrior," Breanne said.

"It's very strange how you treat your men. It is also very strange you claim this man to be a great warrior, yet he – and for that matter all of you – allowed Saria to escape."

Stepping back onto the trail leading to the village, Breanne stopped and turned to Key. "I know our ways are different and probably hard for you to understand, but I've given you no reason not to trust me or my people. So please, Lady Key, hear me now. Saria escaped after kicking Lenny in the face. The maneuver caught us all off guard, and then Saria was gone." She held out her upturned palms.

All of what she said was the truth. Still, it wasn't the whole truth, and deceit made her stomach hurt. Her father always said not telling the whole truth is still a lie, but telling the whole truth about Lenny, and what he'd just done and why, could get them all killed.

Key stared at her for a long moment, as if trying to read her mind.

Breanne didn't know why, but she couldn't look away. Instinct told her she had to hold the woman's gaze for as long as it took without breaking – like some schoolyard staring contest.

Finally, Key nodded. "Of course. Come. Let us get out of this night air where we can see to our people."

~

Back at the longhouse, the women piled inside, along with Breanne and the others. Paul carried David, and they gave him a place close to the fire. Meats pulled from the provisions stacked in the corner were skewered and placed over the fire, along with a pot of vegetables.

Key sent her second-fastest runner to relay a message to the men, informing them the battle was over and which of the women had been killed. In total, fourteen were lost.

Meanwhile, Paul went to work performing triage as best he could on those most in need. But it was a tall order. More than a dozen women had sustained injuries they would likely die from if they were not healed soon, while nearly all the remaining women had some minor level of injury, whether it be bruises and scrapes, lacerations, or minor broken bones like fingers, toes, noses, or ribs.

Listen, people, Paul said in mind speak. *We really need David to wake up. Have you ever tried to wake the kid after?*

Define "tried"? Lenny asked, moving toward David. *Like gently nudged, sure. I've also shaken the kid's shoulder, rolled him over, and moved him around. I've even yelled his name right in his face.*

Breanne watched as Lenny knelt next to David and gave a backward glance over both shoulders to see if the women were watching. Apparently satisfied they weren't, he slapped David hard across the face.

Breanne winced.

But I've never done that! Lenny laughed.

David stopped snoring, but he didn't wake.

When the slap didn't work, Lenny glanced around again, grabbed a corner of David's mustache, and pulled. When David didn't wake, Lenny pressed his lips tight and pulled harder.

Jesus, Lenny, don't rip his cheek off! Breanne warned.

Don't worry, Bre, his mustache will pull off long before his cheek does, Lenny said with confidence, as if he had experience ripping off facial hair. Getting into it, he started pulling up and down on David's mustache, causing his mouth to twist and distort. *Look at him!* Lenny laughed.

Len, if you keep it up, the kid's face is going to hurt like hell when he wakes up, Garrett warned.

Fine, fine! Although, Lenny said thoughtfully, *I still haven't tried slapping him good and hard in the nutsack.* Wrapping his entire fist around David's whiskers, he twisted and wrenched.

Suddenly, David's eyes popped open, and he slapped Lenny across the face.

Breanne startled back, not expecting the slap, but it was Lenny who really didn't expect the sudden strike. The blow must have carried some hefty force because Lenny fell backward off his feet and nearly landed in the fire.

Gabi laughed for the first time that day and ran to David's side. *Are you okay, David?*

Is he okay? What about me? What the hell, David? Lenny said, rubbing his face. *My face is already messed up thanks to Saria! Jesus, bro!*

David rubbed the sleep out of his eyes.

I think you had that coming, Lenny, Gabi said.

I liked her better when she didn't talk, Lenny said.

Lenny! Breanne said.

I'm kidding!

Key approached from the other end of the longhouse. "Is everything alright?" she asked, looking at Breanne and then the others.

"Yes, Lady Key. It seems my healer has awakened."

"Excellent. Your man Paul has done the best he could for my people, but I am certain one will die soon if not helped. Some others are close to death as well."

"Where is Tell? Is she okay?" David asked.

"She is fine, thanks to you. Your queen would like you to please heal the rest of our people," Key said, glancing at Breanne.

Breanne blinked. Key had not referred to her as queen until this very moment. Why now? Why at all? She was too exhausted to think.

In her mind, the others were all talking.

Queen? So you're a queen now, Bre? Lenny said, smirking.

Wait, does she mean our queen or everyone's queen? David asked.

Sis, I don't know what this means for the mission, but play along for now.

I think Paul's right. We need a minute to figure out our next move, Garrett said.

Pete, who had been sitting in the corner talking to the now-potted shrub that used to be Governess said, *I don't need any more minutes to think. The next move is saving Governess!*

"My, such conversation that must be taking place within the magic you weave. I hope your secret discussion is productive," Key said, eyeing Breanne.

David stood on wobbly legs, his sleepy eyes brightening. "Is that meat over the fire?"

Key reached over and lifted a skewer of dripping meat,

handing it to the boy. "Yes, David. Eat as much as you like as quick as you can. Then please save your queen's people."

David reverently took the skewer as if being knighted by a queen. Closing his eyes, he bit into the still-smoking meat and chewed. A smile spread across his face as big as any Breanne had seen. Then, with cheeks puffed out like a chipmunk, he pointed at the pot steaming above the fire. "Whaths thath?" he asked through a full mouth.

Tell nodded. A woman came forward and filled a wooden bowl with vegetables. She smiled awkwardly as she handed it to David.

As David shoveled another bite into his mouth, Breanne and the others served themselves. She wondered how long it had been since a woman had made up a bowl of soup for a man in this society. Most societies on Earth were so sexist in the other direction. She couldn't help but wonder how she could influence this society as their queen. Perhaps she could use what she'd learned in her study of ancient and modern civilizations and all her father had taught her to bring about true equality. Obviously, the men and women of Sky needed someone to help them compromise. Then she immediately told herself this thought process was absurd. She had to remember why they were here. They had to save Earth. Her father and brother were depending on her. A wave of guilt washed over her.

A woman from some unseen shadow near the back of the longhouse let out an awful moan, pulling Breanne from her thoughts.

David, still chewing with his mouth open and eyes closed, froze, one eye popping open. He swallowed. "She hurt?"

"As I said, several of my people are close to death. Others are severely injured."

David looked longingly at the meat stick, then at the

bowl of vegetable soup he'd yet to taste and sighed sadly. Breanne thought he might actually tear up, but finally he looked away from the food and nodded. "I better get to it then," he said, handing the soup and partially eaten skewer of meat back to Tell. "Hey, will you save me some… for after?" he asked pleadingly.

"Of course, we will save you plenty," Key said, smiling.

David smiled back and headed off toward the back of the room.

"Hey! Wait up," Lenny said. "I better tag along and make sure you don't pass out."

"Yeah, Len, and what if I do?" David asked.

"Well, you little fur baby, now I know just how to wake you up."

"I'm coming too," Gabi said.

"Good. You can make sure he doesn't rip off my mustache or slap me in the nutsack if I pass out."

Gabi allowed a slight smile to slip, and Breanne felt instantly better. Maybe Gabi was finally getting her mind off Zerri.

As the three vanished into the crowd of women, Pete approached Key, pulling Breanne back from her thoughts.

"Excuse me, but you promised when we returned from this battle, you would tell me how to cure my friend," Pete said, pointing at Governess.

"Breanne, I must say, your men are very brazen with their tongues."

Breanne started to apologize, but Key waved her off. "Love is a powerful emotion, Peter. Your devotion to your female is admirable. Yes. I did say I would help you. As you may not realize, we are at the edge of Shadow Forest. Osonian is on the opposite side. Hills shelter our rear and make this location good for defense. We can easily escape through a secret path out the back that leads to a complex cave system, perfect for hiding. This is where I sent the men and children. However, beyond these hills are the Cragarmour Mountains. The mountains of the dwarves. Should you venture far enough or travel in the wrong direction, you may be lost forever among endless mountain ranges, discovered by dwarves. Or worse, you could reach Thunder Keep, which has been overthrown by the elves. But rest assured, you won't need to go far into the mountains to find what you require."

"Wait, we have to go into some mountains full of dwarves? How far and to get what?" Garrett blurted.

Tell raised an eyebrow toward Garrett. Clearly she was not appreciating her mother being interrupted by a boy.

Garrett! Don't do that, Breanne warned in mind speak as she held up a hand for silence.

Shit! Sorry, Bre, but journeying into the mountains?

"I'll go by myself," Pete blurted. "Just, please, Lady Key, tell me what I need to do."

Key smiled. "Not to worry – it is relatively safe as long as you don't get lost. You will travel out the rear of the village as if you are going to the caves. When you see the first valley that appears to lead downward rather than upward, turn west and descend into the Dark Narrow. When you come out the other side, you will see two snow-capped mountains. Stay in the valley until you reach a stream. What you seek, you will find there."

Garrett shook his head, asking in mind speak, *Can we please consider that the leader of Sky – a deadly warrior, I might add – just described finding your way into something called the Dark Narrow as RELATIVELY safe?*

Ignoring him, Pete asked, "And what do I seek?"

"You remember how you traveled here with my daughter?"

"Beneath the forest, yes, of course. That's where this happened," Pete said, gesturing toward Governess.

"Yes, but did you see how Tell convinced the trees to help her?"

Pete frowned, and Breanne couldn't remember seeing anything, but she remembered Tell explaining to Key that she'd made an offering to the forest, which allowed her to pass. "She made an offering, and she spoke words of power," Breanne guessed.

"Very good. We don't call them words of power, but I suppose they are indeed just that. The words are the language of the gods, and we guard them with our very lives. You see, we've long lost most of the ancient language, but with the words we remember and the offerings we provide, the Shadow Forest protects us. This has allowed the people of Sky to hunt safely in this forest for many generations."

Breanne remembered something else. When she was below the ground, Tell mentioned she was afraid of being discovered by other humans. "King Deep understands this too, doesn't he?" she asked.

"I'm afraid he does. And this makes traveling beneath the forest a risk. King Deep and the people of Sky hunt this forest. Altercations are, unfortunately, frequent. But it is an acceptable risk, for we, as women, are smarter, faster, and more skilled than Deep's men. He has the numbers, but his army doesn't hunt in force, giving us the advantage." Her expression turned to a glower, then brightened suddenly. "But alas, I digress. Let us speak of the offering."

Pete nodded, listening intently as they all did.

"You see, the ancient language we can help you with, but the offering you must retrieve on your own. This is our way. The one who makes the offering must also be the one who mines it. This is important, Peter. We believe your aura will infuse into the offering, and the forest will know if you are worthy. Please understand, what you are planning to ask the forest to do is something untried by our people. Thus, I do not know what will happen, but if there is to be any hope, you must be pure in your intentions. Do you understand?"

"I understand. What is it I must get? How do I do it?" Pete asked eagerly.

Key motioned Tell forward. "Show them the offering."

Tell removed a small, heavy-looking pouch from her hip and turned it upside down in her palm. Three small opaque stones, no bigger than human teeth and just as bright, spilled into her hand.

Pete leaned forward. "What are they?"

Key smiled. "Those, Pete, are the secret to the Shadow Forest, the life of Osonian, and the only hope you have of saving your friend."

22

Fish Fingers and Fire

God Stones – Moon Ring 2
A lake at the edge of the Nightshade Desert

Before mounting Cerb, Jack had him blast a load of dragon fire into the water.

"That's good!" he shouted above the roar of flame. He only wanted to boil some fish, not the whole damn lake.

Above, the two Karelian suns were both shining brightly now, their warmth and the heat already drying his clothes. In the distance, the stupid sandstorm or mist storm or whatever they called it raged on, never seeming to get any closer. He pulled his gaze back to the water, where the steam quickly cleared as fish popped up, one after another, like ice cubes dropped in a glass of water. First only a few, but then more and more, until hundreds of dead fish of varying sizes and colors littered the area. *How do you like that, Rán?* Jack thought as he knelt next to the shore and felt the water. It was hot but not scalding, which meant it was cooling fast.

Send a few dozen of the prisoners in to collect the fish. They need to eat too if they're going to survive long enough for me to give them as gifts, Jack said, eyeing a large fish jostling against the shore as the small waves lapped at the beach. Jack reached down to retrieve the fish, but then paused. The fish, with its eyes closed, had very human-looking facial features. And come to think of it, were there even fish with eyelids back on Earth? The fish didn't really have scales either, but instead something like catfish skin. Grabbing the brown-and-black–skinned fish by the tail, he heaved it onto shore. Then he dropped it, reeling back. *What the shit!* The fish had arms and legs, complete with toes and fingers.

What is it, Jack? Did you get burned? Cerberus asked.

What? No. This fish is just really weird. It has fingers and a face!

So what? Probably tastes the same as the other fish.

Well then, you can eat it.

Cerb laughed. *Thanks, brother, but my belly is still full of dead nephilbock.*

Jack knew the time might come when he had to eat dead nephilbock, dragon, or maybe even an elf, but that time would not be today. He made up his mind that if he couldn't find something more… well, normal, he was going to eat this, whatever it was. He looked back at the water. This time, he braved the hot water and waded in, searching around until he found a fish that looked closer to what he expected. This one had scales and fins – maybe a few extra fins, but it didn't have fingers and its eyes didn't have eyelids. With his fish in hand, he made his way onto shore, found a nice flat rock, and pulled the thing apart. It separated easily to reveal white flaky meat still steaming on the inside. As he ate, he watched the elves collect their fish and return to their huddled groups to share with the others.

With his own belly full, Jack called to his dragon. *Time to do this, Cerb!*

Cerb landed on the shore near Zerri and Ahi, who both lay sprawled out, sunning themselves. "Perhaps we should just let our horde feed on the elves now?"

"What? Why would we do that?"

Ahi stood, shaking the sand off his scales like a dog shaking off water. "I think what Cerberus is suggesting may result in more of us making it through the storm, my lord."

"They're both right," Zerri commented. "If you make the dragons carry the elves through the storm, you will lose more dragons. You will probably lose a great number even without the added weight. You must remember, these are juvenile dragons, Jack. It will be all they can do to keep themselves alive."

Standing on the shore with his back to the water, Jack assessed them one by one. "You know what I find interesting?" he asked, but he didn't wait for an answer. "You have no faith in me. You call me lord because I have this crown upon my head, and you know that with it I could destroy you all. And let's be honest here, I know you all want something. Zerri, you want power as the rightful Queen of Queens. Ahi, you are the snake who just wants to stay alive, right?" Jack got closer to him, not breaking eye contact. "No, that isn't really all you want, is it, Ahi? No. Not you. Not the great and wise, Ahi! You probably have ten plans that all end up with me dead." He whipped around now to look at Cerb. "And you, my own brother. You're the other half of me. Without me there is no you, and without you there is no me, but you question me, and by doing so, you… well, you suck."

"No! This is not how it is, Jack. I care about you!" Cerb said. "But…"

"Go on! Say it. Say what you feel, Cerb!"

"You sound more like him all the time, Jack."

"Like Apep?"

"Yes. Apep... at the end," Cerb said, his heads dropping low as if he were ashamed.

"How many times do I have to tell you, I'm not Apep! I'm not stupid either. I have a plan. But before I tell you, I just want to say you should all feel like shit. Ahi, you're not the only one planning five steps ahead. And if you think for one moment this whole thing ends in you somehow killing me and Cerb, you're badly mistaken!"

"My lord, I have done nothing but obey you. I assure you I have no plans for betrayal."

"Yeah... whatever, bro. Just know there are two ways this ends for you. You stay in line, or you step out and die." The truth was, he already knew Ahi was planning to betray him, and he'd already told Cerb as much. It was all too convenient, him showing up when he did, suddenly wanting to help – to be part of the team. Well, Jack might have been born at night, but it wasn't last night.

"Jack, you need to stop with the paranoia," Zerri said, rolling from her side to her feet and standing. "Now please tell us of your plan."

Jack looked over at the crowd of elves, then back at the dragons. He'd never felt more alone than at this very moment. "I am going to use my power to get us through the storm."

"That's your plan?" Zerri asked.

"Yes, it is, as a matter of fact. Cerb and I will lead the formation, but I need you and Ahi on either side. Stay behind us but stay tight. We will need the hordes to do the same. We must fly in a tight formation. I'm talking wing tip to wing tip."

"You're going to what, try to form a shield?" Cerb asked.

"Don't you know me by now? I'm not the defensive type. No, I'm throwing haymakers."

"What does that mean?" Zerri asked, stretching her back into a catlike arch.

Jack smiled wickedly. "I'm going to punch a hole through the son of a bitch. And as long as you do what I've just explained, I'll protect you all. But we'll need to go fast. I don't want to use Sentheye any longer than I have to."

"Are you sure this is safe, Jack? Your overuse is so evident now. What will this do to you?" Zerri asked.

"This is the only way," Jack said. "Now, prepare the hordes." Then, looking up at Cerb, he said, "I will be right back."

Jack walked through the group of elves with his chin up and his hands clasped behind his back. It was the walk of a king, and it was, come to think of it, the same way Apep had walked. It was effective too because the elves, larger and physically stronger than he, quickly scurried back, some nearly falling over themselves to get away from him. Then she was there, standing in the space emptied by the others. Nyana.

"I want you to ride with me," Jack said in dökkálfar.

"Why?" Nyana asked.

"I need to keep you alive in case your god returns. I'm not sure you will live if it is not me who carries you through the storm."

"I thought you had a plan?"

"I thought you knew better than to question me?" Jack countered.

Nyana stared at Jack for a long moment, then bowed slightly.

∽

Jack sat in his usual spot, straddling the hump that ran down Cerb's back just below where his three necks joined his torso.

Nyana sat behind him, her arms around Jack's waist. Something inside Jack stirred. Despite this creature not being human, she was very attractive. As they approached the storm, Jack found he quite enjoyed having a girl's arms around him – even if they were elvish.

Cerb! he said, making sure his connection was private and only his brother could receive his telepathy.

What is it, Taker?

After I do this, I... I don't know what I'm going to be like.

Cerb's voice strained with concern. *What do you mean?*

I think I'm losing it, Cerb, and I can't get this crown off. Not even if I wanted to.

Taker. It isn't too late to stop this. We can turn back and go around, or at least dump these damned elves. Then maybe you wouldn't need to use the Sentheye.

Jack adjusted his grip on Cerb's spurs. *We can't go around, and we're not dumping them. Besides, Zerri's right. Even without the elves, we could lose hundreds of our horde, maybe more. For all I know, maybe all of them. I have to do this, Cerb. I just need you to do something for me,* he said, knowing that what he was about to ask could kill him.

What is it? Cerb asked.

When this is over, I need you to pull the crown from my head. Do it by force.

And if you change your mind?

I won't. And if I do it, it isn't me.

Silence stretched out between them.

Cerb?

As you wish, brother.

Danny's voice filled his mind in warning. *You are going to ruin everything if you take this crown off.*

I don't have time for you right now, Danny, Jack thought to the voice.

Since when do you not have time for me? Danny asked.

Since there is a big-ass storm – I got to get my dragons through!

Fine, little bro. But you better hope I'm not the one calling the shots when we get to the other side, or the Sound Eye will be staying right where it is.

Suddenly the strange presence was gone, and Jack wanted this crown off now more than ever.

Cerb, when we get through, you've got to take it off, but be careful, okay? Don't accidentally break my neck or pull my head off. At the thought, an image of Apep's head rolling across the temple roof flashed through his mind.

Do not worry, Jack, I will do my best not to kill us.

Thanks, Cerb.

Jack had never been sure who the voice he was hearing really belonged to, but the way he figured it, there were three possibilities. The first was that it really was Danny – that's what the voice wanted him to believe. In truth, he'd wanted to believe it too – goddamn, he'd wanted to believe it so bad, and until this very moment he'd been telling himself it really was Danny. The second possibility was that the voice was his own. A figment of his imagination brought on by his grief or anger or… shit if he knew, he wasn't no shrink. Then there was the third possibility: that this was the God Stones themselves somehow taking him over. The truth was, he still didn't know for sure, but he knew one thing. His brother was dead. This voice pulling at him, making him want to do what it said… it wasn't Danny. But if Danny really could hear him from the afterlife, Jack needed his brother to hear him now. *Danny, if you're watching this, I sure could use some help!*

Ahead, the wall of black drew closer as a low rumble filled his ears.

The thunder grew to a deafening roar, sounding more like he was standing next to a train or maybe a jet engine. He glanced up one more time, only to feel the sting of sand against his face. Behind him, Nyana buried her face in his back and squeezed his waist.

Jack primarily pulled power from others, and he was damn good at it, but this wasn't that kind of party. There were no powerful monsters to draw life from – no kraken or ancient trees. The mist storm wasn't a living thing. No, Jack needed to pull from another source, and he knew where he had to get it, sure as the Sound Eye crown sat fused to his head. Jack splayed his fingers just as he'd seen Apep do when he'd poured Sentheye into mountains, into the tree army miles away.

Jack closed his eyes. There was only one place to pull the power he needed. Reaching out with one hand, fingers spread, he screamed. Pain pierced his mind as he drew the black Sentheye from the Sound Eye down into his head and body. From his splayed fingers, he fired long ribbons of black.

As the ribbons pierced the wall of the mist storm, Jack imagined the Sentheye creating a hole that punched through the storm.

Cerberus shouted, his gruff voice somehow reaching Jack through the fracturing of his own mind. *Jack! What do I do?*

Finally, unable to bear the pain, Jack dropped his hand and opened his eyes, squinting to see. The wall of sand stood solid before them, wind and lightning stirring inside. The only evidence of the magic Jack had dumped into the storm was a black circle on the face of an already dark storm. It reminded him of the stain left behind from motor oil dumped in the dirt. But it wasn't a hole, and it didn't look like something they could fly into.

Jack! Cerberus begged.

There was nothing else to do. It hadn't worked. He had expelled Sentheye to the point he'd felt something in his head pop, and it hadn't even worked. The way he saw it, there were no choices left except one. Jack had sworn to himself that he would never back down from a fight, and he sure as hell would not back down from this. Nyana's arms squeezed his waist, and he could feel her body shiver against his. All the other elves would probably die, and who knew how many dragons?

About to call Cerb's name and order him through, Jack stopped short. A voice whispered something. It wasn't Danny or Cerb, and it wasn't any other voice he'd heard. But what had it said? He listened. The voice came to him again like a whisper from a ghost.

Fire.

Jack frowned. He looked ahead again at the storm. The wall was there, unavoidable now. And there, directly in front of him, was the large circular stain of Sentheye still discoloring the wall like oil-soaked dirt.

Fire, the whisper came again. And Jack was sure it was the Sentheye itself speaking to him. The thing about oil was that it burned. Could that be it?

Cerb! Breathe fire at the wall! Hurry, Cerb!

Cerb opened his center head and roared. Dragon fire poured from his mouth, hitting the Sentheye circle in the mist storm wall like a sharpshooter hitting a bull's-eye.

Jack ducked his head down as the stain of Sentheye ignited into an instant inferno. What had he done? What had he thought would happen?

Cerb collided with the fiery wall.

Behind him, Nyana screamed.

23

Ice Ember

God Stones – Moon Ring 2
The Shadow Forest

"The greatest city in all the known world is Osonian. But the magnificence of Osonian does not lie in its great wall or the city's incredible architecture. The true magnificence of Osonian is Metsavana."

Garrett frowned, wondering what Osonian had to do with the odd little pebbles cupped in Tell's hand.

As if reading his mind, Key continued. "Some time ago, after the humans lost their God Stone, Turek took them away to a new world. With the possession of two God Stones, the dökkálfar had complete control over the kingdom of Osonian. The problem was that, originally, Osonian was established as a city of trade, meant to be a sort of neutral zone. Once the dökkálfar had our God Stone, they grew in power, deciding the city should be theirs and theirs alone. Soon they banned trading, not just with humans but with all inhabitants who visited the city. Once the city was purged of everyone who was not elvish, the great wall was erected and access to Metsavana was cut off. This meant no more offerings."

"Wait. I'm sorry, but who is Metsavana?" Garrett asked.

"Ah, I forget this would not be common knowledge to you. Metsavana is the father tree. The Cities of Seven, also known as Old Osonian, hang from its branches. Some say it was the gods themselves who built the hanging cities."

"Right! The tree we saw beyond the wall," Pete said.

"A tree so large a city can hang from it! That's unreal," Paul said.

"Not only one, but seven cities, and I assure you the tree and its cities are very real. To our knowledge, the cities themselves were never occupied. They are said to be a symbol of what Karelia could be if peace reigned between all the favorites."

"A symbol of hope," Breanne said.

Key nodded. "Our legends say if peace were ratified, the cities would lower from the canopy, welcoming all creations home. It is a pleasant dream, but peace among the seven favorites could never be, as by nature or design we are food to both giant and dragon."

Garrett swallowed, remembering all too well the overstuffed mouths of the shark-toothed giants he'd fought in Mexico.

Key continued. "Below the great canopy and the seven hanging cities lies New Osonian, which is built around the base of the tree. Despite the name, it isn't new at all. Though there are many differences in the religions and beliefs held by the creatures of this world, it is agreed upon by all how the magical father tree came to be. The creation of Metsavana required the work of all seven gods. Larger than any known life form in all of Karelia, it is truly a sight to behold."

"I'm sorry, Lady Key, but I don't understand. What does

any of this have to do with those?" Pete asked, pointing to the stones in Tell's hand.

"Everything, Peter. Before the walls were erected, the inhabitants of Karelia came from far and wide to bring this very offering to Metsavana. Giants and even dragons came – well, before they were both banned for eating the other gods' favorites. Wandering trees often ventured into the city. And on the back side, a stream reaches all the way to the trunk, allowing for even the creatures of the sea to visit. In return, those deemed worthy would receive a gift from the father tree. It is said the gods empowered the father tree to grant any wish, should Metsavana deem the wish a worthy one."

As Key continued to talk, Garrett shared a look with Lenny, the beginnings of an idea taking shape in his mind. Lenny nodded his understanding, but there was no time for discussion now. He didn't want to miss a word.

"This substance is very special to the father tree. It is how the tree survives, and it must have a regular supply, but with the outside world cut off, only the dökkálfar can give offerings and reap the gifts of the great father tree. And so, they have taken Thunder Keep away from the dwarves to mine the substance for themselves."

Key ran a finger along the stones in her daughter's hand. "But we know something the elves do not. When the city was walled in, we soon discovered the trees of the Shadow Forest also enjoyed the gift of Ice Ember. This led us to a startling discovery. The roots of Metsavana stretch all the way to Shadow Forest and, thus, when we are offering the forest Ice Ember, we are truly helping Metsavana."

"Ice Ember?" Pete repeated.

Key nodded, "Yes. Of course, without making the offering directly to Metsavana himself in the offering garden of New Osonian, we receive no granted wishes. However, the forest returns our gesture by helping to protect us. So you see, Peter, perhaps if you provide as much of this element as you can find, and if your intentions and the intentions of your tree friend are pure" – Key paused and smiled – "maybe the forest will save your friend."

Pete nodded, and Garrett could see the determination hardening on his face.

"Okay. You said to go to the stream and I will find it. What do I do? Is it just lying around?"

"No. There is only one way to find the element that we know of. You will need to enter the stream. The water is clear. Search the center at the bottom. When Ice Ember is wet and under the shine of the white sun, it glows."

"Right. Okay. Wade around in the water, search the bottom for glowing embers, got it," Pete said, nodding.

"You will need to search when the white sun is at its highest. You can swim, yes?"

"Like a fish," Pete said.

Key smiled. "Good, because the water is deep, and Ice Ember is heavy. Show him, daughter."

Tell dumped the three small stones into Pete's palm, which dipped as though Tell had just plopped a brick into his hand rather than the small pebbles.

"Whoa. This is going to be hard to swim with," Pete said, measuring the weight with his hand.

"Yes. This is why Ice Ember is so rare. Even our best swimmers can only collect the smallest pieces. It is also why we think Metsavana may be dying."

"Wait – dying?" Breanne asked.

Key nodded again. "Yes. You see, we know the dwarves were once very good at mining Ice Ember from deep inside the mountain. Nephilbock were also said to know a secret location of the element, but that is only legend. No one knows for sure, but stories say they visited Osonian in the time of tolerance. Back then, many lesser species traded, thieved, or otherwise obtained the element, venturing into the city hoping to have their wishes granted. It was a magical time, when hope was available to all who applied themselves. But once the dökkálfar came into power, walled in the city, and took away the ability of others to bring forth their offerings, there was no point in gathering the Ice Ember. It then fell to the dökkálfar alone to make the offerings. It is our belief that despite the taking of the dwarves' largest mine and trading post, Thunder Keep, as well as the enslavement of lesser creatures used to mine Ice Ember, the dökkálfar still cannot keep up with the demand needed to sustain Metsavana's life."

Breanne pinched one of the stones between her thumb and index finger, lifting it from Pete's palm with a soft gasp. "It *is* heavy. And you're saying this element, Ice Ember, is like food for Metsavana?"

"Fertilizer," Pete said.

"I do not know this word 'fertilizer,' but food, yes, we believe so. Why else would the great tree father grant wishes to those who make offerings?"

Ask her if most people who make an offering get their wishes granted? Garrett asked in mind speak.

Breanne asked.

"No. Only those deemed worthy by the father tree have their wishes granted."

Tell raised a fist. "Yes. And the rumors say those rotten elves haven't received a gift in many cycles. That's what they get for walling in the father tree!"

Paul, clearly forgetting to use mind speak and have Breanne ask, said, "What makes you think the big tree is dying, and how do you know the trees of Shadow Forest aren't just eating this stuff for their own growth? I mean, from what I've seen, this forest is incredibly complex and, vertically, these trees must be as tall if not taller than redwoods."

Garrett caught the look of annoyance on Key's face. But to her credit, she drew in a calming breath and answered Paul. Breanne must have caught it too because she projected, *Dang it, Paul, ask me your questions and I'll ask her for you.*

Right. Paul shrugged, his face sour.

"Long ago, generations before my time, but not long after the elves built their walls, we discovered Ice Ember could be used to gain help from the forest. Imagine the excitement of my ancestors. Imagine how they must have had to learn how to use the offering and what the trees would do and not do. When I led the queendom of Sky, one of my favorite ways to spend a day was by sitting in the library of Cloud reading ancient texts."

"That's one of my favorite ways to spend a day too," Pete said, unable to help himself.

Key raised a curious eyebrow. After sighing at the interruption, she nodded and went on, "In my ancestors' stories, one woman wrote of how they excitedly made offering after offering, eager to explore below the forest. One day, they decided to explore near the edge of the forest on the south side, bordering Osonian Valley, near to where Tell found you and brought you in. This woman – Standfast was her name – wrote of roots that looked unlike anything she had seen. Gnarled black roots glowing with a rich green aura. We now know this 'aura' to be Sentheye. The roots she wrote of must have been the roots of the great father tree, Metsavana. When I discovered this text, we sought the location but found no roots. So, we followed the tree line of Shadow Forest east until we eventually found what we were looking for."

"You found the black roots?" Breanne asked.

"Indeed, we did. We tried to make an offering directly to Metsavana's roots, but he did not accept the offering. No matter how much we offered, no matter who offered it, there was no response. It was as if the great father tree could not hear us. But then—"

From the far end of the longhouse, the room lit with a soft golden light, drawing all their attention.

Key stopped speaking to watch the golden shine.

Women gasped and whispered excitedly as the light faded.

"Praise Turek, your male David is blessed indeed. Now where was I?"

"The father tree would not take your offer," Breanne reminded her.

"Oh, yes, of course. When we were finally ready to give up, I decided to try giving our offer to the roots of the Shadow Forest. The roots accepted, and then something strange happened. The roots of Metsavana glowed brighter. And not just a little brighter – so bright it was almost blinding. Then, after a moment, the light faded. We repeated the experiment multiple times. We even had women make offerings from farther away in the forest while others waited near the black roots. Each time, the result was the same – the gnarled roots of Metsavana glowed brightly. We tried making wishes, but they received no response. Still, we learned that the forest was passing the Ice Ember on to the father tree. So, to answer your male's question, yes, we know the father tree is receiving our offerings."

They all nodded, and Paul opened his mouth to speak again.

"Paul, before you interrupt me again, allow me to answer your second question," Key said.

Paul raised his eyebrows and bowed slightly.

Key inclined her head and pressed on. "How do we know Metsavana is dying? We know because his roots are withdrawing. That's why we struggled to find them. It was only when we traveled to the northeastern point of Shadow Forest near the great wall, in a section of wood closer to Metsavana than any other, that we finally found the roots. Since that time, we check on the roots every tenth moon ring, and each time the roots are farther away from us and closer to Osonian. It won't be long before he has lost his connection with the Shadow Forest and all the Ice Ember we have been supplying will be of no use."

Garrett watched as Breanne's face creased with worry. She set her empty soup bowl down next to her. "How long before the father tree is out of reach?"

Key turned to face her. "Breanne Moore. I believe everything happens for a reason. You come to us in the last ten moon rings of our connection with Metsavana. We believe the next time we go to check on the tree's roots, they will no longer be connected to the Shadow Forest, and the great father tree will be forever out of our reach. If this is true, our inability to make offerings will leave us without a way to travel the forest in secret. We will be at the mercy of dökkálfar and other creatures that hunt in Shadow Forest. But worst of all, the lack of offerings from us will only hasten Metsavana's death."

Tell stepped forward in the same moment that golden light lit the room once again. "But all will be well now, Mother! We can rejoice. Breanne is here! She will save us and our people from King Deep and save Metsavana from the oppression of the elves!"

Breanne gasped, her worried eyes finding Garrett's.

When Tell announced that Breanne and her people were going to rescue the women of Sky from King Deep and save an ancient tree locked behind the walls of Osonian, Garrett thought he might have a panic attack right there on the spot. What the hell were they thinking? Pete trying to run off to the mountains, Lenny trying to meet his grampa, Breanne leading an army of women against some tyrant. They already had one impossible mission: Get a magical item for the trees of Earth and find a way to open the portal back home.

Garrett started to speak, but Pete blurted out, "I will leave at first light, and I'll be back as quick as I can."

Petey, Garrett tried in mind speak.

Don't say anything unless it's that you're coming with me, Garrett.

Garrett could see there was no changing his mind and opened his mouth to speak again. This time, Paul cut him off, stepping forward and speaking aloud. "I'll go with him. You guys should stay and head to the caves, and we can meet you there once we get the Ice Ember."

Key raised an eyebrow. "Yes. That is exactly what we should do. It is becoming clear to me, Breanne Moore. Your men are not subservient under your rule."

"We work differently, that's all," Breanne said.

"I see. And I trust this will not hinder your ability to overthrow Deep?"

"What do you mean?"

"What I mean is that Deep tells the women under his rule what to do. And not just Deep, but all the men who follow him. They treat the women like objects. They are slaves to the men," she snarled.

"Lady Key, I assure you this is not the case with these men. We will travel to the city of Cloud, and we will meet this Deep."

"You will meet him?" Key asked, shaking her head. "There is only one outcome for Deep. He must die! You must see to it that he does – or I will. It will be the only way to bring his people back under our rule."

"Tomorrow then," Breanne said, clearly avoiding the discussion of killing the king.

Finally, Garrett interjected in mind speak, *Pete! If you have to go, I'll go with you too.*

That's a negative, Paul answered. *I think I can be a bigger help to Pete than I can be here. Besides, I would feel a lot better if you stay here with my sister, keep her safe, and figure out our next move. Like Pete said, we'll rest and get moving at first light.*

Part of Garrett felt like he was losing control, and the weight of what they were supposed to be doing felt crushing. But they'd only arrived today. They still had time. He just didn't like the idea of splitting up. On the other hand, part of him knew Paul was right. And besides, he didn't want to leave Bre, not again. This was a simple out-and-back mission. A grab-and-go. He hoped he was making the right decision. Then again, he wasn't even sure the decision was his anymore. He glanced at his sages and nodded reluctantly.

Key looked between them, obviously unable to hear the conversation. Behind them, the longhouse lit golden again. "It's settled then. At the rate your healer is working, our people will be healed and rested by morning. We can accompany you as far as the Dark Narrow. From there, you will have a full moon ring to get back before we move on to the city of Cloud. But if you are not back by the morning of the following moon ring, we will move on to the city without you."

Garrett shook his head. "Now wait a second. I won't leave any of my—"

Key frowned. "Your... what?"

Garrett, careful, Breanne warned.

Garrett pressed his lips tight. "My friends. I don't want to leave my friends."

Key looked to Breanne with anticipation.

Garrett. Please be silent, Breanne said, then turned to her brother. *Paul, if you're going to do this, you just make damn sure you two get back on time.*

Pete nodded impatiently. *So, we have a plan then. Paul and I will go, and we will be back the next day. Then we'll save Governess and go meet this dickhead, Deep.*

Key studied them closely and then gave a backward glance toward her warriors. Their focus was fully on David as he performed the work of healing at the other end of the longhouse. Still, she leaned in, lowering her voice. "It's easy to see you are giving your men a tongue-lashing with your mind. It is wise to restrain them. Breanne, I am truly trying to be understanding of your ways, yet I fear the women of Sky may find it an even greater challenge than I. Turek spoke your name on the wind. Your vision has come to pass. And your people are powerful indeed, even these men. But this is a fragile time, and men behaving the way – well, the way yours are behaving – could cause confusion."

Now Key looked from Garrett to Paul, and finally to Pete. "Whatever your normal customs, I think it best you listen to your queen and let her make the decisions – unless she asks for your opinion. Please understand that this is our way. Here, political matters, finance, education, defense, and religion are discussed and decided upon by the women. We cherish our men, and they play a vital role as builders, farmers, and lovers. Studying you, I don't believe your ways are the same as Deep's, but the more I watch, the more I realize they are quite the departure from our own. For now, I implore you to pretend. Can you please do this for me and for Breanne?"

She was right, and Garrett knew it. He pressed his lips into a tight line and nodded. The others followed suit.

"Good. Now that we have our plans solidified, please make sure you fill your bellies. We've still much to do."

"I thought we would rest for the journey," Breanne said.

"We will rest, but first we must sing."

"Sing?" Breanne asked.

"Yes. We must sing for the dead and for the living. We must sing for the healed and for all the blessings our goddess Turek has bestowed upon us. And we must make your new title official by holding the naming ceremony. Once named, you will become what you are meant to be." Key smiled, raising her scarred arms out to the sides. "You will be the queen of Sky!"

24

The Queen of Sky

God Stones – Moon Ring 2
The Shadow Forest

In the longhouse, the night stretched on into what felt like morning, and Breanne wondered if she would ever be allowed to sleep. But after Key's announcement that she would be named the queen of Sky, she knew she hadn't a chance of falling asleep anyway.

David, however, did not seem to have any issue, having finally healed everyone and eaten his fill of meat and vegetable stew.

Her brother, Garrett, and the others all looked exhausted, but no one wanted to miss the naming ceremony – not that she was eager to be these people's queen. But it took only a brief discussion before they'd all agreed that, for now, she had to play along until they figured a way out of this. *One problem at a time, Bre,* she told herself.

The singing stopped, and Key appeared from the crowd of dancing women, her skin glistening in the firelight. "Breanne Moore, the time has come for you to be named."

The longhouse fell silent as the women of Sky gathered round.

Tell stepped forward and wrapped her mother in a blue silk garment.

Breanne felt strangely nervous. Despite Garrett and the others agreeing this is what she should do, she was feeling something else – a sort of pulling from deep inside her. Almost like she was supposed to be here. Like this was what she was supposed to do.

All the women sat down, some on pelts on the wood-planked floor and others on the sleeping shelves that ran along the sides of the room. Across the front of the shelves were horizontal and vertical poles lashed together with twine, and from the poles hung large animal pelts that could be secured and drawn closed to create privacy for the occupants.

Currently, all the pelts were drawn open and the shelves were filled with women who watched in silence, eager to bear witness to the naming of the queen of Sky.

"Breanne Moore, you come to us on the wind asking for nothing and making no claim of rights to us or these lands," Key began, her voice even and sure. "You tell us you have the ability of sight and then you share a vision, a vision that quickly comes to pass. Further, you and your strange companions aid us in battle using incredible magic and magical weapons to help us defeat the dökkálfar invasion led by Saria the Night Slayer!" Her voice was rising – shouting. "You, Breanne Moore, are she – the one promised to us by our god, Turek! Let any who disagrees stand! Let any who are not satisfied with this judgment, my judgment, Turek's judgment, stand now and speak!"

Key turned in a slow circle.

Breanne swallowed dryly, wondering briefly what a challenge would entail.

No one stood.

Key smiled at Breanne. "Step forward, Breanne Moore."

Breanne glanced at Garrett, finding his eyes. Garrett didn't nod, and he didn't speak – which was good because she wasn't looking for permission and certainly wouldn't want Key to construe the look in that way. No, she was looking for something else, and she found it in the eyes of the boy she loved. She found reassurance. Something was happening inside her. She was feeling something.

All these women were staring at her, believing in her, and Key, a queen in her own right, believed in her too. The others had said she should play along until they figured out their next move, but this felt like more than playing along. After all, something or someone had spoken her name to these women. When told of a prophecy and questioned on her abilities, she'd answered correctly that she could see the future, and then she proved it with a vision, right off the back of her claim. How could all this not mean something? Glancing at Garrett, she could see, without the need for words or nods, that he felt something too. Most importantly, his look told her he believed in her. She cemented her courage and stepped forward.

"Breanne Moore, please kneel before your people."

Breanne went to one knee.

Key placed a hand atop Breanne's head. "Do you promise to protect the women of Sky?"

"I do," she answered confidently, knowing she couldn't make this promise unless she meant it.

"Do you promise to put your people above all else?"

Breanne felt her palms sweating as she set her jaw and nodded. "Yes."

"It is time for you to receive your true name," Key said, turning to her people. "Women of Sky, close your eyes as we call to the ancient ones."

A chant started among the women of Sky, low at first,

The Last Gift

but it grew louder as they banged their spears against the wood floor. Breanne didn't understand the word they chanted, but she didn't need to know what it was. It was a word of power. Louder and louder they chanted, pounding their spears down angrily until the sound became deafening.

Then, with no warning, the chanting stopped and the longhouse went silent. The atmosphere changed, like a collective breath had been drawn in and held. Everyone seemed to listen, but for what?

A moment passed, and Key opened her eyes, a smile stretching across her face. "Of course. Breanne Moore, the girl whose name was spoken on the wind. Your true name is clear to me now. Clear to us all."

All around the room, the women nodded.

"You are hereby—"

In perfect harmony, every woman in the longhouse spoke the name along with Key, "Breezemore, the queen of Sky!"

Key smiled. "Now and forever you will be known to your people as—"

Again, the crowd announced in perfect synchronicity, "Queen Breeze!"

How did they do that? Garrett asked in mind speak.

Right. How did they come up with the same name all at once? Paul asked.

I... I don't know, Breanne managed.

A woman stepped forward with a small ornate wooden box cradled in both arms.

Lady Key opened the lid, reached inside, and reverently lifted something from the box.

A crown, Pete whispered.

Bone spiraled and stabbed upward from twisted black vines. The whole thing was bound together by silver thread meticulously woven in and out in a pattern of crisscrossing braids.

Gently, Key placed the crown atop Breanne's head and took her by the hand, urging her to her feet as she turned to face the women of the longhouse. She lifted Breanne's hand high above her head as if announcing her champion.

Th women found their knees and placed their foreheads down onto the floor or the sleeping platforms upon which they sat. Lady Key smiled at Breanne, and she too knelt down and placed her head on the floor of the longhouse.

After a moment, Lady Key rose, followed by the others, and the crowd erupted in a raucous toast that soon turned into a celebration. They sang to Queen Breezemore, drank wine, and danced. Even Lenny got into it, brandishing his guitar and strumming along. The ladies, having never seen an instrument like this, were wowed.

"Lenny seems to be getting quite a following," Breanne said to Garrett, nodding toward a group of women who sat around the boy, singing along as he strummed.

"Guess he is," Garrett said, smiling.

Breanne grabbed him by the hand and led him to an opening by the fire.

"Oh, um, I don't know if I'm much of a dancer, Bre," Garrett said, allowing her to pull him along.

She laughed, turning to face him, and took his other hand in hers. They danced and laughed and, despite the atmosphere and the strange music, for a moment she felt like she was back home dancing with an awkward boy at prom.

Garrett wrapped his arms around her and pulled her close. She tipped her head, placing her cheek on his shoulder. If she could just stay here, in this moment, how perfect it would be.

Her mind wandered as they slow danced. She wondered what this strange turn of events meant. If they were successful, all those Keepers back on Earth – her daddy included – would come here. What would they think of all this? Garrett squeezed her tight to him, and her thoughts changed. Would she and Garrett ever go on a date? No, she supposed not. Not in the traditional sense, anyway. This might be as close as they would get to a date, until god only knew when. She squeezed him back and kissed his cheek. "Are you okay?"

He drew back, seeming to search her eyes. "Well, no, not really. We still have to find the magical item that will keep the trees of Earth unbound and keep Pando from killing every human on the planet. Then we have to open the portal. And as far as I know, the only way to do that is to find Jack. God, I hate to even guess what kind of trouble he is causing with the God Stones. Now we got Pete running off, and we have to go deal with this King Deep guy... No, I suppose I'm far from okay. But..."

"But?" she asked.

"But there's no place I'd rather be than with you," he finished, his face turning a bright red visible even in the firelight.

Breanne smiled and then pressed her lips to his.

He pulled her body into his, and she didn't think they were dancing anymore.

After a moment, a thought popped into her head. She pulled away just enough to look at Garrett's face again. "Jack!"

"No. I'm Garrett," he replied, giving her the side eye.

"No," she said, slapping his chest. "The dragons and nephilbock were battling the dökkálfar when we fled."

"What does that have to do with Jack?"

"That army was Apep's, but Jack has the crown now. What if he controls the armies?"

"Jack? Leading armies?" Garrett asked skeptically.

"With all that power, what if he is leading them, and what if he beats the dökkálfar and takes Osonian? You know him, Garrett. What would he do?" Breanne asked.

"I don't think I know him at all, Bre – not anymore."

"All those dragons… What's to stop him from destroying the entire city, including the tree?" she asked.

Garrett nodded. "There's something else I've been thinking about," he said, hesitating.

Breanne's eyebrows knitted together. "Go on," she urged.

"The father tree. Key said it could grant wishes to those it found worthy. What if we got inside the city and made an offering, then wished for Pando's magical item?"

Breanne felt a glimmer of hope. "Do you really think it could work?"

"Not if Jack destroys it before we stop him."

"Garrett, we've been here for hours. If Jack is leading Apep's army, the battle is probably over."

"Maybe not. Don't you think it's strange they would have sent Saria here if their walls had been breached?" Garrett asked, stepping back and twirling her.

Breanne couldn't help but laugh as she spun. "Hey, I thought you couldn't dance?"

"I'm a quick learner," he said. "But seriously, doesn't it seem odd?"

"Not if her god told her to come after us. And what the hell does it mean? What are we dealing with?"

"They aren't gods, Breanne. I don't know what they are, but Coach's journal says there are seven of them and they have favorites. Turek told me he wasn't a god, and if he isn't a god, then they aren't either."

"Then what are they?"

"I don't know. Right now, I just wish there was a way to know for sure what happened to Osonian and the father tree. And I think it's best if you tell Key everything about the dragons, the nephilbock, and Jack."

"I was thinking the same. Maybe she can send a runner to gather intel on what's happening at Osonian."

"Gather intel? You sound like Paul," he said, smiling.

"Hey, what do you expect? Both my brothers are military." She smiled back, feeling the moment winding down. Although her feet were killing her and all she wanted to do was lie down and sleep, she didn't want this moment to end.

"Maybe we better get Key caught up and then get some shut-eye?"

She heard him, but she didn't let go. Instead, she buried her face deeper into his shoulder. Finally lifting her head, she said, "Yeah, I think the others are asleep." She smiled, pointing at Pete, who lay curled up in a fetal position next to Governess's pot of soil.

Garrett stared at the boy for a long moment.

Breanne read the concern on his face. "Paul will keep him safe," she said.

"I know. I just hate us splitting up."

"It's only for a day, and I think Pete needs to do this, but if it makes you feel better, go with him. I'll be okay with Key and the others."

The singing stopped, confirming Breanne's fear that the intimate moment they'd shared was over. She stood next to the crackling fire, still held in Garrett's embrace. *Please don't let go,* she thought.

"Yeah, well, leaving you? That's not happening. Besides, you're right, this is Pete's journey. And let's be honest, Pete wasn't helpless even before he had supervision. He's always been the bravest kid I knew. Did I ever tell you the story about how he stood up to Jack in the high school bathroom?"

Breanne smiled. Was he stalling? She hoped so. "No. I don't think you have."

"Well, let's put it this way. He got his ass kicked, but he didn't back down. When everyone else was afraid, Pete stood up," Garrett said. Then he looked around, seeming to notice for the first time they were the only ones left swaying to music that no longer played. He gave her an apologetic smile, and she knew he didn't want it to end either.

Breanne sighed. "Come on, let's find Key. We can get everyone else caught up in the morning."

~

"Lady Key, may I have a word?" Breanne asked, beckoning Key to sit next to her.

"Of course, my queen. Tell me what troubles you?"

Breanne explained everything. She told her about Earth, and about Apep and Azazel. She explained how Gabi killed the Queen of Queens, how Garrett had slain a two-headed dragon, and how she had helped the elven king kill Apep. Then she told Key about the armies of dragons and giants flooding through the portal and attacking the elves. She told of Jack, and how he now held all the God Stones, and that they were still assembled into the Sound Eye.

Key looked suddenly older. Her face paled. "The gods never meant the Sound Eye of Karelia to be connected unless all the gods' favorites reached enlightenment together and peace reigned over the world. My queen, forgive me for being so bold, but why are you only telling me this now?" Key asked, her forehead creased with concern.

"I'm sorry, Key. So much happened so fast, and I needed to understand more about you and the people of Sky."

"I will wake a runner, but I fear the forest will be dangerous to travel through. We have little offering left. I need to reserve what Ice Ember I have for the trip to Cloud, in case we find ourselves in need of escape. Besides, the fastest runners I have left have already departed for the caves."

"The fastest you have left?" Breanne asked.

"Yes. Sadly, I lost several in the battle."

Tell, looking as though she could hardly hold her eyes open, approached and sat next to her mother.

"Why are you not sleeping, my daughter?"

"I overheard you talking about sending a runner," she said.

"Of course you did, and the answer is no. I won't lose you again."

"Mother, you didn't lose me."

"Yes, I did! I saw it myself. You were dead!" Key said, her eyes glistening.

"Oh, Mother, please don't. I have never felt better."

"Let me settle this. The answer is no," Breanne said.

Tell frowned, looking as though she might challenge Breanne, but Breanne quickly held up a hand, waving her off. "No one will go."

Garrett gave her a look and then spoke in mind speak. *Bre, we need to know what's happening at Osonian.*

Breanne shook her head. *It won't change what we need to do. We can't go there now, not with King Deep sending his army after our people and Saria likely coming back. Even if we knew, we couldn't stop it – not yet. And we can't let her risk her life for something we can't do anything about.*

Damn, you're right, Garrett said.

Well, get used to it. She smiled wryly.

Key raised an eyebrow. "Can I ask what you two are saying?"

"Sorry, Lady Key."

"Queens do not apologize," Key replied with a playful smile of her own.

"Well, this one does. Especially when she is wrong or rude."

"Very well," Key conceded. "Shall I send a runner then?"

Breanne shook her head. "No. Do not risk one of our women in order to learn something we cannot change."

"Very wise, my queen," Key said, tipping her head and then turning to Tell. "Daughter, please show our queen to her pallet. We've a long day tomorrow."

At the far end of the longhouse, Breanne was given an elevated shelf thick with soft feathers and covered in hides. It wasn't as comfortable as a bed, but she'd slept on much worse. Best of all, she had Garrett's arms wrapped around her. Outside, the wind blew, whistling through cracks in the longhouse. Breanne found the whistling wind coupled with the soft snores of other sleepers and the crackle of the fire quite comforting, but she could feel the tension in Garrett. "It's going to be okay, Garrett," she whispered, rolling over to face him.

"Are you just saying that to make me feel better?"

"No. No, I mean it," she said. Garrett was usually the optimistic one, but she could hear it in his voice. In this moment he needed her to be the optimistic one.

"How can you be so sure?" he asked in earnest, his voice hoping for something. Perhaps hoping she saw it in their future. But she hadn't, and as much as she wanted to, she couldn't give him certainty.

"Because it has to be. Because anything less means…" She trailed off, not wanting to say it.

Garrett swallowed and finished her sentence. "Because anything less means we fail and everyone we love dies."

25

Mist Storm

God Stones – Moon Ring 2
The Nightshade Desert

Flames flashed across the wall of the mist storm like a magician's flash paper. Jack forced himself to raise his head, fearing his eyes would burn when he opened them, but the fire was spreading away from the center in all directions.

Behind him, Nyana screamed as Cerberus plunged into the tunnel of fire, breaking the plane of the mist storm. Once inside the tunnel, Jack noticed it was hot as hell, but bearable. He wasn't burning. Ahead, the Sentheye continued to spread, fire following close behind like a flame chasing a trail of gasoline. *Cerb! Are we okay?*

Ha! I believe we are, Taker! I believe we are!

"Stop screaming, Nyana. Open your eyes and see what I've done!" Jack shouted.

Nyana must have heard him above the roar because her screaming stopped. Her arms still gripped his waist tightly, but he didn't mind that.

Zerri? Ahi? Report, he ordered.

Zerri's voice came through first. *You've done it, Jack. You've punched a hole through the storm!*

Yes, I am near the rear of the horde, my lord, Ahi said. *The tunnel is narrowing, but we are staying ahead of its closure.*

Any losses, Ahi?

None, my lord.

Excellent! Jack said. Except he didn't feel excellent. He felt sick and his head felt like it might pop. The world around him was growing fuzzy, and he really wanted to lie down. Just hang on a little longer, he told himself. A little longer and he could rest.

Look! Cerberus said.

Jack squinted, forcing himself to see through this new pain. Ahead, the flames dissipated outward, fizzling away and opening to a night sky full of moons and stars.

Jack felt the cool breeze even before they cleared the smoldering tunnel. *I did it, Cerb!*

Yes, Taker! We are safe!

Below him the desert looked dark, like a midnight ocean. Jack's head was making a strange buzzing sound. *Can we land? I need to rest.*

My lord, I do not advise landing in the shadow desert. There are rumors of creatures that live within the sand. Very scary creatures, Ahi said.

Scarier than thousands of dragons? Scarier than you, Ahi? Scarier than Cerb? Scarier than me? Jack asked, annoyed because he just needed the buzzing to stop.

No. Perhaps not, but we are nearing the Mountains of Twelve. You made the journey easy for us, my lord. Our wings are still fresh.

Fine. Onward then.

Are you alright, Jack?

No, Cerb. I don't think I am.

Try to rest. I'll fly steady. Perhaps you should dump the dökkálfar female, so you can stretch out and get comfortable.

No. She's fine. She's… she's keeping me warm.

Very well. Are you…? Cerb asked, trailing off.

Jack knew where this conversation was heading. What his dragon brother wanted to ask was if he'd gone crazy – if he was losing his shit.

I'm fine, Cerb, he said, knowing the big dragon wouldn't believe him. *When we land, I'm going to need to be strong for the next part, but right after, I need you to keep your promise. I need this thing off my head.*

It will be done.

Time passed, though Jack couldn't say how much as he drifted in and out of sleep. The warmth from Cerb beneath him and Nyana sleeping against his back helped make it easy to drift off. Yet it still felt sketchy to sleep on the back of a dragon, even one the size of Cerb. Jack found that by wedging his hand beneath one of Cerb's recurved neck spurs, he could quickly grab hold if something startled him awake. But as promised, Cerb flew steady.

Below him, the desert was gone and all he could see now were puffs of clouds packed in tight, only occasionally breaking to reveal patches of blues, greens, reds, and yellows. Above them, the two suns seemed to have circled the sky and were now heading back toward one another as if playing a game of chicken to see who would swerve first. But Jack knew neither would chicken out and eventually the two suns would appear as one before finally fading away to night.

Soon he saw something else. Something his mind struggled to comprehend. *Ahi, what am I looking at?*

Those, my lord, are the Mountains of Twelve, home of the dragon.

Below them, there were no more breaks in the clouds, only a solid blanket of white so thick and flat Jack felt like he could have walked on it. Above the clouds, an entire world came into view unlike anything Jack could have imagined. A single massive mountain seemed to float in midair. But it wasn't just the floating part – it almost looked upside down, though it wasn't flat on top either. A smaller mountain range spread across the top of the floating goliath. As they drew closer, Jack could see unnatural shapes carved into the mountains themselves, forming... forming what? Jack squinted up, realizing it was a city – a dragon city.

At the sight of the city, a part of Jack felt something strange. A memory took him back to Petersburg. Hanging out with Pete, Garrett, Lenny, and the others in the Z tunnel that ran under Route 123 back by the concrete plant. During those hot summer days, they would set up teams and choose sides, then use sticks to sword fight or paintball guns when they got older. When it got hot, they'd get in the creek to cool off, then sit in the shade.

The conversations always turned to talking about shit like going to another world, or what if magic was real – especially if that super douche David was around. Jack would usually make fun of them all for being pathetic losers but right now, riding a dragon into a strange floating world, he felt suddenly... he felt... Well, he felt lonely and oddly he wished... Well, it didn't matter, did it? *I know you're with me, Danny.*

My lord, Ahi said, interrupting his thoughts, *there are twelve mountains like the one you see ahead. Each is its own queendom with its own queen, and yet all answer to one.*

The Queen of Queens, Jack said.

Yes, my lord. I feel it is my duty to mention we likely will not be welcomed into the fold.

No shit, Sherlock, Jack said. What did Ahi think he was – an idiot? As he felt his sudden irritation rise, his brain began to... to buzz. Dammit. He'd hoped it had passed.

I apologize, but what is a Sherlock, my lord? Ahi asked.

Never mind. Which one do we land on?

Ah, yes. In the center of the twelve mountains is a thirteenth. We will need to fly in between the mountains and then over the lake. The Mountain of Thrones floats in the center.

In the center of a lake? So, like an island?

No. Not exactly. It floats above the lake.

Jack struggled with the concept. *But you're saying there's a lake… up here?*

Yes. The Floating Lake of Twelve or simply the Lake of Twelve. I understand your confusion, my lord. Earth lacks an area of gravitational flux. This must seem impossible to you, but as you will see momentarily, all these things are quite possible here.

Jack's instincts were to ask Ahi to explain gravitational flux, but he hated school and besides, it didn't matter how the mountains were floating because they were. He was looking at a mountain floating dead ahead. So if a mountain could float, why not a lake?

As they drew closer, they rounded the mountain, opening up Jack's view to a massive waterfall, its width stretching from one mountain to the next. It spilled down, disappearing into the clouds far below. *I thought you said it was a lake. This looks like a waterfall.*

Indeed, my lord. The lake is above the falls. We will find the waterfalls in between each of the twelve mountains, denoting the edge of the gravitational flux. Notice how the water is falling slowly.

"Good gods," Nyana breathed into his ear. "You have brought us to the queendom of dragons."

Jack ignored her as he sought understanding from Ahi. *So, we need to go above?*

Correct, Ahi said.

They climbed skyward, higher and higher, until they were above the falls. Jack craned his neck to see in between the mountains. The lake stretched out as far as Jack could see, like a sheet of glass, perfect and still. Staring out across the lake, he only saw more water. If there was a mountain in the middle, he sure couldn't see it.

However, to his left and right, the Mountains of Twelve rose ever skyward, threatening to poke a hole in the atmosphere. Tipping his head back, Jack looked up as they passed in between the goliaths, amazed at their size. He bet half of Illinois would fit on top of that one mountain.

Bracing himself, he wondered if he would start floating when he crossed over the falls and above the suspended lake.

They crossed the threshold, but Jack did not feel weightless. Although… he did feel different. He didn't feel lighter, but he had a sort of strange tingling in his stomach.

Am I going to float like the mountains, Ahi? he asked, realizing the question sounded stupid only after he asked it.

No, my lord. Living creatures are only minimally affected. The Mountains of Twelve have their own gravitation force reckoning. The force between the two bodies includes the Mountains of Twelve and Karelia. Of course, our two suns, seven moons, and a large concentration of Sentheye factor into the equation as well. Though you can't see it, the Mountains of Twelve rise and fall over the course of each moon ring.

So, all of this lowers down to the planet's surface each day? Jack asked.

No, not all the way. The queendom only lowers into the clouds, never through them. The waterfalls ensure the clouds are ever present as the gravitational flux draws the water back into the lake from beneath. It will take some time, but I can explain Sentheye as it relates to gravitational flux on a mathematical level… if you would find it beneficial?

Um, no. I think I understand well enough. What a smart-ass! He could have just said it was magic and been done with it. Instead, he had to be a dick. God, he hated that guy.

Very well, my lord.

Craning his head back to ogle up at one of the behemoths, Jack watched as something launched itself from the top. When he saw wings spread open, grabbing air, he realized he was looking at a dragon. It appeared small in the mountain's shadow as it took flight far ahead of them. The dragon's wings pumped as it raced across the water.

Ahi must have noticed too. *One of the queens, my lord. They will all be gathering at the throne of thrones, preparing for our arrival.*

Tell me what I'm dealing with, Ahi. Will they bring their armies?

Armies? No, there will only be the queens.

That seemed dumb to Jack. *Why wouldn't they bring their armies?*

We are surrounded, my lord. Their armies are already here en masse. Should this go badly, we've no escape, Ahi said.

For once, he didn't say it like a dickhead. He just stated it plain. It shouldn't have pissed Jack off so much, but the goddamned buzzing in his head wouldn't stop! Was he screwing up? Was this damn buzzing screwing him up?

You're fine, Jack. Settle down and take it easy, said the familiar voice of Danny-but-not-Danny. *They don't have the God Stones. They don't have the Queen of Queens, and they don't have Cerberus, the son of Typhon, or Jack the Taker.*

Bzzzz. Bzzzz. Bzzzz. That was true. Yes. That was for sure true. He just needed to stay sharp.

Of course, there is the risk...

What? What risk? Jack asked.

The voice hesitated.

Bzzzz. Bzzzz. Bzzzz. What risk? Jack snapped.

Ahead, a tiny shadow appeared above the lake.

Well, Zerri could turn on you as soon as she is named Queen of Queens. Then she could use her new army against you.

Then she'd have to face me and my army! Jack argued.

Of course... But then again...

Well?

Not-Danny sighed. *Well, she could be secretly in league with Ahi and, after all, your army seems to be growing quite fond of her. I think they would die for her.*

For her?! Jack shouted. *You don't know what you're talking about!*

Of course I don't, little bro. I'm sure you're right.

Shut your face and get out of my head! Jack sucked in a breath and held it. The buzz in his head was pulsing louder than ever. Just calm down, he told himself, letting out the breath. The buzz quieted to background static. He took a couple of breaths, listening to be sure the voice was gone. When he didn't hear not-Danny again, he sighed with relief.

The shadow in the distance grew larger, taking shape above the water. The thirteenth mountain appeared similar in shape to the others, pointed at the bottom and widening as it rose skyward. But as they drew close, there was something clearly different about it. Sculptures of dragon heads as big as buildings protruded from the mountain itself. From what Jack could tell, there must have been hundreds, covering every inch of the mountain.

Damn, that stupid voice had him paranoid. He focused on Zerri. *Zerri?*

Yes, Jack.

What do you want more than anything in the world?

There was no hesitation. *I want to kill Gabi De Leon.*

The Last Gift

It had been a gamble, but it was exactly what he'd hoped she would say. If she had said, "I want to be the Queen of Queens," he might have had a problem. Of course, he knew she wanted that too, but he feared she might not need him to claim her title.

Why do you ask me this now?

Because I want to give you this, Zerri.

Give me what?

Jack smiled. *A promise. I promise you, once you have been named the Queen of Queens and I finish this business with the nephilbock, I will dedicate everything I am and everything I have to killing Garrett and capturing Gabi.*

You're afraid, she said in astonishment.

Jack scoffed. *What? Afraid? What do I have to be afraid of? Hey, I'm offering you something here.*

As long as I don't betray you. Which means you are afraid I'll do just that – betray you.

Bzzzz. Bzzzz. Bzzzz. Dammit! Fine! Do what you want! But if you betray me, you better kill me!

Zerri's voice came back calm and even. *You've nothing to worry about, Jack. You gave me the truth, and for that, I owe you. I will not betray you unless you give me a reason to.*

Jack could almost feel her smiling. *And?*

Even so, it is nice to know you fear me.

∽

Ahi instructed the horde to land in a massive clearing atop the mountain, where they were to wait for further instruction. *Follow me, my lord,* Ahi said, dropping over the edge of the mountain and gliding through the mouth of one of the dragon-head sculptures.

They flew down a long corridor and into a massive chamber, where torches with flames taller than Jack lit the walls.

He'd never been in a room this big. Maybe once when he went to the Lucas Oil Stadium to watch the Colts play. But he was pretty sure this was way bigger than the famous football stadium.

Three-quarters of the way across the big stone room, Ahi landed, followed by Cerb and Zerri. At the far end sat a semicircle of thirteen thrones on a raised platform. All thirteen were occupied, including the center one, the one sitting higher than all others, the one belonging to the Queen of Queens.

Zerri took up position in between Cerberus and Ahi as they walked three dragons wide into the center of the semicircle.

The dragon sitting on the throne of the Queen of Queens stared at Jack and Cerberus with a curious discomfort. Jack did his best to avert his red eyes. Fortunately, the Sound Eye crown was easy enough to keep covered under his hood since it circled his head just above the ears and didn't stick up too much.

The first thing Jack noticed about the dragon – besides the fact she sat on the highest throne – was that she, too, wore a crown. He wondered: Was it odd a dragon would wear a crown? Azazel hadn't worn a crown back on Earth. The peculiar dragon crown was not round, but narrow and long. It twisted, jutting up in wicked points of ornate scales intermixed with rust-colored steel, or something that looked like steel. The crown's odd shape fit perfectly between the dragon's two long horns, which protruded from her forehead only to twist back, their points vanishing somewhere behind her head.

The dragon herself was as strange as the crown she wore. At first glance, Jack couldn't put his finger on it what made her so different. She seemed average size, with red eyes like his own. He stared, trying to see what he couldn't. Until, like a hidden picture within a picture, it became suddenly clear it was her scales that set her apart. All the dragons Jack had seen had scales in the shape of clam shells, rounded at the edges, but this dragon's scales came to sharp points like layered arrowheads. Her black scales glistened as if made of something metallic.

The dragon spoke aloud, her serpent voice echoing through the otherwise empty chamber. "Ahi the Silver. Who are these strangers you've brought to our lands? Where is Azazel?"

To Jack, this dragon had a unique accent, like the exchange student chick from Germany, Ursula. Jack had spent an entire year making fun of that troll, giving her the nickname Ugly Ursula. Truth was, she wasn't even all that ugly, and she was super smart too. But she wouldn't give him the time of day, so he taught her a lesson by getting all the kids to call her Ugly Ursula. Jack smiled to himself at the memory. She was supposed to stay for a whole year but tapped out after the first semester. Yep, Ugly Ursula, and this fake-ass queen sounded just like her.

Ahi stepped forward on shaky legs.

What the shit was he nervous for? He should feel lucky he's on the right side of this, Jack thought.

Ahi bowed slightly, addressing the dragon. "We've returned from Earth with a massive force of dragons and aligned with the nephilbock, just as Azazel planned. If it pleases you, we've already attacked the dökkálfar and freed our enslaved dragons."

"You speak of things I already know. Azazel promised to return with a full army of dragons and nephilbock. Yet here you are, less than three moon cycles having passed, and you show up with an army of juveniles barely old enough to breathe fire. And the nephilbock. They are so small. Why was their breeding not better controlled to produce larger soldiers?"

The dragon didn't give Ahi time to answer. Instead, she plowed ahead. Jack shook his head. It was like the adults back home. They never wanted to hear your side. They just wanted to hear themselves lecture you.

"I'm not sure how you can call these creatures giants when I'm told they're barely half the size of a Karelian nephilbock." The queen leaned forward, her jowls drawing up. "Worse, you have the audacity to attack the dökkálfar before returning here to align forces! Tell me, Ahi, how many were lost to free a mere handful of slaves?"

"A handful," Ahi said.

"There are dozens more behind the wall you failed to breach! Of course, you would have known this had you come here first."

"That was not an option. The dökkálfar army was already standing on the battlefield when the portal opened. They were prepared for our arrival. Syldan Loravaris followed us to Earth, and time works differently there. Much time had passed there when only—"

"Silence your tongue, Silver! With Apep and Azazel dead, the treaty is broken." Then, shifting her snake eyes toward Jack, she huffed, flaring her nostrils and releasing two puffs of smoke. "Why are a human and a dökkálfar sitting on the back of a dragon in our most sacred of places?"

Ahi tried to find words. "My... I... Annas... Well, you see..."

That's enough, Ahi. I'll take it from here, Jack said, injecting his voice telepathically.

What is this? Annas demanded.

Did anyone ever tell you your name sounds a lot like anus?

The queen rose to her feet and hissed.

The Last Gift

Jack waved her off. *Listen to me, all of you,* he said, lifting his chin as he willed his already red eyes to brighten to a startling shine. *I have no patience for explanations, so here is what you need to know. You!* he said, pointing at the crown-wearing queen. *You are an imposter.* There was a better word for it, but he couldn't think of it. Imposter would have to do.

Annas narrowed her eyes. *Imposter? How dare you speak to me through a psychic bond. How dare you challenge me? You, a little human. But no, you're not merely human, are you, little one? You're something else.*

Yes, I am something else. Something the God Stones made and Azazel enhanced. I am dragon and human and god. With a dramatic flourish, Jack threw back his hood to reveal the Sound Eye.

All thirteen dragons hissed, shifting uncomfortably as the room took on a heightened tension. But Jack didn't mind. They looked as though they might shit themselves.

Annas narrowed her eyes. "We knew it was here. We could feel it coming. But you... you hold the Sound Eye? This power is not meant for you, no matter what you claim to be. You are Earth-born."

Jack lifted his chin. "Well, you can try to take my crown. Or you can take that one off your ugly head and give it to its rightful owner. Then fall in line like a good little dog." Jack smiled, showing all his teeth, and added, "But I kind of hope you try to take this one instead."

Jack tugged back on Cerb's spur. Cerberus twisted one head back as Jack leaned forward and whispered into his brother's ear.

The pretender Queen of Queens stared down at Jack and Cerberus, her lips curling into a snarl. "I don't care what happened on Earth. I don't care how you came to be or what

OTTO SCHAFER

the abomination is you sit upon. You will never leave the Hall of Queens alive. There are thirteen of us."

Another dragon queen, larger than Annas, broke in, her voice sounding older, like a grandma. "Please, my queen, wait. Let us not be so hasty. I should like to hear of this creature you sit upon."

"Oh, you mean my brother, Cerberus, the son of Typhon?"

At the names of Cerberus and Typhon, the hall erupted in gasps.

"You claim he's Typhon's son, the three-headed Cerberus," Annas said, sounding shocked.

"He can speak for himself."

"I am Cerberus the Mighty. I am the god's son," Cerb thundered, his voice reverberating off the walls.

"An abomination. This... this thing has no claim to the crown!" Annas shouted.

"No. I am not ordering you to take the crown off for him." Jack smiled again, pointing at Zerri as he addressed Annas. "That crown you're wearing belongs on the head of this dragon. The daughter of Azazel!"

All eyes shifted to Zerri.

Finally, Annas spoke. "I do not recognize you, dragon. But it matters not. Queen of Queens Azazel herself gave me this crown in her absence, only to be relinquished upon her return."

"As you acknowledged earlier, Azazel is dead," Zerri said evenly. "But I am her daughter and therefore, by law, I am the new and rightful heir to the Mountains of Twelve. Now if you please, Annas, you are in my seat."

"I do not recognize you as the heir," Annas hissed.

Another dragon, with lemon-yellow scales that darkened to burnt-orange edges, spoke in a nervous tone. "Annas, if she is a female and came from Earth, then she must be the heir. Only Queen Azazel could have birthed this dragon."

"You think your Queen of Queens a fool? She could have come from any of the twelve queendoms. She could be any of yours – any of you could be conspiring against me!"

"Annas, to what end?" another asked.

"Ahi was with Azazel when she left for Earth. This could only be what they claim," said yet another.

"The queendom should have always been mine!" Annas spat. "If not for a lost challenge, it would have been my mother who held the crown, not Azazel! My lineage is the oldest bloodline of the dragon! I and I alone am of a pure bloodline! No, my queens. I will not yield the crown to outsiders! Now choose your side wisely, for there is only one way this moon ring will end."

Jack glanced at the stunned expressions plastered across the faces of the other queens.

No one spoke.

Jack smiled. "Good. Then, as my dad used to say, I think your mouth must be tired from all that running it's been doing. Time to shut it, Anus." Jack drew upon the Sentheye.

"Jack, what are you doing?" Zerri asked.

"Showing them who's in charge!"

Cerberus shifted, lowering himself onto his belly as Jack stood.

"Jump, Nyana!" Jack shouted.

Nyana jumped, landed, and rolled before springing back to her feet and running away from them toward the shadows.

A low roar built as Annas's mouth stretched open.

Thinking about the story Apep had told him of drawing dragon fire into his hand and spitting it out of his mouth, Jack focused. He was no coward, but he wasn't a wizard either. Apep knew words of power. *I'll look pretty dumb getting burnt up after talking all that shit,* he thought.

Jack splayed his hands, pretending his sole focus was on Annas, but from his periphery he saw what he knew would come.

Ahi charged at Cerberus.

"Now, Cerb!" Jack shouted, not taking his eyes off Annas as he leapt to the floor.

Cerberus, already squatting, launched himself sideways at Ahi, driving the dragon across the room in a clash of talons and teeth. Jack could only hope the element of surprise was enough to give Cerb a quick upper hand over the traitor bastard.

In his mind, Zerri shouted, *Ahi, stop! What is the meaning of this?*

Good. Then maybe she wasn't part of Ahi's betrayal after all. As for Ahi, Jack had known for some time, but there was no time to think about that now. Beneath the scales of Annas's metallic neck sparked the glow of dragon fire.

With the trap sprung for Ahi, Jack focused in earnest, splaying his hands and drawing in all the Sentheye he could. Before he had the God Stones, Jack drew his power from those around him, diseasing whatever life he wanted to take and then releasing it all. Sometimes he released it through Cerb. Sometimes though his own fists. But now, with all the power of the gods sitting atop his head, he needed only to draw it directly into his mind, and the flood of magic spilled forth like water flowing over the old, busted dam down at the Sangamon River. The Sound Eye dumped as much as Jack could stand right into his mind, and when he thought his mind might catch fire, it poured on more.

In front of him, the angry dragon's roar was reaching a deadly pitch.

Through the pain of Sentheye in its purest form, Jack shouted aloud, "Come on, Anus! I hate you!" His mind burned like fire, but he didn't care. Switching to English, he kept on, "I hate you, Dad! I hate you, Garrett!" His eyes narrowed as he pushed the Sentheye from his mind into Annas. "I hate you, Danny! Damn you! Damn you! Why did you leave me? Why did you all leave me?" Tears, unwelcome and unexpected, poured down Jack's cheeks.

Annas's face shook, her eyes bulbous and bulging out of her head.

His peripheral vision filled with movement as the twelve other queens rose to their feet, their own eyes bulging but for different reasons as they witnessed the horror that had become their Queen of Queens.

Jack squeezed his splayed hands into tight fists. "Why? Why? Why!"

Annas's roar turned to a sudden and horrifying screech. She choked back the dragon fire, unable to breathe it out – unable to breathe at all.

Through blurred eyes, Jack watched as the head of the false Queen of Queens exploded. The gory scene wasn't unlike the time he and Danny stuffed an M-80 in a watermelon and lit the fuse. Bits of teeth, scales, and bloody mist filled the air.

The dragon's body collapsed from the throne, rolling off the platform before finally coming to rest, still twitching and flopping on the stone floor. The room went still and silent. But not for Jack. In his mind, the noise buzzed electric. Blinking rapidly, he felt something wet trickling down from his ears and nose. Jack let go of the Sentheye, but the buzz didn't fade. Instead, it grew louder, filling his mind like a thousand bumblebees.

The Sentheye wasn't letting go of him.

Around him, dragons went into motion, but through the noise and pain of his own mind, he could no longer see what was happening.

Behind it all, he swore he heard laughter.

When the pain peaked and he couldn't take any more, a horrific crack snapped from somewhere inside him – from in his own head.

Pain followed. Horrible, unbearable pain, and it took him away into unconsciousness. The last thing Jack heard was laughter, and the last thing he felt was the cold stone floor rushing up to meet his face.

26

Soul and Ellis

God Stones – Moon Ring 2
The Shadow Forest

Paul woke before first light, feeling better than he should have after only a few hours' sleep. For a moment, he lay on his side, unmoving. Had it only been a few hours? He glanced over at the slatted windows, but only the dimmest flicker of light shone through. How long was night here, anyway? They'd danced for hours into the night, and he'd danced with more women than he could count. *Ed, bro, how I wish you were here,* he thought.

He was missing Ed, bad. This must be the worst one brother could miss another. They'd been apart plenty in the service, but this was different. This wasn't like being deployed. It was seeing him held hostage in that crazy tree cell and not knowing if he was okay – he couldn't stand it. And his dad, stuck in the wilds of Mexico, waiting and wondering what had happened to his son and daughter. Just knowing how worried his pops must be was driving him nuts.

This was, in part, why he'd been so eager to go with Pete. He needed a mission – an objective. Something to get his mind off Ed and his pops. Garrett and Bre didn't need him. Not for this trip to the caves. Besides, this kid, Garrett, loved her. Weird as it was, he could see it clear as day. Garrett would die before he let anything happen to Bre.

He reached over to draw back his blanket, realizing only then that a woman lay on either side of him. Quietly, he pulled back the blanket. He still had his underwear on, but the woman in front of him seemed to be missing even those.

He carefully lifted an arm belonging to the woman behind him from around his waist and crawled over the one in front. Finally, drawing open the curtain, he eased himself down off the platform and made his way across the longhouse, stepping carefully between dozens of sleeping women.

He shook Pete's shoulder.

"Hey. What's wrong?" Pete said aloud, startling awake.

Shh, use mind speak, kid. The others are still sleeping.

"Women of Sky, rise. It is time to depart," Key's voice called across the longhouse.

Well, looks like everyone is awake now, Pete said, stretching his arms high above his head.

~

Paul walked next to Pete and behind Breanne and Garrett. Around him, nearly two hundred women walked with them, quiet and alert, spears at the ready.

As the morning wore on, the white sun brightened first. It seemed less like it rose and more like it just came closer. Then, as the trees thinned into rocky terrain, the yellow sun seemed to peek out from behind the white one.

"There she is." Key pointed to the sky. "Do you see her? We call this time of moon ring 'asunder.' Asunder is the pulling away. There are many stories of our suns, and I suppose they all have their place among the religions of the varying creatures of Karelia."

Paul knew from time spent on dig sites around the world that many societies worshiped the sun.

"Would you like to hear the story we tell?" asked Key.

"Please," Breanne said.

"First light until the yellow sun is fully revealed is the time of Ellis. When they are fully separated, we will move into the mid moon ring, which is known in our ancient religion as the time of Ellis and Soul. When the two sinful lovers reach their greatest distance apart, we pass the brightest part of the moon ring. Ellis and Soul will then reach for each other, slowly journeying across the sky to join once again. Then, all the way up until they touch, we are in the late moon ring known as Soul. When they finally touch, we might say it's getting very late. Once Ellis eclipses Soul, we enter the latest part of the moon ring known as the banishing, just before darkness sets in. Now Ellis and Soul have fully embraced and for their sin they are banished, and ebon night will soon follow."

"You said, 'sinful lovers.' Who were they, and how have they sinned?" Breanne asked with the genuine interest of a scholar.

God, how she reminded Paul of his pops, but damn if she didn't look like Mom. A pang of hurt shot through his heart. *Mom, what would you think of all this?* he wondered.

"This goes back to the history of Turek. You see, Ellis, a human, fell in love with Soul, a dökkálfar woman, and together they bore a child. The gods strictly forbid this most taboo of sins. To punish the lovers' unthinkable offence, Ereshkigal slew them and their child. It is our belief that Turek didn't share this view, and she became angry at the dökkálfar god."

"And so, the story fits the movement of the suns?" Breanne asked.

"Ah, yes. But it is said that before the gods were angered, Karelia only had one sun, and after, there were three."

"Wait. Three? I don't see three." David shielded his eyes with his hand as he peered into the sky.

Paul noted that Key only bristled a little when David spoke out of turn. Perhaps she was getting used to the kid's outbursts.

Key pointed.

Paul and the others followed her finger skyward. There, far beyond two of Karelia's more distant moons, was what Paul thought was another moon, smaller and farther out. It shone red.

"You see the red sun?" Key asked.

"I thought that was a moon," Pete said.

Garrett nodded. "Me too."

"Not a moon. That is the child covered forever in the blood spilled by Ereshkigal. A stark reminder of what happens when we fail to follow the laws of the gods."

It's like many other societies back on Earth, Gabi said in mind speak, her hand sitting on her brow as she too squinted to see the red sun. *The Aztecs, for example, were known as the people of the sun. And my own Maya ancestors worshipped the sun god Kinich Ahau.*

Breanne nodded in agreement. "Back on Earth, we only have one sun and one moon, but many religions involve both."

Key bowed her head slightly. "Only one sun and moon? I can't imagine."

"Wait a sec, I don't understand at all. What's it all mean, and how are the red one and others reminders?" David asked.

"The blood sun is so small and far away. Forever out of reach of Ellis and Soul. So far away, in fact, they may never hold their child. Instead, both are caught in a perpetual looping cycle, forced to spend eternity unable to embrace not only their child but each other as they pass across the sky. When finally they come close together, Ereshkigal extinguishes their light, symbolizing their deaths. This happens each moon ring as a reminder to us all of what will happen should we ever be so bold as to fornicate with a race other than our own."

Paul glanced at Lenny, who shifted uncomfortably, looking about as out of place as a sheep among a pack of wolves.

"But you said this decision angered Turek. Do you believe their love was wrong and they deserved to die, or do you believe they should have been allowed to live?" Breanne asked.

"I believe in Turek, and she believed love transcended. But I don't believe she is powerful enough to defeat all the gods, so she saved who she could and left. Since that time, others have tried to erase the truth from our history. Horrible people like Deep would want you to believe something else entirely. My faith is strong. Still, there could never be a crossing of races. We hate the dökkálfar and, as far as other races, we would never breed with them, nor they with us. Until we heard your name on the wind, Turek was gone and no other god believed crossing the race boundaries was anything less than blasphemous. Even if the thought occurred, no one would dare act on it."

"Well, maybe times are due for changing," Breanne said.

Key frowned. "I do not understand why, in this, we should consider changing."

Don't push her on this, sis. Not now, Paul said.

Yeah, let's just drop it, Lenny urged.

Maybe ask her why it didn't get warm until the yellow

sun peeked out. I'm getting pretty warm now, but it was flurrying this morning, Paul said.

Breanne did ask.

"Ah, yes, Ellis. Ereshkigal allows no warmth to come from the white sun. Ellis is not allowed to bring forth warmth, nor assist with the crops, nor help the trees to bloom. He is to be a reminder of cold and death. Just as Soul is to be a reminder of Ereshkigal's love for Karelia, the dökkálfar, and the law of the gods. Each night when Soul is put to death despite Ereshkigal's love, it is to be a stark reminder of the life the gods provide us all and that no one is above their laws."

They had been climbing up a rocky slope, and if they were on some sort of trail, Paul couldn't see it. However, this made sense enough to him. A trail to the caves would be a bad thing. Fortunately, the rocky terrain, speckled in only sparse vegetation, would make it almost impossible for even the best trackers to follow.

"Ah, here we are," Key said, pointing.

The terrain leveled, and Paul noticed a narrow valley descending steeply to their left. On either side, the walls rose to form vertical cliffs on both sides.

"The Dark Narrow. Proceed through quickly and reach the Valley of Ember before nightfall. You will be wise to camp at the river, where you will have fresh water."

Key nodded to a woman with two braids wrapped into buns on either side of her head. The woman reminded Paul of Princess Leia if her hair had been braided and her skin was darker, and she was thick and strong. He recognized her as one of the women he'd shared the sleeping compartment with last night. The woman stepped forward, handing him a small satchel.

"These supplies will allow you to catch fish," Key said, as

another woman stepped forward and handed Pete a waterskin.

"Thank you," Paul said.

"You are welcome. Now go. Make haste through the Dark Narrow," Key said.

Why am I getting the feeling you don't want to be caught in the Dark Narrow after dark? Lenny asked in mind speak, then turned to face Paul. *Hey, are you sure you don't want me to come along?*

Negative. We'll be fine, Paul said, then added, *I'd rather you watch my sister's and Garrett's six.*

Lenny nodded, giving Paul a dap and Pete a slap on the shoulder.

Garrett gave Pete a hug and rubbed a hand through his shaggy black hair. *Try to stay out of trouble, Petey.*

Just be careful, Breanne said, giving her brother a hug.

You know I got this, sis. And I know he has you, Paul said, pulling Garrett in close and giving him a slap on the back.

Garrett kept a hand on Paul's shoulder, almost like a father would. *You two be careful and get back here quick. I will run all the way to the river to find you if you're not back here when you're supposed to be. Don't think I won't.*

Paul met the kid's eyes and smiled. He'd known for some time that there was something about this kid, and in that moment, he saw it clearer than ever. Garrett was growing. Not in a physical way, but he was displaying leadership on a level many adults never achieved.

Paul had spent enough time in the military and in the field to have seen some of the best leaders the United States military had to offer, and the good ones – the really good ones – made you want to follow them. They made you want to be your best self. It was an almost unexplainable skill. No, that wasn't right. It was more than a skill. It was who they were on a fundamental level combined with skill obtained over time, over mission after mission of being in the shit.

At this moment, with Garrett's hand on his shoulder, Paul wanted to be his best. He wanted to make Garrett... Jesus, he wanted to make him proud. *Don't worry. We'll beat feet in, grab the target, and get back – quick time.*

Garrett squeezed Paul's shoulder and let go. *See you tomorrow then.*

See you tomorrow.

⁂

Paul led Pete into the Dark Narrow, realizing quickly how the passage had gotten its name. The descent was uneven, steep, and dark. The farther they descended, the taller the walls seemed to grow.

"It's really chilly and dark down here," Pete said nervously.

"You'll be fine, kid. Just stay close." Paul felt uneasy himself, but unease was an asset. While it was the military who'd trained him to never get comfortable, he'd spent plenty of time in high-risk situations and learned to keep his head on a swivel. You had to be ready for anything.

Paul felt good being in this with Pete, though. He was a good kid, and when things had got hairy, the kid never froze up. Plus, Pete was determined to save Governess, and Paul respected that. Given that he'd watched the tree woman run Garrett's sword through Ed's chest, it might have seemed odd for him to volunteer for this mission. After all, he'd never wanted to kill another living thing more than he'd wanted to kill her in that moment. But now Paul understood that she'd never wanted to kill Ed, and the placement of the blade had been surgically precise, missing all his brother's vital organs.

He still wasn't sure about this strange love between Pete

and the tree woman, but who was he to judge? The fact was, he didn't care about that. He'd volunteered to help a friend save a friend, and besides, Governess was critical to the mission. She was an asset in battle, and if Paul knew nothing else, he knew the road ahead was likely a bloody one.

They hustled best they could for a few more hours, descending deep into the Dark Narrow. In places, the space became so tight, Paul nearly had to turn sideways to get his wide shoulders to pass. Finally, after descending what must have been the distance of a mountain, they spilled out onto a mix of rock and sand.

Instinctively, Paul looked at the sky to gauge how much light he had left before they would need to make camp. But this wasn't Paul's sky, and those weren't his suns. However, he remembered something Key had said. Something about when the two suns pass back across the sky and touch, it would be late evening, just before dark. He held up a hand and squinted. Near as he could tell, staring into the bright shine of the two suns, they were close to touching.

Taking his eye off the sky, he assessed his surroundings. In the distance towered a mountain range with two peaks standing taller than all the others. To his left and right were sheer cliffs stretching high and running off into the distance until they vanished in both directions around bends. The only way he could see was forward. He felt like he was standing at the bottom of the Grand Canyon. Across the valley, more cliffs and mountains rose toward the sky.

"Come on, Pete. We need to double time it to the river," Paul said, handing Pete the waterskin.

"I hate the sound of that," Pete said, taking a large swig.

"Look." Paul pointed. "We need to go that way. Right in between those two mountains there in the distance. You see there?"

"That's far, bro. I can't run all that way."

"You won't need to. They're just a guide. We should find the river along the way, but we'll have to hurry. One sun will soon eclipse the other, and once that happens, it's going to get dark fast."

"Damn. You're good at this," Pete said.

After at least a full hour of alternating between walking and jogging across the open valley of rolling hills, Paul heard something. "You hear that?"

"What?"

"Water! Come on." Paul broke into a run, again jogging forward over a slight sloping rise until he crested the summit. A large lazy river came into view, flowing from directly between the two mountains they'd been using to navigate. The river bent in a U shape, turning back toward the mountains to run along a cliff. Key had been right to point them to this spot. A deviation to the right and they would have missed the river altogether, while if they'd gone to the left they would have reached it, but it would have taken them far out of the way.

"It's so much bigger than I thought it would be!" Pete said, stooping to put his hands on his knees. "It's three times as wide as the Sangamon."

"Maybe so, kid, but at least it's moving slow," Paul countered, happy that for once there were no surprises. They'd made it in good time. There was still plenty of light to work by. And there wasn't a soul in sight.

Paul stepped into the water along the edge of the river. "Well, we better get to it."

"Wait!" Pete said, waving Paul off. "Key said it was important I collect the offering. I think I need to do this. At least let me try."

Paul looked down into the water. It was clearer than any water he'd seen, even clearer than the waters of Torii Beach where he'd trained when he was stationed in Okinawa. It looked deep, though. Paul scanned the rocky bottom, where a few fish were swimming this way and that. Nothing that looked too big or dangerous, but how was he supposed to know? He supposed if there were man-eating fish or some other threat, Key would have warned them. Then he spotted something glowing. "Look there!" he said, pointing.

"Yes! That's it, isn't it? Look at it! It's glowing just like Key said it would." Pete stripped off his clothes down to his underwear.

Paul saw three other spots that were glowing. Could it really be this easy? Something in his gut felt wrong. He wished he had a rope. He usually had a damn rope! "Listen, kid, I'm going to be watching you like a hawk, and if I see one hint of trouble, I'm coming in after you. And stay in contact. We should still be able to use mind speak while you're down there. Oh, and grab only small pieces!"

Pete nodded as he waded forward. "The water isn't bad!" he said and dove in.

Paul ran after him to where the edge dropped off and watched as Pete swam headfirst toward the bottom. It was even deeper than it looked.

As Pete neared the bottom, Paul thought he saw something. He frowned. That wasn't right. His eyes must have been playing tricks. He looked up at the sky, thinking a cloud must have passed over the suns, causing what he could have sworn was a shadow, but the sky was clear. He looked back down, searching the water, searching for the shadow.

There it was again, heading right for the kid!

Paul didn't hesitate. He dove.

27

Love Ember

God Stones – Moon Ring 2
Cragarmour Mountains

As soon as Turek's little human entered the river, Rán felt his presence. But after her experience with the boy, Jack, she wasn't much in the mood to reason. So why not just kill this one? Why not just drown him? Yes. She would show Turek just how silly all this was by killing one of his little chosen humans. After all, if Turek were right, and the Great Mother truly chose this little band of humans, then how could Rán kill him?

She took the form of a mermaid, smiling as she reached for the child's ankle.

Strong arms wrapped around her waist, surprising her with a sudden squeeze. Another human? This one would be no match for her, no matter his strength. She laughed, knowing there was no danger to her. This was her domain. Still, the nerve of this one to attack a creator. And that was what this was. She was being attacked. She giggled as she became excited, almost thrilled.

She opened her mind to his. He tried to shut the door to his mind, but she moved through it like a ghost. Ah, this one was called Paul, she thought, reading his mind, his heart, and his soul, all in the same instant. She wanted to learn everything she could before she killed him. He squeezed with incredible force, a force no human should possess. This one was using the Sentheye to increase his strength. Amazing. She smiled, intrigued but unconcerned.

Rán spun, slippery as a fish, in the human's muscular arms.

She met him eye to eye, their noses practically touching. His skin was dark, his eyes brown. They went wide at first, then something happened – they changed and his expression did too, his grip loosening.

Rán stared, and when his eyes changed, her smile slipped. What was this… this feeling? Suddenly she no longer felt his Sentheye; instead, she felt herself pressed into him.

Without conscious thought, Rán pressed her lips to his, her own eyes going wide, then closing. Her mind reeled. Her chest fluttered. What was happening? Was this magic? No. No! This was something else. She pulled her lips away from his and sneered.

Paul's forehead creased, and he let go of her.

She grabbed him and pressed into him again, kissing him harder this time.

Now the human tried to pull away, glancing up. He needed air. She could hold him – kill him here and now.

Rán let go.

The human swam up for air.

Spinning back, she realized the other one, Pete, was gone. He must have swum up while she was… What? She wondered at herself as she, too, swam upward.

Carefully, she broke the surface just downstream from

where the two humans stood. The boy, Pete, handed Paul a small piece of Ice Ember and dove back in.

Paul waded back in, but he didn't dive. Instead, he scanned the water – searching for her.

She lifted herself out of the water up to her shoulders. "Looking for me?"

The man spun, raising his fists. "You're a mermaid."

"Am I?" she asked, drawing closer.

"I've heard stories of you back on Earth. How you draw sailors in with your beauty and then drown them. Is that what you were going to do with me?"

"Maybe," she answered honestly.

"But you let me go. Why?"

She didn't know. "You ask too many questions. My turn."

"Okay," Paul said.

"Why did you look at me the way you did? Why did you kiss me?"

"I don't know. I… I felt something."

Rán smiled, but she didn't know why.

"What's your name?" Paul asked.

"Rán," she answered, sure that wouldn't mean anything to him.

"You're a mermaid then?"

"I'm much more than that, Paul."

Surprised, he asked, "How do you know who I am?"

"I know more than you can imagine."

The human, Paul, looked down into the water. "He's coming back up. You're not going to hurt him, are you?"

She was going to kill him, actually. But now she just wanted to feel that feeling in her chest again – that flutter. What she really wanted was another kiss from this human, Paul. "Perhaps. Perhaps not. That depends on you."

"On me?" he asked.

"Do not speak of me. Stay in the water until he dives

back down, and I will let him live," she said, vanishing into shadow below the water.

Once again, Pete surfaced. "It's hard swimming that deep, but I'm getting some," he said, handing a tiny piece of Ice Ember to Paul. Grabbing a breath, he dove back under.

Rán broke the surface. "Kiss me above the water like you did below," she commanded.

Paul frowned, bent at the waist, and placed his hands beneath the water, gripping her waist tightly.

She gasped in sharply at his touch, but she didn't resist. He lifted her out of the water up to her hips and kissed her again. This time, it was even better than before. Then, their tongues tangled, and he sank into the water with her up to his neck.

Finally, he pulled away. "What do you want?"

"You," she answered before she could stop herself. "I don't know why or what this is, but I know I want you."

Pete's voice filled her mind. *I'm coming back up! Man, I can only find tiny ones, but I don't think I could lift them if they were much bigger, anyway,* the boy said telepathically.

Keep looking, Paul said, not letting go of Rán.

Interesting. They possessed the ability to touch the Sentheye, and they could use telepathy. This would be rare in one human, but both? *What other secrets are you keeping, Turek?*

They both looked as Pete approached the surface again.

Despite the increasing flutter in her chest, Rán pushed away and vanished beneath the surface.

As she held herself under the water, she remembered something Turek had said. "Each of you should have the experience of living at least one lifetime as your creation. I lived many. I experienced both life and death as a human many times."

She reappeared for a third time, realizing she didn't want

to leave this man. "I am going to leave you now, but I need you to promise me something, Paul Moore."

Paul nodded.

"Promise me you'll find your way to water again soon?" She smiled.

He smiled back. "I will. I... I promise."

Her smiled stretched her face almost painfully. She didn't remember ever feeling so excited – so alive.

"He's coming back, and this time he's empty-handed," she said. Then pointing, she said, "Have him dig beneath where you stand. Under your right foot. It's my gift to you, Paul Moore." She kissed him softly and quickly. "Find me in the water," she said, then she splashed away, allowing her tail to slap the water. She heard him yell after her, promising to find her.

Pete broke the surface, speaking telepathically as he gasped for air. Rán faded to a shadow, listening. *I got nothing that time, and I don't think I can swim anymore today. Do you think those two little pieces will be enough for an offering?*

I... I don't know.

Hey. You, okay? It sounded like you were splashing around when I was coming back up.

I'm... I'm fine, Paul said, nodding toward the water. *Do you see that, Pete?*

See what?

Right below my foot. I thought I saw something shining.

What? Seriously? Pete asked.

The boy was right to be shocked. The water was only waist deep where Paul was standing. Ice Ember wouldn't occur there naturally.

Pete sucked in a breath and dove, cupping his hands as he dragged them over the pebbled bottom. Almost immediately, a bright orange glow emitted from the riverbed.

Brighter than any they would find, even in the deepest parts of the river.

Pete burst upward, pulling air. *Paul! Jesus, bro! It's huge! The size of a baseball, maybe a softball. You got to help me lift it!*

Paul smiled, and from beneath the surface, she saw him searching the water for her. She felt herself smile too and then she... she blushed?

Okay, kid. Let's get you that offering.

In the moment, Rán realized something else. Ice Ember Orange was her new favorite color in all the universe, and she knew it would forever remind her of her first kiss.

28

A Promise Kept

God Stones – Moon Ring 2
The Mountain of Thrones

Jack opened his eyes to a room that seemed to spin. The buzz in his head was gone. But the pain... Jesus, the pain. It felt like someone had ripped half his head off. He reached up to touch his head when he heard Cerb.

Don't. Just lie still, brother. Everything is fine. You're fine, Cerb said.

Jack hitched a sharp breath. The pain from Cerb's telepathy was almost too much to bear. He needed to gather himself. What the hell had happened? He lay still, trying desperately to remember. After a moment, he opened his eyes again. The room slowed, coming into focus. The high ceilings, cold stone, and sudden smell of blood told him he was still in the throne room. He tried to push himself up onto his elbows so he could see what had happened after. Yes, that's right... he'd killed her. He'd killed the fake queen.

Jack's arms tingled, and when he tried to move them to push himself up, he couldn't muster the strength. "Cerb," he groaned. "What happened? And please… speak out loud, my head's killing me."

"You did well, Taker. And then I kept my word to you."

"What? What does that mean, you kept your word?" Jack asked.

"I took the crown from your head."

Instant panic surged in Jack's chest. His heart thudded as a boost of adrenaline kicked in. Raising his arms, he touched his scalp and forehead with his fingers, wincing at the sudden sting of touching an open wound. Despite the pain, he forced his fingers to feel around. Even though he'd lost most of the sensation in his fingertips days ago, he could tell hair was missing in large patches and he was sure the bone was exposed. "What have you done? Where is the Sound Eye?" He pushed himself fully into a sitting position. Again, the room spun as he fought to stay upright until it passed.

"I kept my promise to you and because of this, we are alive. You are alive."

"And the crown?" Jack asked, trying not to puke.

"Disassembled back into the God Stones."

"Disassembled? And who has them, Cerberus?"

Hesitantly, Cerberus said, "The Queen of Queens."

But Jack had killed… "Wait. You gave them to… to Zerri?"

"I did. She is our Queen of Queens, Jack."

"You idiot! You… my own brother! You betrayed me to Zerri!" Jack tried to stand but fell back onto his ass.

"She is our queen, Jack. This is the way it should be. And besides, if I didn't take them from you, they would have killed you! That means they would have killed us. I'm sorry, but this is the way of the dragon. The Queen of Queens should hold the power of the God Stone."

"Don't you talk to me about the way of a dragon! I used Sentheye to make you!"

"No, Jack. You enhanced me with Sentheye. You did not make me. Azazel made me, and she made us brothers. She made you dragon. Zerri is her daughter, and we owe it to our Queen of Queens to help her."

"What the hell is wrong with you? Where is all this coming from?"

"The path, Jack... The path we were on could only lead to death and ruin for all dragonkind."

A long silence stretched out between them before Jack finally said, "That's not what I wanted, Cerb. I just wanted us to have it all. I wanted us to make them all pay."

"You think that because you don't have the Sound Eye, we can't have it all? Look at everything we did before."

Jack furrowed his brow, and pain raked across his raw scalp. He winced. "What are you talking about?"

"We defeated an army of trees to make way for the nephilbock army! You slew an ancient kraken! We punched a hole through a damn mist storm! We are legends!" Cerb's laugh rumbled through Jack, causing him more pain and making him smile at the same time.

"I had the Sound Eye for that last one."

"Yes. But I know in my heart, brother, you didn't need it."

Maybe Cerb was smarter than Jack gave him credit for. "So now what, Cerb?"

"Now? Now we do everything we planned. We join the nephilbock as you promised. We defeat the elves and burn the city to the ground once and for all time. Then we have our vengeance on Garrett, and our Queen of Queens gets her vengeance on Gabi."

"And where is Zerri?" Jack asked.

"She's briefing her queens on what's happened and the plan going forward. I brought you to this side of the chamber so we could sort this alone."

"In case I didn't understand?" Jack asked.

Cerb nodded.

"And Ahi?"

"He is alive. They have a dungeon here. It's deep in the bowels of the mountain. A dungeon is like a prison. It's—"

"I know what a dungeon is, Cerb."

"You were right about him being a traitor."

"Of course I was. But the final clues were even more obvious. Like having our army wait atop the mountain. There was plenty of room to bring hundreds of dragons in here with us," Jack said, glancing around the vast space.

"Hmm, yes – very smart, brother."

Jack smiled and winced at the pain of it. "The next clue wasn't Ahi's, it was Annas's. She said Azazel and Apep were dead. Well, none of us told her. Even if she had been watching us since we arrived, only someone on Earth could have known, and the only person here from Earth who knew Annas from before was Ahi. I figure that snake must have warned her before we got here. Probably as soon as we were within telepathic range."

"You are quite wise, Taker."

Jack paused in thought.

"What is it?"

"What happens after this is over, Cerb? What then?" Jack asked, having never really given much thought to it. And if he had thought of it, he hadn't ever asked Cerb what he wanted after Garrett was dead.

"Then we've a whole new world to explore. This is our home, Taker. We will spend our days exploring, hunting, and defending the Mountains of Twelve. We'll terrorize the species of this world, filling our bellies with them! We'll live wild lives and die legends!" Cerberus laughed again. "Every species on this planet will know who we are, and even the gods will write songs."

Jack forced a smile, but inside he still felt an emptiness – a void he didn't understand. "That sounds good, Cerb. That's sounds real good. But... I can't stand up and I feel like I might pass out."

"Right! You need to heal." Cerb swung one of his enormous heads around behind Jack.

A woman's voice cried out.

Jack tried to turn and look behind him, but the pain was too great.

Nyana staggered into view, nudged by Cerb's big head. The woman collapsed onto her hands and knees next to Jack.

Drool spilled from Cerb's mouths and pooled onto the stone floor. His voice entered Jack's mind in a whisper. *You remember, after you killed the kraken? You were in terrible shape, but I made sure you had two human women there when you woke. Just like back in the village, Taker. Use this dökkálfar woman's life and heal yourself before you lose too much blood or your fingers fall off.*

Tears spilled down Nyana's cheeks as she looked at Jack with horror. Did she know what he was about to do, or was the sight of his missing scalp that revolting?

Jack reached for the Sentheye. Not the Sentheye inside the God Stones, but the Sentheye within all living things. The old way. The way he'd used before he'd taken the Sound Eye from the top of the pyramid back on Earth.

Jack thought of disease, pushing it out as he pulled for life.

29

A Sister's Secret

God Stones – Moon Ring 3
The Creators' Mountain, Karelia

In the Great Hall of Creators' Mountain, Turek watched as Rán reappeared, seated in the circle of her brethren of light. He smiled. "Well, it seems you made little more progress with Jack than Typhon did."

"Your human is a monster," Rán answered, but there was little anger in her voice. In fact, Turek quickly noticed there was something different about his sister. Had Jack shaken her? No – it wasn't fear, it was something else.

"Well, you're just in time to hear news most dreadful," Turek said.

"News? What news?" Rán asked.

"Is it true, Eresh?" Turek asked, a knot forming in his stomach. He'd wanted to wait for them all to be together before he confronted them. It would be easier to see who really knew of this atrocity if he could see the way the light danced in their faces.

"Is what true?" Ereshkigal asked.

"What? Don't sit there and act like you didn't hear what my humans said. Is it true Metsavana is dying?" Turek demanded.

"I think she exaggerated," Ereshkigal answered, crossing her arms.

"It took all of us to create Metsavana, and because of the tree, Karelia flourishes."

"If the tree dies, we will make another," Eresh said.

"Eresh, you can't mean that! What has happened to you? All of our creation came after we created Metsavana. If we allow him to die, we allow the world to die! That's how we designed it! Are you saying we start over? From scratch? I thought this was the very concern you hoped to avoid?"

Druesha cleared her throat, which was odd, for as a being of Sentheye, she didn't need to clear her throat. Obviously, she wanted the floor. "It started after you left, when Eresh locked all of our favorites out of the city. The father tree is no longer receiving enough Ice Ember in offerings to maintain his life and, as such, he is dying. The limited offerings from the elves and the small offerings from your humans to the Shadow Forest haven't been enough to stay the retreat of the great Metsavana's roots. They are withering. The only way to stop this is to remove the wall and allow the city to be open to all for all to make offerings. But Ereshkigal won't do that. She wants only her favorites, the dökkálfar, to receive the favor of Metsavana."

Ereshkigal huffed, but she didn't deny it.

"Soon enough, it won't matter. My dragons have the God Stones," Typhon said.

Rán laughed. "If you think that little monster or his Earthen dragons care about a tree, you're a fool, Typhon."

Eresh pointed a glowing finger of light at Turek. "You wanted this! You set us on this course!"

"This is, after all, your game," Aurgelmir added.

The Last Gift

Eresh shook her finger like an angry parent. "Now spin the knife, brother! Your human monster has awoken and is about to devour my dökkálfar! Spin the knife and let it land on me so I may end this creature properly."

"Yes, spin the knife. Let it land on me, and I will ensure the tree remains intact when my dragons overthrow the city," Typhon said.

"Your dragons? Your Queen of Queens is dead, and this Earth-born has already denied you once, Typhon," Druesha warned. "Spin the knife, Turek. The secret agreement between the Shadow Forest and humans has been keeping Metsavana alive this long. When the knife points at me, I will set the Roaming Forest of the Southland on a course to Osonian and ensure the wall falls and the father tree is saved."

"You'll do no such thing! My dökkálfar yield to no one! Osonian is mine!"

Turek straightened, his lip curling. The last time he was this disgusted with Eresh, she'd broken his heart and killed an infant for no other reason than having been born. He tossed the dagger into the circle. The blade and wooden handle clanged against the polished gemstone floor, silencing the bickering and pulling everyone's attention to the knife. "Since Rán won the last round, I think it is fitting that she spin the dagger," Turek said.

Rán's glow brightened as she sat with legs crisscrossed, knees bouncing. "Oh, yes. Let me!"

Turek frowned, skeptical of her odd… enthusiasm. "Sister, before you spin, tell us, what were you doing with your time on Karelia?"

Rán gave him a cutting glance. "Now, brother, you all saw me. I tried to talk to that dreadful Jack – to get a read on him, but he's rotten to the core. I even offered the hateful little monster Karelia's water-born armies, and then he had the audacity to threaten to kill me. Not just me, but all of us. Starting with the next one who tries to form an alliance with him. Oh, why do you force me to think of this ghastly creation of yours? He has no mind for reason, Turek. I'm still unconvinced our best course wouldn't be to kill him outright and be done with this mess." She stared down at the end of her fingers as if assessing her fingernails. Except she didn't have fingernails – not in the form of light.

Turek and the others stared in silence.

"What?" Rán asked, looking up.

"The situation has changed, sister. As you heard, Jack no longer has the Sound Eye, but also the Sound Eye is no more," Druesha said.

"No more? But that's impossible. Even now, I feel its power out there in the world."

"No more, meaning the dragons have disassembled it back into the God Stones," Ereshkigal explained. "Great Mother, Druesha, you are so dramatic."

Turek waved Eresh off. "We know you were with Jack, Rán, but what else were you doing with your time away?"

"Yes, sister, we lost you after your encounter with the abomination," Typhon said.

Durin nodded. "Yes, and we didn't see you make a play at Garrett or Breanne. You didn't go to Osonian, and you left Jack alone after the incident in the water. So, where were you?"

"Well, good to know you were paying attention. He's losing his mind, you know? Can you believe he threatened to kill me? Threatened to kill us all. And did you see the little weasel kill hundreds of my beautiful fish?" Rán asked.

"We saw, and then you vanished. Now stop stalling. Where were you?" Durin asked.

"After that disappointing encounter, I thought it best to

leave mortal affairs alone. So I spent the rest of my time swimming with my creations."

"No. I think not," Aurgelmir said.

"Excuse me?"

"You weren't swimming with your creatures. I saw you, Rán."

"Well?" Typhon demanded. "Where was she?"

"You were all following the wrong creatures. But not I. I paid attention, setting my gaze in the right direction."

"The right direction? What is that supposed to mean, Aurgy?" Turek asked, just as confused as his brethren.

"It matters not. Look at him. He will not tell us," Druesha said.

Turek looked from Aurgy to Rán, whose eyes begged her brother not to tell what he'd seen. And he could see it clearly. Druesha was right. Aurgy wasn't going to.

"Well," Turek said, "there are no rules compelling him to tell us anything. It was her moon ring to do with as she pleased. Now let's move on."

Durin eyed his sister. "Whatever you were doing will come to light, dear sister."

"You seem so sure of yourself, little Durin," Rán sneered.

"All things done in the dark eventually come to the light. I may not have witnessed your meddling, but I saw where you went after your encounter with Jack. Oh, it took me some time to pinpoint you, but eventually I felt you there, splashing around in my domain."

"The water is not your domain, Durin!"

"No, but the Cragarmour Mountains most certainly are. That's right, I know exactly where you were. You should pray to the Great Mother the knife tip does not fall to me, dear sister," Durin said.

Rán looked down nervously at the blade and gave it a flick.

With the blade set spinning, Turek concentrated, ensuring no one interfered. As the blade scraped lightly against the jeweled floor, he found no foul play. The blade slowed, and it appeared as though Ereshkigal would get her wish, but as the blade came to a stop, Turek watched curiously as Rán's face fell.

The tip of the dagger nudged forward to point decidedly at Durin.

30

The Dark Narrow

God Stones – Moon Ring 3
The Shadow Forest

Garrett woke before Breanne. He'd been awake for some time, lying there on a pallet of furs, the coolness of the cave floor still finding its way through the insulated layers. He wasn't cold though, not with Breanne's body snuggled against his, radiating warmth. But as cozy as he was, he couldn't go back to sleep. All he could do was lie there in the dark thinking about Pete and Paul. Well, unless he was thinking about his mom, James, and the way Pando's soldier had encased Ed in that wooden chest.

Desperate for sleep, he closed his eyes and counted backward from a hundred. *One hundred, ninety-nine, ninety-eight...*

By the time he and the others had arrived at the caves, they were all dead on their feet, especially David. The day's hike had been mostly uphill. Fortunately, the men were quick to prepare food and prep pallets for sleeping. Key and Tell had called a meeting to bring the men up to speed, introducing them officially to their new queen – Queen Breezemore. Garrett still didn't know what had driven Turek to whisper Breanne's name, but it was fine with him. These women would never have followed him, anyway. Maybe that's why old Turek whispered her name – he must have known if they'd walked in there with Garrett in charge, they'd have been doomed.

But all that didn't change their true mission. He had to find a way to keep the trees of Earth unbound, and he had to find a way back. Right now, their biggest lead was this wish-granting Metsavana tree. Could the tree help them? He wasn't sure, but Key had said you had to go to the tree itself. And the tree was locked behind an enormous wall guarded by an army of dökkálfar and enslaved dragons. To make matters worse, if they didn't get back there soon, Jack might ruin everything.

He needed to stop worrying about things he couldn't control. *Okay, Garrett, stop thinking and just close your eyes and count. Seventy-three, seventy-two, seventy—*

A memory Garret wished he could forget invaded his mind with sudden unwanted clarity. Danny's visage filled the darkness. The older boy had a look of terror on his face as Garrett launched him out of the tunnel and into the raging Sangamon River.

Fifty-eight, fifty-seven, fifty-six... Ugh! This was pointless. He needed to get up. Carefully, he lifted Breanne's arm from around his waist and eased himself sideways.

Breanne let out a quiet moan and lifted her head, squinting up at him. "Garrett? Where are you going?"

"It's okay, Bre, go back to sleep."

She rolled onto her back, and Garrett covered her in a fur blanket. Carefully, he crossed the cave and went outside.

"Gabi? What are you doing up already?" Garrett asked.

"Same as you, I suppose. I couldn't sleep either," the girl said, sitting with her knees drawn up, staring up at the sky. "The sky is so different here... so foreign. On Earth, no matter what part of the world you were in, at least you would always find comfort in the sky."

"Gabi, are you okay?"

"No, not really. I miss my mamá y papá. I miss Fredy and Manuel. I miss María and Sarah, and you know what else?" The girl's voice was choked with emotion. "I miss Zerri."

"The dragon?" Garrett asked, sitting down next to the girl.

"Sí, I miss her so much. I felt like she understood me, but more. I felt like we shared something. And I betrayed her."

"You did what you had to do to survive," Garrett said, putting an arm around the girl's shoulders. "If she really ever cared about you, she would forgive you."

"She won't. Not for this. I couldn't if I were her," the girl said, putting her head on his shoulder.

Garrett nodded. "Well, maybe you're right. Maybe she will never forgive you. Maybe she would kill you if she could."

"Hey," Gabi said, lifting her head. "I thought you were trying to make me feel better."

Garrett smiled. "I'm not going to tell you what you want to hear, Gabi. I hate it when grown-ups do that, so I'm sure not going to, but I will tell you this. You have a group of friends who love you – who already know how special you are. Don't shut them out, okay? Especially Bre. She's more worried about you than anyone on this entire planet."

Gabi pressed her lips tight and nodded. "If not for Bre, I wouldn't... I wouldn't have anything. She saved me. She is like the big sister I never had. Garrett, if not for her… I would be lost." She leaned her head back on his shoulder.

"I feel the same way. Hey, have you tried to talk to her?"

"Breanne?"

"No. Sorry. I meant Zerri."

She hesitated then said, "I haven't stopped trying, but I can't reach her. I can't even reach Paul and Pete."

"You tried them?" Garrett asked, failing to hide his excitement.

"Of course. I wanted to see if Pete found any Ice Ember for his offering."

"Dang! I've been trying too, but if you can't reach them in mind speak, no one can." He glanced down at the girl's face and caught a hint of a smile. "Hey, I can't tell for sure, but I think the suns are about to come up… come forward… or turn on." Garrett shook his head. "However it works, I think it will get light soon."

Gabi laughed. "I'm not sure how it works either, but I think you're right."

"Will you do something for me, Gabi?"

She nodded.

"Keep trying to reach your dragon friend. Don't give upon her just yet. But in between, can you please keep trying Pete and Paul? I'm worried about those guys, and if anyone can reach them, it's you, Gabi."

Gabi's whole face seemed to stretch into a smile. "Yes. I promise, I'll keep trying."

∼

Two hours later, Karelia's two suns were just pulling apart, ready to begin their lazy journey across a sky of deep blue. Garrett didn't think he'd ever seen a sky so blue on Earth. In fact, he was sure he hadn't. On the descent down the mountain, the men and children stayed in the center of the group. The men carried all the supplies while the women guarded them from both the rear and the front. Breanne and Gabi walked together with Key and Tell at the head of the procession. This didn't bother Garrett as much as it seemed to bother David.

I don't see why we can't walk up front. I'm short, ya know. I can't even see anything, having to walk in the middle like this, David complained in mind speak.

I can lift you up by that face lace of yours, Lenny offered.

David mumbled something, and the back-and-forth bickering began. Garrett didn't mind it, though. The squabbling pair actually comforted him. This was one of the few things here that reminded him of home, of Petersburg. Lenny reached over and pinched David's long mustache horn, giving it a quick tug. The smaller boy yelped, causing spears to rise and the women to frown. The boys laughed while the women stared at them disapprovingly, which only made them all laugh a little harder.

Secretly, Garrett wished he could walk up front with Breanne and hold her hand. But at least they could still talk with their minds, and as the morning transitioned into midday, they chatted on and off. It was during one of these chats when Gabi broke into their conversation, her voice urgent and worried.

María Purísima, I reached Pete! They are in trouble!

Trouble? What trouble? Garrett asked, pulling to a stop.

Breanne and the others stopped too, causing the whole procession to stop.

They are running from something! Something is chasing them!

Where are they? Lenny asked.

They haven't made it to the Dark Narrow yet, Gabi said

as Garrett pushed his way to the front of the group, followed by Lenny and David.

"What is happening?" Key asked.

"Paul and Pete are being chased toward the Dark Narrow!" Breanne announced.

"Chased? What would chase them there?" Tell asked, looking at her mother.

"Dökkálfar?" Key asked, looking at Breanne.

"Gabi, who is chasing them?" Breanne asked aloud.

Gabi looked up at the others. "They said dwarves – dwarves are chasing them! They are calling for help!"

Garrett exchanged a look with Lenny, and they were off. Running to beat hell down the trail. Behind them, David shouted, "I'm coming! I'm right behind you!"

Garrett glanced back to see David and the others running. *Just get there as quick as you can. We're going!* Garrett shouted back.

"Where are your men going?" Tell shouted.

He heard Breanne shout, "My men are fast! They will get there quicker!"

Be careful, you guys. But hurry, Breanne urged in mind speak.

"I will join you," came a voice from just over Garrett's shoulder. "You will probably need a strong and fast woman to protect you."

Garrett stole a glance back to find Tell had crossed the growing gap between them and the others and was matching pace.

"Well, let's see what you got, Tell," Lenny said, leaning forward into his stride.

The descent was rocky and required Garrett to pay special attention to his foot placement as he shortened his stride and picked his way down the mountain at breakneck speed. As the descent stretched on, Garrett picked up his pace, pushing with all he had. Soon, Lenny and Tell were behind him, struggling to stay on pace.

Finally Tell shouted, "You still have an hour or more ahead of you, but if you somehow stay at this pace, simply look for the Dark Narrow on your right side. Wait for us there!"

Panic propelling him, Garrett pushed on, dropping the pair.

They weren't too far behind, but even so, this was the first time he had been alone since coming to this world. Back home, he'd run alone in the woods daily, but this was another world. He felt his body fall into the familiar rhythm of the run. The grade was still steep, and he was bombing it, on the edge of being out of control. This was the zone, the one place where he could reach focus in its purest form. When Garrett tapped into the Sentheye, this was where he went in his mind. And as his focus dialed in, Garrett ran faster still, faster than he had ever thought possible. For the moment, time was lost, and he was lost within it. There was only the cool Karelian air, the blur of his mountain descent, and the rhythm of his own heartbeat, steadily thumping away.

Familiar voices invaded Garrett's mind mid-sentence.

...can't leave it, Pete said.

They're gaining, but if we can make the Narrow, maybe we can lose them, Paul said.

Can you hear me? Garrett asked.

Garrett! Pete shouted.

On Garrett's right, a dark gap in the cliff face opened to a descending passage. The Dark Narrow.

Garrett, we're almost to the Dark Narrow, but six dwarves are chasing us, and one is... I don't know, a wizard or something!

A wizard? Garrett repeated.

We might make the gap, but if we can't figure some-

thing out, they'll catch us once we get inside! Paul's voice cut in. He sounded distressed. *Garrett, are you close? We may have to ditch the Ice Ember. It's so heavy I can't run with it.*

Can't run with it? How much had they found that Paul couldn't run with it? *I'm close. Entering the Dark Narrow now...* Garrett looked back up the mountain he'd just descended and saw no sign of Lenny or Tell. He was supposed to wait for them. *I'll be with you in a minute.*

In a minute? It took us a couple hours to get through the narrow! Are you alone? Paul asked.

Yes, but the others aren't far behind. They couldn't be, could they? But then again, if Paul and Pete were over two hours away... Damn, he thought. How fast had he been running?

Lenny, if you can hear me, Pete and Paul are in trouble. I can't wait.

Lenny's voice came back to him. *We're running as fast as we can. Sit tight. Don't you go in there. You promised me you wouldn't do this again!*

I know, that's why I'm telling you. I can't wait. I'm going in.

Dammit, Garrett!

It's Pete and Paul in there! Would you wait?

There was a three-second pause, but it felt like three hours. Finally, Lenny said, *No. I wouldn't! Go. Just be careful.*

And you just hurry, Garrett answered, stepping down into the crevice.

The Dark Narrow was just that, dark and narrow. He could barely see his hand in front of his face. The cliffs climbed so high that almost no light reached the bottom. This was not a safe place to run – but he had no choice and ran anyway, hands pressed out in front of him.

Paul's voice came to him now. *Why didn't the others come with you?* he asked, obviously unable to hear Lenny.

They'll be here soon, Paul.

He dropped them, Pete said accusingly. *They couldn't keep up with you, and you dropped them, didn't you?*

They will be here. For now, you have me.

Yep, he dropped them, Pete said. *Well, get your butt down here. The guy with the hammer is yelling stuff at us!*

Did you say hammer? Are you in the Narrow? Garrett asked.

We're in, but they're right behind us! And yes! One is waving a hammer!

Garrett found his eyes adjusting enough that he could see the shape of the ground, and so he leaned in, pushing the descent. Minutes passed in a blur as stone and shadow whizzed by. Twice he tripped but recovered before face-planting. More than a half dozen times, his shoulders raked the sides as the narrow tightened. Still, he ran on recklessly. His friends needed him.

From behind him, a breeze picked up, pressing at his back. There had been no breeze before, only stagnant cool air. Despite his speed, the breeze outran him, blowing faster and harder against his back.

It's the wizard! He's pulling us back... making it almost... impossible for us to move... forward! Pete groaned in mind speak.

Get in front of me and I'll keep you from being sucked backward! Paul shouted.

For Garrett, the wind made his descent easier, carrying him faster toward Pete and Paul. *Please! Let me get there in time,* he begged.

Moments later, he rounded a thin crook in the fissure to find the Dark Narrow opened several shoulder-widths wide. Just ahead, he saw Pete leaning forward, pushing into the wind as he struggled up the steep slope leading to Garrett. Paul was behind him with both hands pressed against Pete's back.

Garrett tried to slow by planting his feet. But the wind sucked past him as if it were a tornado.

Skidding down the slope, Garrett feared he would collide with Pete. Turning into a fighting stance, he managed to get sideways and grab on to the jagged rocks, pulling himself to a stop.

The sound of the wind was deafening, forcing him to use mind speak despite being face-to-face with his friend.

Pete! Are you okay? he asked, shouting as if he were speaking aloud.

Yes! But we have to keep going. They're right behind us! Pete shouted back.

What do they want?

I don't know, but they look pissed! You want to stop to ask?

Garrett turned and began pulling himself back the way he'd come when a voice boomed through the wind tunnel as if shouted from a megaphone: "Yous can't escape a god, little humans!"

Garrett stopped and turned back toward Pete and Paul.

Why... are you... stopping? Paul grunted as he stomped forward.

He said "god," Garrett answered.

So what? Isn't that... even worse... than a wizard? Pete asked.

I want to talk to him. Figure out what the hell is going on, Garrett said.

Pete stopped next to him, his black bangs pasted back by the wind. *That's a bad idea, Garrett. We're outnumbered here, and they might take the Ice Ember!* Pete said.

You're right. Just keep going, I'll stall them!

Negative. I'm not leaving you, Paul said, struggling forward. The wind alone shouldn't have been enough to make a muscle-stacked guy like Paul, whose magical ability was strength, struggle this much.

You can't help me, Paul, not weighed down like this. Just keep going! Let me do this while you get the Ice Ember out of here!

The expression on Paul's face told Garrett he was clearly torn and struggling.

I'll be fine, Paul. I'll just try to talk to them. If it doesn't work, I'll run. Either way, you need the time!

Twenty yards back the way Paul and Pete had come, a dwarf came into view, followed by several others. The lead dwarf had a braided beard hanging midway down his chest, fire-red hair, thick eyebrows, and a wide nose. He wore a dark tunic with a sash around the waist and a sleeveless purple cloak over the top. But Garrett's eyes were drawn not to what he wore, but to what he carried. In the dwarf's right hand was a war hammer.

Strangely, the wind seemed to pull into the lead dwarf and simply end. Behind him, the others walked forward unhindered.

Paul pressed his lips into a tight line. *Just don't be stupid!* he said, and with those words of wisdom, he stomped up into the tighter crevasse.

Garrett focused on reaching for the Sentheye, grabbing it easily.

The dwarves slowed to a near stop.

However, the lead dwarf, the one Garrett presumed was claiming himself a god, marched forward without slowing. Then, of his own volition, he stopped, but only long enough to glance back at his comrades, who stood frozen in mid-stride, motionless.

The dwarf looked back to Garrett and stomped forward again, despite Garrett's concentration.

"You're Garrett Turek!" the dwarf shouted, his Rs rolling like an angry Irishman's as his voice echoed off the jagged stone walls of the Dark Narrow.

"I am," Garrett said, careful not to let his concentration slip.

The dwarf waved his empty hand with a flourish.

The wind stopped, causing Garrett to nearly fall backward. He hadn't realized how hard he'd had to lean back to keep from being pushed forward toward the angry dwarf.

"Interesting yous rocked up here from Donard Caves half past the moon ring. Sooner than ye should. Figure you must be working the Sentheye. This complicates things, I suppose," the dwarf said evenly.

"Complicates what?" Garrett asked.

"Thine own will be watching me now, aye?"

Pete's voice called out from behind him, "We don't want any trouble. Just leave us alone and we'll be on our way."

I thought I told you to go! Garrett shouted back at Pete in mind speak.

Well, Paul's the one carrying the Ember. I can run too… So, I'm staying.

The dwarf stepped up close to Garrett, an angry sneer twisting his lips and cocking his braided whiskers. One eye squinted as if he were looking into the sun, while the other eye seemed to study him. The stocky dwarf looked seriously pissed, but then Garrett wondered if this was how he always looked. Kind of like old man Buster who lived down the street back home. Ole Buster looked mad even when he was smiling.

"You're him then, are ye? The wee kin to me own brother. You don't look like much," the dwarf said. Looking back at the six other dwarves frozen in time, he added, "But then again, the Sentheye comes easy for ye. Easier than it should, to be sure."

"What do you want?" Garrett asked.

"Do you know who I am?" the dwarf asked.

"Turek's brother? You're a…"

"Go on, lad, tell me what I am."

"Well, you're not a god."

The dwarf looked surprised. "No?"

"No. Not you and not Turek. I don't know what you guys are exactly. Turek said he created humans but wasn't a god."

"Did he now?" the dwarf asked, lifting his hammer and resting it over his shoulder.

Holding the six dwarves in place had been easy at first, but now Garrett felt the beginnings of exertion as their will to press forward strained against his own will to hold them. *Pete,* he called in mind speak, hoping the dwarf couldn't hear him, *I can't hold them much longer.* He locked eyes with the dwarf and said, "Maybe you created dwarves, but you're no god, Durin."

The dwarf laughed. "Clever lad! Did me brother tell ye me name as well?"

Garrett didn't answer. Turek had not told him the names of his brothers and sisters. In fact, he hadn't even known they called themselves brothers and sisters. However, Coach's journal had stated the names of all the gods and their favorite creations. Dwarves were the favorite of Durin.

As the strain to hold became too much, the dwarves began to move as if in slow motion. *Guys! I'm slipping here.*

"Leave it be. It makes no difference what me brother told ye. Makes no difference at all. But fear me not, wee Turek," Durin said, looking toward the sky. "I'm right sure me brethren are watching us – watching this very moment. I'll play by the rules. I'll not lend aid to the six dwarven warriors about to rip ye to shreds." The stocky dwarf let out a hardy belly laugh. "You've made a right bags of it, boyo! They call this lot the mad six!"

Garrett, his hold failing, dropped to one knee.

The dwarves' shouts echoed off the walls, filling the Dark Narrow with enraged battle cries.

Garrett drew his sword, falling back into a fighting stance. *Pete, run!*

The lead dwarf swung his ax.

Garrett raised his sword, blocking the mighty blow, but the force sent him sliding back, stunned by the power of the strike.

Still laughing, Durin shouted over the melee, "Did ye think me greatest creations weak because we stand a wee two céim to your three? Oh, lad, ye be mistaken! One of me chiselers be stronger than ten of Turek's!"

Two more flanked him on both sides, blocking the rest of the crevice.

Another dwarf reared back to swing a shortened broadsword, but before the swing came, the weapon blew from his hands into the darkness behind them.

Nice, Pete! Garrett shouted, raising his own sword to block another strike from a dwarf wielding a war hammer as if it were light as a feather. The hammer, however, did not hit like a feather. The force, jarring Garrett's wrists, sent him spinning backward out of control. Amazingly, his sword didn't break.

From the shadows, Durin's laugh continued, rising unnaturally above the battle and reverberating off the walls all around them.

Garrett dodged a swing as two more dwarves crowded in, waiting for their turn to swing an ax, hammer, or mattock. The dwarf who'd lost his weapon drew a knife from his waistband. Garrett couldn't help but notice this dwarf looked younger than the others. Not much older than a kid – not much older than himself.

Garrett kicked the young dwarf in the face, but the dwarf barely flinched. *Pete, we got to run for it. I can't keep this up!*

I'm coming back! Paul answered.

No! Don't! We're coming to you! Garrett shouted, dropping low to plant one hand on the ground as he kicked a foot out to sweep the knife-wielding dwarf's feet. He executed the maneuver perfectly, but he might as well have been trying it on a tree. The dwarf didn't budge.

"Ye wee little footsies won't save ye," the young dwarf said, lunging forward with the knife.

As Garrett scrambled to stand, the ground beneath him suddenly lurched. A great groan released from the Dark Narrow. Feeling like a rug had been yanked from beneath him, Garrett lost his balance, falling back as the dwarf fell forward, knife extended.

The blade of the dwarf's knife grazed Garrett's shoulder, the familiar bite of metal slicing flesh. Garrett twisted to the side, desperate not to be smashed by the falling dwarf. Beneath him, the ground continued to quake.

As the dwarf collided headfirst with the ground, his metal helmet fell askew, loosing long red braids. Grabbing a trailing braid, Garrett yanked, pulling the dwarf's head back. At the same time, Garrett raised his sword, smashing the pommel down on the dwarf's temple.

The dwarf grunted and tried to push himself up, but Garrett struck him again.

This time, the young dwarf collapsed.

Garrett sat up to find the other dwarves were trying to get to their feet as well. Small pebbles rained down, clicking off stone. The mountain groaned as if angry, and a fist-sized stone narrowly missed Garrett's head.

Garrett, we got to go! The whole place is coming down! Pete shouted.

Other dwarfs were shouting now, scrambling backward down the steep slope the way they had come.

Garrett looked up in time to see an enormous chunk of the canyon wall break away.

31

Fistfighting Fire

God Stones – Moon Ring 3
The Mountain of Thrones

Jack could feel the healing power of disease swirling within Nyana. The answer to his relief lay in the blood, tissue, and bone of the dökkálfar girl. All Jack had to do was think of it, and it would be so. Her life would draw into his own, and the pain of his exposed skull and rotting fingers would be no more.

Take her, Jack. We've much to do, Cerb urged.

Nyana sat with her knees drawn to her chest, her body shaking, eyes bloodshot and face smeared with dirt. Tear-stained streaks ran blue trails down her cheeks, and she looked like she'd barely slept in days.

Jack couldn't remember the last time he looked at someone like he was looking at her. In fact, he couldn't remember the last time he thought about how anyone else felt, except for Danny. Yet here he was, inspecting Nyana, not as a meal to devour or as a means to end his own pain but to see if she was okay.

Cerb, for now, this one lives, he said, dropping his splayed hands, shoulders slumping.

Taker, brother, is there something you need to tell me? Cerb asked, pausing as if choosing his next words wisely. *Are you… catching feelings for this dökkálfar female?*

What? No. Of course not! But there is something you should know. The god of the elves, Ereshkigal, took possession of this one. She gave orders for her to stay close to me until she returned.

And you spoke to this god? Cerb asked.

Jack shook his head and winced at the pain. *Well, no, but before… before when we were back in Osonian I… I saw her… in the way she'd looked, but I couldn't get to her before the goddess was gone. She told the female she would return.*

Jack, this female would say anything to live. Are you certain she isn't trying to fool you with some dökkálfar trickery?

Jack looked over at the visibly shaking girl. *No, Cerb. No. She's telling the truth. I need to keep her alive, at least until this goddess returns. I see what Ereshkigal wants. Let the others know this one is under my protection.*

As you wish. But, Jack, your head is still bleeding quite badly. You must heal. Shall I have a few other dökkálfar brought down?

Not taking his eyes off of Nyana, Jack said, *No. I have a better idea. Bring me Ahi.*

Cerberus laughed. *Brilliant! I shall fetch him myself!*

While Jack sat, waiting for Cerb to return with Ahi, he could just barely hear the murmur of Zerri's voice as she spoke aloud from across the cavernous throne room. Most of what the dragon said he couldn't make out, but he caught some words: Apep, Sentheye, dragons, nephilbock, Pando, and trees. He didn't need to hear how it all fit together to understand she was briefing her queens. He wondered if she would tell the part about Gabi taking over Zerri's mind.

Absently, he stared at Nyana as she sat, arms locked around her knees. "It's okay, Nyana. I'm not going to kill you."

Her words came thick with fear. "You... you thought about it though. I saw that look in your eyes. I saw you reach for your power."

"I am... I am in bad shape here and I wasn't thinking clearly." Was he really explaining himself to her? To an elf. Jack Nightshade didn't explain himself to anyone. But he felt... he felt different. He'd thought losing the Sound Eye would drive him insane, like in that story where the little hairy foot guy, Frodo, had a magical ring and when it was gone, he had like, withdrawal or something. But Jack didn't feel that way at all. Actually, he didn't feel any craving. Now that it wasn't on his head, he realized the power wasn't really gone at all – he could still feel it.

"Your head looks bad. Very bad," Nyana said.

He wanted to snap back, "Tell me something I don't know," but he held his tongue. "It will be okay. Help is on the way," he said. Then, sitting up a little straighter, he added, "Have you heard any more from your god while all this was happening?"

"No. But I'm sure you'll be the first to know when I do."

He wondered if that was supposed to be a threat. He smiled. "Good."

"Good?" she asked.

"Good," he said, smiling even wider. The gesture hurt his face, and he could feel the dried blood over his lips and cheeks cracking.

Nyana seemed to relax a little, and Jack even thought he might have glimpsed a smile.

Falling forward, Jack caught himself with one hand as a

sudden and intense wave of nausea passed through his middle. Swallowing dryly, he fought back the urge to puke.

The elf girl shuffled cautiously over to him, placing a hand on his back. "Are you alright?"

Jack looked up at the girl, her strange, swooping brows knitted together in worry. Worry for him. "I'm fine," he said, trying to right himself.

Nyana didn't retreat. Instead, she stayed, her hand rubbing his back.

Jack let his eyes fall closed. He knew he shouldn't. Not when he was this vulnerable. Nevertheless, he did. This strange creature whose people he'd ordered attacked could kill him right now – right here while he sat dumbly exposed, eyes closed. Even knowing this, Jack kept his eyes closed, waiting to see if his neck would snap or if he'd feel the death blow to the back of his head. But after a moment, Jack relaxed into the feeling.

Nyana's hand rubbed up and down on his back ever so softly while the two sat, saying nothing. Despite the pain, Jack wanted to stay here in this moment, feeling the light caress of the dökkálfar's hand, for as long as he could.

It wasn't until Jack heard Cerberus approaching that he finally opened his eyes, the death blow having never come.

Cerb and Ahi must have caught the attention of the others; following them were twelve queens and Zerri, the Queen of Queens.

"Why have you brought Ahi back to the throne room, Cerberus? He is to stand trial and when found guilty, he will burn in the flame of a thousand suns."

Jack struggled to his feet as a combination of dizziness and pain threatened to overtake him. "Yeah… well I… I don't know about a thousand suns or whatever… but he's going to die right now instead."

Nyana backed away, fear gripping her once more.

Jack glanced back. "You will be okay, Nyana. I gave you my word and I plan to keep it."

Staggering forward, Jack reached for the Sentheye.

The other queens seemed confused, but not Zerri. Her bright white eyes cut into him, telling him, "Don't you do it," with a single sharp look. She said, "Jack, he's to stand trial! Use the dökkálfar to heal yourself. If you fancy this woman, then use the others."

Mind your own business, Zerri, and don't forget who grew you into what you are! he snapped back telepathically. Maybe Zerri didn't want the others to see how powerful he was without the Sound Eye. Didn't they know what Azazel had known? What even he had heard her say more than once, way back in Peru? The power of the God Stones belongs to all who have the ability to reach out and touch it.

"I beg of you, my lord," Ahi groveled. "Spare me! Please, I can be of use to you!"

"You pathetic weasel! Lift your eyes and breathe your fire, Ahi! Fight me like a man… er, like a dragon! I'll fistfight your fire with my bare hands, you coward!"

Ahi did not lift his eyes or breathe fire. Instead, he groveled and blubbered. "Please throw me in the dungeons of the Mountain of Thrones. Just please! Please don't!"

Jack snatched the Sentheye and poured disease into Ahi. Into the dragon's heart, his brain, bowels, and guts. He pushed in all the sick and the vile and the hate.

As Ahi's life faded away, Jack drew it all in. Power. Energy. Life. It pulled in from the dragon in a flow of wonderful strength. And like a sponge, he absorbed it into every pore.

The queens, seeing Jack's power without the Sound Eye crown for the first time, backed away.

Zerri and Cerb stood their ground, one on each side of the dying dragon, as Ahi screeched out a last plea for mercy.

"Pleeeease!" Ahi begged aloud, his death cry echoing through the chamber.

But there would be no mercy. Ahi's eyes sucked in, and his forked tongue dried up like a two-day old turd left in the sun – its pink flesh blackened, hardened, and crumbled in the dragon's mouth. The dragon's silver scales turned putrid and sloughed off his rotting muscle and onto the floor. The big dragon collapsed onto his side, his body convulsing, racked in seizures.

Finally, the silver dragon exhaled a final breath and went still.

Jack smiled up at the others, feeling better than he had since he first donned the Sound Eye. The buzz he'd thought was gone when he woke up was completely gone now. He realized only now, the white noise had still been there, just at a low hum. This new quiet in his mind felt nothing short of amazing. He looked down at his hands and smiled, surprised to find his skin was flesh-colored all the way down to the tips. Then he noticed his pinky, and his smile suddenly faltered as he realized there was something odd. Part of a pinky was missing. It had probably rotted and fallen off, but the weird part was... something else had grown in its place. It looked like a dragon pinky with a curved talon on the end. Okay, so what? At least it no longer hurt. The way he figured it, no one really needed their pinkies, anyway.

"Jack, your head!" Cerb said.

"What?" He reached up, expecting to find all his hair missing. But his hair wasn't gone... it was... different. Thicker and longer. He pinched some locks between his fingers and pulled them around in front of his face. They were shiny as silk and black as night but otherwise normal. Then his fingers brushed the hairline of his forehead, and he froze. Where his scalp had been torn away were... "Cerb! Are those scales?"

"They are beautiful, Taker. Blood red in color."

"They match your eyes," Zerri said.

A frightening thought passed through Jack. Each time he suffered an injury, would the damage be replaced with dragon parts? Was he eventually going to turn into a freaking dragon?

"How are you feeling now, Jack?" Zerri asked.

Jack glanced at the gooey shell that had been Ahi. "I've never felt better."

Zerri followed his gaze. "We have laws here, Jack. Ahi would have died a horrible death despite your interference. I will forgive this action as you were severely injured and not thinking clearly. Now, you need to eat and rest," she said, and then turned her attention to her queens. "Queens, will one of you show Jack to his quarters?"

The queen with the yellow scales tipped with orange stepped forward. "I am Queen Pimra the Golden. I will show you."

"Yeah, no. That's okay," Jack said, waving off the colorful dragon. Then, pointing at Ahi, he looked at the other queens. "So, you want me to believe you're fine with this? And you all are just all okay with the fact I killed that crotchety old hag, Anus?"

The dragons shifted, but when none spoke right away, Jack went on. "Did you tell them how I led you, Zerri? Or how I saved you, then turned you into a full-grown dragon?"

"It is my belief our alliance was, and remains, a mutual affair, Jack."

"So, we're all good then?"

"Yes. We are aligned," Zerri said, glancing to her queens. "The queens accept me for who I am and who my mother was. Surely you see the crown atop my head, yes?" Zerri said, tipping her head.

As if placed by magic, one of the seven God Stones was now embedded in the front of Zerri's crown.

"Sure, I see it and I see the shining God Stone you've mounted to it."

"The dragon's stone has been returned to its rightful place."

"And where are the other six?"

"They are safe here with us. You needn't worry. You are dragon, and you will always be dragon. Besides, their power nearly destroyed you. The one you see in my crown doesn't touch me physically. I am safe. The others will stay here where they, too, will be safe."

"No," Jack said flatly.

"No?" Zerri asked, raising a scaly brow.

"When we leave, you need to bring them. Cerb can carry them."

A jade-colored dragon lowered her sleek head. "Why would we do that?"

"Yes, will they not be safer here?" asked another, with deep ocean-blue scales.

For creatures that loved to use fancy talk, these dragons weren't all that bright. Jack locked eyes with the jade dragon. Her eyes burned like two emeralds set ablaze. "Well, for starters, we may need to draw on their power, which will be harder to do from so far away. Two, they aren't safe here at all. Not when your entire army is halfway across the planet!"

Zerri tipped her head in agreement. "It is fine, my queens. There is no one on this planet with the power to depose us en masse. When we return to Osonian, we must free every enslaved dragon – I will accept no compromise in this. Keeping the God Stones close will only enhance our already great power."

"Good, then it's settled," Jack said.

The Last Gift

"Now may we eat?" Cerb asked. "I'm told the lake has an endless supply of fish."

"Yes, I'm starving," Jack said. When it came time to ransack the city of Osonian, he'd need to remember to grab as many supplies as he could haul back here before burning the place down. He was craving bread and, as much as he hated to say it, he was longing for some vegetables – well, potatoes anyway. He wondered if they even had potatoes here.

"Excellent," Zerri said, a toothy smile spreading across her face. It was like watching a dog smile. It looked out of place. "While you have your fish, we will feast on the dökkálfar prisoners you were so wise to bring along."

32

Kilug

God Stones – Moon Ring 3
The Dark Narrow

High above Garrett, near the top of the Dark Narrow, a chunk of stone as tall as a building broke loose and tipped toward the opposite wall.

"Garrett! Move!" Pete shouted.

Tell rounded the corner. "Oh my," she gasped.

Garrett scrambled to his feet, turned, and ran forward, back up the path toward Pete.

Above, the slab of stone struck the wall of the canyon with crushing force, exploding the tip into fragments and wedging the larger piece between the two canyon walls.

Stone rained down around him, but Garrett knew he had plenty of time to get out from underneath the bigger boulders if he just hustled. Go, go, go, he told himself, scrambling forward. Pete was safe, and the falling stone would block the dwarves from getting to them.

"Kilug! Wake up, lad! Wake and move!" Durin shouted.

The Last Gift

From somewhere lower in the crevasse, other voices rang out, "Save me boy, Lord Durin! Please!"

Garrett stole a glance back over his shoulder. Durin stood over the young dwarf who had attacked Garrett with the knife. High above, the larger stone fractured with a loud pop, then another. It wasn't going to hold.

"Get up, damn ye! Before it's too late!"

The other dwarves were shouting from where they had retreated deeper down the narrow, beyond the falling stone. They were begging Durin to help. Garrett stopped, not understanding why Durin wasn't saving the young dwarf.

Ahead, Pete and now Tell stood where the canyon narrowed, motioning frantically.

Why are you stopping? Come on, Garrett! Let's go! Pete urged in mind speak.

Durin stomped his feet. "You's thick as a plank, lying there acting the maggot! Get up or be dead, you will. I'll not break my word, lad! Not while me own kin is sure to be watching!" Durin pleaded. He sounded angry at first, but as a basketball-sized chunk of stone dropped onto Kilug's shin, smashing it, Durin's anger quickly turned to sobs.

The young dwarf's eyes popped open, and he let out an anguished wail.

"Oh, if I save ye, I'll lose the game for sure! Now get up! Get up, lad!" Durin shouted, choking out another sob.

But the young dwarf's pain must have been blinding because he didn't move.

"Oh, lad, I'm sorry for ye, but I'll not lose the game!"

He's not going to save him, Pete! Garrett shouted, turning and bolting back down the slope.

Garrett, what in the hell are you talking about? Pete called.

"Why is he turning back?" Tell shouted.

But it was too late. Garrett had made up his mind. He was going.

Above, the large wedge of stone gave way, breaking apart as it crashed against the walls. Smaller chunks of stone rained down, a prelude to the massive boulders still to come.

Sliding like he was crossing home plate, Garrett collided with the young dwarf, then rolled atop him, back to chest. He extended his hands toward the sky as if to catch the massive stone slabs about to crush them flat.

Giant stone chunks plummeted downward. In the fragment of a second before Garrett was to be crushed, he reached for the Sentheye. The last thought flashing through his mind was, *This is the dumbest thing I've ever done, and I've done some pretty dumb shit!* Then as the smell of spring's wet foliage filled his nostrils, all conscious thought faded away. Seasons passed in an instant. The heat of summer's sun warmed his face. Fall leaves rustled in his ears. A snow-covered trail cooled his toes. Absolute focus pulled it all together as Sentheye filled his mind.

Above Garrett, everything slowed.

"Now, what be this?" Durin asked, kneeling down beside Garrett as he peered up.

In the distance Garrett heard rocks falling, and below him the ground shook. But above him – above him he held time and everything within it, including the stone boulders, some bigger than a car, bigger than a house.

Below him, the young dwarf spoke. "Ye got to be codding me."

"Um, Kilug, right?" Garrett asked with effort.

"I be... him," the dwarf said, his voice strained.

Below him, the ground went quiet.

"Well, listen, don't kill me, okay? If you do, all the rocks floating above us are going to fall and you'll be dead too."

"Aye, I hear ye," the dwarf grunted.

"I'm going to slide off of you. Can you move?"

"Something is wrong with me leg, but I'll manage," Kilug said.

Pete! Can you and Tell get over here, please?

Garrett closed his eyes, holding the focus as he slid carefully onto the ground.

Up the Narrow, Garrett heard Pete scrambling over rocks and opened his eyes. When Pete came into Garrett's peripheral vision, Pete exclaimed, "Uh, holy shit, Garrett! How are you…"

"Just help me get him out," Garrett said, grunting with effort.

Going back to mind speak, Pete said, *Um, Garrett. That angry-looking dwarf guy with the hammer is staring at me.*

Yeah, I don't think he can do anything, Pete. Listen, I can feel the stone straining my will. Help Kilug, okay?

"Kilug, right?" Pete said, squatting down. Pete cautiously pushed a floating stone the size of a beach ball. The pressure changed the stone's trajectory. It appeared to float away until it reached the edge of Garrett's focus, then dropped heavily to the floor. *Woah!* Pete's eyes widened as he shared a look with an equally shocked Tell.

Garrett couldn't think about the impossibility of what he was doing. He couldn't think about anything. He had to stay focused.

Together, Tell and Pete pushed several more floating stones out of the way as Kilug crawled forward, dragging his badly broken leg. Finally, taking the dwarf's hand, Pete and Tell pulled him clear.

Okay, now what?

Garrett hurriedly scrambled back, trying to maintain his focus, as one massive stone fell, then another, and another. Finally, as Garrett cleared the edge of the floating stone field, he lost the focus altogether. Slabs of stone crashed to the ground in a deafening avalanche of rubble, sealing the canyon and separating Garrett and the others from the rest of the dwarves.

"Jesus, Garrett, can you imagine how much weight you were holding?" Pete said, speaking aloud for Tell's benefit.

Garrett shook his head, still struggling to understand it himself. "No... I... I..."

Guys, what's happening? Paul asked in mind speak.

We're fine, Paul, Garrett answered, brushing himself off as he stood and stared at Durin.

Kilug couldn't stand. His head was bleeding but worse, his leg was badly busted. Maybe even crushed. Garrett figured bone must have come through his flesh because his fur boot was soaked with blood.

Finding his voice, Kilug looked at Durin. "Me lord and maker, forgive me for failing ye."

Durin smiled at the young dwarf. "Yous are safe now, lad." Turning to Garrett, the dwarf approached, leaned in, and whispered so only he could hear, "What is it in you that made you save a life that tried to take yours? To risk yourself for this creature even though it meant you might die as well?"

Garrett frowned. The dwarf no longer sounded like... well, like a dwarf. His accent was gone, and so were the strange slang words he'd used. "I don't know."

Durin tipped his head to the sky. "Turek, is the Great Mother truly at work here?"

Garrett looked up, almost expecting to see Turek descending from the sky, but there was nothing, only dust-filled air. And what did he mean, "great mother"? Then he remembered the dream where Turek had said the great mother was the one who created Turek. Why was this Durin asking Turek? He looked back down at the dwarf. "Can't you help Kilug? Can't you heal him?" Garrett asked.

"So strange, this creature of yours," the dwarf said, still

talking to Turek as if he were standing right there. "He worries for one he doesn't even know. And his use of the Sentheye... incredible."

"Hey. Mr.... um... Durin, right? Hey, do you even hear me? Kilug needs help."

"I do not know what this means, but I no longer desire to harm this creature, nor do I desire the Ice Ember." Durin smiled through his thick beard. "You may continue on your journey, young Turek."

Confused and a little pissed, Garrett turned back to Kilug and pointed. "This guy's leg is smashed, and he's bleeding out." He turned back, but Durin was gone.

Guys! Lenny's here, Paul said.

Yes! Took you long enough! How far back is David? Garrett asked.

Lenny's voice filled his mind. *He's right behind me. I felt bad for dropping the kid and was afraid he'd get himself lost, so I slowed up.*

What'd we miss? David asked.

Just get your asses down here, Garrett said, doing nothing to hide his panic.

Paul's voice came through next. *Unless you need me to do any heavy lifting, I'm going to keep on mission. The package is heavy enough, and I don't want to backtrack.*

A look on Pete's face told Garrett something was wrong.

"What is it?"

"I just worry about him going it alone with the Ice Ember. Look, I'm not sure why that dwarf guy wanted it in the first place, but what if someone else attacks Paul while he's alone?"

"Go, Pete. Tell and I will be fine."

Tell shook her head. "I'm not sure I should allow this strange behavior to continue, Garrett. As the only female here, I feel it is my decision. We should stay together until we can all leave together."

"Sorry, Tell, but I am sure. Pete's going. Paul is out there alone. Now you can go with Pete, or you can stay here and help me until David gets here."

Tell pulled a face, but to her credit, she held her tongue. Still, Garrett could see she was pissed. He nodded toward Pete, who nodded back, turned, and ran.

Garrett assessed the dwarf, who was getting paler by the minute. Luckily, it didn't take him long to find what he was looking for. Kilug wore bracers made of leather strapping. The thick leather wrapped around his wrist over and over all the way up his thick forearms. "Can I see your arm, Kilug?" Garrett asked.

The dwarf held it out and Garrett went to work, unwrapping one of Kilug's wrist straps.

Tell nodded. "Yes, that's good. Binding the leg should help with the blood loss."

Garrett nodded. "This is going to hurt, Kilug," he said, stuffing the strap under the dwarf's leg and tying it into a constrictor knot. Then, grabbing the loop with both hands, he leaned back with all his body weight, cinching the strap down tight.

The dwarf gasped, grunted, and lost consciousness.

"Holy shit!" Lenny announced, appearing from the pathway with David in tow. He pointed at the dwarf. "David, I didn't know you had a brother on this planet!"

"Real funny, Len." David gave Len the bird before turning his attention back to the unconscious dwarf. "Man, look at him – a real live dwarf. Like in the video games." David knelt down next to him.

"Yeah, and look at those arms! This guy is jacked," Lenny said.

David's eyes assessed the dwarf, stopping on the bloody leg. "That leg is mangled."

"Yeah, I need you to fix it, David," Garrett said.

"Well, sure, Garrett, but it won't work. I can only heal humans. You've seen me try to heal Dagrun and then Governess. It doesn't work."

"But you haven't tried a dwarf," Garrett said hopefully.

"Yeah... but..."

"You just got to try, David. Please?" Garrett asked.

"Well, sure, but don't get your hopes up is all," David said, squatting down next to the unconscious Kilug.

"Hey, he isn't going to wake up trying to kill us, is he?" Lenny asked.

"No. I don't think so," Garrett said.

Lenny raised a brow.

Tell shook her head, her dark eyebrows scrunching. "I've met this dwarf. My mother has traded with his clan in the past. I don't understand. Why were they pursuing you in the first place? We've no quarrels with the dwarves. They've always made great allies and trading partners. We traded goods with them only seven moon rings ago. It's true that since the dökkálfar took Thunder Keep, it's been harder, but there is no bad blood between us."

"It's complicated, Tell," Garrett said. "Pete and Paul found a huge piece of Ice Ember and, for some reason, the dwarves wanted it."

"Ice Ember? But to what end?" Tell asked.

"It was their... god, Durin," Garrett said.

"Yes. I heard you refer to the other dwarf as 'Durin.' Do you really believe that was their god in the flesh?"

"Yes, I think so," Garrett answered.

Tell put her hands on her hips. "What you're saying is that dwarf – the one who stood by and did nothing while you held half the mountain suspended in the air – was Durin? And it was Durin leading the dwarves in pursuit of Ice Ember? Then rather than killing you and saving his own dwarf, he just let you go? I'm sorry, but this is… well, this simply can't be."

"I know it sounds crazy but… but you saw him standing here and then vanish?"

"I saw a dwarf, yes. And yes, it's true, he vanished when no one was looking, but that hardly makes him the god of dwarves."

Frustrated, Garrett said, "Look, there is much more going on here than we understand." Then, turning to David, he nodded. "Please, just get him healed. Maybe he will have some answers."

"What makes you think this dwarf will tell you anything?" Tell asked.

"Because I saved his life," Garrett said.

David knelt, placed a hand on Kilug's leg, and glowed.

At first, David's glow was dim, and Garrett thought surely the healing wouldn't work. But then, like curtains being thrown back on a bright day, the canyon lit with David's shine. Garrett shielded his eyes, trying to see what was happening, but it was like looking into a sun being born.

From within the blinding light, Garrett heard a bone crack, followed by a loud pop and a scream.

Lenny winced. "That sounded awful."

The light faded like a candlewick at the end of its life, but Garrett had to wait for his eyes to adjust before he could see. When finally they adjusted, Garrett gasped at the sight of Kilug standing over a sleeping David, his war hammer cocked on his shoulder.

"Kilug, don't!" Garrett shouted.

"Aye, I won't hurt the wee creature," Kilug said, cocking his head. "This lad's hairier than any human I've laid eyes on."

Lenny laughed, but Garrett knew it was more in relief than at David's expense.

"What ye laughing at? Yer 'bout the ugliest of 'em I seen! Hairless like a new babe and lanky as a bag a dem bones."

"Hey, watch it!" Lenny started.

Garrett waved him off, walking toward Kilug. "Are you alright?"

"Aye," Kilug said, looking back down the Dark Narrow.

Garrett followed his gaze. "Listen, I know you want to get back to your friends, but it's going to take some time to dig through all those stones."

"What's yer point?"

"My point is I need your help."

"Me? What fer?"

"I need you to answer some questions for us. Like why you were chasing my friends. Then I promise, you can get back to your people."

"I'll answer ye questions, but I ain't going back."

"What?" Garrett asked.

"I don't even know who ye are, what be yer mission, or where in the bloody hell yer off to," Kilug said, his thick unibrow flexing curiously and then lifting thoughtfully, "but I know I owe ye my life twice over. Ye gave the order for dis wee sleeper on the floor to give me da healing. I be a good dwarf. I may be a wee bit young, but I be the best warrior in my clan, a good hunter too, and loyal. Aye. I've made up me mind. I will join ye."

Garrett stepped forward and extended his hand. The dwarf locked forearms with Garrett in a tight embrace. "Thank you, Kilug. I accept."

At that moment, Tell stepped alongside Garrett. "I require a word."

Garrett frowned. Now what? "I'll be back," Garrett said, excusing himself.

Kilug nodded, turning his attention back to a sleeping David and cocking his head like a curious cat.

"What is it, Tell?" Garrett asked.

"What are you doing?"

Garrett thought his intentions should have been obvious. "I'm aligning with the dwarf. He wants to join us."

"I am the only female among you. You should take your lead from me. All this talk about a mission and owing you his life," Tell said, frowning.

"I don't understand. Do you disagree with my strategy?"

"It's not about whether I agree or disagree. You are a male and as such you should know your place. If you have suggestions, disclose them to me for consideration. If I deem them worthy, I will act on them. I'm sure your queen" – Tell paused thoughtfully before continuing – "our queen will not be happy if I report back on your performance."

"My performance?"

"That's right."

Garrett sighed. "Listen, Tell. I'm sure by now you realize things were different where we came from?"

"Yes. Well, you aren't there anymore."

"No, but my queen doesn't follow your rules. I'm sorry. Maybe it isn't my place to tell you this, but we don't operate like that."

"You think you will come here and force us to be subservient like Deep? Is that your plan, to betray us to Deep?" Tell asked, her nostrils flaring.

Garrett looked down at the woman's hands. Her fingers were wrapped around her spear in a white-knuckle grip. "Tell, listen to me. We can talk about this all you want when we get back to the others, but I'm just going to say this. We don't want you to submit to us. Where we come from, we decide together. If you have a better idea, I'm listening, but I need to know what this dwarf knows, and considering he owes us his life, that makes him a valuable ally. Do you disagree?"

Tell stared at Garrett for a long moment. "No. I do not disagree."

"Then can you please just pretend for now that whether I am a male or female doesn't matter?"

"Pretend?"

Garrett nodded.

"Perhaps I will just pretend you are a girl," Tell said, and Garrett was sure he saw the slightest hint of a smile playing at the corner of her mouth.

"Okay?" he asked, smiling back.

"Fine. But if I see something I disagree with or if I have an idea—"

Garrett cut in. "Then I want to hear it and together we will give whatever your concern is fair consideration."

Tell sighed. "Fine."

Garrett turned back to the dwarf. "Kilug, can you start by telling us about Durin?"

Kilug stroked the thick braid of his beard thoughtfully. "Aye, our god, Lord Durin, came to our keep and told us to intercept ye. As you know by now, Durin himself led the charge."

"Your god? The same Durin we saw standing next to you?" Tell asked skeptically.

"Aye, he was. On me life he was."

"But to what end?" Tell asked. "We have been diving in the river for many moon cycles. Your kind have never objected in the past."

"Lord Durin said if we could catch yous before ye reached the Dark Narrow, we could claim a prize greater than any. He said we could take from yous an Ice Ember larger than any dwarf had ever seen."

"And even then, you would attack us?" Tell asked in disappointment, as if hurt.

"I didn't know these strangers were tied to yous women of Sky. Lord Durin said these was criminals."

Tell crossed her arms. "And a stone bigger than any ever found would be a good trade with the dökkálfar."

"What do yous expect? Since they took Thunder Keep, me clan has suffered. Food is scarce. Sickness be on the rise. We lost plenty in me own clan to a bad dose. Maybe if the ember was truly as big as Lord Durin said, we could trade it for Thunder Keep. If we's could, we's could get trade going again."

"And Durin promised to help you? What did he want you to do with the humans?" Tell asked.

Kilug fidgeted uncomfortably. Finally, he shrugged his wide shoulders. "Who am I to question me lord god, Durin?"

"So he wanted you to kill them?"

"Anyway, it matters not now. Ye heard me lord. We no longer have Durin's permission to take the Ice Ember. Yous is off the hook."

Tell stared at Kilug, shaking her head. "You couldn't take it now if you wanted to."

"Durin said yous is off the hook!"

Garrett waved Tell off. Making the dwarf admit he'd intended to kill them wasn't important. Whether the dwarf was to be believed, Garrett wasn't sure, but he felt there was something genuine about this Kilug. He wanted to trust him. Besides, he'd heard Durin himself say he no longer wanted the Ice Ember. "Kilug, do you think your kin will come looking for you?"

"Once every stone be turned, me father will come. Can't say how long they'll look before they bang on, but I've no doubt about it. They will come."

The Last Gift

Garrett nodded, hoping by then they'd be long gone. "Well, welcome to the party, Kilug. Now come on, guys, let's jog. It shouldn't be too hard to catch up with Paul."

"What about David?" Lenny asked.

Garrett had forgotten about the sleeping boy. It was odd that he'd passed out like that. Garrett had thought David was past falling unconscious when he healed, but then again, he'd never healed a dwarf. Maybe that's why the healing looked different. Garrett supposed the fact David could fix the dwarf's severe injuries at all was curious. How had he pulled it off? Well, it didn't really matter – not now, anyway.

"I got the wee lad." Kilug lifted David and flopped him over his shoulder like a bag of rice. Once secured, he picked up his war hammer and started jogging.

Dwarves' strength is no joke, Lenny said in mind speak.

Despite the shadowed crevice of the Dark Narrow, Garrett felt slightly overheated from his run. Without giving it a thought, he pulled off his knit hoodie, intending to tie it around his waist. He had a damp T-shirt on, but removing the sweater left his arms exposed.

Um, Garrett, Lenny said, nodding toward Tell.

Tell stood, eyes wide, staring. "By the gods! What are those markings on your skin?"

Garrett sighed, instantly regretting the error. Well, at least she didn't seem to know. Maybe this was good. Maybe he could just say they were tattoos.

Ahead, Kilug spun. "Runes! Ye have runes etched into your skin!"

Shit. Garrett suddenly felt naked and that he'd made a horrible mistake.

Kilug walked back toward him. "I knew ye be a sorcerer when ye saved me from the rockfall, but dragon runes – on a human? Ye be codding me?"

"You know what these are, Kilug?" Garrett asked.

"They be dragon runes all right. I ain't seen none meself, but I heard tell of 'em in stories from me grandfather." Kilug lifted Garrett's arm to exam the runes. "Me grandpa tells stories of dem dökkálfar dragon masters using dragon runes to control the dragons – to enslave them."

"It seems there is much you have failed to share with my mother, Garrett," Tell said with an expression of unease. "How did you get these markings?"

At first, with so much already happening, like Bre's name being whispered on the wind, it had seemed like a good idea to keep this piece of the story hidden from Tell and the others. In hindsight, maybe this had been a mistake. Regardless, at this point, there was no reason to hide the truth. "Back home, I killed a two-headed dragon. After I cut off its first head and it bled all over me, its second head doused me in fire."

"Doused you in fire? And you didn't die?" Tell asked skeptically.

"Obviously," Garrett said, frowning. She clearly didn't believe a word of it.

"Me thinks this makes sense. Me grandpa told a story of a ritual with dragon blood and dragon fire. The way me grandpa tells it, the dökkálfar bleed dem dragons, coat themselves in blood, and have fire breathed on 'em. He told it went wrong much as it went right, killing half who tried, while making dem ones who lived dragon masters. If ye be speaking the truth, and me is thinking dem runes are proof ye are, then blood before fire is what saved ye and gave ye dem runes," Kilug said, letting go of Garrett's arm.

"You slew a two-headed dragon? I've never even heard of a two-headed dragon," Tell said.

"Yeah, well then, you probably haven't heard of a three-headed dragon either, but one came through the portal with us," Lenny said.

"When we catch up with the others, you will show my mother these runes and tell her of how you received them. Unless, of course, you have something else you're hiding?" Tell asked, raising her spear. "And if that is the case, you will need to kill me now to keep your secret."

"What? No. No one is killing anyone. We're all on the same side, Tell," Garrett said.

Tell nodded, relaxing a little. "Let us run then," she said, motioning up the trail. "I'm sure my mother will be eager to see these dragon runes of yours."

33

You Could Be the Hero

God Stones – Moon Ring 3
The Mountain of Thrones

Maybe it isn't smart to eat the dökkálfar, Jack said, looking from Zerri to Cerb.

What do you mean it isn't smart? What else are we to do with them? Cerb asked.

If a dragon could frown, Zerri was frowning. *What's wrong with you?* She asked.

Nothing is wrong. It's just that you have plenty of food here, and these could make better slaves.

Slaves? Zerri asked.

Yeah, slaves. Or hell, they could make bargaining chips if we get into a position where we need to trade them for our own.

Trade them? Why would we trade them? A queen asked.

We will not barter for ours. We will crush any who stand in our way! Another queen said.

Jack sighed. *Dammit, I'm not saying I would, I'm just*

saying… Just don't be so quick to eat them – they could be of use.

We have taken slaves before, the jade dragon said. *Dwarven dracs shaped these halls.*

And wasn't it dwarven dracs who carved the dragon faces in this very mountain? Asked another of the queens.

Taker, surely you don't have feeling for these dökkálfar? Zerri asked.

Jack steeled his gaze and stared Zerri in the eyes. *Whatever feelings I had died when I became what I am. I require slaves is all.*

Zerri didn't look away, and Jack could swear she was staring right through him. *We will keep them as slaves… for now.*

Jack felt a strange relief.

Taker, did you know my mother was a master at creating dracs? You know what a drac is, yes?

Jack nodded. He hadn't seen one, but he knew that before her death back on Earth, Azazel had been creating dracs. The way he understood it, dracs lost their humanity and turned into monstrous, mindless things only capable of following the orders of their creator. However, because Apep opened the portal early, they'd left behind the dracs Azazel had created.

Good. The ritual of creating dracs is one I desire to learn, and these elves will make adequate practice subjects, Zerri said.

Grand idea, my queen, said Queen Pimra the Golden. *Dökkálfar have a high mental dexterity, typically making the success rate much higher than transforming weak-minded humans.*

Even better, Zerri said.

Jack caught the dig. Weak-minded? He could crush her with a single thought. A more childish version of himself might have challenged her to a fistfight on the spot. But not Jack the Taker. *Whatever! Can we just get going? We've a long journey back, and the nephilbock are waiting.*

Zerri nodded. *Yes, eat and rest. Queens, gather your armies. We will leave in full force at first light, before the suns separate.*

As Queen Pimra prepared to lead Jack to his quarters, she turned to him and asked, *And what of the female dökkálfar? Shall I have her delivered to the dungeons along with the rest?*

No, Jack answered quickly. *This one stays with me. She is... she's my personal slave.* Then speaking aloud, he turned to the elvish woman. "Come, Nyana. You're with me."

The girl nodded hesitantly but obeyed.

Pimra led Jack and Nyana to quarters that had once been used for enslaved dwarves. It was the closest thing Throne Mountain had to accommodations fit for a human or elf to rest. Although the small space didn't look like it had been used in a hundred years, a single cot covered in dusty animal hides looked comfortable enough.

The yellow dragon, far too large to enter the small chamber, poked her snout into the room.

Nyana cowered back, squatting into a corner, shutting her eyes tight.

"Even after all this time, I can still smell the dwarf who occupied this space," Queen Pimra said with disgust.

"I think we're good now," Jack said, turning to Nyana. "You've nothing to fear from them when you are with me," he said, offering the dökkálfar a hand.

Uneasily, Nyana took the offered hand and stood.

Pimra withdrew her snout. "Yes, well, I will have the slaves put to work collecting fish. We shall bring you some soon."

Jack lifted a furry red hide from the cot. "Make sure it's cooked. I don't get down with sushi."

"Sushi?"

"You know, just boil the water in the lake with dragon fire. Or ask Cerb – he knows how I like it. None of that raw stuff."

"If you wish yours to be flavorless, it shall be as you wish," Pimra said, withdrawing from the doorway.

Jack lifted a pelt and started for the door. "Help me shake out these furs."

Nyana obeyed, lifting a second pelt from the cot. After shaking off centuries-old dust, they made the cot back up. Despite the use of magic to heal, he still needed rest, and the cot looked inviting. Magic might postpone the need for sleep, but it didn't replace it, and while he felt okay physically, his mind was tired.

Once the fish arrived, he and Nyana sat on the edge of the cot's wooden frame and ate until their stomachs were full.

"What will happen to me now?" Nyana asked.

"Well, I was thinking we'd get some sleep before we go back to Osonian."

"I meant what will become of me after the battle?"

Jack looked at her for a long moment. "I am going to crush your city, Nyana. Everyone who doesn't die will become mine to do with as I please."

Silence filled the tiny chamber. Finally, Nyana said, "I don't think Ereshkigal will allow this to happen."

"I disagree. I think she may try to stop me, but I will kill her too."

"You think you can kill a god?" Nyana asked in genuine surprise.

"I guess we'll find out."

"You could change your mind," Nyana said.

"Change my mind? Why would I do that?"

"Do you even know what is behind the wall? Do you know what Osonian is?"

Jack frowned. "A city."

"Not just a city. Osonian is the oldest city in Karelia. It was created around the trunk of Metsavana, the father tree. Metsavana is said to be the first creation of the gods. It was meant for all to share, but my people took it for themselves after claiming the humans' God Stone and tipping the balance of power. Jack, this is important. The tree, when given a magical mineral called Ice Ember, grants wishes to those it deems worthy. My people were greedy and wrong for locking all other creations out of the city, and now we fear the tree is dying."

Jack's mind raced, trying to understand the implications. "Why are you telling me this, Nyana? What do you think giving me this knowledge will change?"

"You, Jack. With your armies, you could destroy the wall and free the city from my people and give it back to all species of Karelia. You could be the hero, Jack."

"Why would you want your people to be overthrown?"

"There are many of us who do not agree with our king and his council. The tree can't be allowed to die. If you are successful in overthrowing my king, that's one thing, but destroying the tree would change the course of Karelia forever. The legends say it took all the gods to make Metsavana. The legends say there is a piece of each of them in the father tree."

"Can this tree bring back the dead?" Jack asked, trying to hide his hope.

"Well, no. I have heard stories of those who have asked, but never has such a wish been granted.

Jack's hope sank into the pit of his stomach. He nodded. "I understand." And he did understand. With a new clarity, he understood exactly what he must do and why he was here. He had to destroy Metsavana.

That's where he would find the gods. The gods who let his shitty dad treat him like crap. The gods who let his mother abandon him. The gods who let Danny die. And somehow, Jack just knew when it came time to burn the oversized tree to the ground, Garrett would be there to stop him.

"So you will save the tree and free the city?"

Jack looked at Nyana, smiled, and said, "I'll see what I can do." And he would see what he could do. One way or another, he was going to find out just how powerful he was.

Nyana smiled. She covered her mouth, hiding a yawn.

Jack kicked off his boots and crawled onto the cot.

Nyana eyed him. "May I have one fur to lie on the floor?"

Jack looked at the blue-skinned woman. She was quite attractive despite what she was, and part of him knew he could make her do whatever he wanted. "You can sleep up here with me."

"I won't be forced to—"

Jack pulled a face, feeling his face flush and his ears burn. "I never said you had to do anything, did I?"

"No. You did not," Nyana said, looking down.

"Okay then, either sleep on the floor or sleep under a fur with me, but I'm not giving you anything. It's cold enough in here as it is," Jack said, taking off his jacket and placing it atop the furs.

Nyana slid under the furs and rolled on her side, placing her back to him.

Jack rolled onto his side, facing the elven woman, whose long hair fanned out in front of him. He tipped his head forward and breathed in the scent of her hair. She smelled like a flower he couldn't place. The room was frigid and as

Jack positioned himself closer to her, he told himself it was purely because he was cold. Slowly, he slid his arm around her waist, then froze, waiting to see what would happen.

Nyana scooted back, pressing her back into his chest. She placed her hand atop Jack's and went still once more.

Sharing her warmth, Jack closed his eyes and went to sleep.

34

Only Skin Deep

God Stones – Moon Ring 3
The mouth of the Dark Narrow

Breanne stood at the mouth of the Dark Narrow, staring down into the blackness between two walls of stone rising high into the deep blue sky. The two suns were far apart now, and she guessed they would soon draw toward each other – or perhaps they already had, she wasn't sure. She hadn't been here long enough to read the sky. She guessed it was mid-day. Behind her, hundreds of the women, men, and children of Sky were resting, eating, and hydrating to prepare for the next leg of the journey. Onward to the city of Cloud.

"My queen, I have a question to ask of you and your small one," Key said carefully.

Breanne guessed she had never explained her and Gabi's relationship. Did Key assume they were friends, or perhaps sisters? "Of course, Lady Key, what is it?"

"Can you teach your women how to speak with our minds?"

"Are there none among you with this ability?" Breanne asked.

Looking embarrassed, Key said, "Well, no. We have heard of this ability among the nephilbock, and we've all heard the legends that say dragons can communicate over great distances, but I have never heard of a human with this capability – not until now."

"Dragons can speak over great distances?" Gabi asked, and Breanne sensed a flare of hope surge up in the girl.

"So the legends say, yes."

"Teaching this isn't something I can do," said Breanne. "We were exposed to the Sound Eye, and we—"

"I might be able to teach you," Gabi interjected. "But it will take time and practice. Plus, well, you are old, so—"

"Gabi," Breanne said, trying to suppress a smile.

"Sorry, I only meant that, well, like with Paul – it's harder is all."

Key waved a hand. "It is alright. The young learn many things faster than the old. Despite the difficulty, I would very much like to learn… if I can."

Gabi? What's up? Breanne asked, wondering why she had the sudden desire to teach.

I can't get my mind off Zerri, and I fear she is hearing me but not answering. I need to busy my mind, the girl said.

Of course. I'm sorry, she said, feeling bad for the girl. *But, Gabi, I'm not sure it's such a good idea to teach them. Not now anyway. We have a lot of secret conversations using this method of communication.*

Gabi nodded. *It's okay – I will just get her started with the basics. It will take a long time for someone so old to get her mind nimble enough to learn.* Then, speaking aloud, Gabi said, "Let's find a quiet place to sit." As Lady Key and Gabi turned away from Bre and the Dark Narrow, Breanne heard Gabi say, "Pretend your mind is a room, and in the room is a door."

Breanne turned her own focus back to Garrett and the others. They had brought her up to speed on the dwarf, and Pete and the others hadn't stopped talking about what Garrett had done when the cliff fell into the Dark Narrow. Then, of course, there was the description of the Ice Ember. Lady Key still didn't believe it was as big as described, but Paul wasn't the type to exaggerate, and if it were so heavy that it was taking her brother this long to carry it back, it must be huge.

Reaching with her mind, she asked, *How much longer, you guys?*

Can't be much farther. We've caught up with Paul and Pete, and we're moving as fast as Paul can go, Garrett answered.

What about David? He wake up yet?

Garrett chuckled. *Yeah, he and Lenny are going at it.*

What's so funny? Those two are always going at it.

Yeah, but now Kilug is coming to David's defense.

The dwarf?

Yeah. Garrett laughed again, and it made her smile. *They're double-teaming him and it's hilarious. Hey, there's one other thing I didn't tell you.*

What's up? she asked, her smile slipping. She could tell it was bad.

Well, after I did all that running, I started sweating and… well…

What the heck was so bad he was afraid to tell her? *Garrett—*

Hey! Garrett called suddenly.

What is it?

I think I see light up ahead.

Breanne ran forward. There! Far down below, she thought she saw movement in the darkness. *I think I see you.*

I see your silhouette, Bre, Garrett answered, running up from the darkness.

A moment later, Garrett wrapped her in his arms, hugging and kissing her. Bre's heart fluttered just like the first time his lips had touched hers, and she didn't want him to pull away.

They turned around as Paul and Pete appeared, looking utterly exhausted. Lenny and Tell emerged next, followed closely by David and Kilug.

The dwarf looked different from what Breanne expected as she thought back to the cartoon *Snow White and the Seven Dwarfs*. Kilug was as wide as two people, with broad shoulders. He was pale, and his arms looked as though they belonged on an Olympic body builder. While he wasn't exactly what she expected, some of the dwarf's features met her expectations. He was short, four feet tall or so, and he had a red beard braided into one thick plait, with long red hair dressed into several matching red braids. His nose was wide, and one eye seemed to squint at her as if in a permanent wink.

Gabi ran to David and jumped into his arms.

"Glad to see you too, Gabi!" David laughed.

"Kilug Redforge of the clan Oakenstone, it was you who attacked the humans I sent to dive for Ice Ember?" Lady Key asked. "Does Kalmur know his eldest son is out attacking humans?"

"I'm sorry, Queen Key, but we were ordered—"

"Ordered! Are you trying to start a war? I've been trading in good faith with your father for the last twenty moon cycles! Just because it has been a few moon cycles, don't think I've forgotten the Ice Ember he still owes me for the wagonload of hides and leathers we provided. Now I learn it was you, Kilug Redforge, the once-tiny dwarf I bounced on my knee, who tried to rob and kill my people! Look at you! Half of your clothing came from the hides my women hunted and my men stitched. Oh, you just wait until your father learns of this," Key said, wagging her finger like an angry mother.

Kilug straightened. "Aye, me father was with me, as were me brother and two of me cousins."

"What?" Key gasped. "Where are they now?"

"The Dark Narrow was sealed when the mountain collapsed. Figure me kin are on the other side digging through, or Durin help 'em, crushed below. Though I suppose if me kin are trapped, Durin won't be helping 'em. Me leg was crushed at the time, but I remember ole Durin crying to the heavens, something about rules and interfering."

Key shook her head, not understanding. But her confusion was to be expected. Breanne and the other sages had chosen not to divulge any details of what happened in the Dark Narrow until they were all back safely together.

"Your god ordered humans attacked? But why?" Key asked.

"Aye, Queen Key. It is so. The order came from Durin himself, and I'm sorry, but ye don't be questioning a god when he be given ye orders. Ye best to obey. I never wanted to hurt yers, I promise I didn't, but Durin wasn't having it no other way until... well, until this one stopped the mountain from falling on me," he said, cutting a glance to Garrett. "Then ole Durin forgave whatever he was angry about in the first place and called off the order."

Key looked at Garrett, her brows scrunching. "Stopped a mountain from falling?" She glanced to Breanne. "My queen, how is it your man can do such a thing?"

"Queen?" Kilug asked, squinting his one eye even more if that were possible.

What should I say? Breanne asked in mind speak.

But before she could answer, Tell stepped forward. "Mother, there's more about this Garrett you must know."

Key's frown deepened as she held Breanne's gaze. "Go on."

"Dragon runes mark his skin," she said, pointing accusingly at Garrett.

Garrett! How does she know that? Breanne asked. Garrett was wearing a sweater and his runes were completely covered.

I was… I was hot from all the running, and I pulled off my sweater without thinking, he answered apologetically.

Key and Tell were still going back and forth.

"On his arms?" Key asked. "Show me!" she said, turning on Garrett. "Remove your tunic!"

Suddenly, several of Lady Key's personal guards shifted from a casual stance to a ready one. They didn't lift their spears, but they were prepared to.

This is bad, Breanne said.

Garrett looked at Breanne. "My queen, do you wish me to show them?" he asked aloud.

Good, Garrett. Remind them who the boss is, Paul said.

"Queen, ye say?" Kilug asked again, still assessing Breanne. "This one? Aye, come to think of it, ye ain't wearing yer wee crown anymore, Queen Key. What's happened?"

"No, Kilug. We have named a new queen. Queen Breeze, whose name came to us, whispered on the wind by Turek herself." Key straightened as if just realizing she might have overstepped in ordering Garrett to remove his shirt, but her eyes stayed locked on Breanne's.

Breanne needed to salvage this. She knew what her father would say. She could practically hear his voice in her head.

When in doubt, always choose honesty as your path forward. "I've intended to keep no secrets from you, Lady Key."

"Yet you have," Key replied sharply.

"Yes. Some. You understand we come from a society different from your own. We don't rule over our men – we partner with them. If I am to be fully honest, in many cultures, women have had to fight to be treated equal to men."

Key stepped forward, frowning as she lowered her voice to an urgent whisper. "I advised you that it was best to keep quiet in front of your followers about the way you treat your men."

"My apologies – your issue isn't with secrets, but only with the secrets you don't approve of?"

The muscles in the woman's cheek flexed as she clenched her jaw. Raising her voice again, she said, "So you were once enslaved by your men, yet now you partner with them? You allow them to give their opinion on womanly matters? Matters of the house?"

Breanne raised her hands. "Listen to me, all of you – there is more than one way. There is a way where one gender doesn't rule over the other."

"And is this what you want for your new queendom? You want to partner with Deep?"

The faces of the women changed from curiosity to anger as they hung on Breanne's next words.

Careful, Bre, Paul warned.

For a long moment Breanne said nothing, and then finally she said, "I want to meet with Deep. I want to tell him what I've told you. There is a greater threat that gathers at the wall of Osonian. It threatens to destroy the city and the father tree, Metsavana, which you know is already dying."

The crowd exchanged looks.

Lady Key shook her head. "You think Deep will listen to you? He will enslave you or kill you unless we kill him."

"We have to try."

"And if I am right?" Key asked.

"Then I will fight with you, just as I fought alongside you when the elves attacked. I won't allow any of you to be enslaved," Breanne said, and she meant every word. "I am here for a reason, and I bring with me sages of great power. Both female and male. Show her your dragon runes, Garrett," Breanne ordered with confidence.

Garrett bowed. "Yes, my queen." He removed his sweater, exposing arms etched in black and red lines. The lines crossed, twisted, and spiraled around one another before disappearing beneath the cuffs of his T-shirt.

The women gasped, crowding forward to see.

Key held up a hand for silence and approached Garrett. "Remove your shirt."

Garrett gave Breanne a pleading look.

Just do it, she urged in mind speak.

Don't be shy, bro, Lenny snorted. *I'd take off my shirt in a heartbeat if these chicks wanted me to.*

Garrett sighed, lifting his shirt to expose the pattern of runes zigzagging down from his shoulders, red on one side and black on the other. The lightning bolt–shaped lines intersected, spiraling around each other in the center of his chest, ending abruptly before reaching his navel.

"Turn around," Key said.

Garrett did so. The lines on his back held the same design as the ones on his chest. But the black and red came from opposite sides to meet between his shoulder blades and twist downward.

"Yes. These are indeed dragon runes," Key said.

The women gasped again. Chatter broke out as the women whispered to each other.

"Silence," Key ordered. "These are as the legends say and as I have seen with my own eyes."

"There have been others like me?" Garrett asked.

Key nodded. "Others, yes. There are others. Like you? No. There is no record nor legend of a human having been dragon marked."

"But you said—"

"I said others. Dragon masters. The dökkálfar who enslave dragons are dragon marked. I've seen one myself once, but that's a story for another time. There has never been a human with these markings. Tell me, Garrett, how did you get these?"

"I severed the head of a two-headed dragon—"

Hundreds of women and men gasped, crowding forward, ready to hang on every word.

Garrett told of killing the dragon, the blood, and the fire.

"Unbelievable that you, a male, could have achieved such a feat," Key said in wonder.

Frowning, Garrett jerked his shirt, then his sweater, on over his head.

Breanne lifted her chin and scanned the crowd. "As I said, we are powerful sages, and despite how different we may seem, we are here to help you. Not hurt you."

Key nodded sagely and turned to the crowd. "You heard our queen. Now prepare to move out. We are going home to Cloud."

"Um, wait! Lady Key!" Pete said, his voice urgent. "We did it. We found a huge chunk of Ice Ember. I'm ready to make the offering for—"

"Ah, yes," Key said, her eyes narrowing skeptically. "My queen, may we have a look? If this ember is as big as I'm told, it should have been impossible to carry, but impossibility seems to be the word of the day."

Breanne smiled. "Paul, please show Lady Key what you carry."

With some effort, Paul stepped forward and eased his pack off his shoulder, dropping it to the ground. He unzipped the pack and heaved out a softball-sized rock.

Key's eyes opened wide. "That cannot be Ice Ember," she breathed.

Kilug knelt down. "Aye, 'tis ember alright."

"But you carried this here – how?"

Breanne smiled. "As I've said, my friends are powerful and my brother is no exception."

"But how did you find it?" Key asked, shaking her head. "Did you use magic? Did the Sentheye show you where to look?"

Pete grinned. "Nope. It was just right there in the shallow water next to the shore! Paul noticed it, but I pulled it from the shallows."

"In the shallows, ye say? I ain't never heard of ember being found in the shallows," Kilug said, stroking his long chin braid.

Breanne saw something in her brother only a sister would notice as he shifted uncomfortably. *Paul? What is it?* she asked in mind speak so only he could hear.

Nothing. It's nothing. It's like Pete said. I just looked down and there it was.

Aloud, Pete continued, "Well, that's where we found it. Paul glimpsed it when he wasn't even looking for it, and there it was, just below the sand. Tell them, Paul."

Paul nodded. "It's like he said. We just got lucky. But it doesn't really matter, does it? It was there, and we found it. The real question is what to do with it. How do we get our friend back?"

Pete nodded. "Right!"

"This will make a fine offering, Peter. To my knowledge,

this will be greater than any single offer of Ice Ember in the history of Sky," Key said.

"Aye, bigger than any found by the dwarves, to be sure," Kilug admitted.

Garrett's voice filled Breanne's mind. *Guys, I was thinking about this. Pete, did you find any smaller pieces?*

A few. But they are very tiny. Honestly, if it hadn't been for Paul's find, I would probably still be there trying to get more.

Okay, well, Paul, do you think you can break it in half or maybe in fourths?

What? Why? Pete asked.

Stay calm, Pete. I'm just weighing our options.

Options? What options?

"Lady Key, is it possible to break this into two or maybe even four pieces?" Garrett asked.

"Ah, you desire to save some, perhaps for a wish with the father tree?" Key asked.

Kilug shook his head. "Na, 'tis not the way Ice Ember works, boyo."

"Kilug is correct. If you were to take this behind the wall to the father tree, for each piece you get one wish. Often, even then, wishes are not granted. Though it is common to compile more pieces into one wish, it is impossible to separate Ice Ember to get more out of it. If there is some other wish you desire, I suggest you choose wisely."

"There is no other wish!" Pete seethed, his eyes boring into Garrett's.

Garrett held up his hands. "It was just a question, Pete." Then in mind speak, he added, *In case you forgot, we are also trying to save all of humanity. And to do that, we need to get the portal open.*

And is any one of us a fair trade for opening the portal, Garrett? Pete asked, crossing his arms.

"Hmm. It seems you are once again having a private discussion," Key said. "I very much look forward to Gabi teaching me this incredible gift of yours, my queen."

Paul, Pete, Lenny, and Garrett all shot Breanne a look.

Don't ask.

"Well," Key continued, "do you wish to try to save your friend, or will you be saving the Ice Ember for the father tree himself? I would not fault you if you chose to take this most gracious offering to the father tree. After all, there are no guarantees this will even work."

Breanne watched as Garrett and Pete stared each other down. Finally, Garrett said, "Of course we wish to save our friend."

Everyone, including Breanne, let out a collective breath, drawing the attention of Tell and Key as they exchanged curious looks. *Dammit,* she thought.

"Very well," Key said, looking at Breanne. "Unless you have other secrets you feel I and the ones who have pledged themselves to you should know before we march to the trees and into the enemy's lair?"

Breanne swallowed dryly. There were still far too many secrets she hadn't shared with Key. The biggest one involved Garrett's true identity. She was starting to feel like this was a mistake. But why had Turek spoken her name on the wind? "No, Lady Key. I think it is time we move on. Let's save our friend and go see Deep."

35

Dragon Runes

God Stones – Moon Ring 3
The Creators' Mountain, Karelia

A moment after Durin vanished from the Dark Narrow, Turek looked on curiously as the dwarven creator materialized in the circle among the six other creators.

"You're back early, brother," Ereshkigal said.

"Don't act bloody surprised, and don't act like yous weren't watching me down there!" Durin said.

Typhon leaned in. "Well, I guess we now know what our beloved sister was up to. But tell me, Rán, why would you break the rules and give the humans a giant piece of Ice Ember?"

"Rules? I broke no rules," Rán snapped. "I gave the humans nothing."

"You expect us to believe this? Durin saw your treachery, or how else would he have known to pursue the Ice Ember?"

Turek watched as Rán cut Durin a pleading look. For someone who had little stake in this, she seemed overly concerned with being disqualified, but why? Why *did* she give Paul and Pete the Ice Ember, and why did she want to win another spin so badly?

Aurgelmir lifted his hands from his knees, holding them palms up. "Well, brother Durin, your testimony can eliminate Rán from this brief experiment."

"As could yours, Aurgelmir," Durin said.

Aurgelmir said, "Now tell us of the rule breaker's misconduct."

Durin looked at Rán for a long moment, as if contemplating something. "I saw nothing of what she did, only that she was there near the shore talking to the one of the humans."

"And what did she say?" Typhon demanded.

"I turned my gaze on these humans near the end of Rán's visit. I only saw her turn away and vanish beneath the water," Durin said, still holding her gaze.

He was lying. Turek was sure of it.

"I told you," Rán said, lifting her chin condescendingly.

"I don't believe you," Typhon said. "There is no way Ice Ember that large could exist in water so shallow."

Durin shook his head. "I never said it was in the shallows."

"Well, no human could pull a stone so heavy from the bottom of the river even if one so large existed, which they don't! Not naturally," Ereshkigal said.

"If you are so keen to know, you should have had your sight set on the river," Durin said, waving her off before turning back to Turek. "Brother, I... I need to understand what I saw. I need to understand why your favorite did what he did for my creation."

"For Great Mother's sake, why does it matter?" Eresh asked, throwing her hands up.

"It matters to me!" Durin snapped back. "There was no logic in it. No reason to save my creations when they were trying to kill him. And how did he do it? He's but a wee human, and so young! To command the Sentheye like that! To slow time and hold up a bloody mountain's worth of stones like they were but wee pebbles!"

Turek smiled. Durin always spoke with an accent reminiscent of a mix between Ireland and Scotland. But when he became excited, the slang really came out. Turek had done his best to influence the one entire region his humans occupied throughout time in an attempt to perfect the dwarven accent, but he could never get it exactly right. Of late, when he was missing Durin, he would find himself spending time in a Belfast pub. The closest he could get to his brother was listening to two heavily inebriated Irishmen argue.

"What me be needing to know – have to know – is whether this was the Great Mother. Is this what me be seeing, Turek?"

As Turek opened his mouth to speak, Typhon interjected, "Nonsense! Foolish nonsense."

Ereshkigal gasped, holding up a hand. "Hold, Typhon! Look at the boy!"

All the creators, including Turek, turned their attention back to the Dark Narrow, where Garrett was removing his sweatshirt. He quickly saw the reason for Eresh's gasp.

"Dragon runes!" Typhon bellowed.

"I told you Garrett was blood marked," Turek said.

"Blood marked! You said nothing about dragon runes! How can this be? How can he be marked with dragon runes?"

"It happened in his fight with Sylanth," Turek explained. "After he severed one of the dragon's heads, it coated him in blood, then the other breathed fire upon him, giving him the boon of dragon runes."

"Never have I seen a human blessed with dragon runes," Typhon said.

"It was fine when the dökkálfar created conditions to bless themselves, but then it happens naturally and you take issue, brother?" Druesha asked knowingly.

Long ago, when Typhon created the dragon, they'd all known he had created a creature of long life, incredible intelligence, the stamina to fly great distances and, of course, the ability to breathe fire. As a sort of handicap, Typhon had agreed to create a way for the worthiest of creatures to receive a boon in the form of dragon runes. However, the only way this strange anomaly could exist was if Typhon himself built it into his creation. Of course, Typhon could never have known that Ereshkigal's chosen dökkálfar would exploit the gift and use it to enslave his dragons. Turek suspected Ereshkigal was the one who had provided this forbidden knowledge to her favorites. Surely Typhon must have suspected too.

Turek shrugged. "Well, Typhon, doesn't Druesha have a point? This is, after all, why you agreed to design the boon, so that some creatures, if worthy, could secure dragon runes, making them impervious to dragon fire."

"Yes. But it does more than just make them impervious. It—"

"Yes, we know. It gives some the ability to control your creations' minds," Aurgelmir said.

"No. It doesn't give them anything. The runes weaken my creations' ability to think for themselves."

"Isn't that the same thing?" Rán asked.

"No. It isn't the same thing," Typhon snapped.

"Remind me, brother Typhon, why were you agreeable to this?" Aurgy asked.

Typhon gave Aurgy a knowing look. "You out of all of us do not need to be reminded, but very well. As we agreed in the beginning, I designed it so that only the most powerful of warriors could gain dragon runes, and only under perfect circumstances. But should it happen, a bond could be formed, a way to bridge gaps to foster an alliance. I meant it as a sort of safeguard to make you all comfortable that my superior creations wouldn't simply eat all of yours."

"Funny, I remember it different," Durin said. "The hope was this gift would help our favorites get to a place of peace so the God Stones might be shared and eventually allow our favorites to open portals and explore beyond Karelia."

"That too," Typhon admitted, his eyes cutting daggers at Ereshkigal. "However, I had no idea the dökkálfar would learn the steps to create the conditions artificially and use my own creations against one another."

Perhaps there had been a time when his big brother actually cared about all creation – a time when he had hoped for peace across Karelia. Though for any of them to claim blood marking as the single idea to create peace across all species was farfetched.

"Anyway," Typhon continued, his gaze focused back on Garrett jogging next to the dwarf Kilug, who had a sleeping David slung over his shoulder, "this human killing my two-headed dragon was something no other human had ever accomplished. The way you described the conditions under which he became dragon marked is nothing short of..."

Turek leaned in. *Go on,* he thought. *Say it. Admit this could be nothing short of a miracle. Nothing short of the Great Mother herself!*

"Suspicious," Typhon finished, boring his eyes into Turek's.

Turek sagged back, his hope smothered.

"He possesses the ability to wield Sentheye, unlike any of our creations. Now we find out he is also marked by dragon blood and fire? You expect us to believe this additional power isn't the result of you breeding with one of your own creations?" Typhon stood, looming over Turek. "Well, he may be impervious to dragon flame, but that doesn't mean the runes will give him the same ability to soothe a dragon that it provides for dökkálfar, who are strong of mind. Now know this, my brother. At some point, if he doesn't get himself killed by some other means, your abomination will answer to the full force of my creations. As far as I'm concerned, this trickery of yours is unlawful and means nothing to prove your cause!"

Durin stood next. "It means something, Typhon. By the Great Mother, you weren't there. You weren't standing two paces away, watching it play out. Forget that he is ten generations from Turek. Be damned if all of our creations didn't come from us in the beginning anyway, and I never seen nothing like this. He knew he was going to die and still he went! The boy had not an ounce of fear for himself. He had not a moment's hesitation. Forget the runes! Forget the Sentheye! Aye, the lad should be bloody dead! I just can't get past why he'd do it."

Everyone looked at Turek, as if expecting an answer. It was true. He knew what he hoped was the answer, but he needed to choose his words carefully. No. That was exactly what he didn't need to do. He needed to be honest. "I… I do not know why, brother Durin."

The room fell silent, but it wasn't to last. Durin shook his head. "No. I know what I witnessed. The boy is pure of heart. Good in every way. And, by the Great Mother, it bloody well means something."

"Good in every way, says the creator of dwarves and other small ground-dwelling rodents," Typhon mocked. Then, laughing, he added, "Yes. Good, like the mice and the rats. Pure like your pigea and giant capybear."

Ignoring Typhon's insults, Aurgy shook his head. "No creation is pure, Durin. No creation is without shadow."

Aurgelmir turned to Turek. "I'm sorry, brother, but yours are not pure. This one, too, can choose darkness."

"Aurgy, I never claimed he could not," Turek said.

Durin nodded. "But I made claim of it. Maybe ye be right. I'll say this and I'll say no more. Despite what he is capable of, he committed a truly selfless act. Shamed as I am, I was there, standing right next to the boy, ready to let my little lad die just to stay in this bloody game a yers! Now I'm telling yous, Garrett did not know he was going to live. But I could see it clear in his eyes – something compelled him to try, to risk it all. What, if not the Great Mother, compelled him?"

Druesha shook her head. "This does not matter. Metsavana is dying. The Ice Ember could help save the father tree."

Taking a breath, Turek nodded. "Yes. We need to discuss this."

"Discuss the tree father? Why does it matter? If the tree dies, we create another." Typhon shrugged as he sat back down onto the bejeweled floor. Near them, the stream meandered through the Hall of Creators, its invisible water babbling over diamonds and rubies. "Should we not be discussing Jack and the fact he has been stripped of the Sound Eye once and for all? Thank the Great Mother my dragons had the good sense to separate the Sound Eye back into the seven God Stones. The human and his three-headed abomination are less of a threat now. And I, for one, believe this merits some relief."

Less of a threat? Some relief? Turek wondered. Could it be that Typhon was more fearful of Jack than he let on? Turek looked at his brethren, their expressions just as curious as his own.

"Relief for whom, Typhon?" Druesha asked.

Ereshkigal laughed. "Yes, Typhon, explain your relief."

Typhon shifted uncomfortably.

"You are afraid of him," Rán accused.

"Nonsense!" Typhon snapped, embarrassment radiating through him in a wash of burnt-orange energy.

"It is alright, brother. I think we've much to be concerned about. Do you remember creating Metsavana?" Turek asked, changing the subject back to the father tree.

Typhon nodded. "Of course I remember. What kind of question is that? You were there. We were all there," he said, looking around the circle.

"Yes. But why did we create him?" Turek asked.

Typhon frowned.

Ereshkigal frowned as well.

Turek looked to Aurgelmir, whose energy told Turek he was frowning. "You see? It was so long ago that none of you remember it well. I have thought on this, and there is so much I too can't remember. Aurgy, you have the best memory of us all. Why did we decide to make Metsavana?"

Aurgelmir sat staring ahead for a long moment, then finally turned to Turek. "Brother, I… I have not thought of this memory for a long time. The making of Metsavana isn't the first memory I have, but it is one of only a few. The memory itself is clouded. If I concentrate" – he closed his eyes – "I can see it, but it comes to me as if looking through a thin veil of smoke. This was the first task given to us by the Great Mother just after the last of us was born. After you were born, brother Turek. This was the first being we were to create." Aurgelmir frowned.

"Go on, Aurgy. Why did the Great Mother desire this? Tell us what you see," Turek urged.

"You cannot tell me you remember the Great Mother giving you instructions! I cannot even remember seeing her! I cannot remember her voice! Great Mother, I can barely remember the light that shone from her visage!" Druesha said.

"No, it wasn't like that. It was a calling. We were compelled to create this magnificent creature as a gift to the Great Mother, to show her we were ready. It was… it was a test."

"Oh, dear Great Mother, I remember," Ereshkigal said. "In the end, she was pleased. I know this because I felt her smile upon us. That is the only memory I have of our Great Mother."

"But… I remember something else," Aurgelmir said, scanning the group to rest his gaze on Turek.

"Please, go on."

Aurgelmir nodded. "We placed a piece of ourselves in Metsavana."

"Well, I knew that. Everyone knows that," Durin said.

"Yes, just like the God Stones we bestowed upon our favorites. We each filled a stone with Sentheye," Rán said.

"No, you don't understand. This is not the same. The God Stones are not alive. We infused the stones with Sentheye. We gave Metsavana a piece of our spirit. Metsavana is part of us."

Typhon, suddenly looking very uncomfortable, shot Aurgelmir a strange look. He remembered it too.

Turek frowned. He wished he could remember her smiling, but he couldn't remember feeling it.

"That doesn't… doesn't make sense. A piece of our spirit? I wouldn't even know how to do that," Rán said.

Nevertheless, it was true. Turek didn't need to remember to know – it was all true. "What are you saying, Aurgy?"

"The creation, Metsavana, is tied to us. It is what binds us to this place. In this way, it is our anchor. It is as immortal as we are."

"Then he cannot die, right?" Rán asked.

For a second, no one spoke.

"Right?" she asked again.

"I think… if the father tree dies… I think we cease to be."

Silence filled the Creators' Hall.

In the silence was the truth. Everyone felt it and whether or not they remembered, they knew Aurgelmir was right.

"We cannot allow Metsavana to die. Even if it means we go down there ourselves and protect him," Typhon said.

"I agree. This far outweighs some experiment to see if the Great Mother still watches," Ereshkigal said.

"I understand," Turek said. "However, I would just like to point out, even without knowing how our immortality may be tied to Metsavana, a piece of Ice Ember larger than any ever discovered will soon be offered to the Shadow Forest feeding the father tree. In addition, the Sound Eye has been disassembled. And finally, the greatest threat, Jack, no longer holds the God Stones," Turek said, though he was under no illusion about the threat Jack still posed. Jack had held the God Stones, all of them. This meant he had a special connection with the Sentheye contained within each, no matter who physically held them now. "Therefore," he continued, "I ask you, my brethren, do we need to intervene now?"

Durin was quick to answer, "No. I suppose not."

"No. I agree, Durin," Rán said.

Ereshkigal nodded. "The Ice Ember's delivery to Metsavana is inevitable."

"And Jack is not a current threat to Osonian," Aurgelmir said.

"I suppose no immediate intervention is required," Typhon agreed.

With a final nod from Druesha, they all agreed.

"Well then, can we please spin the knife?" Rán asked.

Turek studied his sister as she clearly struggled to contain her excitement. *What is your game, Rán?* he wondered. "Yes, let us get on with it. Durin, the spin is yours."

The Last Gift

Durin reached into the center of the circle, lifted the knife, and flipped it in his hand from blade to wooden handle. He placed the knife back on the floor and set it spinning.

When the knife finally slowed, its point indicated Rán might get her wish.

Rán's eyes widened. "Please, oh please stop... stop. Oh, please stop," she begged in a soft whisper. Her voice was quiet, but they all heard her pleas.

The knife continued to spin ever so slowly past Rán and past Durin. Turek's eyes brightened as he thought perhaps the Great Mother would persuade the tip to name him the winner. But no, the knife did not choose him. Instead, it moved on toward Aurgy and Druesha. What would Aurgy even do if the knife named him? Would he seek out Ogliosh? Would he send all the might of his armies to kill Garrett and the others? Maybe he would turn his anger inward to his own creation and punish Ogliosh for his part in the Earth-born nephilbock's creation? Turek really couldn't tell where his brother stood in all this.

And what about Druesha? Her trees were close to the father tree, Metsavana. Until recently, their roots were tied to his, but now he had withdrawn. What would she do if the knife landed on her? Governess was hers, after all, and the beautiful creature was here to fight for the freedom of Earthen trees. Governess's alliance with Garrett and the others was interesting, and what about this relationship with Peter? What of Peter's relentless determination to save her? What must Druesha be thinking? Oh, he would very much like to find out what she would do if she won the spin, and so Turek prayed the blade might choose her.

However, the knife chose neither Aurgelmir nor Druesha. On it spun, slower still. All the way back around it went, past Typhon, before settling with finality to point at Ereshkigal.

"No!" Rán breathed, tears filling her eyes.

Ereshkigal smiled. "Finally! Now, my brethren, watch and learn!"

Turek closed his eyes. *Great Mother, I've faith you have a plan.* And why wouldn't he have faith? For all their skepticism and all their attention to detail, not one of them questioned why David, the little human no one seemed to notice, was able to heal a dwarf when until that very moment he'd failed to heal anything other than a human – well, and that time he'd healed a giant rat.

36

The Offering

God Stones – Moon Ring 3
The edge of the Shadow Forest

Garrett peered into the blue sky where one Karelian sun overshadowed the other in a tangle of forbidden love. Soon, Ellis and Soul would be banished to darkness, another day on Karelia coming to a close. Another day, and he felt no closer to getting a magical item and getting back to Earth to free the trees and save humanity. Even now, Pando's last words echoed through Garrett's mind. *Do not forget your promise, Garrett Turek. Six months from this day. Fail me, and humanity dies!*

As Garrett and the others crested another barren hill of loose rock and dirt, a uniform row of trees came into view. Their solid canopy stretched up into a darkening sky. They looked less a forest and more like a wall expanding in both directions as far as his eyes could see. Finally, they had reached the Shadow Forest, a forest as tall as a mountain.

Pete darted forward, unable to contain his excitement.

Garrett and the others ran after him. Even Paul, still carrying the Ice Ember, hastened the last twenty yards.

"Does it matter which tree I offer it to?" Pete asked.

"Wait!" Garrett called after him.

"What now?" Pete asked, unzipping Paul's pack.

Stopping alongside him, Garrett placed a hand on the boy's shoulder. "Listen, Pete, I've been thinking, David healed Kilug," Garrett said, pointing to the dwarf.

"What's your point?"

"Maybe something has changed! Maybe David can heal other creatures besides humans now."

Pete frowned, but Breanne and others were nodding.

Garrett's mind filled with Lenny's voice. *Yeah, but David has used the glow on me before. And I'm not fully human, but I am part human. Governess is all tree bush.*

Watch how you talk about her, Len, Pete warned.

Easy, buddy, I'm just saying...

He's just saying I shouldn't have been able to do it, David panted, bent over, hands on knees. *But I did it and you know what? It felt right. I mean, it was hard at first and it took a lot out of me, but it felt right.*

But, David, Kilug's a dwarf – he's not part human, Pete said.

You sure? Have you asked him? Paul asked. *'Cause I don't see how David pulled that healing off if he's not.*

Kilug, Tell, and Key were all there now.

"It be bloody weird the way ye be looking at each all the time like ye got something to say, but ain't none yous saying a ting," the dwarf said, looking from Garrett to Lenny and then to Pete.

"Kilug, are you part human?" Lenny asked.

Kilug's hammer came off his shoulder like a cocked baseball bat swinging at a fastball.

"Hey!" Lenny shouted, jumping back. The hammer swished past Lenny's left thigh.

Kilug heaved the hammer back onto his shoulder, cocked and set to swing again. "Ye insult me unprovoked!"

"What? No. Just trying to understand how our healer, who can only heal humans, somehow healed you!" Lenny said.

"Well, ain't no part of me pumping human blood!" Kilug spat. "All dwarf! Me lineage is a testament to the purity of me clan!"

Lenny held out his hands. "Easy, little big guy. There must be some other explanation."

Garrett nodded. "Well, there you go. I think it makes sense for David to try to heal Governess one more time. Maybe something changed."

The others nodded, and reluctantly, Pete agreed.

But when David tried, the outcome was the same as last time. A dim glow and then nothing. "Dammit – sorry, Pete."

"Can we please just get on with making the offering?" Pete asked, looking at Key.

Key nodded. "Yes. It is time." She walked toward what appeared to be a random tree along the edge of the Shadow Forest. The people of Sky approached, forming a half circle in front of the forest. Then, on their hands and knees, they placed their foreheads on the rocky dirt.

Garrett turned around, looking at the hundreds of people now kneeling before the forest edge. Garrett nodded to Lenny and together they lowered themselves onto the ground. The others followed, even Kilug. Breanne, seeming unsure if she was supposed to assume the position or not, shrugged and knelt.

"Come, Peter Ashwood, bring forth your offering," Key ordered. Then, searching the crowd, she called, "Shine, bring the plant forward."

Garrett looked back as Shine appeared, walking between a row of kneeling people. The guy's muscular arms were extended out, holding a wooden pot full of dirt with a not-so-good-looking Governess listing to one side. If the plant looked bad before, she looked downright dead now.

Shine set the pot on the ground next to Pete.

"Wait! Just one question. Are you sure we shouldn't be going directly to the father tree to ask him for this wish?" Pete asked nervously. "I mean, we only got one shot, right?"

"It is a good question, Peter. Normally, yes. The Shadow Forest does not grant wishes. The Shadow Forest only opens its secret passages to us. However, the offence from your friend was on the Shadow Forest herself. I think in this case, it is wise to seek forgiveness from the very forest your friend offended, the very forest that placed your friend in the state she is in."

Pete nodded slowly. "That seems logical."

Key smiled and nodded toward the backpack containing the Ice Ember. "Peter Ashwood of Earth, did you and you alone pull the Ice Ember from the Ember Stream?"

"I... I didn't know it was called the Ember Stream," Pete mumbled nervously.

"Did you and you alone retrieve this very piece of Ice Ember from the stream?" Key asked again. This time, her voice carried an accusing edge.

Pete straightened. "Yes."

Key smiled. "Good. Say it, please."

Pete bit nervously at his lower lip and nodded. "I and I alone pulled the Ice Ember from the stream."

Shine produced a tool that looked like a trowel and handed it to Pete.

"Dig a hole and transplant your friend into the hole. Ensure you fully bury the roots," Key said.

The Last Gift

Instinctively, everyone seemed to understand the burden was Pete's and Pete's alone.

Feverishly, Pete dug the hole.

"Good. Now remove your friend from the container, but be careful. She has become brittle," Key warned.

Pete lifted Governess from the pot and planted her in the hole, carefully covering her roots with the rocky soil.

Around him, the people of Sky were absolutely silent and still.

"Apologize for your friend's actions. Explain she meant no harm and beg for forgiveness. Beg for a blessing upon your friend."

Pete stood and looked at the trees. He looked back, unsure.

Key nodded. "Go on."

Pete looked up at the trees and spoke, explaining that Governess had meant no harm. She only wished to speak to them. She was sorry... he was sorry. Pete's voice broke, and Garrett's heart broke for him as the boy tried to keep it together and not cry in front of hundreds of people as they lifted their heads from the ground to watch.

"Good," Key said. "Now, Peter, present your gift to the tree."

Pete squatted down, lifting the orange-colored stone from the backpack. With the Ice Ember held down between his legs, Pete duck walked toward Key. It was all he could do to carry the thing ten paces.

You got this, Pete, Garrett encouraged in mind speak.

Pete shuffled forward and pressed the ember to the tree.

Key walked forward and whispered words only Pete could hear.

Pete nodded and said the ancient words of the gods.

A hole opened in the tree's trunk.

Key smiled. "Good, Peter. Place the ember inside."

Pete tipped the heavy stone into the opening, and the trunk grew back together.

Garrett couldn't help but feel sick. Like they had just given away their only hope of saving humanity, all to save a single tree. But he wasn't sure if the cause of his twisting gut was the fear they'd made a horrible mistake or guilt for questioning the use of this incredible gift to save a single being – to save Governess. He could have ordered them not to use it. As the leader, he could have insisted they use the Ice Ember to ask for a magical item capable of allowing the trees of Earth the ability to remain unbound. But somehow it didn't feel right. Besides, even if he had, there was no guarantee the father tree would have granted the wish and even then, they'd still need to open the portal back. Plus, Pete would have never forgiven him, and honestly, he would never have forgiven himself.

Pete stepped back, his eyes darting to Governess. "Is it working?" Pete asked.

"Patience, Peter," Key said, and no more did the words leave her mouth than the forest seemed to come alive. The ground rumbled while the canopies began shaking violently as if suddenly struck by a hard wind, but there was no wind. Leaves as big as paper plates fell from the swaying trees to dance lazily down, some spinning, some rolling end over end as they made their way to the ground.

"What's happening?" Pete shouted.

"It's fine! Focus on your wish, Peter! Focus on saving your tree friend!" Key shouted over the swaying and creaking of the impossibly tall forest.

Garrett watched as Pete closed his eyes, his lips moving in a silent plea.

The forest went still.

Do you see that? Breanne asked.

See what? Garrett said.

The Last Gift

The tree Pete gave the stone to, it... it's glowing.

Garrett squinted his eyes. It was hard to say, but when he glanced at the tree to the right and then to the left, he realized, sure enough, it was glowing. Not a lot, but... but wait... it was glowing even more now. Like a dimmer switch being turned up, the tree grew brighter and brighter until it became blindingly bright white.

"Key, is this normal?" Breanne asked.

"No, it is most definitely not normal."

Garrett shielded his eyes and looked down, only then noticing that the single tree at the forest's edge was not the only one glowing brilliantly. "Look!" Garrett pointed.

Governess was radiating.

Pete knelt down beside her, his eyes hopeful. "Please. Please. Please," he begged.

The light faded from the large tree first, then it faded from Governess.

The scraggly tree in the pot changed shape. Its twigs, no longer dry and brittle, twisted and stretched as slowly the unmistakable silhouette of a woman came into view. At first, she was brown with dark streaks of wood grain, but seconds later, her skin and then clothes filled with color until the auburn-haired beauty they had all come to know was standing before them.

Pete lunged forward, throwing his arms around her in a tight embrace. "Oh my god! I thought I'd lost you!" he cried.

Governess stepped backward, pulling herself from Pete's embrace. Out of nowhere, she backhanded the boy across the face.

"Ugh!" Pete grunted, spinning a quarter turn and dropping to one knee.

"You fool! What have you done?" Governess demanded.

37

The Mazewood

God Stones – Moon Ring 3
The edge of the Shadow Forest

Garrett and the others ran forward as Governess stepped toward Pete, intent on striking him again.

What the hell? Pete said in mind speak, holding his jaw with one hand.

Governess, stop! Garrett ordered, fearing she might strike again.

Around them, the people of Sky watched from their kneeling positions.

"What is wrong with her?" Key asked.

Breanne got to Governess first, throwing herself between the tree woman and Pete. This threat to the queen of Sky seemed to pull the people from their disbelief of what they'd seen and into action. Garrett watched as the women jumped to their feet, spears instantly at the ready.

Balls, Lenny said.

Breanne threw her hand out toward the crowd now moving in with spears pointed. "Hold!" Breanne ordered aloud. Then, switching to mind speak, she projected, *Governess, what's wrong with you? Pete saved your life!*

Governess made the motion of spitting at the ground, which seemed quite dramatic for a tree. *I know what you did! I could hear everything!*

Pete's confusion turned to apparent embarrassment. *You heard all those things I told you when we were alone?*

Governess's face softened for the briefest of moment. *Yes, of course, but that is not what I am talking about, Peter Ashwood. You traded the only hope we had of freeing my people, you damned fool! You should have listened to Garrett Turek! We could have traded this Ice Ember to the father tree for a gift to keep my people unbound! You threw it all away – for me!*

Pete's face hardened, and he stepped forward, wagging an accusing finger. *You are the most stubborn creature I have ever met in my life! You don't understand a damn thing about friendship, loyalty, or... or love. And you call me the fool!* Pete turned away, hiding his eyes as he stomped back into the crowd.

"What is happening?" Key asked.

"It's alright! Just hold," Breanne ordered, her hand still raised.

Breanne switched back to mind speak. *Governess, what the heck?*

Governess did not look at Breanne; instead, her eyes bore into Garrett's. She spun on her heels, marching toward him.

Gov? Garrett asked in a warning tone.

The woman stopped within reach, and Garrett prepared to grab for time in case she attacked. *You! Garrett Turek! Why would you allow this to happen? Do you know what you have done? The great father tree is dying. That piece of Ice Ember could have been exactly what we needed to keep the trees of Earth unbound, and what do you do? You waste it! You waste it on me!*

First, calm down, Garrett ordered.

Governess's eyes flared.

Second, stop calling me by my full name. Key doesn't know who I am, and if these people find out, it's going to cause a mess.

Garrett Tur... Garrett. I am speaking only telepathically. A capability unknown to these people.

Actually, I started training Key earlier this morning, Gabi said.

What? Why? Governess asked.

She wanted to learn. She wants all her people to learn, Breanne said.

What if she overheard everything? Garrett asked.

Everyone looked at Key.

"What is it?" Key frowned. "My queen, why are you all looking at me like that?"

Gabi giggled. *She doesn't know. She hasn't learned how to hear mind speak, and it will probably be a long time before she does. She's really old, probably like forty – maybe older.*

"It's nothing, Lady Key," Breanne answered, turning her gaze back to Governess.

"I will be glad when this child teaches me the magic of mind speak," Key said, frowning.

Yeah, well, don't get in any big hurry to show her, Gabi. *We need this to stay within the sages and the sages only, at least for now,* Paul said.

Garrett dragged a hand down his face. *Listen, Gov, it hardly matters now. But just maybe everything happens for a reason. Fact is, Pete chose to save you because he cares about you, and we chose to support his decision because he's our* friend and, well, you're our friend too... and dammit, it just felt right.

Governess frowned, her face twisting and flashing wood grain. *But you warned them against this course of action! You should have ordered Peter Ashwood not to use the ember in this way. If you are to be their leader, you must learn to lead!*

Something about that rubbed Garrett wrong, and it really pissed him off. *You know, Gov, maybe being a leader isn't always ordering people to do what you want all the time. Sure, there's some of that, but maybe it's more about listening to others' ideas. Maybe it's about compromising. Maybe it's taking all the information you have from those around you who might know more than you do and making the best decision you can.*

Gov's eyes were still flashing anger at him, but at least she was listening.

Pete loves you. He would never have forgiven me if I let you die and, dammit, maybe that isn't enough of a reason when we are talking about humanity and all the trees of Earth. Garrett felt his face turning red and his eyes welling up. He feared they could all see it, and that pissed him off even more. *You know what else? Maybe it isn't a this or that. No one is doomed – not yet. We just have to find another way. So now that you threw your little fit, yelled, and hit Pete in the face for saving your ass, why don't you try to be helpful? Maybe tell us what you learned so we can figure out what to do! Then how about you go find Pete and tell him you're sorry for being a shitty friend!*

Governess stared at Garrett for a silent moment and then said, *Perhaps you are right, Garrett. What is done is done. The fact is, I have learned a great deal from these trees.*

Paul gave a sharp nod. *Well. Now we're talking. What intel can you provide?*

None of it is good, I am afraid. The father tree is dying. The single piece of Ice Ember you gave the Shadow Forest will not be enough to save him.

Damn, Garrett thought. *I thought surely it would help.*

The Ice Ember will help, but unfortunately every piece of ember shrinks as it is transported to Metsavana. Every tree who moves the ember along its roots consumes a small amount. This is the nature of Ice Ember. For a tree to pass it along, they must consume some of it. This piece you found is still very large, and the father tree is very appreciative. Which is why they not only healed me, but they also taught me the Karelian tree language. I may now root and speak to the trees at will. Thanks to this gift, we are now in Metsavana's good favor.

Breanne smiled, looking hopeful. *Governess, this is great! If you can talk to them, then you can find out if an item exists on this world that will save Earth?*

Governess nodded. *Of course, I have asked this question, Breanne Moore. As I said, what I learned is not good. There is no knowledge among the trees of an item that can grant such power save the God Stones themselves.*

Garrett's heart sank. *Did you ask Metsavana?*

Garrett, one does not simply ask Metsavana.

But he's a tree, right?

Governess shook her head. *That is incorrect. He is much more than a tree. He is the first living being created. The trees tell me it took all seven creators to bring him to life. He is for all the favorites – a special being made for the sole purpose of fostering peace and harmony.*

"Queen Breeze?" Key asked, clearly unsure if she was interrupting or not.

Breanne stood with her eyebrows knitted in concentration, considering Governess's words.

Um, Bre, she's talking to you, Garrett said.

"Oh, sorry – I'm still not used to the name. What's wrong?" Breanne asked.

"I am glad your creature was saved and that we could deliver this most impressive gift to the father tree. However, we should not linger here at the forest's edge for long. The danger of elves or even Deep's army finding us is high, as I am sure by now Deep's men will have returned to our village and burned anything left standing. And we do not know when Saria will return with a battalion of elves."

Governess rooted to the ground.

Key's brows shot up. "What is this?" she asked in fascination.

"She's checking for us."

"Checking?"

Governess unrooted. "I can find no sign of humans or elves in the Shadow Forest."

"You can see the whole of the forest?" Key asked.

"Indeed."

Key nodded skeptically. "If this is true, they could be skirting the forest using the foothills as we are."

Garrett didn't like the sound of that. *Hey, if we're sure they're not in the forest, then couldn't we cut through, Bre?* Garrett asked in mind speak.

Breanne asked, "Lady Key, if the forest is safe, should we not use it?"

Key looked grave. "Are you sure they are not in the forest?"

"I am sure, Lady Keyhold. We are clear all the way to the Mazewood," Governess said.

Key raised an eyebrow. "If you know of the Mazewood, then you must be telling the truth."

Governess bowed her head. "Indeed, Lady Keyhold. Through the forest's eyes, I can see everything."

"Then let us make haste," Key said.

Garrett, his sages, and the people of Sky walked into a night made darker by a canopy too dense for starlight to pierce. Governess made dozens of torches lit not by flame but by the green glow of Sentheye, her ability astonishing the women. They took it as yet another sign Turek had sent Queen Breeze and her companions to the women of Sky to retake the queendom of Cloud and make right a wrong known as King Deep.

Breanne was getting all the attention as the chosen one of her people, and Garrett didn't mind one bit. In fact, he welcomed it, but he knew from his dream with Turek that this wasn't "the" ancient wrong. It simply didn't feel right. Call it a gut feeling or intuition, he didn't care. He just knew he had to get to Osonian. He had to stop Jack and his armies from destroying Osonian, but even more importantly, he had to get to this ancient tree, Metsavana. For he knew whatever the answer turned out to be, he would find it in Osonian.

Hey, sis, can you ask Key if there is a river or a stream in the city of Cloud? Paul asked.

Why, you thirsty? Lenny asked.

Thirsty? Paul asked, his voice pitched weirdly. If Garrett didn't know better, he'd think the guy was embarrassed.

Sure. Here you go. My waterskin is plenty full if you're out, Lenny offered, shaking the waterskin a man had given him back at the caves.

Oh. No. I would just like to clean up, maybe go for a swim, Paul said. *Can you ask her, Bre?*

Sure, Paul, Breanne said. *Hey. You sure you're okay? You're quiet. Even for you.*

I'm good. Just want to wash up is all.

A moment later, Breanne said, *You're in luck. Key said*

there's a river and some amazing waterfalls you can shower in.

Garrett looked back at the big guy. He was nodding approvingly and smiling. Man, he wished he could get so excited about a shower, but the fact was he couldn't stop trying to puzzle out what they were going to do. He supposed it was possible a magic item existed that the trees didn't know about. But how was he going to find it? What he really needed was another big-ass chunk of Ice Ember, then he needed to give it directly to Metsavana and make the wish. Maybe being related to Turek would make him worthy enough to get his wish granted. What were the odds they could find another one like the one they'd just given away? Slim to none. Dammit! He felt the stress overwhelming him – like he might have a panic attack. He was freaking seventeen! Seventeen-year-olds aren't supposed to have panic attacks. He needed…

Len? Can I ask you something? he asked, speaking only into the mind of his best friend.

Shoot.

What do you feel like we need to do more than anything?

I don't understand. I mean, obviously we got to find this magic item you promised to Pando.

No. I know that. I mean, what is your gut telling you we need to do specifically?

Honestly?

No. Lie to me. Yes, honestly.

Dick, Lenny said, and Garrett could see his friend's smile cast in the soft green glow. *Okay then. Every bit of my soul is telling me to get my ass to Osonian. That was my father's home, Garrett. My grandfather is there, and if Jack hasn't already crushed the city, he's going to.*

Unless we stop him, Garrett said gravely.

Lenny nodded. *I just know we got to get there.*

Thanks, Len. If it makes you feel any better, I feel it too. From the bottom of my gut, I feel it. Garrett felt a strange relief the instinct wasn't his alone. But a new panic quickly replaced the relief. They had to get this business with Deep behind them, and they had to get to Osonian as fast as possible.

Around him, all the women and men stopped.

What's happening, Bre? Paul asked.

Key says we're here. We're at the Mazewood.

Garrett and his friends pushed themselves forward to join Bre, Key, and Tell. The green light from several torches illuminated a wall of solid wood stretching at random jutting angles in all directions. As Garrett stared at the wall, he realized all the weird angles were triangular, like some crazy art design. Directly in front of them, a single triangle was missing, leaving an opening in the wall plenty big enough for them to pass through.

Lenny leaned in toward Tell. "So, what is this exactly?"

Tell smiled. "Just like the name suggests, the Mazewood is a solid grove of trees whose trunks grew together, forming walls that in turn form a maze."

"But what's with the shapes?" David asked.

Key frowned. "It is the way the trees have grown. Who are we to question the trees?"

"Touché," David said.

"To what?" Key asked with annoyance.

Lenny's voice filled their minds. *I may have mentioned this before, but in case I forgot, you're an idiot.* Lenny raised a hand to slap David on the back of the head.

Breanne cleared her throat. "It means 'good point,' and David thanks you for educating him."

"I see," Key said, raising an eyebrow. "Well, be warned, the journey through the Mazewood to Cloud is difficult as the maze is ever changing."

"What? How long has it been since you have been through here?" Breanne asked.

"I'm afraid it has been a great many moon cycles," Key answered, but she didn't seem concerned.

"How will we find our way?" Breanne asked.

Key smiled. "I used to know every combination and could navigate this forest with my eyes closed, but alas, I am long removed from this place. I will do my best to guide us, and where I cannot, we will trust the forest to take us home. Remember my queen, it is your name Turek whispered in the wind, and I doubt she spoke your name only for us to be lost in the Mazewood. Now come this way," Key said, vanishing through the dark opening in the tree.

"Right," Breanne said, stepping through after her.

You guys seen Gov? Maybe she can help? Garrett asked in mind speak, stepping through behind her.

She's with Pete, Gabi answered. *They've been walking by themselves near the back for a while now.*

Garrett had never really thought about it before, but Gabi somehow seemed to always know where each of them was. *They make up?* Garrett asked.

Not sure. But she hasn't whacked him again, Gabi said.

Oh good. I'd hate to miss Pete get another solid backhand, Lenny said, chuckling.

Just so you guys know, I can hear you, Pete said.

Well, good. Bring your barky babe up front. It's dark in here and we could use a few more of those Green Lantern torches of hers.

Lennard Wade, I too can hear your insults and would advise you to stay your tongue. I assure you I am not in the mood for your contumely.

Lenny jabbed Garrett in the ribs to get his attention and gave him a sinister smile.

"You knock it off, would you?" Garrett whispered.

"Sheesh! Hey, we gotta have some fun. Where would you be without my humor?"

Garrett opened his mouth, but Lenny went on whispering. "I'll tell you where. You'd be in the same place, but a whole lot more pissed off about it."

"No way. You're so wrong."

"What? You telling me I'm not making this at least a little fun?"

"If you'd shut up long enough, I'd tell you I wouldn't be pissed off because I'd have been dead a long time back without you, Len."

Lenny went "cat got your tongue" quiet. It was so dark in this strange space between wooden walls that Garrett could only see a vague outline of his friend's face in the green glow of torchlight. High above hovered a thick canopy, blotting out the sky. Even one familiar with the strange Karelian sky couldn't use it to navigate by.

"Len?" Garrett said.

Lenny patted Garrett on the back. "Thanks, man."

"Of course." Then, switching to mind speak, Garrett focused hard on Pete. Garrett found speaking directly to a single person took a bit more care than speaking to the group. It was like whispering took a little more thought than speaking normally, probably because you didn't normally whisper. *Pete, can you hear me?*

I hear you, Garrett. What's up?

Also, when someone spoke to you and only you in mind speak, you knew – somehow you just knew. The tone... no, not tone, feeling – the feeling was different. Garrett didn't need to say, "Hey I'm just talking to you, okay," because Pete would just feel it.

Are you okay?

There was a long pause. *I am now. But I was really pissed. No, that's not true. I wouldn't say this to the others, but it really hurt me. Not physically – the hit wasn't that bad. I think she was holding back. What I mean is I was embarrassed.*

And what about you and Governess?

I don't know how I feel now. But she has apologized to me like a dozen times. I think she really cares about me, Garrett. She's just so different, you know? And what I love about her also drives me crazy.

For what it's worth, I think that's normal, whether you are with a tree, a human, or any relationship where love is involved, Garrett said, recognizing as he spoke that maybe he wasn't experienced enough in relationships to be giving love advice.

The line of people, three and sometimes four or five wide, stopped abruptly. Garrett looked ahead to see they had apparently come to a dead end. Already near the front, Garrett pushed forward with Lenny on his heels.

"What's happened? Did we go the wrong way?" Garrett asked.

"Wrong way," Key repeated, smiling. "No, we haven't gone the wrong way. It is here where the maze truly begins."

Garrett and Lenny exchanged confused looks.

Key pointed. "Now we go up."

38

What Good Are Gods?

God Stones – Moon Ring 4
The Mountain of Thrones

Ereshkigal opened her eyes. The room was fuzzy as she began blinking away the sleepiness of mortality. Occupying one of her creation's bodies wasn't her favorite way to present herself. Of course, she could have just appeared as a dökkálfar, but this was more... physical. In flesh and bone, she could touch and feel in a different way.

For example, as she assessed herself, or rather Nyana's self, she realized she felt warm breath on her neck and an arm hugging her waist. What in the Great Mother was wrong with these humans of Turek? It seemed they were all quick to want to fornicate with other species. This would never have happened before he arrived. Well, not since he left. So, it seemed the common denominator was Turek himself.

Turek – oh, how she had missed him. The sacrifices she had made to hold true to the creator's code had been great. To break the heart of her brother was to break her own soul. But she'd done it. Self-sacrifice for a greater cause. The Great

Mother tasked only seven lifeforms in all the universe with the responsibility of creation. This was not to be taken lightly.

Why couldn't Turek understand this? Their responsibility wasn't to be tossed about by their creations in the name of a chemical emotion called love. He'd added too much of this element to his creations, and now they seemed to be falling in love with everything! No. What these humans needed was discipline and accountability – consequences. Sadly, before this was over, she would be forced to break Turek's heart once more. For she knew but one certainty. All this had to be erased. They did this forbidden breeding in the shadows of Earth and now, like a plague, it was spreading over Karelia.

She lifted the boy's arm from around her waist and rolled toward him. Her face was but a few inches from his. So, this was Jack the Taker up close. She had only glimpsed him for a moment the last time she had occupied this dökkálfar's body. This dökkálfar who had told Jack to keep her close for when the goddess of all dökkálfar returned. However, Ereshkigal had never asked the child to do any such thing. Very clever. In her deceit, she had earned herself a place in Jack's bed rather than a cell in the mountain's dungeon. Note to self: kill this dökkálfar if she survives what's to come. How dare one of her own lie in the goddess's name, then have the audacity to lie down with this human scum.

Jack opened his eyes.

Ereshkigal's breath hitched. She knew the boy's eyes were red, but to see them this close was startling. They looked like two rubies, bright with an inner glow. But more than that, the eyes were a perfect combination of the red of a dragon, with the crystal pupils of a sea monster, yet they were a human's shape. Great Mother, this was… well. This was not the work of Turek, Typhon, or Rán. Those eyes, could they really be achieved by chance through a blood bonding and the death of Hafgufa?

"How long did we sleep?" The boy moaned, stretching his arm above his head. His tongue spoke perfect dökkálfar.

"Long enough," she answered.

"Long enough, huh? Well then, I think it's time to check in with the others."

"And I think it is time you and I have a talk," Ereshkigal said.

The frown of irritation on the boy's face told her he didn't like being spoken to in this way by a slave. Ereshkigal realized then she'd made a mistake possessing this weak peasant girl. She needed this creature, Jack, to see her in her dökkálfar goddess form. She needed him to know just how magnificent she was. Then she could twist him around her finger and bend him to her own will. *Well, my brethren, I hope you're paying attention.* She left the girl's body and materialized next to the bed, behind Jack.

Nyana's eyes widened as she sucked in a gasping breath. "Goddess Ereshkigal."

Jack sat up, turning to face Ereshkigal.

She decided to make an impression, appearing in all black with knee guards, wrist bracers, a chest plate with spiked shoulders, and a helmet to match. Two swords crossed her back with pommel and grips sticking up above her shoulder spikes. "Hello, Jack."

"I figured you'd show up eventually," the boy said, sounding unimpressed. He didn't seem as scared as she had hoped he would be. Jack threw back the blanket and swung his feet off the bed.

"Splendid. I have alighted on your emplacement so we may discuss the rather precarious situation you find yourself in, Jack Nightshade."

"Oh, hell no. Listen, lady, and you listen good. I'm

likely going to kill you before this talk of ours is over, but if you want to push me into a fight right here and now, just keep talking fancy. I ain't got no use for it and ain't about to sit here and pretend I understood a bit of what you just said. But I will tell you this. I ain't embarrassed either. Not even a little, because you see I killed just about every godlike monster I came across. And I told that little mermaid chick back at the lake that the next one of you wannabees who tries some bullshit with me is as good as dead!"

Nyana crawled off the bed and pressed her forehead to the floor. A rambling of begging and prayer spilled forth, but she would find no forgiveness. Ereshkigal raised a hand to kill the girl but paused. A look on Jack's face hinted at something. Oh, well, how delightful. The boy's visage turned to concern. He cared for this peasant slave girl.

Ereshkigal smiled. "Let me speak slow and plain so even a tiny child could follow along."

Jack's face twitched with irritation, his lips curling into a sneer.

"You will return to Osonian, taking every one of my people you've brought here with you." Ereshkigal folded her hands and began to pace back and forth in the small chamber. "You will order your dragons to turn on the nephilbock – destroy some, but not all. They, in turn, will turn on the dragons. You will kill the Queen of Queens. Do you understand?"

"Are you high?" the boy asked.

Ereshkigal thought this a strange question but answered without hesitation. "I am the god of dökkálfar – there is no one higher."

"No. I mean, are you crazy? Why in the world would I do anything you tell me?"

"Ah," she said, understanding. She stopped pacing and

straightened. "If you live through this, I will personally see to it you get what you wanted all along."

"Garrett," Jack said, his face a sneer.

"Yes. Garrett and all his companions. Yours to do with as you wish."

"Well, here's the thing, elf chick. I don't need you to get that. I don't need any of you. Besides, you're wrong. That's not what I want more than anything."

"Oh, then tell me, Jack. What is it you want?"

"Thought you being a god and all, you would just know. You are a god, right?" he asked.

"Indeed, I am," Ereshkigal answered.

"Well, this should be easy, then. You give me this one thing, and I'll do whatever you want without question," Jack said, his face an expression of promise.

Whatever he wanted, this would be the play to win it all! Ereshkigal could practically see her brethren leaning into the circle holding their breath. "Go on, Jack. Name your price."

"Bring my brother Danny back from the dead. Give him to me just like he was before he died," Jack whispered, tears welling in his eyes. "Can you… can you do it?" the boy managed, clearly trying to hold back the emotion.

Ereshkigal sighed, her hope for this creature's easy obedience dashed away by an impossible request. "No. Even gods can't bring back the dead."

The boy moaned, squeezing his eyes shut. A moment passed, and when he opened them again, they hardened into something hateful. "Then what good are gods?"

"Excuse me?" Ereshkigal asked.

"No. No, I don't think I will. I said, then what good are gods?"

The audacity of this mere mortal. "I can give you anything else you want, but I cannot bring back the dead."

"Then you are worthless."

"Stay your tongue!" Ereshkigal said, lifting her hand to show splayed fingers encircled in black Sentheye.

"You raise your hand to me. You better be ready for me to raise mine."

Between their feet, the peasant elf remained with her forehead to the floor, shaking uncontrollably.

"You dare to threaten Ereshkigal, god of the dökkálfar," she warned.

"I don't dare shit! And I don't know what you are, but I know you're no god. That means you can die just like everything dies… just like Danny died! Now, I am going to give you one chance to leave."

Anger rose within Ereshkigal, and even though interfering physically would break the rules of Turek's little experiment, blinding rage decided for her. In the heat of the moment, she didn't care if she were to be included in future spins of the blade or not. She was going to end this vile creature here and now.

"On second thought, screw it," the boy said, lifting his hands. "No more chances!"

A devious smile stretching across her face, Ereshkigal sent Sentheye forward from her hands like the exhalation of a breath.

Then she felt it. A faltering. A twisting of her insides as blinding pain filled her head. What? How? She didn't understand. She'd never felt anything like this. It was… horrible. The pain was so terrible she lost the Sentheye altogether, her hands going to the sides of her head. This could not be!

∼

Jack drew in so much power so fast he thought he was going to blow apart. It felt like every muscle fiber in his body was seared, every cell overflowing with Sentheye. He screamed, needing to release the power... and so he did.

Eyes bulging, Jack focused, intent on blowing the fake god to smithereens, but as he released the stored power, the wannabe goddess vanished.

Sentheye poured from Jack, crossing the small chamber and striking the roughhewn mountain wall, blasting a hole through several yards of stone before exploding out of the mountain to reveal a man-sized hole with a lake view.

Jack dropped to one knee, looking around the room but finding only Nyana still cowering on her hands and knees. *Cerb, get to my room now!*

A breeze blew in off the lake through the new hole in the wall, but Jack saw no sign of Ereshkigal. "That's what I thought," he said, pushing himself back onto his feet. He looked down at Nyana. "You can stand up. The goddess you cower from ran away like... well, like a coward."

The girl stood, and Jack noticed she was no longer crying. In fact, she didn't look scared at all. "You think you can kill me so easily?" Nyana snapped.

Jack's eyes went wide. "Ereshkigal." He reached for the Sentheye again but hesitated.

"Well, what are you waiting for, Jack? Go on, send your poison." Nyana smiled.

Jack held out his hands, fingers locked like talons gripping the air.

"No. I didn't think so."

"You think I won't kill her in order to kill you," Jack snarled.

Nyana stepped forward.

Jack stepped back, the back of his leg hitting the cot.

"No, Jack, I don't think you will."

"Well, what would be the point – you will probably just run away like a chickenshit anyhow."

Nyana smiled. "As I suspected. Now that we are past that little fit of yours, let us get back to your instruction. You will go back to Osonian, taking with you the dökkálfar you have stolen. You will free them. You will then attack the nephilbock, and you *will* start a war between them and the dragons. You will ensure my city stays in the control of the dökkálfar."

"And then I get Garrett?" Jack asked.

"No. You don't need my help for that, remember? No, instead you get to live, and this one I am occupying – she gets to live too. But if you betray me, Jack… the next time you see me, this one dies painfully while you watch. Then you die next."

Jack could feel himself losing it. Screw this elf girl! Why in the hell did he care if she died! He focused, drawing on disease once more.

Behind him, wood splintered.

Jack looked back in time to see several black talons protruding through the heavy wooden chamber door. With the sound of fracturing wood and stone, the door ripped outward. Cerberus reached inside, his talons gripping one side of the doorframe, jerking, and ripping the wall apart.

As one of Cerb's heads entered the room, Jack looked back to Nyana, reaching for his concentration once again and with it the Sentheye.

Nyana stared at him, her glistening eyes wide and full of fear.

"Nyana?" Jack asked, just short of unleashing a deadly dose of sick.

The girl nodded, tears spilling down her cheeks.

A strange feeling came over Jack. He grabbed the girl, wrapping her in his arms.

Nyana buried her face in his neck and sobbed.

Taker! What's happened?

Ereshkigal was here. I tried to kill her, but I failed.

You tried to kill a god and you're still alive? Cerberus laughed.

She's no god, Cerb. Jack released Nyana and, speaking aloud, said, "We need to go."

"Are you going to do as she says?" Nyana asked.

"Hell no!"

"But she will—"

"Listen, Nyana, you and I need to get something straight right now. No more cowering on the floor. These things aren't gods, that much I'm sure of."

"These... things?"

"Yeah, this isn't the first one I've dealt with since coming to this planet," Jack said, pulling on his boots.

"But Ereshkigal said if you don't do as she said, she will kill me."

"First of all, this isn't about you, this is about the kingdom of Osonian and who rules it. If you think she is going to let you live, you're an idiot," he said, cinching down his laces and straightening. "I almost killed her. Damn, I was so close."

Nyana nodded. "Yes, I think... I think maybe you were."

"What? Why do you say that?"

"The last two times she was inside my body, it didn't hurt, but this time, oh the pain. My stomach, my joints, but especially my head. I thought if she didn't leave me soon, I would surely die."

"I knew it. They're not gods at all," Jack said, feeling surer than ever. He turned toward the destroyed wall where Cerb's big head still poked through. "And if they're not gods, they can die! Let's go! I have a city to take and some fake-ass gods to kill!"

39

Cloud

God Stones – Moon Ring 4
The Mazewood

Breanne stared up at a sloped crevice in the wall of trees. It didn't look like much of a climb, but it twisted out of sight, disappearing around a corner high above.

"You didn't think a city called Cloud would be down here, did you?" Key asked with a wry smile.

Governess and Pete had made their way forward, collecting Kilug, David, and Gabi along the way. Kilug and David seemed to have hit it off pretty well; Lenny joked it was their ability to bond over facial hair, but maybe he wasn't that far off. The 'stache seemed to give David some instant respect with the dwarf warrior. Breanne felt good knowing Gabi was happy to walk with David and Kilug. The little girl seemed to laugh more when she was with David. After first losing her parents and then falling out with the little grey dragon, to see her laughing or even smiling was a win.

Two of Key's guards entered the crevice first. These women had thick, muscular thighs and arms to match. They scaled their way up with ease, disappearing around a corner only to signal back with what sounded like a sort of bird call.

"Come, now we climb," Key said, entering the crevice while beckoning Breanne to follow.

Garrett's warm voice entered her mind. *I'm right behind you, Bre.*

And we're right behind him, Lenny said.

"Aye, dwarves don't much care for climbing about in trees," Kilug called nervously.

"It isn't like climbing any normal tree, Kilug," Tell said. "It's much taller and weirder."

Kilug made a noise like something between a growl and belch as he pulled himself up into the crevice, falling in behind the others.

And so they climbed, weaving their way up and up. Sharp bends split off in different directions, some leading downward, some straight ahead or around corners, while some continued up. Tell was right; nothing about this was like climbing a tree. Sometimes they were hiking up inclines steep enough they had to use their hands, grabbing for whatever tree knobs, hunks of bark, or gnarled knots they could grasp. However, there were no branches, only bark-covered wood, bending and twisting.

Frequently, Key would raise a hand, calling a halt as she tried to remember which path to take. If she hadn't been told the trunks of many grew together to form the maze, Breanne would have guessed it all belonged to the same tree. There was no way to differentiate the seemingly seamless transitions from one tree to the next.

"Should we worry about guards?" Breanne asked.

"No. I do not believe so. Especially since we expect Deep's army to be busy invading our village," Key said.

The plan made sense. After one of Key's own, a spy of Deep's named Gateman, had escaped, Key knew he would run here and warn Deep. King Deep would then send his army to crush Key and her people once and for all. Obviously, Deep's men would find the village empty, and by the time the army returned, Lady Key's new queen and powerful friends would have already taken the city, forcing the returning army to surrender at the gates.

Still, with every step they took, Breanne became more and more nervous.

I don't have a good feeling about this, guys, she said in mind speak.

I'm with you, Bre – plus, if this goes on much longer, my legs are going to cramp up, David complained.

Suck it up, David, Lenny chided. *Or wait, why don't you have your new whisker warrior carry you on his big-ass back? I know, maybe if you sit on his shoulders, you two can equal the height of a normal person.*

Len, buddy, you don't seem like the jealous type, David countered. *Stop hating on Kilug. There's enough of me to go around.*

Lenny laughed. *There's enough of you to go around alright, just not enough to go vertical.*

Breanne was going to tell them to cut it out, but she found herself strangely comforted by the squabbling boys. Ahead, Key stepped into a steep tunnel of wood. The opening was surrounded by triangles that all pointed in, but it was neither round nor uniform, reminding her of the toothy mouth of a giant. She felt herself becoming more and more nervous. But nervousness was to be expected, wasn't it? After all, they were about to confront the man who'd overthrown Key and her people.

She exited the steep tunnel and, for the first time since they had started climbing, she noticed a breeze. It was dark, but high above, the skies opened, lighting everything in a wash of otherworldly moonlight. *Garrett, look.*

Garrett stepped out behind her. "Whoa," he breathed.

What is it? David asked.

You guys got to see this, Garrett said.

Breanne spun in a slow circle, unsure what she'd expected to see. Behind her, a forest stretched out in every direction. It was hard to fathom a forest of trees growing from atop the Mazewood, but there they were, a strange tangle of trees with crooked trunks, bending back and forth, like a crowd of contortionists. The trees were intertwined so tightly she couldn't tell how deep the forest went.

A creaking and twisting drew her attention. "What is that?"

"A portion of the maze is shifting," Key explained. "When you are inside, you don't see this happening unless you are in the shifting section. It seems my memory is sound, my queen. No wrong turns. Fortunately, we didn't encounter any portions shifting on our path, nor did we encounter a single maze sprite on our journey. Turek has certainly blessed our journey on this day."

Wait. Did she say sprites? David asked, his voice pitching even in mind speak.

What the hell is a sprite? Lenny asked.

"Lady Key, I'm sorry, but what are maze sprites?" Breanne asked.

"It's a broad term for the fairies, pixies, and other like creatures of the Mazewood. There are many varieties. How many? No one knows for sure. Some, like goblins and kobolds, are quite devious creatures. There are also many formidable creatures in the maze, often hunted by the warriors of Cloud. The deadly creatures, coupled with Mazewood's confusing and dangerous passage, both protect and provide for those of Cloud. This ability to hunt in the Mazewood means less frequent trips to the Shadow Forest below."

So, what she is saying is we could have all been killed? David asked, appearing from the tunnel, hands on hips.

Settle down, David. You're fine, Garrett said.

"Where to now?" Breanne asked.

Key pointed behind her. "This way."

Breanne turned. She didn't see a forest in this direction, only a path worn into the smooth wood. It wasn't a steep climb, but it was pitched enough that she wouldn't be able to see what was on the other side until she reached the top. She nodded and began following Key and her guards upward, Garrett on one side and Paul on the other.

When they crested the wooden structure, Breanne found herself standing at the edge of the Mazewood, looking down. In the distance, water roared. Hundreds of feet below, a river glistened in the moonlight as if alive. White water crashed over rocks, but she shouldn't be able to hear the water, not from up here.

Paul pointed. *Look! Twelve o'clock.*

"Is that a bridge?" Breanne asked aloud.

"That, Queen Breeze, is indeed a bridge," Key said, smiling.

Behind her, the rest of the people of Sky were emerging from the tunnel and taking a moment to gather, hydrate, and rest from the climb.

"But I don't understand. It seems to twist... or turn? I can't see where it connects to the other side."

"Ah, you expected a straight bridge? But this bridge is not built here, my queen. This bridge was grown. Directly across are sheer cliffs. The bridge winds around. It will reach the other side, and then you will see the city we were banished from – your city."

"Cliffs – so we're leaving the woods?" she asked.

"Of course. Come. You shall see very soon," Key said, and Breanne could sense the woman's excitement.

The structure in front of Breanne was like a rope bridge but formed from vines that stretched and twisted through branches protruding upward on both sides, like curling fingers. The footway consisted of a narrow plank of worn wood growing in one continuous piece rather than many planks placed crosswise along the span. The bridge swayed slightly when she stepped onto it, causing her heart to jump.

It's okay. I'm right behind you, Garrett said.

Nodding, she drew in a calming breath and walked forward. The long plank of wood kinked, bent, and sometimes pitched down only to climb back up. Breanne felt like she was on a bridge made by Dr. Seuss.

As they walked, three things remained constant. They were winding to the left. The sound of crashing water was growing louder, and the cliffs, now on her right, were growing taller. Finally, the bridge turned, cutting back sharply to the right.

Then she saw. They all saw. "Oh, wow!"

In front of her, the mountain parted into sheer cliffs rising ever upward on the left and the right. But what stole her breath lay ahead in the near distance, where a stone city scaled a terraced mountainside. The city appeared lit by hundreds of orbs containing a combination of moon and starlight. The otherworldly illumination reminded Breanne of the glow from lightning bugs on a summer night back home in Indiana. Only this lightning bug glow was oversized and unmoving.

The city itself was unlike anything she had ever seen. The stone walls appeared carved into the mountain face, but when she looked more closely, she could tell the buildings protruded onto terraces of impeccably shaped and stacked stone. On both sides, waterfalls sparkled and spilled quietly from the mountains, pouring over in volumes that rivaled Niagara Falls. Quiet as the falls were, the crashing of water far below gave off a constant rumble. This was the source of the sound she'd heard when she first stepped onto the bridge.

"Behold the city of Cloud!" Key announced.

They continued forward along the strange, twisting sky bridge until they reached a stone landing outside the city's massive wooden gate. The gate was several yards wide, spanning the width of the landing.

"Look at those planks. They must be thick as trees!" David shouted aloud as he pointed toward the gate.

"Aye, those iron lashes binding them planks be dwarven forged," Kilug said pridefully.

As Key, Breanne, and three of her guards stepped off the bridge, two men approached from each side of the gate, swords drawn.

"Halt! In the name of the king!" one man shouted.

The men were not what Breanne expected. They wore colorful outfits that looked like they were right out of the 1970s on Earth. Their pants belled out at the bottom, with matching sleeves that flared at the cuffs. The material of their uniforms reminded her of velvet, and each of them wore black capes like they were Elvis Presley impersonators.

Oh, hell no! Lenny laughed.

But when the men drew their swords and leveled them at Key and Breanne, Lenny's mind laughter stopped short.

Breanne glanced back to find Garrett was right behind her, with Lenny and Paul in tow.

"Do not point sharp things at your betters, lest you wish to find yourself the one impaled, Glass," Key said evenly.

"I see you haven't changed, Key."

"That's Lady Key to you."

"Really? Have you given up on calling yourself a queen, then?" Glass asked, grinning at his companion. The younger man grinned back stupidly.

"I've neither time nor desire to explain myself to you,

peasant! I demand an audience with Deep. Now step aside, or shall I take the city by force?"

"By force?" Glass laughed. "You couldn't take it last time. What makes you think you will fare any better now? Is the ebon night concealing some grand army we've yet to learn of?"

Key stepped forward, within reach of the portly man. "It is quite attractive for a man to carry extra weight – quite impressive. But a man's weight should be paired with strength from building, from working fields, from tanning hides, butchering, and splitting firewood. However, I see no strength here. Only pathetic examples of men. You have grown lazier than even I could have predicted. Now, stand aside or be slain. I already know Deep's army is out there trying to hunt us down. But his plan failed, Glass. I have brought the entire might of the women of Sky to his doorstep. Now stand—"

"You are mistaken, Lady Key," Glass said, his face twisting into an ugly smile. "Our army is right here."

Behind the two men, the gate creaked as the sound of a chain clicking filled the night air. Slowly the massive wood gate rose, firelight flickering from beneath.

Damn, Paul said.

Breanne glimpsed a row of feet a dozen yards wide. Each foot was partially covered in the same flaring bell-bottom pants worn by the gate guards. As the gate continued upward, the feet became legs, torsos, and arms – arms holding shields and swords. Finally, the gate clunked with finality, revealing not a single row of men, but dozens of rows – every soldier staring directly at them with anger and resolve.

40

King Deep

God Stones – Moon Ring 4
The City of Cloud

Garrett and his sages stood staring down an army of men clad in weird uniforms, holding strange-shaped shields, and brandishing crude swords. To the trained eye, the weapons looked heavy and unwieldy.

Garrett drew his sword. *Lenny, get ready to play your guitar. David, spin that staff and get ready to swing. Focus like you did before with the giant. Pete and Paul, draw guns and get ready to shoot. Maybe if you shoot in the air, it will scare the crap—*

"Well, well, well!" a voice shouted, drawing Garrett's attention.

In the center of the rank and file, men spun on their heels, one group taking a synchronized step to their left, the other to their right, forming an aisle. At the opposite end of the courtyard stood a bulbous man in a ruffled blouse. Over the blouse, he wore a long cloak of blue with gold embroidery. His too-tight pants were bright red, belling out like his men's. He started forward, his shoes clacking on the stone. Garrett squinted at the shoes and realized they were designed with a sole several inches thick. But even with the extra inches, the man didn't appear to be very tall.

Deep reached the front row of his men and brushed back a lock of salt-and-pepper hair. His ornate crown held the rest back. The crown looked like metal of some kind, but it was in the shape of... antlers, maybe? Now that he was close, the man reminded Garrett of a rat. He had beady eyes and a pinched face with teeth that stuck out of his mouth.

Garrett? You sure I shouldn't just give this guy my guitar? I mean, look at that outfit! Lenny laughed.

Kid, how about you focus on how we're going to get out of this alive and forget the fashion show, Paul said.

I know, I know, but I'm just saying... those shoes, though! And I have to get a pair of those pants!

King Deep narrowed his eyes at Key. "I've been waiting for you," he said, his voice creepily sinister.

Garrett shivered.

"You didn't expect my army to still be here." He smiled, lifting a shoestring arm to point at Key. "You expected me to send them chasing after you like a fool."

"You look well, Deep—"

"King Deep!" the man screeched, his eyes flashing.

"You're no king of mine," Key said flatly.

"Yes, well, I was good enough to be your lover until you tossed me aside for that scoundrel, Shine!"

Whoa, eww. Key is way too hot to be with that guy! Lenny said.

You know it isn't always about looks, Len, Pete said.

I know, but come on! Her... and him... Yikes! I'm just saying yi—

Stow it! Paul said.

"You have never been better than me, Keyhold. You and

your women have never been better than us," King Deep said, gesturing with a flourish. "Now state your business here and prepare yourselves for what comes next."

"And what is it you think comes next, Deep?"

King Deep smiled. "What comes next is a celebration. What comes next is your surrender, be it voluntary or by force. Personally, I prefer the latter. By force is how I plan to treat you in all matters of this kingdom."

"Ah, but I know something you do not. Oh dear Deep, do you really think I would come here knowing the risk without knowing the outcome? Do you think me the fool?" Key glanced over at the crowd of soldiers, raising her voice so all could hear. "A name has been spoken on the wind! A name spoken by Turek, the one and only god of humans! We all heard the name and soon after, the chosen one appeared! This chosen of Turek is here with us now!"

"Good. Very good!" King Deep said, raising his own voice to match Key's.

Key's brows knitted, and she laughed. "Good?"

"Yes, of course! Most glorious of moon rings!" King Deep held his hands out to his sides, palms up. "Not only do we get our new emperor, whose name was spoken on the wind for all of us to hear, but Turek saw fit to hand-deliver the women of Sky back home to serve under the rule of man!"

With a sudden flourish, Deep's army jumped in the air, stomping down with one foot, then the other.

"As it should be!" Deep shouted.

The men jumped again, landing on one foot, then stomping the ground with the other.

"As it should have always been!" Deep shouted.

Again, the men responded, this time by stomping their feet twice, raising their swords high in the air, and stomping their feet twice more.

Are we being challenged to a dance off? I feel like these fools want to dance battle! Lenny said, laughing.

No one else laughed.

King Deep smiled and raised his own sword high. "Bring forward he whose name was spoken!"

He? Breanne said in mind speak, her eyes finding Garrett's.

Oh no, he said, closing his eyes.

"He?" Key repeated, her face a visage of confusion.

"Of course! Come forward, Garrett Turek! Descendant of the one true god of humans! Claim your place among your men!"

"Garrett Turek?" Key repeated, her face twisted as if she'd bit into a lemon thinking it an orange. "You! You are of... of Turek?"

Garrett opened his eyes to find Breanne's own were still locked on his. He did his best to express how sorry he was.

Tell stepped forward, looking at Garrett anew. "The runes, the way you levitated the collapsing mountain..." Her face was a combination of horror and awe. "The way they look at you, the way you commanded them in the Dark Narrow!"

"But the name! The name spoken was not Garrett Turek," Key argued.

"I have over eight hundred soldiers standing before you who will testify that the name spoken on the wind was in fact Garrett Turek! Now, I ask you again, Keyhold – vagrant of the Shadow Forest, leader of a filthy rebellion, and let us not forget, dethroned and exiled peasant – send forward the one whose name was spoken by the wind. Let him be named and take his rightful place as emperor of the land of Sky!"

Emperor? They want to make you an emperor! David said in mind speak.

Garrett, still looking at Breanne, ignored the comment.

The Last Gift

"Answer the question," Key demanded. "Are you him? Are you descended of Turek?"

Garrett swallowed, finding his voice. "You know the answer, Lady Key."

Key's eyes flashed, and she recoiled as if he had struck her. "I trusted you! We trusted you!" But she was no longer looking at Garrett – her attention was on Breanne. "You lied to us!"

"No! I... I... it isn't like that," Breanne started.

"It is exactly like that. You with your easy ways. Letting men partake in womanly decisions!"

The women of Sky raised their weapons. "This is it then! Today we die or we take back our queendom," Key shouted. Then, turning to the women, she shouted, "Kill them all! Fight unto you fall or every man is dead!"

Garrett spun in a slow circle as the women raised atlatls, the men high on a courtyard wall drew back bowstrings, and the soldiers on the ground lifted their iron swords. There was no time! No time for words. No time for Lenny to play the guitar or the others to use what skills they could to stop the approaching battle.

As Garrett turned, a bird with wings spread wide glided down onto the ledge separating the landing from the sheer cliff's edge. The bird was strange, stranger than any bird he'd yet seen on Karelia. It was tall, maybe two feet in height, with red and black feathers that looked chinchilla soft and sparkled as if dusted with diamonds. It reminded him of an owl, but this was no ordinary owl.

Suddenly, his mind flashed to the time he got to pet a chinchilla at a pet store in Springfield. It had been the softest fur he'd ever felt. What a stupid thing to think about now. Besides, it wasn't this strange bird's fluffy feathers holding his attention. It was the thing's face. It looked more human than bird. Like a woman's face, and she was looking right at him – smiling kindly.

The mysterious bird's eyes looked as if they were made of something... something his mind struggled to see but also saw clearly. Sentheye? Yes. Sentheye in its truest form. Garrett didn't know how he knew, but he did – he knew.

The bird inclined its head toward him – or perhaps toward the armies behind him.

Garrett frowned, his head whipping around to steal a glance over his shoulder.

∼

Breanne's heart had broken when Key accused her of lying. After having spent hours talking with Key over the last few days and learning about her people, her culture, and Key herself, something dawned on her that she hadn't realized until this very moment. She'd lost her mother years ago, and then Sarah only a few days back, but Key... Key reminded her of them... of something she'd lost. She didn't want to lose Key too.

Scrambling, she had tried to explain, but Key wasn't listening. What else could she say? She didn't understand what was happening, and she hadn't meant to lie. She hadn't meant to hurt anyone. Back at the longhouse, it had all spun out of control so quickly when... when Key said it was Breanne's name, whispered on the wind. They'd all heard it, hadn't they?

Why would Turek do this? Why would he whisper her name to the women of Sky and Garrett's to these men? *Think, Breanne. You can solve this. There must be a logical explanation!* But there was no time. Key was yelling now.

Breanne wanted to shout, "Wait! No. Don't."

The Last Gift

The women were lifting spears, and the men were angry, drawing their bows and raising swords.

Lenny was trying to get his guitar untangled.

David looked scared as he clumsily spun the staff.

Governess stood next to Pete, who looked like he didn't know who he should focus his eyes on. Paul was beside her, his jaw clenched as he drew his nine and racked the slide.

Instinctively, Breanne's hand went to her hip, gripping the handle of her own handgun. Her eyes found their way back to Garrett, only to find him with his back to her, to all of them, looking… looking at… at a bird.

Suddenly, he whipped his head back around.

Breanne gasped. In front of her, a hundred bowstrings released with a collective *thunk*. Simultaneously, the crowd of women behind her grunted as they let fly hundreds of spears.

And in the middle of it all, Breanne stood next to Key, Tell, and the others, a hundred arrows bearing down.

Reflexively, she slammed her eyes shut and threw her hands up to protect her face, as if a hand could stop an arrow.

41

The Chase

God Stones – Moon Ring 4
The Creators' Mountain, Karelia

Ereshkigal appeared, collapsing onto her hands and knees, gasping.

"Eresh!" Turek shouted, gliding forward, his arms cradling her.

"I'm fine," she managed.

"No, you are not fine, Eresh," Turek said.

"How is this possible? The boy doesn't even have a God Stone!" Typhon shouted.

Aurgelmir shook his head. "No. You are wrong. Do you not see? He has them all."

"What are you talking about?" Druesha asked. "Clearly, he has nothing."

"How could we be such fools?" Aurgelmir said.

"Aye, what are ye saying?" Durin asked impatiently.

Turek looked upon his brethren, still kneeling next to Ereshkigal as she struggled to push herself up from the floor. "What Aurgy is saying is that we are thinking of the physical relationship between the God Stones and Jack, when we should be thinking of the magical one. Jack doesn't need to hold the God Stones. He has transcended the need for a physical connection in order to harness their power."

"But that's not possible, is it?" Rán asked, her face swirling in alternating light, a sure sign she was frightened.

"No. Of course not," Typhon said firmly.

"Fool," Ereshkigal said. "Of course it is possible. Not just possible, but it is a fact, and I have just proven it. Or do you think my near-death experience a ruse? The creature nearly killed me!"

"Are you... are you alright, sister?" Druesha asked.

Rán and Druesha glided forward, landing softly beside her and Turek.

"I will survive, I think. The pain – if indeed this strange sensation is pain – well, it seems to be fading," she said, gathering herself. "Now, enough of this. What is important are my orders. I have given the boy very distinct instructions, and as long as he believes I will follow through on my threats, I should be able to control... what?" she asked, trailing off. "What is it?"

Pulling his attention from Ereshkigal, Turek glanced at his brothers. They were peering into the circle – into Karelia.

"Well, this is interesting," Aurgy said.

"Come, let me help you," Turek offered, and the four joined the others back in the circle.

"Yes, interesting indeed. Jack and Zerri are leading their armies away from the Mountains of Twelve toward Osonian," Durin said, pointing into the circle.

"So what? The creature is doing as I directed. I have a feeling he will follow my orders to the letter," Ereshkigal said, wincing as she leaned forward.

"You may want to recant that statement, sister," Typhon said. "Or do you not see what is missing from this picture?"

Ereshkigal frowned, searching the scene below, but Turek had seen it instantly. "What?" she asked again, shaking her head. Ereshkigal's scowl deepened, then her eyes flashed with revelation. "Where are my dökkálfar?"

"Jack left them imprisoned in the dungeons of Throne Mountain," Durin said.

"No. No! This means he plans to ignore my warning!"

Typhon stood. "Turek, my brother, I know we have not agreed on a great many things, but I think it is time we abandoned this experiment of yours and intervened. I respect what you had hoped to find, but the risk to Metsavana, and therefore to all of us, is too great."

Turek nodded solemnly. How could he continue to argue for this? How could he allow the entire world of Karelia and even their own lives to be at risk in order to prove the Great Mother was here watching them even now, manipulating everything? No. Typhon was right. As he looked around the circle, he could see they all knew it. But Typhon was asking his opinion – not forcing him. Perhaps, if he were stubborn in this, they *would* tell him to abandon this fool's errand, but the fact they were asking… well, it filled his heart with love. "I… I know in this you are—"

"Wait!" Rán blurted. "Change your vision to Garrett!"

Turek did so, and the others followed suit. All looked into the circle as if it were a crystal ball, but in fact it was just a floor – bejeweled as it was, it was just a floor. Still, they focused, the Sentheye pooled, and they saw.

Garrett and the others had arrived in Cloud. King Deep's army had greeted them at the gate. Bowmen were drawing down on Garrett, his sages, and the women of Sky. In turn, the women were about to launch spears.

Turek's heart sank. Death was about to befall not only his sages but so many of his humans. "This is unfortunate," Turek said.

"No, look!" Rán said again. "The bird."

Turek frowned, watching as Garrett turned his back on the doom of what was to come and focused on the bird. "Typhon. Birds are your domain. Did you send this one?"

"No," Typhon said, as they pulled the view closer. "Wait."

"What is it?" Druesha asked.

"This is not one of mine," Typhon said.

"Well, whose is it then?" Turek asked, his eyes flashing around the circle.

"That creature is not of my making," Druesha said.

"It seems to have the wee face of a female human, dökkálfar, or like creature. A fairy perhaps?" Durin asked.

"A fairy bird?" Turek asked.

"Perhaps a fairy casting a spell?" Ereshkigal offered.

"No. I don't think so," Druesha said.

Skeptically, Turek glanced around the circle, but no one claimed the creation of the mysterious fowl.

"Look!" Rán gasped. "Look at the boy!"

Turek watched as Garrett nodded at the bird, then glanced back over his shoulder.

In the moments that followed, excited commotion broke out as the creators watched what unfolded below.

Turek should have been watching too. Above all else, it was he who had the most vested in his sages and his humans. But he could not turn away from the real mystery. He could not so much as blink for fear of losing what no one understood.

Turek watched the bird.

The bird opened her wings and glided from the stone railing. Turek followed, intent on staying with the strange aberration. What was this creature? Why was she here now, at this very moment? And where was she going? He had to stay with her. He had to see where she went. The bird dipped low, swooping toward the falls. Very well then – there was nowhere on Karelia that Turek couldn't follow.

As the owl-like creature dove, Turek's vision dove after her. When she banked, his vision banked, and when she twisted, he too twisted. Far down the mountain, mist roiled up from the crashing water below, thick as storm clouds. The bird plunged downward like an eagle in pursuit of prey, faster than water fell and faster still until… until it vanished, swallowed by the mist.

No! Turek thought, panic rising as he zoomed in closer. Yet, close as he was, he couldn't see. Wait! There! A blur. Just a small streak, but then a flash of feathers, then gone again. Sentheye surged through his body like blood from a quickening pulse. He felt alive – truly alive! He couldn't lose her. The thought of what this meant – of what this creature meant! For if not of their making, then whose?

Another flash of silver, then white! Wait! Was that the bird or the mist itself? *Dammit.* Turek panned back above the mist, watching, hoping. Praying he would see her when she came out. But she never came out.

The bird was gone.

"Well, brother Turek?" Aurgy asked.

Turek blinked. "What?"

"Your humans! Did you not see what just happened?"

"What?" Turek repeated.

"Did ye not see? If not in the city of Cloud, where have ye been, brother?" Durin asked, studying Turek's face.

"I… I was…"

"Plotting something, no doubt," Rán said.

"You're one to talk of plotting, sister," Turek answered. "In fact, I was following the bird."

"The bird?" Typhon asked. "And where did the bird go?"

"I followed it for several minutes but lost it in the mist of a waterfall. But please, what did I miss?"

"You missed the death of your human—"

"Wait!" Aurgy interrupted. "A simple bird outwitted a creator?"

"I've a feeling this was no simple bird. But please, tell me – who died?" Turek asked, a sick feeling filling him as he turned his vision back to the city of Cloud.

No one answered. Instead, their conversation centered on the bird, which Turek suddenly regretted having followed.

"Another altered creation? Perhaps this one slipped through the portal from Earth," Ereshkigal offered.

"That would explain why we couldn't identify it," Aurgelmir said.

"Perhaps, but please tell me. Who died?" Turek pleaded as he peered into the circle. "Oh, dear. Oh Great Mother, she didn't?"

Druesha placed a hand on Turek's shoulder. "She did. But it matters not, brother. Let us focus on the dilemma at hand. Considering what just took place in your human city, I think we can agree an alliance of the humans is unlikely. Not that they stood any chance at defeating the forces of dragon, giant, and dökkálfar anyway."

"Then do ye all agree? Once the gates to Osonian are breached, we should intervene?" Durin asked.

"Yes. Of course. Metsavana must not fall lest we all die," Ereshkigal said.

The others nodded.

They were right. There was no denying the risk to their very own existence. Turek wanted to have faith. In their Great Mother, he did have faith. But his faith wasn't strong enough to risk the destruction of not only Metsavana but themselves.

Great Mother, please forgive me. Turek nodded sagely. "Then it is decided. If Jack and those he leads are not stopped before they breach the wall, we shall descend to Karelia and stand united in defense of the father tree."

"It is agreed. But..." Rán started.

Eresh narrowed her eyes. "But? But what?"

"She wants to spin the knife," Turek said, a grin forming on his face.

"Well, we still have two moon rings before Jack will arrive with his army of dragons. Might as well have some fun." She smiled innocently.

"I don't know your game, sister, but two moon rings are two more opportunities for us to influence the outcome," Typhon said.

"Yes. And knowing what we know now, it would be in our best interest to work to influence an outcome best for Metsavana rather than ourselves," Druesha said.

"I don't disagree," Turek said, feeling excitement swell inside him. There was still time. *Oh, Great Mother, are you there guiding this? I think you must be.* Still, why was Rán so invested? Jack wasn't good for anyone and, of course, one God Stone was hers, but all his instincts told him she was up to something else. There was more to her excitement than the prospect of getting back her stone.

"Spin it!" Rán blurted.

"Eresh," Turek said, placing the knife in the circle, "I believe the honor is yours."

Ereshkigal frowned, reached into the circle, and spun the knife with a casual flick of her wrist.

The spin stopped on Aurgelmir.

PART II

THE PROMISE AND THE SACRIFICE

42

The Failure of James Paul

Saturday, May 7 – God Stones Day 31
Rural Chiapas State, Mexico

Standing atop an ancient pyramid in southern Mexico, James Paul wept silently, a rage building in his chest, threatening to turn his tears to fire. Above him a full moon hung, unconcerned with mortal affairs as it shone brightly, daring the star-filled sky to do more. Below him, a wreck of carnage littered the stairs in the form of dead giants, dragon scales, blood, and a broken tree that still lay smoldering. But none of that mattered. What churned the bile in the back of his throat were the bodies of his friends… his Keepers… Annie… all strewn amid the chaos of hot ash and charred wood.

From the forest below came a flood of tall faceless creatures, marching on creaking stick legs. The army of tree monsters stomped from step to step in an assured cadence, each brandishing a wooden shield for one arm and a sword for the other.

For James, the moment slowed into a surreal nightmare.

The Keepers who had survived the giants' attack on the pyramid stairs were now fleeing upward, their faces visages of horror-stricken fear as they screamed. Some ran upright, others clambered on hands and toes, all scrambling away from this new threat.

James blinked, everything slow, everything distant, Pando's words echoing in his mind. "You asked what now, Commander. I will tell you. You will listen as your people scream and die. You will learn what it is to be truly helpless."

Even now, his head shook from side to side. Even after he pleaded, "You can't do this."

He closed his eyes, her next words gutting him. "Oh, but I can. I am going to kill your people, James Paul. I am going to kill them while you watch."

"No, please no," he rasped, opening his eyes.

But the woman before him was no woman. Pando the Trembling Giant, tens of thousands of years old, was the queen of Earth's trees. Until the God Stones were unleashed, she was simply a colony of quaking aspen rooted in Utah. Now she was the greatest monster Earth had ever seen wrapped in the form of a beautiful human goddess similar in appearance to Nefertiti.

Behind him, more people screamed – his people.

Spinning, James found the entrance to the temple fully blocked by more of the tree creatures.

Keepers were panicking, some collapsing at the trees' stick feet, begging for their lives, while others ran. But with nowhere to go, fear drove them to do the unthinkable – leap over the side of the pyramid. A few controlled their descent, staying on their backs as they slid. However, most immediately lost control, tumbling head over heels or going into a sideways roll.

"Oh, dear god," James breathed. Even if they survived

The Last Gift

the slide down the mountain-sized pyramid, the forest waited for them below.

"Please! Everyone, stay calm!" Elaine pleaded as another Keeper screamed and leapt over the side.

Holly the Hammer and Bloomer, now Sir Spider, appeared at the top of the stairs – disheveled and bloody, but alive. Lady Hammer's face was set in a grimace, her war hammer in one hand, sword in the other. Sir Spider's face seemed to match his crazy beard as he held a two-handed broadsword coated in giant blood.

Pando followed James's gaze and smiled a twisted inhuman smile, grains of wood radiating across her perfect skin. "You think they can save you? Or perhaps you think you can save your Keepers." Pando held out her arms, and the trees went still where they stood. Hundreds of the strange shape-shifters now crowded the stairs, while hundreds more crowded around the temple, filling the entryway. "You can save no one, James Paul." Pando dropped her arms. "Fell the humans!"

"No!" James shouted, raising his bastard sword.

"Now just hold on!" Dr. Moore shouted at the tree queen, but James knew there was no bargaining, no compromising – and no more begging.

The tree shifters raised and swung their long wooden blades, chopping down his helpless Keepers as if whacking through thick brush.

Elaine's eyes widened in horror.

James lunged at Pando, swinging his bastard sword with every ounce of strength he could put behind it.

The tree woman caught the blade in her hand and snapped it, idly tossing the metal shard onto the stone stairs. The broken blade bounced downward, from step to step, strangely silent. James watched the blade, as to look in any other direction was to witness a horror he could neither stop nor bear. Nor could he hide from the reason for the silent descent of the broken blade. The sound of metal on stone must have been there somewhere beneath the ocean of screams.

James stared down the ancient pyramid's stairs, somehow aware he'd departed sanity. Pando still stood at the top of the stairs, her back to the forest, but he wasn't looking at her. Nor was he focused on the hundreds of tree people marching up and up, their woody limbs creaking as they trampled the smoldering chunks of wooden shards, leftovers of some battle fought before James arrived – before Garrett left them all behind. No. James didn't see them, relentless in their determination to claim their pound of flesh.

The screams were there too – many at first, but one by one the screams were snuffed out like a candlewick under a douter. The place where his sanity once lived was hollow now. In this new emptiness, all that remained was the echo of his own emotions. His gaze was fixed far away, far below this nightmare of murderous death. Then he saw them: a group of humans appearing from the trees. They reached the stone stairs as a man turned and ran from one side of the stairs to the other, doing… doing what?

A strange wall of… of smoke shot up into the air, disappearing into the night sky.

A man yelled, pointing.

James realized he must truly have gone mad.

Another man threw something and shouted, but James couldn't make it out. Oh, he'd really lost it. He almost laughed at the spectacle, but then gunshots pulled him back.

James flinched.

Farther up the stairs, something exploded.

A group of tree people splintered into shards.

James's ears rang.

Pando twisted, shouting something.

Hands gripped his shoulders. Charles was shaking him. Yelling something.

James blinked again, another explosion... Boom! And another... Boom!

James shook his head. Maybe he wasn't insane or maybe he was, but either way, those were real people on the stairs! A real force field and real frags detonating.

The men appeared through the smoke, guns firing rapid rounds into the trees. James could hear a man shouting orders. "Bill! Fire eyes! Light them up!"

A short man took off his glasses and seemed to just stare at a group of trees. A second later, they burst into flame. "DeKeyser, when we get to the top, we need to separate the target! You get a wall up, and I mean fast!"

A woman James hadn't realized was a woman until now shouted, "Shawn, the target is loaded with mojo! She's so full I can't even nail down her attributes!"

"What are you saying, Jenna?" a man in a boonie hat asked.

"I'm saying, I've never felt anything like this!" She jerked the pin from a frag and threw it like a baseball, high over James and the Keepers who were gathered behind him, still fighting for their lives.

The frag landed in a group of trees near the corner of the pyramid temple.

"Heads down!" she shouted, just before the explosion shook the pyramid beneath his feet.

Tree people blew off the ledge outside the temple.

Finally shaken back into the moment, James looked over to find the tree queen's face flashing woodgrain.

"Enough of this!" Pando hissed, turning away from James and the others to face the six soldiers on the stairs. Thrusting out her hands, she chanted a language James hadn't heard in nearly a thousand years. This was the language of the gods, spoken by Apep the night Turek, the templar, was killed.

James looked at Sir Spider and nodded.

The bearded man tossed James his longsword and drew his sidearm.

James caught the sword by the hilt. Was this Turek's doing? Was this the last chance he'd prayed for?

Dr. Moore racked the slide on his forty-five. The man's eyes were enormous, his cheeks flexing under the strain of a clenched jaw.

Elaine drew back on her bowstring.

Live or die, it was time to end this. James raised the broadsword and charged Pando.

43

The Sentence

God Stones – Moon Ring 4
The City of Cloud

There was a truth Garrett hadn't understood until this very moment – this very nanosecond – as his head whipped around to find arrows loosed and spears in flight.

A revelation dawned as time ran out. Breanne was going to die. Lenny, Pete, David, Gabi, and probably even Governess were all going to die, and for no other reason than time. Time they no longer had.

Garrett understood something else. He didn't want to be a leader, but he'd always known that bit. Truth was, he'd never wanted this responsibility, and he'd tried all along the way to do everything he could not to lead. All the way back in the dojo, he'd begged Mr. B to help them, tried to convince him he'd gotten this all wrong. He tried again with James and Phillip. Even with Ed. Back then, he'd probably have been okay with Ed just leading the whole way if the others had been, and if things hadn't gone so badly. And what had all his leadership gotten them? Failure. He'd failed to save Ed or the Keepers, and by the time this was over, he would have failed to save humanity. If Bre died... Jesus, if she died... none of it mattered. Damn it all.

This was how he spent his nanosecond of thought.

They were out of time.

But Garrett had one more revelation. Time was the only thing he could control. And so he reached.

The poor kid from nowhere Illinois, who slowed dragons in flight, giants in mid-stride, and once even stopped a mountain from crushing a dwarf, grabbed time once more.

Above them, hundreds of arrows and spears halted, suspended in their flight.

Lenny jerked his head up, filling Garrett's mind. *Bro! did you just stop—*

Nearly slipping at the abrupt entry of Lenny's words into his mind, Garrett replied, *No time, Lenny – get that guitar unstrapped.*

"Whaaaat?" Deep shouted.

Breanne slowly lowered her hands. *Garrett!*

Garrett had stopped the arrows and the spears, but not the armies.

Pete, focus on the arrows and push them away, Garrett ordered.

I... I can do that?

You can, Garrett said assuredly, noticing the bowmen on the wall shaking off their amazement to nock another round of arrows.

"Aye, who's me fighting, Lord Garrett?" Kilug asked, spinning the massive war hammer as if it were a baton.

"Hold, Kilug!" Garrett shouted out loud and then in mind speak, *Play, Len!*

Lenny did play.

Garrett looked at Pete, who was focused intently on the sky.

The Last Gift

All at once, the arrows dropped from the sky, clattering onto the stone. Pete spun, a smile stretching across his face. Shifting his focus to the spears, they too were pushed away until they fell from their slowed flight, dropping harmlessly onto the stone floor of the courtyard.

"What is the meaning of this?" Key asked.

The women scrambled, bending to pick up what spears they could.

Lenny, playing a song by an artist who shared his first name, was now singing horribly at top of his lungs, "Are you going to go my way!" but there was so much shouting coming from both sides Lenny either couldn't focus or wasn't being heard.

"What is that incessant sound?" Deep bellowed, as he spun back to his bowman. "Dammit, what are you waiting for? Fire again!" Then, pointing at the women, he shouted, "Men of Cloud, charge!"

But the men faltered, unsure.

Paul! Bre! Fire your guns in the air! Garrett shouted.

Roger that! Paul said, nodding to his sister. They lifted their weapons, each firing three rounds.

Clack, clack, clack!

Clack, clack, clack!

The thundering reports echoed off the mountain walls. The shouting ceased, everyone going silent, trying to understand what was happening. Some even fell to the ground covering their heads while others, having never heard the concussive blast from a gun, looked up as if expecting the heavens to open.

It was all the time Lenny needed. His voice lifted, becoming clear and pitch perfect.

The bowmen were the first to falter. They dropped their bows and sat down. Deep's ground soldiers went next, their iron swords clattering to the ground.

"Look! They're dying. Take them now," Key ordered.

Lenny spun, changing his attention to the women and singing, "I just got to – got to know... yeah!"

The women of Sky stumbled in sudden exhaustion.

King Deep trudged forward, his long cape trailing behind him, finger wagging angrily at Key as she started forward to meet him.

They were farthest from Lenny, but with every step they were moving closer.

Key was brandishing a short sword. Garrett wasn't even sure when or how the woman came to possess the sword, but nevertheless she had it, and she was preparing to use it.

Governess! Garrett said in mind speak.

Governess ran forward, her hood falling back to reveal loose hair the color of autumn leaves blowing with the wind as she moved. Roots shot from Governess's hands, tangling the two as they neared one another.

Lenny walked toward them as he played, and the two went into a strange slow-motion collapse.

Governess withdrew her roots.

Both armies were subdued in the sleep of Lenny's spell. After a final strum he announced, "We're badasses!"

"Pete, that was awesome!" David said, lowering his staff. "Kilug, did you see..." But he trailed off when he noticed the dwarf lying in a fetal position, cradling his war hammer, and snoring.

The rest of the sages continued talking, but Garrett ignored them.

Breanne was looking at him, and he could see the distress in her eyes. "It's okay, Bre. We can fix this." Turning to Paul and Governess, he said, "Can you guys carry Key and Deep this way? I see an inner gate. If we can lock the armies out here, we can deal with those two one on one."

"Won't the armies just kill each other when they wake up?" Pete asked.

"Probably. That's why we need to hurry," Garrett said. Then he looked at Lenny.

"I already know what you're going to say. Yes, I would be happy to stand guard and yes, I will make sure if anyone wakes up, I rip some chords and lullaby them back nighty-night," he said, jumping into the air and scissor kicking as he strummed the guitar.

"Show-off," David said.

"Thanks, Len," Garrett said, slapping him on the shoulder.

"Don't thank me. I get to hang out here and play guitar while you go play marriage counselor with angry grown-ups. I think I got the better deal on this one," Lenny said, walking toward a stone bench.

Paul lifted Key, and Governess lifted a snoring King Deep. Garrett, Breanne, and the rest of the sages, save David, who insisted on staying with Lenny to keep him safe, made their way across the courtyard and into a corridor, where several sets of stairs led up and down into various parts of the city.

The first thing Garrett noticed was that despite the darkness of early morning, the halls were well lit with wall sconces that were fueled by neither electricity nor fire.

Down the hall, two women carrying baskets of colorful produce gasped, dropping their goods as they turned and fled back the way they'd come.

"We need privacy," Garrett said.

"Here!" Paul said, pushing open a thick wooden door.

They hustled inside.

The room was large, with a long table along one side. Atop it sat food in various stages of preparation. The smell hit Garrett, causing his empty stomach to complain instantly with a deep growl. Garrett glanced around at the plain room, which, oddly, didn't contain chairs or other places to sit. The only thing resembling furniture was the long countertop.

A voice called out, "Girls, have you brought the chelios and vebainia sprouts?" and a woman wearing an apron appeared from around a corner, her eyes focused on a tray of cooked meat in her hands. When she looked up, her eyes widened.

Garrett held up his hands. "It's okay."

The tray dropped with a crash, its contents scattering across the stone floor. The woman screamed, turning back and fleeing from the room.

"Here." Paul pointed, pushing the food to one end of the long counter. He and Governess laid the sleeping pair on the long surface.

Garrett ran to the door the frightened woman had vanished through and peeked around the corner. The smell of fresh bread filled his nose. All along the wall were stone stoves glowing bright with hot coals. A kitchen. No chairs in there either. Man, David was really going to regret not coming along. At the opposite end was another door. The fleeing woman must have gone that way.

Garrett turned back, sliding shut a pocket door between the two rooms. Pete had already closed and bolted the other door.

King Deep sat against the wall, propped awkwardly atop the counter, listing to one side, his cape twisted around him. Key lay flat, one leg flopped over Deep's knees, the other hanging off the counter. Deep was already stirring.

"I think he's waking up," Gabi said.

"Well, here we go," Garrett said, reaching across the counter and slapping the king in the face. He didn't slap him hard, but hard enough.

The king's eyes popped open. Deep's thick brows

bunched immediately, his eyes shifting left and then right, then down to the leg lying across his lap. "Where am I? What's happened?"

"King Deep, I don't think we've been properly introduced. I am Garrett Turek."

"You? He whose name was whispered on the wind? So you say… Well, you don't look like much, and you show up with this ilk," Deep said, pushing Key's leg off his lap as he sat up straighter. "Even if you had come here alone, I would have been suspicious. I would have tested you, putting you through the rigors to ensure you are who you say you are, but you show up with my enemy?"

Key stirred.

"And what is this?" Deep asked, glancing at Key with irritation. "Where is my army? What have you done to them?" He pushed forward, swinging his legs off the counter.

Paul stepped forward, placing a hand on Deep's shoulder. "Just take it easy."

"What's happened?" Key asked, pushing herself up to a sitting position. She rubbed at her eyes, confusion setting in as they darted around the room. "The buttery? But what… why?" She looked to Breanne, "Where is my army? What have you done?"

Governess stepped forward next to Paul. "I advise you to remain calm, lest I be forced to restrain you."

Key frowned. "You think you can restrain me?"

"I am quite certain of it, Lady Key."

"Okay, enough. You two are going to knock it off and whatever problems you had are no longer important," Garrett said.

"No longer important?" Deep repeated. "If you are who you say you are, allow my army to imprison these women!"

"Over my dead body!" Key shouted.

"'Tis fine with—"

"Enough!" Garrett shouted over them. "No one will be enslaved, King Deep. We will work this out so that everyone is equal!"

"Equal?" Deep laughed.

Key shook her head. "Equal is not our way. Men are too intellectually inferior to women! They have their place. This is simply the way it is! The way it has always been!"

"Well, it is time for a new way, Key, and considering you named Breanne as your queen, it isn't your decision," Garrett said, looking at Breanne.

Breanne wore a sorrowful expression. "I'm sorry, Key. I really am, but women can no longer be treated as superior."

"Ha," Deep laughed. "You see! Even your own chosen one sees the folly of your ways, Keyhold."

"Shut up, Deep," Breanne said, clearly surprised at her own forcefulness, but she pressed on. "Key may be set in ways that need to change, but you, tyrant, have enslaved women into servitude of labor and god only knows what else. You, Deep, are a criminal. And today your tyranny ends!"

Garrett blinked, awed at her choice of words.

Key opened her mouth to speak, but at Breanne's words, she stopped short, listening. When Breanne finished, she asked. "And what exactly are you proposing, Breanne Moore?"

Garrett noticed Key no longer addressed her as Breezemore or queen. He looked to Breanne, ready to hear her plan, but nothing could have prepared him for what she said next.

Breanne narrowed her eyes. "I propose we execute Deep."

44

No Escape

Saturday, May 7 – God Stones Day 31
Rural Chiapas State, Mexico

The queen of trees, Pando the Trembling Giant, stood in human form, casting a magic spell down an ancient flight of stone stairs. As James drew back to swing, he realized that striking the dense and powerful tree with a sword would likely have little effect. Then his eyes fell on the tree woman's dress, which trailed all the way down what might very well have been a thousand stairs to writhe and root in the dirt below. Which begged the question, which part of Pando was up here, and which part was down there in the dirt?

A strange sensation filled James's chest. Something he hadn't felt since before he realized the portal was closed.

James felt hope.

This new hope surged inside him as he dove forward past the queen's human form and onto the stairs. Then, swinging from overhead like a crazed man with an axe, James chopped down with all he had, severing the trailing dress from Pando's human form.

The effect was instant. The human form changed back into a tree. Specifically, a small aspen only seven feet in height. Its leaves were dried as they would be in fall, and its roots were a tangled ball that neither wiggled nor writhed. The whole thing stood still for a moment, but the moment wasn't to last. With nowhere to root, it slowly tipped, falling uneventfully onto the stairs.

The six soldiers were with them now, engaging with the trees blocking the entrance into the temple, but still more came around both corners.

A tall bald man who looked to be chiseled from stone whispered into the leader guy's ear. The leader, a man with a salt-and-pepper beard, nodded and started giving orders. The tall guy ran forward, then fired at a tree until his magazine was empty. He dropped it and slapped in another as if he'd done this thousands of times.

"Bill," the leader shouted. "Get fire on that corner! Jenna, frag the other corner until we've nothing left to throw! Dexter! I want suppressive fire! DeKeyser, when we clear that entrance of those bastards and get the survivors in, I want a shield on that door, small and thick. How long can you hold one?"

"Maybe two minutes," answered a wiry man.

The guy shouting orders fired his weapon first into the air, causing the crowd of panicked Keepers to duck low onto the ground. Next, the man fired into the trees in front of the door of the temple, where dozens of dead or dying Keepers were still under attack. "Hold it for three!"

James stepped forward, intent on attacking and saving as many as he could, but something compelled him to look back over his shoulder. God, how he wished he hadn't done that.

Where James had severed the trailing dress stood a growing tangle of vines and roots in the shape of Pando.

James's heart thudded against his chest.

The tree woman met his eyes in a glower as she grew upward, larger than before. "Your efforts are futile, James Paul. A mortal wielding a strip of metal cannot kill me." Behind her, the forest moved forward, filling the stairs once more. "There is no escape for you!"

James turned back to the temple entrance, which was still blocked by stick people. "Come on, we have to get through!" he shouted, grabbing Dr. Moore by the sleeve.

Keepers were trapped, crowded in like cattle. Their only choices were to turn back to the stairs, jump off the pyramid, or fight the trees.

Behind them, Pando was still speaking. Above the chaos of screams, gunfire, and death, James could hear her plain as day. She was speaking to him telepathically, somehow, just like Garrett had.

Watch them, James Paul. Watch them all die because of you. Then, speaking to someone else but letting him hear, she said, *Go, my little ones. Let them feel our wrath.*

From across the crowd, James heard the bearded soldier shout, "Jenna, we need a frag on the entrance!"

"Negative! I'll kill civilians for sure!"

"No choice!"

James, Dr. Moore, and Elaine pushed forward through the crowd, chopping at the stickmen blocking their path. They had to get to the temple entrance. At least then he could fight and try to lead his people inside.

A concussive blast rang out. Wooden shards sprayed in every direction. James felt the wooden projectiles piercing his skin and face, but still he pushed forward – swinging, hacking, hoping, and praying. "Please!"

The temple entrance was their only chance.

45

Not a Single Chair

God Stones – Moon Ring 4
The City of Cloud

"Wait, what?" Garrett asked. "Sis? Are you serious?"

Breanne couldn't put it together at first, but now she knew exactly what she needed to do, and she knew precisely why Turek had spoken her name on the wind. "I am one hundred percent serious," she said, stepping toward the king.

Sweat beaded on Deep's brow, and he licked his lips, eyes darting. "You can't kill me! My army won't allow—"

"But your army isn't here," Breanne interrupted. "They are fast asleep, and by the time they wake, you will be dead." Breanne's words came with assured confidence, leaving no question.

Paul switched to mind speak so only she and the sages could hear. *Sis, what the hell are you doing?*

It's okay, Paul. Go on, Breanne, Garrett urged.

Of course, she wasn't actually going to kill him. But just knowing that Garrett trusted her completely, without even understanding, gave her a warm feeling inside. Breanne pulled the pistol from its holster and pointed it at Deep.

The rat-faced man cocked his head sideways, clearly confused by what he was looking at. Oh yeah, he'd never seen a pistol before and even though they'd fired it outside, he probably hadn't known where the sound had come from. She holstered the gun and drew her Toledo sword, then whipped it through the air, the blade whistling before it stopped abruptly against Deep's throat.

Deep reeled back across the counter, slamming himself against the wall, his eyes terror stricken. He reached up and touched his neck, his eyes going wider still as he looked at his now-bloody fingers.

Jesus, Sis! Give us a warning next time!

It's only a flesh wound... so far, Breanne answered back in mind speak, pressing the sword closer to the king's throat.

Deep's face twisted in fright as he whimpered. But Breanne's eyes were on Key and the unexpected expression of concern the woman let slip. *Just as I suspected,* Breanne thought. Then she spoke aloud so both Key and Deep could hear. "Garrett, your name was spoken on the wind, just as mine was. After I kill this disgusting scum, you will replace Deep and lead his army."

Garrett blinked. "Right. Okay."

"And what of my army?" Key asked.

Breanne narrowed her eyes at Key. "I think you mean my army, which I will lead as I see fit. The better question is what is to become of you, Keyhold."

"What? My people are victims! Outcast from our home! We've done nothing wrong... broken no laws!"

"I'm not talking about your people, Key, I'm talking about you. You, who accused your queen of deceit, called her a liar, and went against her orders and attacked!" Breanne drew back her sword and thrust it his time toward Key, stopping it as the point touched the woman's chest.

Key gasped, pushing herself back against the wall, her shoulder touching Deep's.

"Now, I ask, who dies first?"

Finding his voice, Deep pleaded, "You may have my army! Please, I beg of you, do not do this, do not kill me!"

Breanne's eyes gave a deadly flash. "No! You will turn on Garrett the first chance you get."

"No! I won't. You have my word," Deep said, leaning forward onto his hands and knees.

Garrett, Breanne said.

Garrett drew his sword, stepping forward to join her, his blade now leveled at Deep's face.

Deep scrambled back to his place against the wall.

Breanne glanced at Garrett. "Deep can't be trusted. He should die first. Do you want to kill him, or may I have the honor?" Breanne asked.

"No! Wait!" Deep pleaded. "The wind spoke the name Garrett Turek! Please! You *can* trust me! I give you my word, I will order all the citizens of Cloud to obey! The city is yours!"

"You always were a coward, Deep!" Key said.

"Silence, Keyhold of Sky. I am still deciding your fate," Breanne ordered.

"You think if you kill me, my people will follow you? You think my daughter will follow you?" Key asked.

Breanne swallowed the emotion threatening to spill down her cheeks. She could not kill Keyhold, but she hoped Key didn't know that. "Keyhold, I don't want to hurt you. Just like I don't want to hurt our people or your daughter. But I am here for a reason." She switched her sword to her left hand and took Garrett's free hand in hers.

Pete and Gabi stepped up close, crowding around them.

"We are here for a very important purpose, Key. We are trying to save a planet of humans and get our people here safely. And if you can't see by now that we were chosen to be here, then I'm afraid you're blinded by your own vengeance. I'm sorry, but we just don't have time for this. If that means I need to kill you... I will."

"You say this and yet you expect me to believe you have the good of my people in mind?"

"Yes. That's exactly what I expect, because if we fail, there will be no Osonian, no Shadow Forest, no Mazewood, no city of Cloud, no Metsavana. Maybe no Karelia, at least not one anyone recognizes, because I promise you whatever is left will be in ruin."

"What? Is this true?" Deep asked.

They all nodded.

Deep looked at Key, his brows knitted.

Key's expression turned grave. "Breanne Moore is telling the truth, Deep. Dragons and nephilbock may be attacking Osonian even now."

"Please, let me live. Let me help. Whatever you want," Deep begged.

Breanne hesitated, then looked at Key. "Do you still want to be my advisor?"

Key pulled in a long breath and let it out. "Yes, Queen Breezemore. I... I would very much like that."

"Then advise me, Lady Keyhold. Decide what we do with Deep, and it shall be so. Shall we let him live? Shall we allow him to help us mend this and get his people in alignment with ours?"

A new fear filled Deep's eyes, but they no longer begged. It was as if he knew his fate before Key spoke the words.

Gabi spoke in mind speak. *Um, Breanne, Garrett – maybe she shouldn't decide.*

Paul nodded. *We still need him to order his armies to follow you and Garrett.*

But it was too late for that. She'd already extended the offer. Key would make the right decision. Breanne had seen the expression of concern when Key thought Breanne was going to kill the man. *No. Let her choose,* Breanne answered in their minds.

Garrett nodded. *Agreed.*

"I think... I think it best if..." Key hesitated, her eyes glancing around the room, frowning before finding Deep once more. It was almost as if the words pained her. Maybe despite it all, she still loved him. Maybe her sadness was because she felt compelled to let the man live. Because she knew she couldn't kill him.

"I think we must hold him accountable for what he has done to my people, I mean... our people," Key said, but her voice was calm and sad. "Do you know why there are no chairs to sit upon in this place, my queen?"

Breanne's eyebrows knitted at the odd timing of the question. She glanced around. "No. I don't know why."

Key's face became determined. "A chair is a place to sit and take rest. But, you see, the women whom Deep has enslaved get no rest. For there is no room for laziness under the rule of Deep. Not for women. Therefore, you will find no chairs in this buttery, nor near the cook fires, nor in the bakery, nor the pantries."

Breanne's attention turned to Deep. She still held her sword out in front of her, though its point was withdrawn slightly, no longer pressing against Key's chest.

Deep's eyes filled with shame. Unable to meet Breanne's eyes, he looked away.

Key twisted suddenly. The motion was fast and precise. Her hand grabbed Breanne's sword hand, pulling with a jerk.

Then, with a slight push, the woman changed the trajectory of the sabre's clumsy thrust.

Still holding the hilt of the sword, now stuck through Deep's throat, Breanne gasped. Instinctively, she let go. The sword dropped, the blade pulling free to reveal a mortal wound.

The man's hands went to his throat as he tried futilely to stop the bleeding. Deep's head twisted, eyes searching for Key's frantically.

David, can you hear me? You better get in here quick! Pete said in mind speak, running for the door.

But Breanne knew there would be no saving Deep, not from this. Too much blood was flowing between the man's fingers. She had punctured his jugular. *Hold, Pete,* she managed.

Pete stopped, looking back over his shoulder.

Key leaned forward. "I'm here, Deepman," she said, her voice breaking. "I'm here and I'm sorry. I truly am."

King Deep took one hand from his bloody neck and flailed for her.

Key took Deep's hand, holding it in her own. "You banished us from our home. You left us out there, moon cycle after moon cycle, to fend for ourselves in an unforgiving forest. Many of my people died, many more you captured. You did this not because you wanted men to be treated differently. You did this because you wanted vengeance against me, because I love Shine and not you."

A moan escaped Deep's mouth and crimson spilled down his chin.

Key pressed on. "Even though you never forgave me, perhaps I could have forgiven you your jealousy. Perhaps, since I and the women of Sky chose to leave rather than be forced to stand all day in your butteries, I could have forgiven you even now. But what of those left behind or captured? What of those forced into your servitude? What of them, Deepman? What of those never allowed to rest? What of those with no chair?"

Deep's eyes begged forgiveness in place of words he couldn't form.

Key shook her head and firmed her gaze. "No. Instead, you will die knowing I never forgave you." She let go of the self-proclaimed king's hand. "Die now, Deep. Die, knowing I hate you for what you've done."

Tears spilled down King Deep's smooth-shaven face. As his eyes grew heavy, he found enough strength to take his other blood-soaked hand away from his throat and reach for Key's cheek, hoping to give it a last caress as he exhaled his final breath.

But Key drew away, not allowing him even this.

As King Deep exhaled his final breath and died, Breanne looked from Key to Garrett, her stomach turning. She'd made a grave error in judgment. An error that might have just cost them everything.

46

Step Up

God Stones – Moon Ring 4
The City of Cloud

The man who had just promised Garrett his obedience and the allegiance of his army was dead. How was he supposed to get an army of men he'd never met to follow him to a war against giants, dragons, dökkálfar – and Jack? A feeling of despair filled Garrett's guts.

War was only one obstacle. He didn't know why, but every ounce of him knew the tree in Osonian was the answer. They had to get there. Even if the army wouldn't follow, he still had Key's army and, frankly, these women appeared three times tougher than the men. Then again, the men had swords and bows, which would be a nice complement to the atlatls the women warriors carried.

Garrett! Breanne said.

Sorry, he said, coming back to the moment. King Deep lay on his side in a pool of his own blood, and they all stood staring at him. "What?"

"Will you allow my people to live after what I have done here today?" Key asked, concern in her voice.

Garrett blinked. "You think the fate of you and the women of Sky is my decision to make?"

"You are the descendant of Turek, are you not?" Key asked.

Garrett's eyes glanced at Breanne. Her face was a visage of concern. She had just fallen into her role as leader of the women of Sky.

Garrett nodded. "Yes. But you still don't get it, Lady Key. We decide together," he said, looking at Breanne and Paul. "But I think I can answer for all of us when I say we will not kill you or the women of Sky."

"You agree with what I have done, then?"

"I didn't say that. Deep had just promised me his allegiance. You understand we are about to go to war with giants, dragons, and possibly even the dökkálfar if we can't find a way to show them we're on their side before they kill us. Now how am I supposed to—"

"On their side?" Key interrupted. "The dökkálfar? They would as soon see us dead as speak to us."

"You don't know that. By the time we reach them, they may need us," Garrett argued. But in the back of his mind, he hoped Lenny could somehow help when the time came.

"You are an optimistic male. Shine is a lot like you, always believing the best outcome, even when the worst is imminent." Key looked back at Deep, her expression stony. "If you want to lead his army, you need to step up and take it. Remember, it was your name the men heard whispered by the wind. They will follow you if you command them to do so."

Garrett wasn't so sure, but he nodded. "And what about you, Lady Key?"

The former queen of Sky looked away from Deep, her

eyes meeting his. "I have taken my vengeance," she said, shifting her gaze to Breanne. "If you would still have me, I will follow you, my queen, fully and completely. If your orders are to join with these men to war on Osonian, then it shall be so. We must do everything within our power to save Metsavana. Even if it means we all die."

Breanne switched to mind speak. *You guys, I'm sorry. I misjudged. Really, I didn't think she would do it,* she said, her voice stressed and apologetic.

Garrett squeezed her hand reassuringly. *I saw what you saw, Bre, and I thought the same thing. Your plan was a good one, and it almost worked.*

What's done is done, sis, and there is no point second-guessing it now, Paul said, nodding toward Key.

"Will you still have me, my queen?"

"Of course," Breanne answered, embracing the woman with a hug.

Outside, the suns were separating once more as a new morning greeted Garrett's tired eyes. The men and women strewn about the courtyard were waking up to find he, Bre, Key, and the others standing high above them atop the archer's wall. As for the unconscious archers, Pete, Lenny, and Paul used strands of vine grown by Governess to bind the men's hands and feet so they couldn't try and attack when they woke. The archers on the wall now sat behind them, grunting as they struggled with their binding to no avail.

Garrett stared down sixty feet to the courtyard below. "Everyone, stay calm. The fighting is over!"

"Where's King Deep!" a bearded man shouted up at him in a gruff voice.

"Where's our king!" shouted another, shaking an angry fist in the air.

As the armies in the courtyard below woke from their

sleep, more men and women staggered to their feet, the two groups still massed on separate sides of the space.

"What have you done?"

"Where is our king?"

The crowd below, quickly turning into a mob, focused their anger on Garrett and the others high upon the archers' wall. Hundreds of fists and swords shook angrily as they chanted, "Where is the king? Where is the king? Where is the king?"

The women looked as angry and confused as the men, prompting Key to step forward, her hands held out, motioning for calm as she tried to shout over the mob. "Women of Sky, stay your spears. We are at peace until we conquer the greater threat!"

Beside him, Kilug's hands flexed on his war hammer. "Aye, looks like we be about to go down there and crack some skulls."

"Garrett, this is looking bad, bro," Lenny said. "Maybe I should put them all back to sleep?"

The woman lifted atlatls and gathered up in a defensive formation.

"Where is the king?"

"Where is the king!"

The men drew their swords, many facing the women, the rest facing the inner gate. Once the inner gate fell there would be nothing to keep hundreds of men from climbing the stairs and flooding onto the archers' wall in overwhelming numbers.

Key nodded toward the angry mob and shouted, "Descendant of Turek, you must take control before they kill each other!"

Garrett felt terrified. What if they didn't listen? What if he failed?

From somewhere in the mob, a man threw a stone.

Reflexively, Garrett ducked. The rock hit just above and behind Garrett's head.

A group of twenty men were at the inner gate, counting off one, two, three, and shouldering in unison. The gate flexed inward but held.

"The inner gate is nothing like the outer one. It isn't meant to withstand an army," Paul said, studying the gate and the men charging it. "Once it goes, we're compromised."

"Where is the king!"

"Where is the king!"

Behind them, one of the restrained archers broke loose of his bindings and charged, his raging cry giving him away.

Paul grabbed the man by the shoulder and squeezed. The man cried out and dropped to his knees. His eyes rolled up in his head, his body going slack.

"Um, you got to teach me that," Pete said.

Another stone flew past them. This one nearly hit David.

"Hey! Watch it!" David shouted, crouching down behind the short wall of stone.

Below, a man ran forward toward the wall. He snatched up a bow that must have been dropped over the side when Lenny had sung everyone to sleep.

"Should I play again?" Lenny asked. "I'm feeling some Jimi Hendrix."

"No. They will just wake up and be pissed all over again," Garrett said.

Garrett! Do something, Breanne urged in mind speak.

Garrett stepped up onto the short wall. "Stop!"

Surprisingly, the chanting stopped.

"Your king is dead!" Garrett said.

That wasn't the something I had in mind, Breanne said.

Way to rip off the Band-Aid, bro, Lenny said.

The crowd below shouted curses, their swords shaking angrily in the air.

Garrett tensed.

The man with the bow turned to the crowd. "Silence!" he shouted.

The crowd silenced.

Then, turning back, he let the bow fall slack at his side. He called up at Garrett, "Who killed our king?"

The man was dressed slightly different from the others. No, not different. He still had the 1970s-style pants, but in addition, he wore a ruffled vest with a flared collar. His hair was long and braided into small braids. The smaller braids were drawn up tight and plaited in one large braid, which ran like a mohawk down the middle of his head to hang thick as Garrett's wrist down the man's back. This man was important.

"I killed him," Garrett said, drawing in Sentheye and with it the dirt trails of his mind.

The man dropped the bow, his shoulders slumping. Then, with a sudden jerk, he threw his hand forward.

Garrett tried to slow the man's arm, but the man managed to throw something before he could. Focusing, Garrett instead slowed the object and at the same moment leapt off the wall.

The fall was at least sixty feet. Far too high not to break a leg, or far worse. Behind him, his friends shouted.

He turned his focus inward, trying something he had never attempted. In fact, it might not even be possible. Great. Just perfect. His big leadership moment punctuated by a leap to his death in front of two armies, his friends, and the girl he loved. He couldn't have tried this with both feet on the ground?

Garrett had jumped out and up, but he dropped... fast.

The Sentheye was there though, as Garrett focused it on himself. Still, he couldn't focus it all on himself while the object was flying toward him.

The strange sensation of gravity changing around him was weird. But he knew it wasn't gravity slowing him or the object – it was time. Therefore, for him and the small object, time was equal and everything around him sped up.

To everyone else, the object and Garrett slowed. This was a problem he had to solve in a nanosecond and on an instinctual level. It came to him like a reflexive jerk, almost without thought. Garrett slowed the object even more than he slowed himself. Tipping the balance allowed him to see the object was in fact a knife flying at his face, blade first. Garrett reached for the knife's handle as it closed in, snatching it from the air.

Great, he had the knife, but now he had a new problem. Jumping from a wall and slowing time would not change the landing or the gravitational force when he hit the ground. What an idiot! Instead of landing like a superhero in a cool kneeling pose, all his friends were going to see him splat against the stone courtyard below. Only they'd be seeing it in slow motion.

Holding the knife, he focused fully on himself, slowing time to a near stop. He needed to think. He couldn't control the pull of gravity when he hit the ground, but he could control how he landed. Never had anyone had this much time to think and react to the ground coming at them. Mr. B had spent a significant amount of time teaching him and Lenny how to jump, flip, throw, and land, but never from a distance this high.

Nearing the ground, Garrett braced himself. His toes met the stone and the balls of his feet compressed. His ankles flexed and his calves tightened.

He made his move.

Shifting his weight, he threw himself forward. This wouldn't work in real time, but he wasn't in real time. He was in slowed time. His legs compressed, but he leaned into it, launching himself, curling his shoulder and twisting. His kick off of the pavement combined with his forward momentum countered some of the gravitational force. Garrett rolled hard across the stone, but because time slowed him, he could tuck, twist, and shift in all the right places at precisely the right time.

Springing to his feet without so much as a scratch, Garrett changed his focus, letting the Sentheye shift from him to the man with the vest, who'd thrown the knife. The man stood still as a statue, staring at him with knitted eyebrows. Everyone stared, probably wondering how he'd just done the impossible.

He wondered, too, but there was no time to think about it now. Garrett ran forward at full speed toward the vest man, whose face was slowly changing, eyes slowly widening. Garrett grabbed the man, placing the knife to his throat, and released the Sentheye.

The man dropped to his knees.

Dozens of men rushed forward.

The man held up a shaking hand, staying the men.

"Are you a general or something?" Garrett asked.

"A... a... I... I don't know what that is," the man said, his eyes shifting down to the blade, then back up to meet Garrett's. He licked his dry lips.

"Are you next in command?"

"Yes. I am Deep's second," the man said.

"What's your name?" Garrett asked.

"Stone... Stonebender," he said.

"Really? That's a cool name," Garrett said, as if now was the time for small talk. Now, while he held a knife to the kneeling man's throat while behind the man, an angry army prepared to charge forward.

"My... my family's lineage goes back to the time of Cloud's creation. Their hands laid the stonework you see all

The Last Gift

around and above you," the man said, swallowing hard. Then, looking back at the knife, he asked, "Why are you doing this? Are you going to kill me like you did Deep? Why? Why did you do it? We heard your name on the wind! We thought you came to save us, and you bring them!" he was shouting now, his body shaking, spittle in his beard. He twisted his face to see the women of Sky nervously awaiting their queen's orders. "What have we done? What did Deep do to deserve this?"

Garrett looked down at the bearded man. "Deep paid for the mistreatment of his people with his life."

"Mistreatment? But he was good to us!"

"Maybe. But those women are also your people," Garrett said, nodding toward the crowd. "Your king forced them to submit to slavery or be cast out. This is not the way."

Stone closed his eyes. "He wasn't always this bad, you know. It's true, he always felt like we were better than the women, but as time went on he treated them far worse than they ever treated us. I told him… I told him he was pushing this too far. I told him Turek wouldn't have it. But he wouldn't listen to me."

Beside Garrett, Paul landed hard, fracturing one of the stone tiles. He was kneeling like a freaking superhero. Dang. He made it look easy.

Paul stood. *They're starting to worry about you, so they sent me down to help,* Paul said in mind speak.

Garrett nodded and looked back at Stone. "You can't do anything about Deep. He is gone. You know that Turek spoke my name on the wind because you heard it, and so did they. Now I ask you, Stone, are you going to help me? After all, it is what Turek expects."

Stone nodded slowly.

Garrett removed the knife and stepped back.

The men behind Stone rushed forward, swords raised.

Garrett prepared to slow as many as he could, but he didn't have to. Stone raised his hand, staying the men for the second time. He turned to his men. "Stay your swords, good men of Cloud. This is Garrett Turek, descendant of Turek, whose name we all heard spoken on the wind."

"He killed King Deep!" a man shouted, and the others shouted too.

"Silence! Deep is dead. And the chosen has told me he was punished for the treatment of the women of Sky."

"What of us? You would have us bow down to the women again."

"No," Garrett said, raising his voice above the noise.

The men quieted.

Garrett said, "But the old way is gone. For both women and men. A great threat has come to the land of Karelia. The father tree is dying, and if we don't march to war, Osonian will be destroyed and, soon after, the forest, the Mazewood, and this very city – all destroyed, and all of you will be killed."

A thick man with arms the size of Garrett's legs stepped forward. "And who would you have us fight?"

"It doesn't really matter who. If we don't fight, we die anyway."

"Elves then? You expect us to fight them?" another man, this one holding a crude iron sword, asked.

"I hope we can partner with them. They will likely need our aid."

"What? Partner with the elves? They will kill us!" a man shouted. "What threat could the elves face they would require our aid?"

"Half-giants and dragons," Garrett said with a flat seriousness.

The man blinked as murmurs spread through the crowd.

I'm not sure this is convincing them to follow you, kid, Paul said.

"Listen to me, all of you. Turek himself sent me and my sages here to help you."

"Himself!" a woman shouted, pushing her way forward. She was at least six two, with muscles that rippled beneath her ebony skin. "We heard the name spoken by the wind, and it was Breanne Moore! Do you deny this?"

A wave of tension spread through the women of Sky as hundreds of hands stiffened on spears.

Breanne, can you get down here, please?

Sure, Garrett.

"Sure, Garrett"? That didn't sound good. Had he done something?

"Well? Do you deny it?" the woman repeated.

"No. I don't deny what you heard. I don't deny Turek may be female or male or something else altogether. The truth is, I don't know."

"You claim to be of him, but you don't know?" a male voice asked, but Garrett couldn't see the source of the question. More voices started in, everyone talking over everyone else.

Dammit, he was screwing this up. Garrett held out his hands, trying to quiet the crowd and the pressing questions.

A moment later, the inner gate opened as Breanne and the others appeared.

Breanne stepped forward, taking a place next to him, but she didn't look at him. "It *was* my name you heard on the wind," she said, looking at the crowd of women. Then, turning to the men, she said, "Just as it was Garrett's you heard. I suspect Turek knew it would take a woman to convince the women of Sky to follow us. I am not of Turek any more or less than any of you. However, Turek chose me nonetheless."

"But we named you our queen?" one said. "You, who lied to us?"

"That's not true. Breanne Moore never lied. If anyone lied, it was me," Garrett said, finding himself getting angry at the accusation.

Breanne held up a hand. "I never lied to you. You heard my name spoken, and it was you who tested me and you who made the decision to name me your queen."

The massive man with the leg-sized arms looked down at Garrett. "You would have us follow you against dragons! How can you protect us from them? We will surely die."

"Don't you understand? You will all die anyway." He pulled off the knit hoodie, exposing his arms.

The crowd of men gasped at the sight. "Dragon runes!" a man shouted. The words repeated over and over, spreading back through the ranks like ripples on a lake.

Garrett held out his hands again, quieting them. "I can't promise you won't die, but you saw what I did with the arrows. You saw how powerful my sages are. And now you see, I am dragon marked. At least with us you stand a chance." Fixing his eyes on Stone, Garrett said, "Stone, speak for your men. Be my advisor, as Lady Key is to Queen Breezemore. Will you and your men help us save the land of Sky, Osonian, and the father tree?"

Sweat was beading on Stone's brow. The nervous man looked over his shoulder to find several hundred men staring back at him, faces angry and expectant. Stone wiped a billowing sleeve across his face and turned back to face Garrett squarely. For a second, Garrett thought the man might get sick.

Finally, Stone nodded.

Garrett shook his head. "No. A simple nod is not enough, Stonebender. I need you to swear your fealty to me. Not just you, but the fealty of your entire army."

The Last Gift

The crowd fell deathly silent, hanging on Stonebender's next words.

Stonebender swallowed thickly. "I... I swear it. I swear the fealty of myself, and I swear the allegiance of these men—"

"How dare you!" a short, stocky man said, pushing himself forward. "You can't speak for us! You're not our king, Stone!"

Stone started to speak, but now it was Garrett who held up a hand for silence. "Those who choose not to follow us to war are free to do so."

Several heads in the crowd nodded in agreement.

"However, you will be banished to..." Garrett stopped, trying to remember the name of the mountains or the desert he'd heard Key speak about.

Key stepped forward, nodding sagely. "May I suggest they be exiled to the Shadow Forest, as was the fate of the women of Sky? At least this will afford them the same chance at survival we've... enjoyed," the regal woman said, a smile stretching across her face.

Garrett nodded. "Fine, you will be banished to the Shadow Forest. Now, what is your decision?"

Stone wasted no time falling to one knee. "My answer is unchanged... my... What do I call you? Are you our king, then?"

"Just call me Garrett, okay?"

The man frowned but nodded. "My answer is unchanged, my... Garrett."

Murmuring broke from the ranks as many men took a knee while others stood firm. Finally, a man from the crowd shouted out, "And what of these women – are they to bend the knee to you as well?"

Now the women grumbled under their breaths as they

shifted uncomfortably. Garrett looked to Key, then to Breanne.

Breanne raised an eyebrow and looked back at Key. Now he was sure she was mad.

"No. I'm afraid Queen Breanne's women of Sky will not bend the knee to a man," Key said, crossing her arms.

"They don't have to," Garrett said, sighing as he addressed the crowd. "Turek has whispered the name of Breanne Moore to the women of Sky." He chose his next words carefully. "Breanne Moore is a powerful sage and has been named queen of Sky," he said, daring a glance over at Bre.

Breanne diverted her narrowed eyes, nodding to Key and the women of Sky. She still looked pissed. What the hell?

"Are you ordering us to follow her, then?" a man shouted.

"We swore nothing to her, only to the chosen," Stonebender said.

Key's lip curled into a frightening sneer, better fit to a wolf than a woman of her beauty. "Pay care to your tongue, Stonebender. For if you cannot, I will deem it feral and cut it from your mouth. You are, after all, addressing Lady Key of Sky in front of Queen Breezemore, whose name, as your own chosen has just informed you, was spoken on the wind to all women of Sky."

Garrett held up his hands for the third time. "We are all together in this. Stop worrying about the semantics right now. Let's just agree we are fighting the monsters out there." He pointed for effect but then realized he wasn't sure he was even pointing toward Osonian. "If we survive, we can figure out the rest after. Do we agree?"

Garrett saw a few men turn, heading for the main gate. A dozen, maybe two dozen. Great. He'd probably just given the worst inspirational speech in the history of pre-war speeches.

For the rest of the men and women, reluctant heads nodded.

"What now?" Stonebender asked.

Please say food. Please say food. Please say food, David chanted in mind speak.

Garrett looked at David, then the others, and finally back at Stone. "My sages are tired and I'm sure the women of Sky are as well. I'd like to see your city and get some rest."

And food. Please? Oh god, please! David's chanting continued.

"Oh, and we would like to eat," Garrett said, giving David a wink.

"Yes!" David shouted aloud, throwing a fist into the air.

Stone flinched, then nodded. "Of course, we will be your hosts. I will have the kitchen prepare you something, my lor... um... Garrett."

"Thank you, Stone," Garrett said. Turning toward the gate, he paused. "And who would cook for us?"

"Well, the servants cook the food."

"He means the women he's enslaved," Key said in disgust.

"Stone, you don't have servants anymore."

"Well... um, we will..." the man sputtered, running a hand across his face.

"My men will prepare food for us," Key said assuredly.

Stone stopped, turning toward Key. "So it is acceptable for you to order your men to cook, but not for me to order our women?"

"It is not the same at all! You force women into servitude, but we have an agreeable arrangement with our men!" Key said.

"How is this any different?" Stone protested.

Breanne's voice filled Garrett's mind. *Well, Garrett, did*

you really think you were going to fix this with a little magic and a speech?

Garrett shouted over them. "Enough! We know the way to the kitchen and are perfectly capable of cooking our own food. If we have questions, we can ask."

"You're going to cook your own food?" Stone asked in disbelief.

Lenny laughed. "This guy!"

Garrett sighed. "Yeah, we are, and you're going to join us," he said, patting the man on the shoulder. "You might actually find you enjoy it."

47

A Restless Night

God Stones – Moon Ring 4
The City of Cloud

The suns had long been up – or out or whatever they did on Karelia – and were now crossing the sky by the time Breanne got to a room with a bed. But this wasn't just any room. This was King Deep's bedchamber. Well, it had been, but now the king of Cloud was dead.

The chamber was elaborate in its décor and had what appeared to be the first proper bed she'd seen since – well, since her camper on Oak Island. The cot she'd spent the night on in Violetta's Mexican village was a close second. But this was proper. It was large and raised off the floor. It had something that resembled a mattress. She pressed on the thick hide-covered bed, her hand sinking into its softness. It must be stuffed with feathers or something like cotton, perhaps. She wasn't sure, and to be honest, she didn't care. It looked amazing and she couldn't wait to crawl atop it and go to sleep.

If she weren't so tired, she would also be amazed by the

many things in the room she recognized: framed pictures hanging on the walls, what appeared to be a wardrobe, as well as two ornate chairs and even a lounging chaise. Briefly, she wondered how many worlds capable of holding life similar to humans might exist in the universe. More importantly, were there chairs on all of them? Was the chair a universal truth? As curious as she was about the chair, she might like to explore the strange items she didn't recognize and discover their purpose. But not this moment. Right now, she just wanted that bed.

Across the chamber, white curtains danced in the breeze from an open balcony door. Dishes that reminded Breanne of a fine china tea set rattled softly. The elegant dishes appeared to be made of a woven glass-like substance forming watertight vessels and then painted with strange designs. Idly, she wondered if humans or someone else had made these. Tossing her pack into a chair next to Garrett's, she kicked off her boots and crossed the stone chamber onto the balcony.

"Hey," Garrett said, turning to look at her. "This place is amazing."

She frowned. "It is."

Garrett's smile faltered. "Are we going to talk about why you're mad at me?"

"Who said I'm mad at you?" she replied, her tone sharper than she intended.

"Come on, I know you well enough by now to know you're mad."

"You couldn't have talked to me? You couldn't have included me or the rest of your friends – your sages – in the decisions you were making?"

"I was—"

"No. You had to do what you wanted. All along, you've talked about us being a team. The sages stick together no matter what. We will figure this out *together*." She felt her face flushing. She was getting really pissed. "Was it all bullshit, Garrett? Were you always going to just do what you wanted?"

Garrett blinked, then opened his mouth to speak. Again, she cut him off.

"What if that little stunt you pulled jumping off the wall hadn't worked, and you splatted onto the stone? That would have been quite the dumbass ending to all that we've been through – you jumping to your death!"

"That isn't why you're mad at me," Garrett said.

"Oh, really?"

"I mean, maybe you're mad at me for that, but you were mad at me before, Bre. You were giving me the side eye way before I jumped off the wall. Tell me I'm wrong."

"I'm going to bed. We have to march to Osonian and fight giants and dragons *and* figure out how we save our parents and all of Earth! Or maybe you have it all figured out and you're just keeping it to yourself like all your other plans!"

Garrett pulled a face. "Other plans?"

"Good night, Garrett!" she said, spinning on her heel and stomping back into the room.

She could feel Garrett on her heels. "Now wait a minute! What are you talking about? I don't have secret plans, Bre!"

She turned around, finger wagging. "Really? Are we really going there to save a tree, or because you know Jack will be there?"

"Bre, we have to get the God Stones back. One, I don't know another way to open the portal. And two, I don't have or know of another item that will let the trees of Earth stay unbound." He shook his head. "Am I missing something? What's this really about?"

She shook her head. "I don't want to get these people

killed. And these women – they heard my name on the wind. Doesn't that mean something?"

Realization lit Garrett's face, his arms dropping to his sides. "This is because I took over."

"You don't get it at all, Garrett. This is about more than you. You made decisions that affected all of us. And what if you had died pulling that stunt of yours? What happens to all of us then?"

"But I didn't die, Bre, and we united the armies."

"You united *them*, not us. You were only thinking about yourself," she said, crossing her arms.

"That's not true. If you hadn't come down off that wall and said what you said, the whole thing would have blown up in my face."

Damn him. "Yeah, well, assuming any of us or them live, what happens after? Are you going to lead them? Are you going to take care of these people?"

"I… I haven't given a thought to after, Bre! I've been busy trying not to fail at the first part! We have to get the portal open and save our parents, your brother, and all the people on Earth – remember?" he said, raising his voice.

"Of course I remember! But these people and what becomes of them matters too! Maybe not to you, but they matter to me!"

"I never said they didn't matter! I think stopping Jack and saving the tree are just as important to their future and the future of this planet as saving the people on Earth!"

Breanne's face was hot. He just wasn't hearing her. Didn't he realize what these people were sacrificing to follow them? She and Garrett were about to lead them into what might well be certain death. They might all die, for god's sake. Didn't he understand how fragile all this was? She held up her hands. "I'm done."

"What does that mean?" Garrett asked.

"It means I need sleep, Garrett. We must've been up for over twenty-four hours. My stomach is full, and I'm exhausted. I want to go to bed," she said earnestly, throwing back a blanket of soft linen to reveal even softer fur. She crawled onto and then across the bed, which was far larger than a king-size bed back home.

She felt the bed move behind her as Garrett climbed in. "I'm sorry I raised my voice, Bre."

"Let's just go to sleep. We're both tired," she said.

She heard him sigh. "Okay, but let's talk in the morning."

"Sure, Garrett." A gust of cool air blew across the room, rattling the tray of dishes. "You didn't shut the door."

A soft snore answered her.

"Great, I'll get it," she said, but Breanne never did close the door. Instead, sleep took her. And as the curtains continued their strange ballet, Breanne drifted into a nightmare.

The fuzzy image of a strange bird sitting atop a familiar altar came into focus. Breanne recognized this place. She was back in Mexico, standing atop the temple. The bird sat with its back to her, but its head twisted 180 degrees to face her. Strange energy swirled in its eyes. This too was familiar. More than familiar, those eyes were reminiscent of something she would never forget. It was like looking into the God Stones.

The bird – an owl, she realized – turned its gaze forward and flapped its wings as it vanished over the south-facing side of the pyramid.

Breanne ran forward, chasing after it.

An explosion shook the temple. The night sky filled with screams.

As she peered over the edge of the temple roof, moonlight and starshine illuminated a large group of screaming people atop the pyramid. They were fighting something… trees… tree people. The stick figures crowded the stairs and surrounded the temple, blocking off the way inside. There, some fifty feet below, was the opening to the temple she stood upon – the spot where she'd first met Gabi so many weeks ago.

With the way inside blocked, there was nowhere to run, but still they fought. Breanne saw them then, the runners she'd met in Mexico. The ones with the special abilities. They were forcing their way up the stairs, shouting orders, shooting guns, and throwing frags. How would they ever get through? There were so many stick men. Then, as the ultrarunner guys neared the top, another group emerged from the jungle. About twenty identical little people… but they weren't people at all. They looked human but were maybe three feet tall. They raced up the pyramid stairs and flooded over the top and into the crowd. She could see them clearly now. They looked wet – like they were covered in something oily. She didn't understand.

Pando was there too, her arms stretched out – perfectly human. She pointed at… at… was that her father? "Daddy? Daddy, run!" she shouted, but he didn't hear her. The shorter tree people overwhelmed the crowd of humans and her dad was… was gone! She strained to see… to find her father in the crowd.

Pando's familiar voice called out, "Welcome to the Devil's Garden!"

What was happening? What did it mean? One of the little tree people looked up and smiled. It was covered in black spots. The black dots fell, crawling as they landed. Ants… they were ants.

"Now, Duroia Hirsuta. Burn the humans. Burn them all!" Pando shouted.

Suddenly the small tree creatures began to spin like tops, flinging the oily liquid onto the crowd. The people screamed out in agony as their skin sizzled and smoked.

Breanne didn't want to see any more. She slammed her eyes shut.

When Breanne opened her eyes again, she screamed, sitting up with a jolt.

"What... what's wrong?" Garrett asked, pushing himself up on his elbow, eyes half-open.

"It was... just... just a bad dream," she said with a shiver, trying to remember the details.

"Want to talk about it?" Garrett asked, covering his mouth to yawn.

"It's fuzzy. I was back in Mexico. At the pyramid."

"Oh, hey, that's good. Maybe that means we will get back there! You think it was like a vision?"

"I... I don't know. I didn't see you or the others. Maybe it was just a dream."

"Tell me what you saw," Garrett asked, sitting up.

"Trees... trees that were shaped like people... like stick people, and these smaller things that looked like humans, but they weren't... and the ants... and acid... I don't want to... I don't want to think about it. I think I might have seen my dad, Garrett."

Garrett's eyes danced back and forth worriedly. "But it was just a dream, though?"

Breanne nodded. "I think so."

The two sat quietly, thinking to themselves. Breanne knew Garrett was wondering if these people could have been his Keepers. But she had never met his brother or mother and wouldn't have recognized any of them.

"I'm sure it was just a dream, Bre," the boy said, forcing a smile.

She nodded. "Yeah, I'm sure you're right. It was just that I saw those runner guys too. You remember them from the farmhouse?"

"Of course. The ultrarunners with powers. How could I forget those guys?"

"I think they were in my dream, fighting the trees. And, Garrett, there were lots of others too. But maybe it was all just my imagination. It was just weird, you know? And that bird—"

"Wait. What bird?" Garrett asked, his thick eyebrows drawing up.

"It was a" – she squeezed her eyes shut, willing herself to see it again – "an owl."

Garrett's eyes widened, the blood draining from his face.

"What's wrong?" she asked.

"I saw an owl right before I slowed time and stopped the arrows and spears."

"That's right! I saw you looking at it. But I didn't get a good look. It was an owl, you're sure?"

Garrett nodded. "An owl with a human face—"

From outside their room, a woman screamed.

Breanne jumped.

"What the hell!" Garrett said, leaping from the bed and not bothering with pants as he grabbed his sword and flung open the door while still in his breeches.

Breanne, still wearing her shirt, bra, and underwear, grabbed her jeans and pulled them on. From the hall, the screaming continued, and it was getting closer. "Tell?" It sounded like Tell.

The young woman burst into the room, half-dressed, tears rolling down her face.

"What's happened?" Garrett asked, tugging his fatigues off the chair and hopping on one foot as he shoved the other into the pants.

David's voice filled their minds. *Guys, um, you better get to Lenny's room, and I mean quick.*

"Lenny!" Garrett said, his face changing from confusion

to fear. "What's happened?" he shouted. He didn't wait for the hysterical girl to answer but grabbed his sword and darted toward the door, snatching his undershirt off the back of the chair on his way out.

Tell threw herself onto the bed facedown and sobbed.

Buttoning her pants, Breanne turned to the girl on the bed. "What happened? Are you okay?"

"Okay? Am I okay?" she cried, lifting her face from the pillow. "I slept with a dökkálfar and you're asking me if I'm okay?" she threw her face back into the pillow and cried.

"Lenny told you what he is?" she asked.

She lifted her contorted face again, shaking her head vigorously. "Told me? No! He did not tell me! After drinking a lot of ale, we lay down together and during that he was human! But what I woke up to this morning was… well, obviously Lenny, but… but not a human Lenny! He must have been using dökkálfar magic to look human, and it slipped in his sleep, for what I woke up to was a pointy-eared elf!"

Breanne's eyes went wide. She jolted from the bed and darted out of the room. Only two doors down the corridor, the door to Lenny's room was wide open. Inside, she found Garrett and David sitting on the edge of Lenny's bed, a much smaller version of the one she and Garrett had shared.

They were all speaking in mind speak now. *Come on, Len. You can't stay under that blanket forever. I mean, how bad could it be?* Garrett asked.

Bad, bro, David said, shaking his head back and forth. *I caught a glimpse of him when I came in. It's bad.*

Garrett slugged David in the shoulder and spoke aloud in a low voice. "Not helpful, David."

"Well, it is bad," David said in a poor attempt at a whisper.

"I can still hear you, David! You little furry prick!" Lenny said from beneath the blanket.

Pete's voice interjected. *Guys, did I hear you say Lenny turned elf?*

You heard right, David answered, rubbing his shoulder.

Oh, I want to see! Gabi's excited voice rang through.

We're on our way! Pete said.

Dammit, David! Why don't you invite the whole city to my room? Lenny shouted, yanking down the blanket and belting David on the same shoulder Garrett had punched.

Ouch! David cried.

Lenny noticed Breanne at the same time that Pete and Governess burst through the door with Paul and Gabi on their heels.

Breanne's eyes went wide at the sight of Lenny's elongated ears and swooping eyes. When he made eye contact, she tried to turn away to hide her shock, but it was too late.

Lenny's strange new eyes went wide too, and the boy let out a yipe, yanking the blanket back over his head and off his feet – feet that appeared dark blue and longer than before. In fact, Breanne was sure his whole body was longer than before.

You didn't tell me Bre was in here too!

It's okay, Lenny, Breanne tried.

Can everyone except for Garrett please just get out? the boy asked, drawing his feet beneath the blanket.

Garrett gave her an apologetic look.

It's okay, I should probably get back to Tell before she runs off and tells Key.

Garrett gave her a weak smile of gratitude.

She nodded back and turned to leave.

Everyone else out too, Garrett said.

Oh, how disappointing. I was looking forward to seeing the dökkálfar's transformation, Governess said.

Screw you, stick chick! Lenny shouted.

Everyone, just please go, Garrett said.

Breanne could still hear her friends arguing in mind speak as she entered her room to find Tell sitting up on her bed. The girl's puffy face was twisted now, her tears replaced by anger.

"What in Turek's name? How could he be... how could he be dökkálfar? I... I mean, I have heard legends of dökkálfar with the ability to use Sentheye to disguise themselves as human or even dwarf, but Lenny? Why? Why would he do this?"

"Just take a deep breath. There is a logical explanation."

"Wait a minute. Did you know? All this time! You did, didn't you?"

"Wait! Tell, listen. I have never seen him transform. No one has."

"He never transformed in front of you, but still, you knew?"

"He has never transformed, period."

"That's not possible. How could he be what he is if he has always been in human form?"

"Lenny isn't pretending to be human, Tell. He is human."

The woman stared, her face looking as though she just bitten into a crab apple. "What I just woke up next to was not human!" she breathed.

"He is. But he is also dökkálfar and yes, I knew. His father was Syldan Loravaris, son of—"

"Of Vulmon Loravaris. The king of the dökkálfar." Tell collapsed back on the bed, her shoulders sagging. "Oh, dear Turek, what have I done?"

"Lenny's a good guy, Tell," Breanne said carefully.

"A good guy? What will my mother say? Gods, I've broken the prime rule of our society, of our lands," the girl said, lifting her head. Her straight black hair was down and loose, long silken strands covering one of her dark eyes, the other dripping tears. "They will put me to death for this."

"No, Tell," Breanne started.

"Yes. They will," she said. "You will have to order it. If not you, then the gods themselves will see to it I die. Don't you understand? I lay down with a dökkálfar!"

"He's half human, Tell! This is the first time Lenny has changed."

"You're telling me Prince Syldan bedded with a human and Lenny is…" She trailed off, her face telling Breanne she was trying to puzzle it out. Tell shook her head, and by the look on her face, the idea must be unfathomable. "No. The gods would never allow this!"

"But Turek would, Tell. You know why your god left this place for so long. It was because Ereshkigal killed the man and woman who had a child that was mixed."

"I know the stories, but—"

"But they are just stories. Turek has chosen us to complete his prophecy," Breanne said.

"Her prophecy," Tell corrected.

"Of course. Her prophecy. The point is, you know Turek whispered my name on the wind, and you know Garrett is the descendant. Despite what Lenny is, he is a sage, chosen by the descendant of Turek." Breanne scooted closer to the barely dressed girl and wrapped an arm around Tell's muscular shoulders. "It's going to be okay."

"Explain that to Key and the women, and for that matter, the men of Sky."

"Let me handle them. Are you going to be okay?"

"Queen Breeze, I… I really liked him, but now… now he's just so… so elvish."

Finding herself sounding like her father, she said, "No formalities between us, Tell. You may call me Bre."

Tell forced a smile. "Bre," she tried, as if tasting the word. "I don't think I could bear to look at him ever again!"

"Did you not think he was cute before?" Breanne asked.

"Yes, of course. He was the cutest! But now…"

"He's still Lenny," she said, smiling. "Listen to me – once he gets his appearance under control, he will still look like Lenny, but even when that happens, we all have to realize the Lenny you woke up to is another part of who he is."

"You don't understand. My people would never accept me being with a dökkálfar! Not even a half dökkálfar!" Tell said, shaking her head.

"Tell, it might surprise you what I understand. Where I am from, humans have a history of doing horrible things to one another just because the color of their skin was different. People were enslaved, tortured, and even killed."

"Well, that doesn't make sense. On your planet, they were all human and doing this to each other?"

Breanne nodded somberly. "It's true, and it took brave people standing up and saying, 'Enough!' to make it stop. Sometimes it even took war."

Tell shook her head, trying to comprehend. "Because of pigment?"

Breanne nodded. "My point is, just like where I come from, this world is changing. It has to – it needs to! The only question is, do you want to watch us change it, or do you want to be the change this world needs?"

Tell didn't speak for a long moment. "He would have made a nice addition as one of my suitors."

"One of?" Breanne asked.

"For a woman, three pursuers are common."

Breanne blinked. "Will you choose one to marry?"

"Marry? Maybe I will marry them all?" she giggled, but then her eyes welled up again. "Thank you, Bre. Thank you for making me feel better."

Breanne nodded, allowing silence to fill the space between them as Tell composed herself.

In the quiet, Garrett's voice filled her mind. *Bre, Lenny did it! He changed himself back to human, or he made us believe he looks human! It's just like Dagrun said. If he focuses hard enough, everyone who looks at him sees a human! It's so weird! You got to get in here and see this! Oh crap. He just blinked back to an elf... You're going to probably want to stay in your room and practice, Len.*

An only slightly calmer Lenny said, *Well, no shit! I'm not leaving until I'm sure I can pull this off without even thinking about it! Hey, uh, Bre? Are you with Tell?*

Yep, she said, looking at Tell.

Don't let her come back in here until I get this under control, okay? If she even wants to see me ever again. Does she?

Does she... what? Breanne asked.

Ever want to see me again? Lenny asked, his voice worried.

Tell, unable to hear any of their mind speak conversation, stared at Breanne, chewing the inside of her lower lip. Slowly, she nodded. "I do."

"What?" Breanne asked aloud, not understanding how in the world Tell could hear them in mind speak.

"I want to be the change, Queen Bre... I mean, Bre."

Breanne exhaled a relieved breath and smiled. She was, of course, relieved, but more, she was genuinely happy to hear this. "Good, because once we save Metsavana and our people, we are going to flip this world on its head!"

Tell wiped her eyes as the beginnings of a smile played at the corners of her mouth. "Maybe we don't need to tell my mother about Lenny just yet."

Breanne smiled back and gave a little giggle. "Deal! Now I want to hear all about last night!" Then, switching to mind speak, she said, *Lenny, I think she's going to want to see you very soon, so you better get your shit together!* Breanne laughed.

Lenny, maybe I can help you with your focus, Gabi offered.

You really think you can? Lenny asked, hope filling his voice.

Gabi giggled. *I think so.*

Well, look at that, Len. There might just be hope for you after all! David laughed.

48

Fragile Alliances

God Stones – Moon Ring 4
The City of Cloud

Lost in thought, Garrett stood next to Bre, staring through Cloud's open gate. Outside the city, the river's falls cried out their endless roar and the sky bridge led away toward the Mazewood. He sure had enough to worry about, but the sound of rushing water pulled him back to Petersburg... back to that night in the tunnel... back to Danny and the river. Despite how awful Danny was, Garrett wished so badly he hadn't tossed the older boy into the river. He wished Danny hadn't died.

Approaching footsteps drew him his attention from his regrets as Key and Stone stomped towards him looking as though they might kill each other.

"What's wrong with you two?" Garrett asked, trying to read their faces.

"This fool allowed one of her women to attack and maim one of my men!" Stone said, his face furrowed with fury.

"Perhaps your man will give thought before trying to take

what he wants next time! For I assure you, if there be a next time, it shall end in more than a maiming!" Key said with steel in her voice.

Garrett pinched the bridge of his nose in earnest. Weren't these supposed to be adults? He looked over at Breanne to find she was staring at him with an I-told-you-so look. "Listen to me. I forbid any harm to befall... anyone," he said, trying to sound more like Key. Then, with frustration he failed miserably to hide, he said, "Do you understand? Stonebender, your men are to keep their hands to themselves, or they will answer directly to me. Key, no attacking the men. If they do something wrong, report it to Bre or myself and we will handle it."

Both frowned.

"Am I understood?"

Stone replied, "Of course, my lord, but the woman who injured my man will need to pay for her assault."

"Over my dead body!" Key sneered.

"That could be arranged," Stone said evenly.

"Enough. Your man should not have touched a woman uninvited, and if that was the way before, it isn't anymore. Now again I ask, am I understood?"

Both nodded, but he could see Stone was not happy.

"Are both armies ready to leave?" Garrett asked, changing the subject.

"Our warriors are ready," Key said.

"As are your men, my lord," Stone said.

"Good. How many days will it take to get to Osonian?" Garrett asked.

Both looked confused, but Key answered, "It will take four moon rings, if that is what you are asking, Lord Turek."

Dammit, he kept forgetting that days weren't a thing on Karelia. "Four moon rings?" He wanted to be there now. "I worry we will be too late. Is there not a faster way? Can't we travel beneath the forest?"

"The forest would never allow so many, even if we could afford it, which we can't," Key said.

"I'm afraid Key is right," Stone said.

Key straightened, a small smirk creeping onto her face.

Stone sighed but continued, "And even if you could, you wouldn't save that much time dragging an army this size single file beneath the Shadow Forest, my lord."

While this news was not what Garrett had hoped to hear, their agreement seemed to ease the tension a little. "Speaking of Ice Ember, do you have any?"

"Of course, my lord. Ice Ember is what we treasure most. It is the substance Metsavana requires to bestow gifts upon those who are worthy to receive them. Of course, no one can get to the father tree since those bastard elves walled it in." Then, interrupting himself with a troubled sigh, Stone looked off toward Osonian and continued, "There isn't a human left alive who has actually ever been to see the father tree in person. For us, Ice Ember's only uses are for trade or to navigate the Shadow Forest."

Key pressed her lips into a tight line and nodded. Then, her brows lifting, she said, "But there is another way, and it could cut our time in half."

"Seriously? How?" Garrett pleaded.

Stone leaned in, seemingly as curious as Garrett was.

"It is actually quite simple, and as long as we don't die, your armies may even arrive rested."

Stone ran a nervous hand across his bewhiskered face. "You're not thinking of—"

"I am," Key interjected, her hazel eyes twinkling.

Garrett keyed in on the "if we don't die" part. "What are we talking about here?"

From across the courtyard, Lenny, Pete, Governess, and

the other sages approached, along with the dwarf Kilug. Tell was with them, and she was walking next to Lenny. Garrett wondered if the woman was still angry over what had happened.

"What did we miss?" a very normal-looking Lenny asked.

"You okay?" Garrett asked.

"Yeah," Lenny said, looking over at Gabi with a smile.

Gabi grinned back shyly.

"Good," Garrett said, slapping Lenny on the shoulder. "Key was just about to tell us her plan on how we can shave a couple days… I mean moon rings off our trip to Osonian."

"That's great! I can't wait to get there!" Lenny said, rubbing his hands together vigorously. "What's the plan?"

Garrett and Breanne shared a look. It was a little strange for Lenny to be this excited to go into what was likely to be certain death.

"We can take the climbing river," Key said.

"That's a death wish, and you know it!" Stone argued through gritted teeth.

"Perhaps for you and yours, but not for my warriors. We have used the river for many, many moon cycles. You need only know the technique for navigating the climbs," Key said assuredly.

"And you will share this knowledge with my men?" Stone asked.

Key, leaning her spear against her shoulder, reached behind her head to tie back her braids. "They are no longer your men, Stonebender. They are the queen's men."

Stone frowned. "I answer to Lord Turek."

"And he answers to Queen Breezemore," the woman said, giving the hair tie a final tug.

Both looked at Garrett and Breanne.

Garrett felt Breanne's eyes burning into him, and he remembered the night before. She was right. This whole thing could fall apart at any moment, leaving him with two armies killing each other before they ever made it to Osonian.

"Listen to me, both of you," he said, looking at Breanne and then the others. "All of you listen. I won't hear any more of this. It is enough to say Queen Breezemore and I are aligned in this effort to stop Jack from destroying Osonian and, with it, Metsavana. That's number one. Number two is opening the portal back to Earth. Turek's Keepers are back there waiting for us. We fail them, and over a thousand die, but even more, a powerful tree queen will kill the rest of the humans on Earth. As for number two, well, once we stop Jack, I am hoping Metsavana can help me with that part."

"Ah, you are expecting a gift from the tree father?" Key asked curiously. "And supposing you can accomplish the first part, what will you give him to receive such a gift?"

Garrett nodded sharply at Stone. "I am hoping you have a surplus of Ice Ember here in the city?"

Stone frowned. "My lord, we have some, but you realize how heavy the substance is, do you not? And if we were to use the river, carrying such a weight would be impossible."

"Well, you must have boats. Can't they carry the weight?" Paul asked.

"Boats? No. Ships do not sail on the climbing river," Key explained.

"Then how do we travel it?"

Key smiled mischievously. "You can swim, yes?"

Pete stepped forward, letting go of Governess's hand.

Hand holding? When the hell had that happened? Garrett wondered. He'd been so wrapped up in trying to unite the armies, Bre being pissed, and Lenny turning into an elf, he'd hardly even seen Pete or Governess. Not since the tree woman had backhanded Pete across the face, anyway.

"Sure, we can all swim, but Governess cannot, and if she can't take the river, then neither can I."

"Peter Ashwood, do not be stubborn. I assure you, where the river takes you, I can follow. For water cannot flow faster than I can run." She smiled at him, took his hand in hers, and gently pulled him back toward her.

Garrett looked around the group, noticing Breanne raise her eyebrows, doing little to hide her surprise at the tree woman's display of affection for Pete. Lenny gave Garrett a light ribbing with his elbow and smiled, while Gabi giggled, and David just shook his head.

Garrett glanced at Paul too, but the older man seemed lost in thought. Probably thinking how bad of an idea the river was. Then he nodded as if in agreement to his own contemplation and cleared his throat. "I think we should listen to Key and take the river. We need to make up time where we can. With my strength, I might be able to carry a little of the ember. Not as much as Pete and I pulled from the river. It would have to be much smaller, but I'm willing to pack some."

Garrett's mind lit up with mind speak as all the sages began talking over each other. Finally, it was Bre who took the floor.

Paul, are you sure you should carry all that extra weight?

I'm sure, he said without hesitation. *The river makes sense.*

Oh, man, David chimed in. *I don't know, guys! Does it have brush piles we could get trapped under? I've been trapped under one and it's no good! Tell them, Garrett!*

"My lord? Are you alright?" Stone asked.

"Oh, they're fine," Key said, shaking her head. "They just don't want you to hear what they are discussing."

"Discussing? But they're not saying anything at all." Stone looked from one sage to the other.

"Oh, they are, Stonebender – they are indeed. It's alright. You will get used to it."

"They are speaking magically?"

"Aye. They've the power of inner speak," Kilug said. "Me people tell stories of giants and dragons possessing such power. 'Tis a powerful magic, indeed."

"Sorry, guys," Garrett said aloud. "We have decided the river is our best option. So, what do we do?"

Key smiled that same mischievous smile. "Oh, I think you will like this next part."

"Dear Turek, please be with us," Stone said.

∽

Both armies gathered in the courtyard, ready to depart for Osonian. Meanwhile, Garrett and the others gathered far outside the main gate near the edge of the falls.

"The first step on our journey is getting to the river," Key shouted over the sound of roaring water. "And to do that, we must get down there!" she pointed over the falls.

"How do we do that?" Garrett asked.

David pushed himself in between the group as they stared over the falls. "Wow. That's far. Is there some secret path, or do we have to backtrack through the Mazewood? Because honestly, I've been hearing a lot about the creatures that live in the Mazewood and I'm thinking we got pretty lucky getting here. Like, did you know there are dire wolves in there? Oh, and I heard there's a pissed-off group of fairies living there too. Now don't get me wrong, I'd like to see a fairy, but not if it's pissed off. Oh! I also heard there's a giant—"

"Shut up, David!" Lenny scolded.

Key barked out a laugh. "No worries, little David. There is no need to go through the Mazewood."

"Well, that's good! I sure like that!" David said, giving Lenny a look as if to say, "Thanks to me, we don't have to go that way! You're welcome!"

"Aye," Kilug said. "But me fear ye won't be liking what she says next none the more."

"Do you see that spot there?" Key asked, pointing over from where they were standing to a small path. Even from here Garrett could see it didn't lead down but only over to another small, flat ledge.

The spot was actually very familiar to Garrett because it was the exact spot where the owl had perched when he stopped the arrows in mid-flight. "Yeah, I see it, Key, but it doesn't seem to lead anywhere."

"Aye. Here it comes." Kilug shook his head.

"Ah, but it does, Lord Garrett. It is the single spot atop these falls from which one can jump with any chance of survival."

There was a gasp from David, followed by an eruption of chatter from the others.

However, despite the roar of water, the fact he couldn't see the bottom, and the fear in the faces of the others, Garrett knew instantly. This was the way. Not because Key said so, but because this was the very spot the owl had jumped from last night. Garrett smiled. Despite how dire this looked, something inside him told him the owl had been a sign from Turek. A sign to show him the way!

Garrett held up his hands, quieting everyone.

The others settled down, but their concerned faces told him they were not on board. Even Paul frowned, his face scrunching as if he'd just gotten a whiff of David's feet.

Garrett swallowed dryly. "Key, I'll go first. Just tell me what to do."

49

Onward to Osonian

God Stones – Moon Ring 4
The City of Cloud

Garrett, you can't be seriously thinking about jumping off this mountain and into... into that! Breanne asked in mind speak so the others could hear. What was he thinking? They couldn't survive a jump like that!

I don't see another option, Bre.

I know how bad you want this, but getting yourself and all of us killed won't save our parents or the people of Earth.

Garrett, listen to her, David said. *This is crazy. There has to be another way.*

Paul leaned out to get a better look. *Kid, I appreciate your willingness here, but I know Army Rangers who wouldn't take that jump with a parachute. You got zero visibility of the lower cliff walls, plus the fall itself could be hiding jagged rock formations. And that's only part of it. You could land wrong or get swept downstream by the undercurrents. Have you ever jumped from anything this high? You have to land perfect or you risk breaking bones.*

Garrett, even if you make the jump, what about Gabi? She's only thirteen!

I'll go second, Gabi said, a smile stretching across her face.

Breanne shook her head. *Not funny. Well, what about Governess? She can't swim, remember?*

Governess raised an eyebrow. *If you choose this suicidal course, I shall simply and quickly descend the cliff face opposite this fall and join you below.*

Garrett, I'm not jumping, David said, his face fear stricken.

Thank god, Breanne thought, hoping that would be enough to deter Garrett from this insanity. *We can find another way, Garrett.*

Garrett shook his head and stepped up atop the stone edge of the path, positioning himself high enough for the others to see. Then he spoke aloud, shouting his words, "Listen to me, all of you. This is the fastest and most direct route! We will jump one after the other over the falls."

The army broke out in shouts, waving their fists in the air.

"Please, listen! All of you hear me now! I know this is what we are to do! Turek has shown me!"

Turek has shown you? Is there something you want to tell your sages, Garrett? Breanne asked in mind speak, crossing her arms. What was he hiding, and why was he hiding it from her?

"We've no more time. You must trust me! This can be done. It has been done. I will go first. As each of you approaches the cliff, Key will tell you what to do. Now if you trust in Turek, then trust in me."

Breanne frowned up at him as he jumped down off the stone and back onto the path. *I'm sorry, Bre,* he said. *I didn't get a chance to finish telling you.*

Telling me what, Garrett? she asked.

The owl. When I stopped the arrows. I saw it jump from the same spot Key is telling us we can jump from! Don't you see what this means?

You believe this is a sign?

Of course I do, he said. *Don't you?*

But if the owl in my dream was the same one you saw, then the people fighting back on Earth – fighting and dying… then it was all real.

Yeah, maybe, but we don't know when that will happen. Maybe it just means we need to hurry.

Well, I don't know about you guys, but I say it's time to fly! Lenny said.

Okay, I can't believe I'm agreeing to this, but if we're going to do it, I say we jump together, Breanne said.

Garrett smiled and nodded.

"Key, we're ready. What do we need to do?"

"Step onto the platform, staying as far back as you can. Then run hard, leaping as far out as you can. Keep your feet pointed down. When you hit the cloud of mist below, suck in as deeply as you can and hold your breath. When you hit the water, kick hard until you break the surface and swim for the shoreline. We will meet there to prepare for the next part."

Gabi, do you want to jump with Garrett and I?

No. I better jump with David. He's freaking out.

David looked green, but he was doing his best to put on a brave face in front of Gabi. Breanne smiled tightly, doing a poor job of hiding her own concern. She wanted to say the stupid things parents would say, like "be careful" and "don't forget to hold your breath."

Bre, do not worry. I'll keep David safe! Gabi grinned.

Breanne's smile was genuine now. *I know you will, Little Lion.* Taking Garrett's hand, she walked down the path onto the stone platform. It looked as though someone had chiseled it flat for the very purpose of running and jumping. She glanced back to find Key was directly behind her. "Have you done this before, Key?"

"Yes, my queen, when I was perhaps your age," Key said, shouting now as the roar of the falls grew with each step. "In the time when the women of Sky ruled the city of Cloud, leaping from here was a rite of passage. It was how we claimed our womanhood. No man has made this leap to my knowledge. For a man and a woman to leap together… well, this makes today a first in our history. I think you might call this progress."

Breanne supposed it might be progress toward equality – if they didn't die.

Farther back, Gabi and David approached. David looked sicker by the moment until he suddenly bent and vomited to the side of the path. Behind him, Lenny and Tell pulled a face. They too were holding hands as they approached together. Behind them, Breanne swore she saw Pete kiss Governess's cheek before turning to walk with Kilug the dwarf, though these two didn't hold hands. The dwarf's war hammer was secured to his back. Her brother Paul stepped onto the path alone. He looked at her and nodded. His assured voice filled her mind. *You got this, little sis.*

She nodded, smiling nervously.

"Are you ready?" Key asked.

Garrett squeezed Bre's hand and nodded.

"We're ready," she answered. Ready as she was going to be, but there was no turning back now. Despite how incredibly pissed she was, she trusted Garrett – trusted him with her life – and she was about to prove it.

With a shared look, they ran forward and jumped.

Breanne had never skydived before, but she imagined if she'd jumped out of a plane, this was what it would be like.

The wind was moving past her so fast it made her eyes water and flattened her cheeks. She wanted to scream. Instead, she focused on keeping her hand in Garrett's, her feet pointed down, and her body vertical.

On and on, they plummeted. The drop was farther than she'd imagined, which meant they were going to hit the water and break every bone in their bodies. This was stupid! This was the dumbest idea Garrett had ever had! *Garrett! We're still falling!* she shouted in mind speak.

I realize that! he answered.

She looked down as a white, cloudlike mist raced toward her, then suddenly she was swallowed inside the thick fog. With sudden terror, she remembered she was supposed to take a breath and hold. As she did, she noticed the wind ripping at her clothes had slowed.

No… she had slowed. She had to have. Why else would the wind slow?

Out of time to think, she crashed into the river, her hand slipping from Garrett's as she plunged beneath the surface like a heavy stone. Down she went, deeper and deeper. She kicked with all she had, slowing and finally pulling herself toward the surface.

Frothing water spun her, rolling her over and over, but finally her head broke the surface, allowing her a water-filled gasp. Somehow, through the choking gulp, she managed to get some air. She rolled again and then her head punched through the surface once more, and this time she held herself there. The current pushed her downriver as she continued to kick. Coughing and choking, she thought she might drown after all when her hands felt soft moss.

"Yes! Oh, dear god, yes!" She crawled forward on hands and knees. An arm suddenly wrapped her waist and helped her to her feet.

"You okay?" Garrett asked through gasps.

"I thought I was going to drown!" she shouted. "Garrett, was that you? Did you make us slow?" She spun back around, staring up at the mist. "Gabi!" The strange cloud hung there a hundred feet above the water. "Did you?" she shouted, knowing if Garrett had slowed them, everyone else who jumped after them would surely be injured or killed from the fall.

"Easy, Bre! It wasn't me!"

From up above, a voice screamed as two more bodies dropped from the mist and plunged into the river.

"That was David and Gabi. I'd know that scream anywhere!" Garrett pointed out into the river. "I'll get them!"

"I'm coming too!" she said, still coughing. She must have swallowed a gallon of water. Nevertheless, she turned, wading back into the river.

Within only minutes of arriving on the bank, Governess joined them and for the next two hours the armies of Sky fell from the mist, landing one after another in the only part of the river below the falls that wouldn't end in their deaths. Breanne and the over a thousand others who jumped that day also learned the ultimate secret Key had already known. As they passed through the mist, their bodies slowed just enough to allow for a safe landing, so long as they landed correctly. By the time the armies of men and women had gathered in full force on the shore, five had been lost. Three died on impact. Two others weren't found, likely washed upriver, never to be seen again.

Breanne knew statistically five out of more than a thousand wasn't bad. Still, five had died today, and she could see Garrett wearing the guilt like a heavy chain around his slumped shoulders.

"Are you okay?"

"Yeah, as okay as I can be."

She wrapped her arms around him and hugged him

tight. She was still pissed, but it would do no good to make him feel worse than he already felt. "If it makes you feel any better, I didn't think half of the people who made that jump would live to talk about it."

Garrett nodded gravely, his expression one of sober severity. Breanne had seen him wearing this look more and more lately, and she couldn't help but worry what the stress and anxiety were doing to him, what it was doing to all of them.

Lenny approached, limping and looking even more distraught than Garrett.

"What's wrong with you?" Garrett asked.

"Worst freaking day ever!" Lenny announced, throwing his pack onto the ground.

Breanne looked at his pack and narrowed her eyes. "Uh-oh... is it gone?" she asked apologetically.

Lenny nodded.

Garrett frowned, looking between them and then to Lenny's pack. "Oh damn, Len, where's your guitar?"

"I don't want to talk about it," Lenny responded sourly.

"Len?"

"Fine! But it shouldn't come as a surprise to you that acoustic guitars and water don't go well together. It's toast, bro! The whole thing came apart. Smashed it to smithereens when I landed! Freaking bruised the hell out of my leg. I can barely walk! You know that was probably the only guitar on this whole freaking planet! But that's not even the worst of it. We've no idea what we are going to be facing! We needed that guitar!"

Lenny's outburst drew all the sages, along with Governess, Kilug, and Tell.

"It's okay, Len," Garrett said consolingly.

"Len, you want your staff back?" David asked.

"No, you better hang on to it," Lenny said, giving David's shaggy head a rub.

David let out a relieved sigh. "Well, at least let me heal your leg and your face. You were ugly before, but that face beating Saria gave you looks worse today than yesterday. Can you even see out of your left eye?"

"Barely," Lenny grumbled.

"Speaking of Saria, I have something you may find helpful," Tell said, nodding over her shoulder to the woman called Push.

Push stepped forward. "Yes, my lady?"

"Do you still have the sword?" Tell asked.

The woman reached back over her shoulder and drew a sword similar to a bastard sword from over her shoulder. The hilt was black with a fine double-edged blade.

"Saria's sword?" Lenny asked.

"She dropped it when she fled. I was saving it with the hope of killing her with her own blade, but perhaps you should have it," Tell said.

"Thank you, Tell." Lenny smiled, taking the sword. Breanne got the impression Lenny's smile was less about the blade and more that Tell was speaking to him again.

Lenny's expression changed as he turned his attention back to David and frowned. "Hey, you could have healed me yesterday, you know."

"Well, I didn't feel sorry for you yesterday. Now sit down," David said, preparing to go to work.

Kilug stomped forward, looking up at Lenny with his squinty eye. "Aye, ye may find comfort in this, lad. The elves be known fer their music. I've seen with me own eyes instruments similar to the one ye carried. Oh, they be fine crafted too, not like that crap you smashed to bits."

"So you're telling me there's a chance they have guitars?" Lenny asked, brightening with hope as he lowered himself to the ground.

"Never heard that word, but aye, thems have stringed instruments to be sure," the dwarf answered.

"Hey, has anyone seen my brother?" Breanne asked.

David pointed toward the water's edge. "I noticed him over by the water when I healed that guy's busted eardrum earlier."

Breanne winced.

"Hey, where are they going?" Pete asked, pointing at a group of women heading into the Shadow Forest.

"A bunch of chicks have been going back and forth. They're bringing out—"

Breanne slugged him in the shoulder.

David yelped. "Bre!"

Chicks, David! Really?

"Wow, bro, you think because you have a 1970s porn 'stache you can talk like that about these outstanding ladies?" Lenny frowned, slugging David on the same shoulder.

"Dick!" David blurted. "Just for that you can go on wondering what they were doing 'cause I ain't telling any of you squat. Now, you want healed or don't you?"

Lenny high-fived Breanne, and she thought she caught just a hint of a smile from Garrett.

Gabi laughed and said, "They're gathering leaves."

"Aww, Gabi!" David protested, placing a hand on Lenny's shoulder. He closed his eyes as his hand began to glow.

"Leaves? Leaves for what?" Garrett asked.

"That ought to do it," David said, then crossed his arms and gave Gabi a "you better not tell" look.

Key approached. "We're almost finished gathering leaves, my queen."

"Leaves, Key? Why leaves? Are they for a fire?" Breanne asked.

"A fire? Gods, no! Why would we light a fire with leaves?" Key asked, her face troubled.

"It's... well..." Breanne shook her head. "Never mind. Why the leaves then?"

Key smiled. "They are the secret to how we will travel to Osonian. The leaves will carry us up the climbing river."

"That seems very unlikely," Pete said.

"That's because you haven't seen the size of the leaves," David said, grinning.

"They're big, Bre. Really big!" Gabi said.

"Aye, bloody leaves on the climbing river!" Kilug groaned. "Me kin would laugh me out of the clan if they heard tell of this."

"When you're ready, we should gather the army up and I'll explain how they work. If we are lucky, we can cover a great distance before the suns die."

Breanne nodded. "Gather them," she said, her gaze falling to her brother, who she now saw sitting on a rock next to the river. Something wasn't right with him. She stood and brushed off her pants. "I'll be right back."

Laughter and chiding voices faded as she left her group of friends.

Paul had his back to her, and when she got close, she heard him talking in a low, urgent voice. She paused, looking around, but no one was there. He was talking to himself. She listened, barely able to hear his whispers, but made out a few words.

"Come on... I'm here... Rán... Sorry... so long... please."

"Paul?" she whispered.

Paul jumped, spinning to face her. "Bre! What are you doing sneaking up on me like that?" he asked, sounding annoyed.

"Paul, I'm... I'm sorry. I saw you sitting over here alone, and I was worried," she said, sounding as hurt as she felt.

Paul's shoulders slumped. "It's okay. Sorry for snapping at

you," he said, scooting down the driftwood to make room for his sister. He patted the spot next to him and she sat, leaning her head against his shoulder.

"Paul? Who were you talking to?" she asked.

"I... I lost the Ice Ember," he said.

She lifted her head, meeting his eyes. "What happened?"

"Stone had given me all he had. It must have been about half the amount Pete and I found. But this wasn't one big stone, it was a bunch of smaller ones, a whole pouch of them. I secured them in my pack. I... I fell so fast. Still, I was determined to keep the package secured and make the swim after contact. I thought sure I was dead, but the mist slowed me. Except I was so heavy. Dammit, I should have stuffed the pouch in my cargo pocket! When I hit the water, the weight of the ember and force of the water was too much. The straps on my pack snapped like overstretched rubber bands, ripping it off my back. Bre, it was gone before I could do anything about it." Paul pointed out into the river. "It's down there right now at the bottom of the falls."

"Oh, Paul. It wasn't your fault," Breanne said.

"I let them down, Bre. Garrett needed that ember. I may have just let the entire world down."

"We'll find another way. I'll tell him."

"No," Paul said firmly. "I'll tell him myself."

They sat quietly for a few minutes longer, Breanne's mind replaying the words her brother had said. Finally, she asked, "Paul, who were you talking to when I walked up?"

Paul turned to her. "Something happened on the trip I took to the river with Pete, sis. Something important."

Breanne frowned. "Well, tell me."

"I will. I promise I will, but not yet. Not... not now. I'm still sorting it out, but I promise I will tell you."

She didn't like this new secrecy, but she knew her brother,

and he meant what he said. He would tell her when he was ready. Reluctantly, she nodded. "Okay."

"Alright. Now c'mon, I think it is time I tell Garrett what happened."

She watched as her brother paused, gazing longingly at the river, and she couldn't help but think whatever he longed for was not Ice Ember.

∼

"Lost?" Garrett said, his face desperate.

Breanne and the others gathered in close as Paul explained. She only hoped Garrett didn't flip his top. She knew Paul had meant well, and no one was going to beat him up more than he was already beating himself up.

"I'm sorry. It was so heavy, Garrett. These packs aren't made to hold that kind of payload and from a fall that far. I... I should have seen the risk."

Garrett shook his head. "What? Should have seen it?"

Breanne felt her face flush and her temper flare. *Don't you blame him for this*, she thought, ready to let him have it. She'd had enough of him deciding without her, and now he was going to blame Paul for something that wasn't even his fault! If he wanted the damn Ice Ember, maybe he should have jumped off the mountain with it!

She opened her mouth to speak, but before she could, Garrett went on.

"If you should have seen it, then I should have seen it," he said, his mouth a pained grimace.

"What?" Paul asked.

"You jumped from a mountain carrying what must have been what, a hundred pounds of Ice Ember in your pack? If you should have known this was going to happen, we all should have known. This wasn't your fault, Paul. I knew what you were carrying and how you were carrying it, and it never even crossed my mind. If anything, you're lucky that pack didn't land on your head! You could have been killed!" Garrett dragged both hands down his face. "We have a whole army with us. Why didn't I pass the ember around to a dozen people, two dozen, a hundred? The truth is, you're the strongest person I know and I trust you. But that didn't make it right to put that kind of burden on you! I'm sorry, Paul. I took advantage of you and gave you an impossible task." Garrett's shoulders slumped as he shook his head. "I hope you can forgive me." His gaze fell to the ground in shame.

Guilt thick as honey filled Breanne's chest.

"I... I don't... I'm. Yes. I mean, there's nothing to forgive. Thank you," her brother said, blinking.

"I don't deserve that," Garrett said. "But thank you." He looked back up at Paul and placed a hand on her brother's shoulder. "You know, whenever I would complain to my dad about having to do my training, he used to say, if it were easy, anyone could do it. What we have to accomplish isn't easy, but don't worry, Paul, we'll figure this out."

"Easy?" Stone asked, approaching from behind with Key at his side.

It appeared the two weren't trying to kill each other for once.

"I assure you, getting to Metsavana will be anything but easy."

"Worrying about the father tree is pointless until we navigate the river," Key said. "We have distributed the leaves, and the army is being trained on how to use them as we speak. We still have plenty of light before ebon night is upon us. Let us use our time wisely. Come, I will show how to use the leaves to make the climbs."

"The climbs?" Paul asked.

"Of course. You mentioned you have waterfalls on your planet, yes?" Key asked.

"Roger that," Paul said.

"Then are you not familiar with waterclimbs as well?"

"No. I can't say that I am," Paul answered.

"Well, just imagine the opposite of a waterfall," Key said, smiling. "Now, please follow me."

Garrett and Breanne exchanged curious smiles. She grabbed his wrist and stopped.

Garrett stopped. "What's—"

She shoved her lips against his, kissing him.

"Mmmm," he tried but then fell into the kiss, pulling her to him and wrapping his arms around her.

Finally, she pulled her head back.

"What was that for?" he asked, his eyes wide but his grin wider still.

"Because I love you, Garrett Turek." She smiled and turned away.

"I don't think I am ever going to understand women," Garrett mumbled, falling in behind her.

She smiled wider still.

⁓

The leaves turned out to be thick and large. Not as long as a river kayak but a bit wider. The weirdest part was they were flexible and, as Key explained, you were to steer by not only leaning and shifting your body weight, but also by tugging on the flexible material of the leaf.

"But won't we tear it if we pull too hard?" David asked.

Key assured him it wouldn't be a problem. After a brief demonstration on land, into the water they went.

A long, winding stretch of river made for the perfect practice section. Still, the current was fast. Breanne felt like she was getting the hang of it pretty easily, and Lenny and Garrett seemed like naturals. Kilug looked quite uncomfortable, but it was David who seemed to struggle the most, spinning in circles and spending just as much time floating backward as forward. "Stop pulling on the leaf so much, David," Breanne offered.

"I think I have a defective leaf!" David shouted, nearly colliding with Key as he spun past her.

"There is nothing wrong with your leaf, stupid boy," Key shouted after him with annoyance. "Listen to your queen and stop trying so hard. We will reach the first climb soon and you will stand a better chance of not drowning or falling to your death if you are facing the climb!"

"Drowning! Falling! What? You didn't tell us we might fall!" David whined.

Breanne felt for him. After that night on the Sangamon River, getting stuck in the brush pile, and confronting the giant rat, she really couldn't blame him for being afraid.

"There, you see it!" Key shouted and pointed.

Ahead loomed what, from a distance, looked like a sizable waterfall, but they were going upriver toward the bottom of the fall. *The climb is a backward waterfall?* Breanne said, in mind speak.

The water is flowing up the fall! Gabi said in astonishment.

Pete steered his leaf between Breanne and Key. "Key, how is this possible? Gravity is still in effect. I mean, the law of universal gravitation is, well, universal?" Pete's voice was one of wonder, begging to understand.

Key shook her head. "I do not know these words, gravity and gravitation, but I assure you, if you do not stay in the water, you will fall. Now listen carefully. When you enter the climb, simply lean forward into the water wall. Your leaf will bite in, and the water below will lift you as it rises. Two things you mustn't do. First, do not lean back. Your leaf will tilt if you lean back. If this happens, lean forward quickly. If you lean back too far, your leaf will slip out altogether and you will fall from whatever point this happens all the way to the bottom. You may live, but you may not. Second, do not tug on the sides of your leaf like your foolish David has been doing this entire time. If you do, you will spin out of control and be thrown from the climbing waterfall back to the bottom." She smiled. "Easy enough. Understand?"

"Roger that!" Paul said.

"Roger what!? No! Not easy!" David said, having brought his leaf under control.

Garrett gently lifted one edge of his leaf, turning it so he faced David. "David, we are going to climb that thing!" He pointed. "I need you to just lean in, close your eyes, and stay still until you get to the top."

"Oh sure, Garrett! That's easy for you to say. You could do this in your sleep!"

"You can do this, David. You know how I know?" Garrett asked.

"No!" David shouted, panic setting in.

"I know because I am going to be right behind you talking to you the whole way up and if you fall, David, you're taking me with you."

"Really?" David asked.

"This is ill advised, Lord Turek," Key said, as if she were obligated to give the warning.

Garrett, are you sure this is a good idea? Breanne asked in mind speak so only he could hear.

Garrett looked across the brief span of water between them. *He can do it, Bre. He has to.* Then he looked ahead at David. "We got this, buddy."

"If he falls just grab him by the face lace and pull him back in," Lenny laughed.

"What is face lace?" Kilug asked.

"You know, his dirt squirrel? Lower brow? Lip cap? Grass grin?"

Kilug's eyebrows rose.

"Flavor savor? Soup strainer? Come on, Kilug, his crumb catcher?" Lenny pleaded.

"If ye are referring to the man's facial fur, I do not advise lifting him by such means. Dwarves have tried this technique with far more substantial growth to grab and the result is always the same. The bloody beard won't hold the weight and it rips out."

"Ouch!" Breanne blurted.

Lenny sighed. "You know, if I'm expected to live on this planet permanently, people are really going to need to work on their humor."

"Brace yourselves for the climb!" Key ordered.

Breanne felt her heart racking her chest as she looked up at the giant wall of water. Unlike the waterfall they had jumped from, there was no crashing of water here, just a wall pulling itself up toward the sky before vanishing over the top.

David's leaf bit into the water wall, and he leaned forward. The water lifted him quickly – much faster than she expected. In only a few seconds, he was halfway up the climb, screaming at the top of his lungs.

Behind David, Garrett glanced back, smiled, and winked. Like David, he leaned in and was gone.

Breanne sucked in a breath, held it, and leaned forward. Water splashed over her as she entered the wall of water. Her stomach dropped as it filled with butterflies and her ears popped. A few seconds later, she was over the top of the climb. Gasping, she laughed and glanced back. Paul appeared next with a giant grin on his face.

One after another, the sages and soldiers appeared over the waterclimb.

The Last Gift

So, the evening went, as the armies of Sky navigated the river along with several more waterclimbs. As darkness swallowed everything, Key led them to shore to make camp. They would rise early to travel yet another full moon ring and part of another. Which, near as Breanne could tell, was like a day and a half, though a moon ring was much longer in hours than an Earth day. How much longer, she couldn't say.

As camp went up, Key sent a few of their fastest women warriors to scout ahead, gather intel, and report back on what the army could expect to find when they reached Osonian.

Settling into sleep, Breanne felt a strange yet familiar anxiousness settle over her. After years of being afraid to go to sleep, afraid to see her dead mother in her nightmares and face the guilt of the accident, she knew this feeling all too well. But she hadn't felt this way since she had made peace with her mother back in Mexico. So what was it then? Well, if she were being honest, she knew exactly what she feared.

Despite her trepidation, she was asleep as soon as she closed her eyes. Exhaustion from the day claimed her consciousness as soon as her head hit the bedroll.

When she opened her eyes, she was no longer on the bank of the climbing river. Instead, she was back in Mexico, in that horrible place, standing atop the pyramid temple. The sun was up, shining in a cloudless sky.

Hesitantly she peered over the side, afraid of what she might see. But the trees were gone and there was no sign of people... save one. For a second, she hoped the man was her father, but even though he was sitting with his back to her, it was clear he wasn't her dad. She didn't recognize him.

The man stood on one wobbly leg, unable to put weight on the other. He looked bad –wounded and starving. One of his hands was swollen, his knuckles scabbed. He glanced up as if to look at her, and she noticed his face was scarred.

James, she thought. Mr. B had told the story of James being burned by Apep. Those scars. This had to be him – Garrett's stepbrother. But then where was everyone else? The Keepers. Garrett's mom. Where was her dad?

"Hello!" she called. But the man didn't hear her. It was like he couldn't see her at all.

Something scuffed the stone behind her. Breanne spun.

A woman was walking across the roof. She was thin, frail, and filthy. Her sandy brown hair was tangled. She was carrying something in her right hand. Breanne started toward her but then pulled up short and gasped.

The woman held Apep's head by a fistful of black hair. The memory of King Vulmon Loravaris swinging his sword and Apep's head toppling to the temple roof flashed through her mind. The head, now mostly skull and a tuft of hair, looked old and rotted. The woman placed it on the altar and smiled. "It's almost time. Soon, my boy will come to take us home. What? What did you dare say? You just wait! You'll see!" The woman let out a soft moan and collapsed to her knees. She picked up a sharp rock and scratched a line into the altar's pedestal. "Six months tomorrow. Six months tomorrow. Six months tomorrow!"

50

Nightmares and Dragons

God Stones – Moon Ring 5
The Eastern Woods

Garrett woke before the suns lit. Maybe nights were longer here? He always seemed to wake before the suns on Karelia – all on his own, without Phillip shouting at him or his mother calling for him. The thought of his parents sent a pang of sorrow through him, followed quickly by a heavy guilt. *I'm sorry, Mom, but I'm trying. I'm really trying.*

Next to him, Breanne lurched upright from her bedroll and screamed, "Six months tomorrow!"

"Breanne!" Garrett shouted, jumping in surprise at the sudden outburst. Her eyes were wild, darting all around. Her hands waved as if fighting something off. "It's okay, Bre!" Garrett said, grabbing her flailing wrists.

"Sis! What's wrong?" Paul called from across the camp as he hurriedly maneuvered between bedrolls.

"I think they're dead! Jesus, Paul!" she said, tears rolling down her face.

"Who?" Paul asked in confusion, but Garrett didn't need

to ask, and he didn't need to hear the answer. He knew by her face it could only be their parents and the Keepers. The question for Garrett wasn't who.

"When, Breanne?" he asked.

Paul frowned. "When?"

The others were up and gathering around them now.

"I... I don't know."

"Did you see anyone specifically this time?" Garrett asked.

Breanne looked at him, her face twisted in horror. "Don't make me say it," she whispered.

Key pushed through the crowd. "What's happened?"

"She's had a bad dream, is all," Garrett said, swallowing dryly. Whatever she saw, he was no longer sure he wanted to know.

"Hmm, yes, well, it's best to take heed. A seer's dreams are always significant."

"We need to get this day behind us, and we need to get to Osonian," Garrett said, his hand rubbing her back softly.

Key nodded. "We should make haste anyway. The suns are lighting and will begin to move soon. Though I suspect with our numbers, we are fine here on the shore, still I would like to get on the water. Trolls are most active at first light and just before the suns die."

David's mouth fell open and his face paled. "Did you say trolls?"

"Indeed. You've heard of them?"

David forced a swallow as if his mouth were full of flour and nodded. "Giant things that eat people."

"Ah, you have heard of them. Good. Yes, they are quite large and very strange-looking creatures. And like many of the creatures of the forest, they will eat us. It's best if we don't have to deal with them."

David had already rolled up his throw blanket, stuffed it

in his pack, grabbed his leaf, and started for the water before Key finished her sentence.

"Where is he going?" she asked.

"He isn't a big fan of danger," Lenny offered.

"No. He is cowardly."

Lenny turned and faced Key. "No. that's where you're wrong, Lady Key. David is brave when bravery is required. In fact, he is one of the bravest kids I know. I once saw him face down an army of nephilbock with nothing more than that wooden staff tied to his pack. No, ma'am, David is not a coward, and I would appreciate it if you didn't call him that." Lenny nodded, turned, and headed off toward the shore.

Garrett looked at Pete with eyebrows raised.

Pete, returning the same look, said, "Well, damn."

"You going to be okay, Breanne?" Garrett asked.

"It was bad, Garrett. So bad."

"It hasn't happened, though. It must be the future, right?" Garrett asked hopefully.

"But it felt so real. Too real. It has to mean something," she said.

"What does your gut say, sis?" Paul asked.

She looked at Governess. "My gut says either Pando didn't keep her word or she's not going to."

"My queen would not break her word, Breanne Moore," Governess said.

"How can you be so sure?" Paul asked.

"Because there is nothing to gain by her doing so."

"Then what?" Garrett asked.

"I am afraid I have arrived at an unfortunate realization," Governess said, looking into Pete's eyes with an expression that looked... apologetic?

"What is it?" Breanne asked.

"Time, Breanne Moore." Governess looked around at the group of sages. "Time, I am afraid, is not passing on Earth at the same rate it is passing here on Karelia. It appears that time passes more quickly on Earth than here."

At those words, Garrett knew it was true. But could it be that different? When Coach and Apep fought in the pyramid, Apep said something about this, but in his fear and desperation he couldn't remember. "What it means is we don't have six months. We have to hurry!"

"But what... what if what I saw already happened?" Breanne asked.

Garrett shook his head. "No. No way! It couldn't have already happened!"

"Why, Garrett?" Paul asked, his face begging for Garrett to provide some hope. Some reassurance they weren't too late.

"Because it would mean I failed, Paul. And dammit, I'm not ready to fail! Look, we don't know what this means, but we have to go. We press on until we find out!"

"Hooah!" Paul said, slapping Garrett on the shoulder. "That's enough for me, kid!"

Garrett and the people of Sky mounted their leaves and pressed on, spending the entire day navigating the river's waterclimbs. By nightfall, they were ready to make their final ascent to Osonian. But clouds were moving in, blocking the light from the stars and the moons. Both Key and Stone agreed it was better to make camp than push forward into only Turek knew what in utter darkness. So instead, they ate dried meat rations and fruit grown by Governess with her use of the Sentheye.

Just one more night – one more, Garrett thought.

Commotion broke out on the other side of the camp as he and the other sages were making their beds.

Garrett grabbed Breanne's hand and hastily led her through camp, careful not to fall over other kneeling men and women as they too prepared their beds for the night.

There's Key and Stone! Garrett said in mind speak as he spotted the two leaders in the middle of a knot of women. As they came closer, he asked aloud, "What's happening?"

"Ah, well," Key said, looking past Garrett to Breanne.

It was clear to Garrett that, when it came to the women of Sky, the women's loyalty was to Breanne, not him. As Garrett stepped to the side to allow Breanne space to move forward, he didn't feel offended by Key's snub. In fact, he was just glad that somehow these two enemies of the opposite sex could come together for a greater cause. Whatever was happening, it was clear that the conflict wasn't between Key and Stone.

"My queen, your scouts have returned with a report," Key said, nodding at two women. The women stepped forward and knelt, their heads bowed, their spears held upright and resting on the ground. Garrett looked down at the women, their black hair braided down to their scalps in rows. In the firelight, he could see fresh scratches and scrapes on their arms crossing old scars.

"You may rise," Breanne said.

The two women rose, standing at attention. Garrett realized then they were identical twins.

"Please, what are your names?" Breanne asked.

"I am Bluraway," said the one on the left.

"I am Blendaway," said the other.

"They are the best at… infiltration," Key said carefully, as she glanced over at Stone.

"She means to say assassination," Stone said, frowning.

"Do not tell my queen what I mean to say," she snapped.

Breanne held up a hand, silencing them. "Okay, Blur and Blend. Got it. Now, enough with the pomp and circumstance," she said, motioning them to relax. "Tell me what you've learned."

God, she is good at this, Garrett thought.

Blur spoke first. "We followed the river north until it vanished beneath the mountains. We then turned west and traveled until we reached the great wall of Osonian. It still stands."

Garrett shared a look with the others and let out a breath of relief.

"The distance from the river to the wall isn't far. When we arrived, we found the wall guarded heavily by dökkálfar."

Without missing a beat, Blend took over. "As we investigated, it became clear that a massive battle took place several moon rings ago. The field was littered with boulders still scorched from having been tarred and lit afire, obviously slung from atop the wall. The ground had been heavily trampled. Also, the road leading in was destroyed."

Blur continued. "But there was no longer anyone on the battlefield nor any dragons present. All was quiet – except…"

"Go on," Breanne urged.

"Except, my queen" – Blend took over the story again – "we saw fires burning to the south, on the opposite side of the battlefield near the Ruins of Turek."

"The Ruins of Turek?" Breanne asked.

"This is the place where it is said Turek escaped with her people, away from this world," Tell said.

Stone nodded. "Yes, it is the place you came to Karelia, is it not?"

Garrett shared a look with Breanne. The strange hollow pyramid where the portal between Earth and Karelia opened.

Breanne nodded. "What did you find there?"

Blur continued. "Using the forest, we skirted the field to get close, and when we did, we found an entire army of giants. These were smaller than the nephilbock we have seen here on Karelia, but their numbers are vast and despite their smaller size, they appeared quite formidable."

Blend pulled a face. "There's more. They must have been

camped there since you all arrived from Earth. They are surviving on dead dragon, dökkálfar, and even on their own kind."

"It was quite disturbing, my queen," Blur said sourly.

"But they aren't attacking?" Garrett asked, unable to help himself.

Ignoring him, the two women stood and remained fixed on Breanne.

"If the battle was over, why are they still here?" Breanne asked.

The two shook their heads in unison. "We are unsure, though it appears the giants are waiting for something, my queen."

Breanne nodded sagely. "Thank you. Please get some food and some sleep. You have done well."

The two women bowed and vanished into the crowd.

Excited at the news, Garrett spoke to the others in mind speak. *It looks like we may just beat Jack to the punch after all.*

As long as we get there tomorrow, Gabi said in a voice that seemed shaken.

Gabi, what is it? Breanne asked.

How would you know Jack is going to be there tomorrow? Garrett asked, feeling his stomach turn.

I know because Zerri just told me, Gabi said.

Garrett could hear her voice holding back a river of tears. *What else did she say, Gabi?*

She said... she said tomorrow she would get vengeance for what I did to her mother. Tomorrow I... I would join my parents. Gabi let loose a sob.

Breanne grabbed her and hugged her tight.

"What's happened?" Key asked.

"The dragons will attack Osonian tomorrow," Garrett said.

"How do you know?" Stone asked nervously.

"We know, Stone, and that's all that matters," Garrett said, not wanting to get into the details.

"Well, do you know when exactly?" Stone asked.

"No," Garrett said turning back to mind speak. *Gabi, I know this is hard for you, and I know you are going to keep trying to talk to her. I won't tell you not to. But whatever you do, don't tell her our location, okay?*

Bringing herself under control, Gabi nodded. *María Purísima, of course I won't tell her, but she said if we are not there, her dragons will burn the city. After that, they will find the humans of this world and destroy them all, starting with the Shadow Forest and the city of Cloud. She knows about Cloud, Garrett! She knows!*

"We leave as soon as it is light enough to see," Garrett said, trying to control his own voice.

"Agreed," Breanne said, sharing Garrett's grave look.

"Is there anything else we should know?" Key asked, looking between them, then at Stone – her expression full of curiosity rather than gravity.

Garrett shook his head. "No. Let's get rested. We've a long day tomorrow."

51

Please, Please, Please!

God Stones – Moon Ring 5
The Creators' Mountain, Karelia

"That was impressive, Turek!" Typhon laughed. "I must say, I didn't expect your descendant to pull off uniting the two armies after slaying the men's king."

"Yes, well, it won't be enough to stop your dragons, Typhon," Ereshkigal snapped.

"No, not now that they have all the God Stones and this Jack thing," Druesha spat.

"Well, not so fast," Turek said. "They are planning to unite with the dökkálfar. If they can get the elves to see the logic in a truce."

Ereshkigal glared at him. "Oh, you are a fool!"

"Hold on, sister," Rán started. "This Lennard Wade is an interesting twist. He reached the age of reveal shortly after mating with the human girl. What is her name – Tess?"

"Tell," Turek corrected.

"Right, perhaps he can—"

"No," Ereshkigal interrupted. "Firstly, he should be slain

outright for existing! I assure you, when King Loravaris gets his hands on him, that is precisely what will happen. No, dear sister, this Lennard Wade makes the case for a truce far worse. They should have kept this detail secret, but instead your Lennard gave Syldan's journal to Saria. By now, it will have been hand-delivered to the king. This was a fatal move. They will find no truce with the dökkálfar, only death."

Aurgelmir appeared in the circle.

Turek smiled at him. "Brother, you have returned."

"Indeed, I have."

"You have missed many happenings in the human queendom of Sky," Druesha said, "but tell us, brother, what did you get up to over this past moon ring?"

"Come now, truly. You want me to believe you were not watching my every move? Not even you, Durin? You, who seemed to be so keen on monitoring all of us?"

Durin straightened, his Sentheye flashing the color of a tangerine sunset back on Earth. "I paid no more attention to your meddling than anyone else. After all, there has been much afoot within the human city. Despite the death of a king, this Breanne and Garrett have united armies!" Durin said, crossing his arms.

"If you wanted us to watch you, why did you not tell us so?" Druesha asked.

Turek peered quizzically at his brother. "Yes, Aurgy. What's happened with your nephilbock? Have you accomplished something?"

Aurgelmir nodded slowly. "I accomplished much, but if it mattered so little to you when I was gone, then it shouldn't matter now."

"Oh, come now. Don't pout, Aurgy," Rán said, poking out her lower lip – it wasn't really a lip at all, but the effect was the same.

"I do not pout, sister, but if you truly did not watch, then why spoil the surprise?"

"Oh, fun! You know how much I love a good surprise!" Rán laughed. "If that's settled, can we please spin now?"

"We should talk about the owl as a group before we spin again," Turek said.

"What's to talk about? It never came back," Typhon said.

"No. But it gave Garrett something," Turek said.

"What are you talking about?" Typhon asked.

"I didn't see it give him anything," Druesha said curiously.

"Nor did I," Ereshkigal agreed.

"Oh, come now. Garrett jumped from precisely the same spot the owl had jumped from. She gave him hope!"

"She, brother?" Druesha asked.

"I… I meant…" Turek stammered.

"You think the owl was the Great Mother," Ereshkigal accused.

"Ridiculous." Typhon laughed, his shoulders bouncing.

Turek rubbed a hand down his face in frustration. "I don't know what she… it was, and for that matter, neither do any of you. No one claimed it as their creation. Don't you find that odd? Odd that we don't know where it came from? Odd that I couldn't catch it? I saw into its eyes, and they swirled with Sentheye."

"There are plenty of other possibilities besides jumping to the conclusion that the owl is the Great Mother herself, Turek!" Durin said.

"He's right. We bless many of our creations with the ability to touch the Sentheye," Druesha added in her soothing voice.

"Agreed. It could simply be a forgotten creation or some blasphemous cross-bred abomination, likely from Earth!" Ereshkigal said, her voice snapping the calm.

"Yes. Earth seems to be where the problems originate," Typhon said, his flinty eyes giving Turek an accusing stare.

"This talk is pointless. Even if the owl was the Great Mother, which I find preposterous, what would we change? Would we not still honor the deal? Would we not defend the father tree if the wall falls?" Rán asked.

"We would indeed," Durin said proudly.

"So… I say spin the knife, Aurgy!" Rán urged.

Aurgelmir looked to Turek.

As much as Turek hated to admit it, his sister was right. The talk about the owl was pointless. There was no way to prove his theory any more than the others could prove theirs. And regardless, in this moment, it changed nothing.

He placed the dagger in the circle and nodded.

Aurgelmir spun the knife.

"Oh please! Ohhh, Great Mother, if you're listening, please, please, please!" Rán whispered.

The point of the blade chose a very happy… Rán.

52

The Sea Goddess

God Stones – Moon Ring 6
The Eastern Woods

Gabi lay awake. Sleep was unable to find her on this night. Not with Zerri in her mind, reminding her with a relentless frequency that she was going to kill her. She could close the door to her mind, effectively shutting Zerri out and ending the torment. But Gabi had spent days begging Zerri to answer her, apologizing for tricking her, explaining she had never meant to hurt her. Finally, only today, and on this very evening, Zerri had finally answered.

The way Zerri answered was as if she was only now hearing Gabi, as Gabi was only now hearing her. *I have been busy claiming my birthright, Little Lion. I have taken my queendom. A whole army of dragons follow me now, and we are coming. Oh, yes. We. Are. Coming. They want to destroy humans and dökkálfar alike. But not me. I don't care about any of that. No. You see, I am saving all my vengeance for you... Little Lion.*

Her voice was unfamiliar. It was more... scary. No, not

scary – mature maybe. And if it were true, and the dragon was only now hearing her, then it must mean Zerri was far away before and was closer now. Scary or not, Gabi couldn't lock her out of her mind – not without saying it all. Not without telling her everything she had said over these last several days all over again. Gabi had learned from Bre to tell stories to El Tule when he wouldn't talk, and it had worked. Eventually, El Tule did talk to her.

And so, like with El Tule, she said it all. She told the stories of their adventure back on Earth and how they had outrun every dragon who had dared to chase them. And when she was finished, she said, *We were both alone, Zerri. But for a little while, we had each other. I never felt more alive than when we were flying together. Outrunning those dragons! And when you attacked Cerb on the pyramid! Well, you were amazing! I love you, Zerri. I love you like a little sister I never had. You understand me, and I know I understand you.*

Finally, with tears streaming down her face, she went silent and waited, but Zerri fell silent too. As Gabi sat there in the dark, she thought the silence was worse than the threats. *Oh, please say something.*

But Zerri never answered.

Sometime later, a shadow moved through camp, only visible under the gentle glow of a fire reduced to coals. Gabi didn't need to see more to know who the silhouette belonged to. Carefully, she tossed back her blanket and followed.

The shadow walked down to the shoreline, then continued out of camp, finally stopping to sit down near the edge of the river.

Gabi frowned, watching as she knelt behind some foliage that reminded her of fan palms back home.

Are you there? the shadow asked.

Gabi's heart jumped, thinking she'd been caught. The

shadow was using mind speak, but she quickly realized he wasn't talking to her, nor to any of the other sages. She shouldn't be eavesdropping, but now she had to know. What in the world was Paul doing? Who was he talking to?

He glanced back over his shoulder, one way and then the other, looking back directly toward Gabi. She ducked down behind the foliage.

When she was sure it was safe, she poked her head back up and watched. She pressed gently into the open door of his mind and listened.

I heard you in my dream. But then I heard you when I woke… I was sure, Paul said.

Water stirred in front of Paul, and Gabi thought she heard a woman giggle. She craned her neck to see.

I am here, my love, the woman said.

Rán, I thought I might never see you again, Paul said.

Rán! Gabi gasped. She remembered Rán from her studies back on Earth. Her father had loved the study of Norse mythology, always looking for similarities between cultures that could point to earlier contact than history understood. She remembered Rán quite well. She was the goddess of the sea!

Gabi crept closer carefully, trying to get a look at the female whose voice she heard in her mind.

I am here now. Let us have this moment, for tomorrow's moon ring will decide not only your fate, but the fate of all.

I… don't understand.

Kiss me, Paul Moore.

Gabi blinked. What was happening? Was she trying to trick him? No, he knew her. He'd said as much.

After their lips parted, Paul asked, *Rán, is there anything you can tell me that will help us save the father tree?*

Rán laughed. *Are you trying to seduce this poor innocent girl?*

Paul chuckled. *I'm sure it's the other way around.*

Gabi smiled. She was sure she hadn't heard Paul chuckle like that before.

Rán's voice became suddenly somber. *In truth, it has been quite difficult for me to get back to you.*

But why? Paul asked.

It doesn't matter, my love. I have important information for you. Come, kiss me again and I will tell you.

Gabi watched as Rán lifted her upper half from the water. Her skin was milky white and glistened with the light of something internal. Her long black hair trailed down her back, and her body – what Gabi could see of it – was nude. Atop her wet hair, she wore a tiara of glistening blue crystals that matched her shining blue eyes. The sea goddess was stunning.

Rán closed her eyes, kissing Paul again, and when she opened them, they were staring directly into Gabi's.

Gabi gasped and ducked back behind the foliage, holding her breath, her eyes slamming shut. She waited there, still as could be, and not daring to breathe. Finally, she peeked out again. Rán was no longer speaking in mind speak – instead, she was whispering in Paul's ear.

What was she saying to him? Suddenly, Paul's head whipped around. *Gabi?*

Gabi's eyes sprang wide open as she leapt to her feet and bolted through the vegetation, running blindly through the darkness. Then she heard Rán's voice again.

She has seen what she has seen. It matters not, my love. Let her go. Our time is limited.

Paul said, *She may tell the others if I don't talk to her. If I don't explain.*

Gabi stopped running and paused to listen. Paul really didn't know she could hear him.

And if she tells them, so what? We may all die tomorrow. But this night is ours.

Gabi started walking, unsure what to think or do. Suddenly, Rán's voice filled her mind, and she knew instantly the sea goddess was talking to her and her alone.

Gabi De Leon, the one I've heard called Little Lion. This is my promise to you. You've nothing to fear from me, and your friend will be safe. Please, give us this night, little one. In the morning, tell whomever you want.

She trusted Paul, and whatever they had seemed to be genuine. Clearly Paul knew Rán before this, though Gabi didn't understand how. Finally, she answered, saying simply, *Good night, Rán.*

Thank you, Gabi. And know you have made a new friend on this night.

Despite her despair over Zerri, Gabi smiled.

53

Karelian Coffee

God Stones – Moon Ring 6
The Eastern Woods

Breanne's heart thumped in her chest as she found herself back in Mexico, walking toward the southern roof of the temple where sat a bejeweled owl, feathers sparkling like diamond dust under starlight. It was all fuzzy, like a dream should be, yet this felt nothing like a dream. The cool night air blew chilly against her cheek, and the smell of human decay permeated the breeze, though thankfully she saw no signs of death. As she drew closer to the owl, she heard a voice.

The owl flew away.

Peering over the side of the temple, Breanne saw James lying on his back, feet dangling over the steps as he peered up at her. No, not at her – beyond her to the stars above. "Where are you, Garrett? What in the hell have you been up to? Did you make it? Are you dead? Shit, I suppose I'll know soon enough, or maybe I won't know anything except darkness. Either way, it will be—"

"Talking to the stars, son?" her father asked as he stepped into view from the temple's entrance.

Tears spilled down Breanne's cool cheeks. Her father was right there, fifty feet below! Breanne blinked, trying to clear her vision of tears. He looked awful and thin! "Daddy! Daddy, up here!"

Dr. Moore did not look up.

"Daddy! Oh, Daddy, I'm up here!"

James sat up. "Yeah, it seems I am. How are you? I think it's been a few days since we talked."

"It's been nearly two weeks," Dr. Moore said.

"Yeah, I guess maybe it has." James nodded.

They couldn't hear her! She spun, searching the roof for the stairwell. She remembered the roof had two sets – one on each side, both leading down into the temple corridor. But this roof had none – it was solid. She turned back to the edge and peered over.

"Listen, James, I need to ask you something," Charles said. Breanne knew by her father's tone that this was serious – important. What was happening?

"What's wrong?" James asked, sitting up.

"That's a funny question, James."

James laughed hollowly. "I suppose so."

"I… I need you to do something for me."

"Not sure what I can do for you now."

Her father sat down on the step next to James. "Listen, James, I just want you to know, no matter what happens, I don't blame you. I mean… maybe I did at first – hell, I think I have blamed everyone at one point or another, but what I've come to realize is there is no one to blame but myself. We all made decisions – decisions that we thought were right in the moment. I guess what I'm saying is we did the best we could with what information we had. Truth is, this could all be worse."

"Worse? Worse how?"

"My daughter and my youngest son could be here with us... about to die. Or they could have been killed a hundred other ways by now."

Tears ran in a steady stream, making wet trails down her cheeks.

Her father continued, "I know what you're thinking, but my children aren't dead. Trust me in this."

"Oh, Dad! We're okay! We're here! We're trying!" She choked on the words, her throat full of emotion.

James nodded. "Okay, Dr. Moore, how can I help you?"

"You can help me by forgiving yourself," her father said flatly.

"I... I don't know what to say."

"You don't have to say anything. Just don't go to your grave carrying guilt for something you couldn't have changed. You did what you thought was best with the information you had. That's it. Maybe because of you and your Keepers, my little girl and my son get to live." Her father placed a hand on James's shoulder and pushed himself up with a grunt.

"Thank you, Dr. Moore," James said.

"Thank you, James," her father said, turning away and vanishing back into the temple opening.

"Wait, Dad! Please!" Breanne shouted.

In the distance she heard the forest creaking. Far below, she thought she saw a dark chasm forming in the forest's valley, almost like a dark river flowing through the center. But this was no river. The forest was slowly making way for something.

A dark shadow emerged and filled the lower steps. Breanne knew this was Pando. The tree queen was moving slowly, methodically – taking time to climb each step. She no longer looked like a perfect human but like something misshapen – something made to look part tree and part human.

Then something else caught Breanne's attention. "Hoo! Hoo! Hoo hoooooo! Hoo! Hoo! Hoo hoooooo!"

It sounded like… the owl?

Breanne followed James's gaze toward the call, and there it was, sitting on the top step, staring at him, its eyes swirling with strange light.

Below, Pando continued to climb.

"Turek?" James asked.

"No, James Paul." The voice was magical – angelic.

"Then what – or who – are you?"

"The next moments will be very bad, James Paul."

"You think I don't know that?"

"In this moment, you choose how you die. Will you beg, or will you die like the warrior you are?" The owl made a swooping gesture with its head. "The sword of your fallen friend, Lady Holly, lies where you left it. Go retrieve it and make your end a worthy one."

"You came here now… to tell me this?" James asked, a clear edge in his voice.

"Go now, James Paul. Go now and suffer the ancient wrong told in the prophecy of Turek."

James frowned. "This wasn't told. This wasn't the way any of this was supposed to go!"

The owl flew away.

"Great! Thanks for nothing! And you're wrong! It isn't the worst part! I already suffered the worst of it when all my Keepers were killed! This… this will be a welcome end!"

∼

Breanne blinked into a predawn morning, rubbing her eyes and wishing like hell for coffee. Another nightmare, and this time she'd seen her father, but she struggled to remember the details. An owl and James... Then suddenly she gasped, remembering her dad was there too. More details emerged, and her heart sank as she remembered Pando climbing ever so slowly up the stairs of the pyramid. The tree queen was changing back into a tree, which meant Breanne must have been seeing James and her father at the end of the six months.

Breanne sat up and stretched, wondering what the owl wanted her to know. Why was it showing her this future? What was she supposed to do? She sat pondering this a moment longer. Then she smelled it, the aroma causing her to question if she was losing her mind. Coffee! That was unmistakably coffee!

She threw back her blanket and hopped on one foot, tugging on one boot, then the other.

Garrett moaned, pushing himself up onto his elbow. "What's wrong with you?" he asked, clearly less excited.

"Don't you smell that?" she asked. She should have told him about the dream, but right now she wanted that coffee! She'd tell him later, after she was fully awake.

"Yeah!" he said, his eyes suddenly going as wide as she imagined her own were. "Smells like bacon!"

"What? No. The coffee! C'mon." They followed the smell to the cook fires, where Stone, Key, the twins Blur and Blend, and many others were gathered, discussing the day's plans. David was there too, sitting with a large wooden bowl on his lap. "Hey, guys! This tastes just like bacon!" he said, holding up a strange-looking disc of meat.

It looked nothing like bacon, but she didn't care. "Coffee?" she asked.

"What is coffee?" Stone asked.

"It's over here." Lenny pointed from the other side of the cook fire, where he and Tell sat together sharing a bowl of food. She and Garrett made their way over and sat down.

"We would be wise to eat quickly, break camp, and go before we draw trolls with these aromas," Key said, frowning at Stone.

"Is that a serious concern?" Garrett asked.

"Probably not with so many of us, but still, we should have eaten our dried goods," Key replied, her face still fixed in a scowl.

"She isn't happy I decided to have food prepared," Stone said. "But as I explained, this may be our men's... *and women's*" – he quickly corrected himself, seeing Key's scowl deepen – "last meal."

"Coffee?" Breanne asked again.

Lenny pointed to the pot hanging over the fire and handed her a metal cup.

"Is it legit?" she asked.

Gabi smiled, holding up her own cup. "It's even better! No bitterness! Seems like it must have caffeine in it too because I'm feeling it for sure! Oh, and look how it's more brown than black. Weird!" she rattled off without taking a breath.

Breanne smiled. She poured a cup and took a sip, her eyes lighting up. "Yes! Stone, what is this stuff called?"

"Jaja. Never start a day without it," the greying man said, smiling.

"Aye, a staple morning drink of the dwarves. After all, 'twas my kind who discovered it long ago in the Cragarmour Mountains," Kilug said matter-of-factly.

"You're mad, Kilug! Man discovered the beans long before the fallout with the gods. A hundred moon cycles before the dwarves took their first piss near jaja, let alone laid claim to it!" Stone argued, shaking his head as he stepped toward the dwarf.

Kilug jolted upright, gripping his war hammer. "And me supposes if me ask an elf he'll lay claim?"

"You're both wrong," Key announced. "Was not man nor dwarf nor elf who discovered the beans of jaja. It was a woman who first found the beans while tracking a wounded mountain rigor."

The camp fell deadly silent as the three stood, hands on weapons, staring each other down.

Just when Breanne thought they might come to blows, the three started laughing hysterically. Others around them started laughing too.

"Mountain rigor!" Kilug laughed, placing his hands on his knees. Trying to catch his breath, Kilug managed, "Ye might as well said ye was slaying me third wife!" The dwarf started laughing again. "Oh stop! Oh, please! Before me pisses meself!"

Breanne looked at Garrett.

Garrett held up his hands and shrugged, laughing nonetheless.

Breanne let out a breath and laughed too. "I think this planet is going to be alright." Then she closed her eyes as she took another sip. When she opened them, she saw Paul walking toward them from the direction of the river. She waved her hand above her head. "Paul, come eat before we go!"

Paul approached, looking tired, like he hadn't slept at all. He glanced around, his gaze pausing on Gabi.

"Maybe you should have some coffee too, Paul," Gabi giggled.

"Yeah, sounds good," he said, giving her a look.

Breanne frowned, recognizing that look all too well. She looked at Gabi, then back at Paul. That was the look he used to give her when he was afraid she would tell their dad something he didn't want told. She handed Paul a cup of coffee, or jaja, then spoke in mind speak, letting Gabi and the other sages hear. *Something you want to tell me?*

No, Paul blurted.

I was talking to Gabi, Breanne said, not taking her eyes off Paul.

Nope. Nothing on my end, Gabi answered quickly.

Um-hmm, Breanne said, narrowing her eyes.

∽

They broke camp, got the leaf rafts back into the river, and made the final waterclimb. Soon the currents pulled them toward a sheer mountain face. Up it climbed, endlessly stretching skyward to vanish into the clouds above.

As for the river, it just seemed to stop against the mountain face, disappearing in swirls of current.

"Where does it go?" David asked, marveling at the vanishing river.

"To our deaths if we don't exit the river here," Key said, pointing toward a wide shoreline. "What you see before you is known as the Craw, and it marks the end of the Climbing River. Many stories are told of those who've been swallowed by the Craw, never to be seen again. Some say it's a direct path to the underworld, others say it leads nowhere at all, while most believe it empties into the bottom of the Roiling Sea. Despite the many legends, no one who has ever entered the Craw has lived to tell about it. Consequently, all one can say for sure is that, wherever it leads, certain death awaits."

Breanne noticed everyone around her tugging nervously at their leaves, ready to get off the river before they were pulled into the Craw. She was glad they were done with the river. She was tired from her restless dreams and tired too of being wet. She just wanted to get to Osonian and figure out their next move.

Before the currents became too strong to manage, Key had led them safely ashore.

Breanne, Garrett, and the others grouped up, stretching their backs and shaking out their legs in preparation for the hike.

"Where's Paul?" Breanne asked, turning in a slow circle.

Lenny pointed. "There."

Paul stood on the shore, watching the river vanish into the mountain wall.

"Paul!" Breanne called.

He turned toward her, his face creased with worry. "Coming."

The armies of men and women gathered in the forest near the mountain wall. All they had to do was follow the sheer wall of the mountain and it would lead them to the great wall of Osonian. Key sent Blur and Blend ahead to check on the status one more time before they made their advance to the front gates.

"How far?" Garrett asked.

"A short walk. No more than a fade," Key said.

A fade, Breanne remembered, was the equivalent of an hour or thereabouts. It was a measure of the sun's light as shadows moved on the ground. She wasn't sure how they measured it exactly, but it seemed to be a learned skill. Above them, purple snow flurries broke from the sky, though it didn't feel cold enough for snow.

Again, Breanne looked for Paul and found him finally making his way up from the water's edge near the Craw.

"Hey. You okay?" Breanne asked.

She watched as he forced a smile and nodded. *Liar*, she thought, studying his face. She started to speak when Garrett nudged her, tipping his head back to consider the sky.

"This means something. I know it does. It's the same as the day we arrived – you remember, Bre?"

She nodded. How could she forget the first time she'd looked upon another world and seen its purple snow? "Garrett, when we get there, what do you plan to do?"

"Talk to the elves. Tell them we are here to help. Tell them what's coming," he said with a shrug. "They have to listen."

"No. The elves won't listen, and they will kill you," Key warned.

"I'm going too," Lenny said.

She and Garrett shared a look. They both knew why Lenny wanted to go, but what they didn't know was whether his presence would make things better or worse.

"No one is going," Paul said.

"What? Why?" Garrett asked.

"It's not…" Paul glanced back over his shoulder toward the river.

"Paul, what's going on with you?" Breanne asked.

"I have to tell you guys something. I… I've been keeping something from you."

54

Bring Down the Wall

God Stones – Moon Ring 6
Outside Osonian

"Helreginn, my friend. As promised, I have returned," Jack said, sitting atop Cerberus the Mighty.

Helreginn stood tall, seemingly unbothered by the flurries of purple snow swirling around him like some strange magic. "Taker, indeed, you returned, and on such a momentous day, but it seems you are now without a crown."

Jack wasn't sure what was so special about this day, but whatever. He glanced around, assessing the nephilbock. They looked rested and well fed, but the place stank of rotten flesh and feces. He desperately wanted to cover his face with his shirt, but to do that would be to disrespect the king. At Helreginn's side stood the taller and broader tennis shoe necklace guy, with that same pair of red Converse All Stars, complete with severed feet. The decomposing necklace hung loosely around the giant's neck. Jack pulled his attention away from the rotten feet and scanned the camp. They had been busy chopping down a

The Last Gift

chunk of the forest to keep their many fires burning. All around the camp, the bones of dragon and dökkálfar lay scattered, gnawed clean, cracked, and sucked free of their marrow.

Next to the king, what looked like a giant wolf sat obediently, pulling tough flesh and scales from a chunk of dragon bone. Behind the big wolf were three smaller wolves growling and pulling, locked in a three-way tug-of-war with an elf leg, its purple flesh giving it away. Though the three wolves must have stood up to Jack's shoulder, he realized these were only pups.

Looking back to Helreginn, Jack said, "Do not let the fact I no longer wear the Sound Eye fool you, King Helreginn. I have never felt better! And I have never been stronger." Jack smiled, feeling Nyana's warm arms wrapped around him, just as they had been the entire way here. "I have traveled far to bring back with me the full might of Karelia's dragon army."

"I see you have!" Helreginn said. "I also see you have removed the crown. This is good. The magic of the God Stones was clearly poisoning you. You have done what the dökkálfar Apep could not. You freed yourself of their power before they destroyed you!"

Jack liked that. He liked that a lot. A wicked smile stretched across his face. "Damn right! And now, it's your turn, mighty king. Now you will see the death of Gato avenged!"

The giant made a horrible face, but it was hard to tell through its ugliness what the expression meant.

Jack frowned. "What's wrong, King? Is this not what you want?"

Helreginn bowed slightly. "Of course, Taker."

"Well alright! Let's make your son proud and finish what we started... what Gato died for! Draw out the dragons while we attack like before, but this time we will take the wall."

"How do we get through, Taker?" Helreginn asked.

"Just draw them out and let me worry about the wall," Jack sneered.

Helreginn nodded, turning to shout orders as he raised his axe and pointed it toward Osonian.

Cerberus flapped his wings.

Hordes, cover the giants as they approach the wall! Kill anything that tries to kill them!

And what of us, Jack? Cerberus asked. *If we try to fly over, we will be targeted by their dragon bolts and burning boulders.*

We wait until the slave dragons emerge, and then we make our move! Zerri, are you and the queens ready?

We are ready, Jack, but perhaps you should tell us this plan of yours?

Jack laughed to himself, shouting into the snow-flurried wind, "It's time they all learned, Cerb! It's time they learn of Jack the Taker and his mighty dragon!"

Cerberus laughed. *Taker, perhaps you should at least tell me the plan!*

Again, Jack shouted aloud, "We aren't flying over the wall, and we aren't flying around, Cerb – we're flying through that son of a bitch!"

Jaaack! This sounds crazy! Like certain death! Cerb shouted into his mind.

What's your point, Cerb!

They both laughed.

∼

The Last Gift

King Helreginn gripped his sword high above his shoulder as he led his army of thousands in a rush toward the wall of Osonian.

"Zebrog, on my command!"

"Yes, my king!" Zebrog nodded sharply, raising his war hammer high above his head.

The false sky god, this Taker, would never see the betrayal coming. "Taker," he sneered aloud. A proper name for the one who'd abandoned him on the battlefield – for the one who'd used him and his people as a distraction, letting thousands of his people die! Letting Gato, his favorite son, die! Even now as he ran forward on this fool's errand, tears for Gato wet his cheeks. But King Helreginn would be a fool no more.

Only one Karelian day ago, his true god, Aurgelmir, had appeared in camp, calling his name. "King Helreginn! Stand before your god and be judged!"

Helreginn had leapt from his sleep, attacking the giant, assuming Ogliosh had sent him. But despite his efforts, he could not hurt the god. He cried out, waking those around him, and they too attacked the giant, to no avail. Despite blow after blow from hammer and axe, nothing harmed the giant. It was then Helreginn realized this creature was god himself. Not a creature claiming to be a god, but true divinity.

Dropping his axe upon the muddy ground, Helreginn had bent the knee and bowed his head. All around him, his people dropped to their knees. The god spoke then, and he and his people listened. Soon he learned there was indeed a place for him and his people in this world, but he wouldn't find it following a false god.

"Helreginn, son of Ogliosh, you may have the city of Osonian, great king, but it must be you and you alone who takes it! You may kill the inhabitants of Osonian and feast on the flesh of those within. You may consume elf, dragon, and man alike until your bellies burst if it so pleases you."

That had sounded good. Very good. But then came the warning.

Lord Aurgelmir had raised his six-fingered hand and pointed down at the king with a grave look. "Pillage and kill, mighty king, but be warned, the tree they built the city upon must not come to harm. It must neither burn nor fall. Fail me in this, and you will have no place in this world!"

Now, as the dragon gates opened in the wall before them and flaming boulders appeared in the sky above, Helreginn gave the order.

"Now, Zebrog!"

Zebrog dropped his axe down from above his head, giving the signal as he banked hard right ninety degrees.

The entire army followed suit, running away from the battlefield and making for the edge of the Eastern Forest.

The king pointed ahead. "Zebrog, the place you spoke of scouting. Do you remember how to get there?"

Zebrog grinned, showing a mouthful of teeth, murder sharp. "Yes, my king. The place where the river vanishes under the mountain?"

The king nodded back, his own grin showing brown and rotten with age, but sharp as ever. "Good. How far?"

"Not far. We need only follow the mountainside. There is a long shore there. It is plenty wide enough for thousands of us to gather."

"Good! We will wait there until the dragons are defeated or the wall falls! Then, when both sides are at their weakest, we shall take the city."

55

The Confession

God Stones – Moon Ring 6
The Craw

"Paul? What are you talking about?" Garrett asked, a sick feeling filling his stomach. He didn't want to believe for one second that Paul would hide something from them.

"It's, well… complicated."

"Paul Gregory Moore! I knew it!" Breanne said, then spun around to Gabi. "Gabi, you know something, don't you?"

Gabi's eyes went big. "No… I mean, yes! But not all of it!"

"You knew something, and you didn't tell me!" David said.

"Okay, everybody, calm down!" Garrett said. Turning back to Paul, he said, "What is it?"

Breanne was glaring at her brother now. "You better start talking, Paul Greg—"

"Let him explain," Garrett said quietly and squeezed her hand.

Paul sighed. "I was told not to go that way. If we go that way, the elves will hot tar us. They have giant vats of the stuff atop the wall, not to mention catapults prepared to throw tarred boulders. They set them on fire, and while we are probably too close for them to use on us, they also have hundreds of bowmen and devices that shoot dragon spikes. Plus, they've more than a dozen slave dragons that will come out of the wall itself. Once the dragons are out in force, they will send out trolls, nasty ones."

Garrett's stomach knotted. It was like the rug had been pulled out from under him. He didn't understand how Paul could know all this, but the look on his face left no question – he knew what he was talking about, and he wasn't done.

"Even if we somehow get even one dökkálfar to listen to us before we're killed, we will have to convince them to let us inside before the nephilbock army positioned only a few kilometers away crosses the battlefield, kills us, and eats us. Trust me when I say that a thousand of us can't win against over ten thousand nephilbock. I'm sorry, Garrett, but if we go that way and stand before the wall of Osonian, we're all dead."

For a moment, no one spoke. Not a whisper, not even a sigh. Key, Stone, Tell, the sages, Governess, and Kilug all stared at Paul.

Finally, Garrett shook his head. "Paul... how could you know all this?"

"Even my best scouts couldn't have gathered this level of detail," Key said, her eyes narrowing.

"I... I met someone," Paul said.

"It's a girl!" Gabi blurted.

"Bro, what girl?" Lenny asked.

"It's complicated," Paul said with a sigh.

Breanne's hands went to her hips. "You already said that!"

Paul winced. "Her name is Rán."

"By the gods!" Kilug breathed.

Garrett exchanged a look with Lenny. "Wait a minute, I've heard that name before."

"This… this isn't possible," Key said, but her voice wasn't sure.

Stone pushed his fingers into his beard, then rubbed his eyes and shook his head. "Yet he knows the dökkálfar's entire defense structure."

Garrett snapped his fingers. "Coach's journal! It listed Rán as one of the seven creators."

"Indeed. Goddess of the sea, creator of all things born of water," Key said. "Every legend of the sea goddess tells of her hatred toward man, and yet you claim to have spoken with her?"

"They did more than speak," Gabi said, grinning now.

Key's eyes went wide.

Lenny's smile went even wider.

Breanne glared at her brother, wagging a finger toward him. "All this time you were—"

Oh no! She's here! Gabi cried out in mind speak.

From the woods, Blur and Blend appeared in a panicked run. "What's happened?" Key demanded as the women slid to a stop in front of them, practically bowling them over.

"The dragons are here!" Blend shouted.

To the west, the distant sky lit with fire.

"Well, balls," Lenny said.

"That's not all," Blur said, gasping for breath.

"Well, spit it out, girl!" Key ordered.

"The giant army isn't attacking Osonian," Blend said.

"Well, that's good, right?" Pete asked, looking from one to the other.

"No! They were charging across the battlefield, then turned!" Blur said, pointing back the way they came.

"They are heading this way!" Blend said.

"Straight for us!" Blur finished.

"How long?" Stone asked.

"Half a fade."

Half an hour, Garrett thought. "Damn."

"We can take the shoreline!" Key motioned. "We'll double back and try to get far enough south to avoid them!" Key advised.

"It's our only chance," Stone agreed.

"That won't work," Paul said.

"It will. It must! Now go!" she said, looking to Blur and Blend. "Send back the order. We must move now."

"You're not in charge here, Key. My sister is… your queen!" Paul said, pointing at Bre.

"Paul, what are you doing? We can't stay here!" Breanne said.

"I really think we should go now!" David said.

Pete, Lenny, and the others nodded.

"Stop! Everyone, just control your fear for a minute!" Garrett ordered, looking at Paul. They were missing something, and whatever it was, the look on Paul's face was enough for Garrett. "What is it, Paul?"

"My lord," Stone urged. "If we're to outrun the coming onslaught, we've no time to debate."

Garrett held up a hand for silence. "Go on, Paul."

Paul loosened his clenched jaw and nodded sharply. "Right. Rán said the river will lead into Osonian. All I have to do is jump in and swim under."

"That's madness!" Key said. "If we jump, we'll be washed to gods only know where, but it won't matter, for we'll surely be drowned before we get there!"

Stone swallowed thickly. His black curly hair was slicked back with nervous sweat. "If you were truly speaking to the goddess of the sea, Rán, how do you know she isn't tricking us into killing ourselves?"

"I don't believe that. Besides, for what? We're already facing impossible odds!" Paul countered.

"Paul, I need more than that," Garrett said.

"I trust her, Garrett. I trust her with my life," Paul said.

"Well, I will not jump in, and I will not order these men to kill themselves," Stone said, then turned to Garrett. "I am sorry, my lord."

"Nor will I," Key said, her expression apologetic but firm.

Paul shook his head. "If you'd all just let me finish, you would understand. I'm not asking anyone to jump in. Rán told me that once on the other side, I need only look left and there would be a set of stairs cut in the stone leading out of the water. They will lead me to a steel door hidden in the rock above. The door can only be opened from inside. She said the door looks like stone from this side, but once I open it, we can all file through."

"Paul, I don't like this," Breanne said.

"It must be me and me alone. Rán is waiting below to guide me through. Sis, I promise I will be fine."

Breanne's eyes filled with tears. "I don't feel good about this. We should just run. Garrett, tell him, please?" she begged.

Garrett felt like an absolute jerk for the words that came next. "Are you sure, Paul?"

Paul drew in a deep breath. "I'm one hundred percent sure."

Garrett put a hand on his friend's shoulder. "You better be. Because I won't leave you behind, and if you don't show up and I mean fast—"

"I won't let you down." He placed his hand atop Garrett's shoulder. "Just get organized and watch for the door to open somewhere along this wall. I'll be right back."

"Paul! Dammit, if you don't come back, I will never forgive you!" Breanne said, tears spilling down her cheeks.

"I promise, sis, I'll be back in a minute." His face turned stone solid with determination. He turned toward the vanishing river, glanced back over his shoulder and shouted, "I love you, sis!" then dove headfirst into the swirling madness of the Craw.

"Guy's got balls big as coconuts," Lenny said.

Stepping close to Breanne, Garrett reached to wrap his arm around her shoulder.

She slapped his arm away.

"You could have ordered him to stay! You could have told him not to go!" she cried, then threw herself into his arms, burying her face in his chest. "You could have ordered him!"

Garrett didn't say anything; instead, he just held her.

"How long do we wait, my lord?" Stone asked.

Garrett glanced down the shore, understanding something Stone and the others did not. It didn't matter how much time they gave Paul. Even if they fled right this very second, there was no outrunning the nephilbock.

56

Fatal Error

God Stones – Moon Ring 6
The Craw

The river's current wrapped Paul like a massive snake and yanked him beneath the water, slamming him into the mountainside and raking him down the underwater cliff face as if he were a piece of sharp cheddar being grated. The impact forced the air from his lungs and tore the skin open on his face, palms, and chest.

Three violent seconds passed as Paul's body raked across stone, then... nothing. With the cliff face gone, Paul rolled through absolute darkness, feeling only the throbbing pain of his new wounds and a pressing urge to breathe in the cold water that enveloped him. The only hint he was still descending was the pressure building in his ears. There was no light in this place, and as he tumbled out of control, it seemed there was no bottom either.

Lungs burning like fire in his chest, Paul realized he'd made a fatal error. He'd trusted the goddess of another creation. He'd believed with his whole heart this goddess of the sea wanted him and, in his utter infatuation with her, he'd convinced himself she might truly love him – convinced himself he loved her. For days, he'd thought only of the woman of the water and the brief kiss they'd shared. Then, finally, she'd come back to him just as she promised she would. They spent a sleepless night together talking, holding each other, and kissing. He'd told her his life story, things he'd never told anyone. And she'd told him the secret to getting Garrett and the others into Osonian. Now he realized it was all for show, nothing more than a clever ruse, and he was the idiot. He deserved this – to die horribly. His pops, Ed, the fate of the world was hanging in the balance, and what did he do? Fall in love.

Paul flailed, fighting the urge until he could fight no more.

He wanted to use mind speak, to tell Breanne he was sorry. Sorry he hadn't listened to her. But there was no time – no focus to be found as his body convulsed.

Paul opened his mouth to suck in the water.

Soft lips sealed over his, and as he gasped in a breath, what filled his lungs was not a flood of water but precious air. Soft hands held his damaged face, and even here in the icy bowels of the Craw, Paul felt their warmth.

Darkness pushed back to his periphery as bright light illuminated the face before him and he saw her – he saw Rán.

Paul exhaled through his nose and drew in again and again and again. Finally, his slamming heart slowed.

Her arms were wrapped around him now as her tail flipped feverishly through the darkness.

Paul looked into Ran's eyes, and they smiled back at him. Strangely, he was thankful for the water that hid his tears. And the tears no one would see were tears of joy and of love. He would not die alone and betrayed in this awful place.

A long moment passed, but he felt like he could have

stayed there with her, breathing her in forever. They broke the surface. And she pulled her face back from his.

"Are you alright, my love?" Rán asked.

"I am now," he said.

"Did you doubt me?"

Paul looked away, unable to lie but not wanting to say the truth.

"It is fine. I would have doubted me too. But you did it! You believed in me – in us. You loved me enough to jump. Now you must hurry. You can still save your friends, but the giants are bearing down, and you must get your army through the door." Rán pointed. "You are in a natural spring fed by the Craw, a sort of well. Climb up, look left, and follow the stone stairs up to the door. It opens at ground level on the other side. There will be a dökkálfar guarding it, but only one. Stay quiet or you will draw others."

"When will I see you again?" Paul asked.

"I hope very soon, my love," she said, leaning in close to him. Her lips caressed his cold wet ear as she whispered, "If the wall falls, retreat across the bay."

"The bay?" he said, frowning.

"Yes. Now hurry!" she said, urgently pressing her lips to his. Warmth filled him, wrapping him in a blanket of comfort. After only a few seconds, Rán pulled her face back and smiled longingly. Her eyes begged for him to stay and oh, how he wished he could, but they both knew he could not.

Rán's eyes flicked upward. "Go, my love."

Paul went, climbing up and out of the natural spring well. He noticed right away that he felt no pain from his torn face and hands. Glancing down at his palms, he realized they were fine. Rubbing a hand across his torn face, he found it, too, was fine. Rán had healed him.

Behind him, the mountain rose high into the sky.

Glancing right, he found a stone building, a guard shack perhaps, carved from the mountainside itself. It blocked his view of the city. This was good, as more importantly, it blocked anyone else's view of him. He guessed he was behind the building. Looking left, he found the stairs carved into the stone. In the distance he heard the noise of commands being shouted, heavy chains being cranked, the loosing of a catapult, clicks and *thunk*s – the sounds of war.

Hastily, Paul ascended the stairs.

He didn't have to go far or climb high before the winding stairs led to a dökkálfar, just as Rán said they would. Behind the tall elf stood a single steel door, three men wide and at least eight feet tall. The problem was that the elf was facing Paul.

Clad in armor and a silver helmet, the elf's face scrunched in confusion. It was a look of surprise, one that said he couldn't possibly be seeing what he was seeing, and it was all the hesitation Paul needed. Leaping forward with superhuman strength, Paul cleared the last five stairs and shouldered the elf before he could draw his sword.

The elf guard fell back into the steel door.

Paul felt bones break and heard the elf's head thud off the door.

Despite the protection of the helmet, the elf's body went slack, slowly sliding down the door. Paul hoped he hadn't killed him; he couldn't imagine murdering a dökkálfar would be a good way to begin peace talks.

Quickly, he pulled the unconscious guard out of the way and slid back the three bolts, unlocking the secret door. Paul heaved, pushing mightily against the steel. The door responded, swinging wide.

Again, just as Rán said, the door opened level to the forest floor beyond. Paul stepped out, looking first to the right. He saw nothing, only a cliff wall and the woods.

"Paul!" Breanne shouted.

Paul looked left to find his sister, Garrett, and the others going through a rapid transformation of facial expressions from relief to panic.

"I told you I had this, sis." Paul smiled, but behind his smile he fought to hold back tears. He never wanted Bre or the others to know just how close he'd come to dying in the Craw.

57

Chain, Bone, and Scales

God Stones – Moon Ring 6
Osonian

Jack! Look! What are the nephilbock doing? Cerb asked.

Jack leaned forward, peering over to the battlefield below as Cerb dodged a flying boulder coated in burning tar. Below, the nephilbock banked hard to the east, toward the forest.

I don't know! Maybe they have a different strategy from last time. After all, they lost over half their numbers! Maybe Helreginn is trying something new. I bet that's it. Maybe he's going to try to skirt the edge or use the forest for cover until he gets the army close enough? Jack guessed, but something felt wrong.

Why wouldn't he have told you of this plan? Cerb asked, as he pulled up to avoid another boulder, then twisted onto his side to avoid a bolt. *And if he planned to use the forest to advance, why not split the army and use both sides of the battlefield?*

Below, at the base of the wall, several gates slowly lifted.

The Last Gift

Damn, they're about to send out the enslaved dragons! I wanted the nephilbock there to distract them.

Jack, came Zerri's voice, *why is your army running from the battle?*

I don't know, Jack said. *I think they may have some plan we don't know about.*

A young juvenile dragon spoke from the horde. *My lord Taker, they have entered the forest and are fleeing deeper still. It appears they are moving northeasterly past where the wall ends and along the mountain's edge. It's hard to say for sure because the forest is so dense.*

What's back there? Jack asked.

A wide river, then more forest as far as the eye can see.

Jack, perhaps we should abandon this plan, Zerri urged. *There is no reason we have to take the wall head on! In another day's time, we could circle the mountains and attack Osonian from the ocean.*

A whole day? Jack asked, knowing, as Zerri knew, that a day here was much longer than a day on Earth.

We would need to rest our wings. Your dragons are tired already, and flying around the mountains and circling into the ocean will require rest.

Forget that. One thing you better know about me, Zerri – I'm no coward. This wall is coming down with or without the nephilbock! We got to show these elves we can't be stopped!

What's the plan, Jack? Cerb asked.

The plan is to throw my haymaker!

Arrows filled the sky, intermixed with dragon spikes and flaming boulders from the trebuchets hidden somewhere behind the wall.

The gates below clanked open one after the other as over a dozen dragons emerged.

Suddenly, several of Jack's dragons closest to the wall turned back and attacked the others.

Jack, the dragon masters are taking control of some of our dragons and forcing them to attack their own! Zerri shouted.

I have eyes, Zerri!

Cerb let out a gout of fire toward the ground, trying to be careful not to hit the enslaved dragons, but Jack knew this was not the answer. The dragon masters were hidden somewhere in the wall, watching and controlling from their cowardly hiding places.

They think they've gotten smarter since last time. But they haven't seen what we can do, Cerb! Dive! Let's get this party started!

Jack, what are you doing? Zerri asked.

Jack had never played chess. He was more of a checkers man. But during all those days spent with old Apep, he'd learned some of the lingo. *Sometimes, my queen, you've got to sacrifice your pawns.*

Jack! What are you sacrificing? Zerri shouted.

As Cerb closed in on the ground, Jack focused his mind on the dragons chained to the wall below. He sent in the sick and disease and in return he pulled the life from the three closest elder dragons. Power flowed into him, flaring his eyes into two bloody stars.

The three dragons collapsed in a rattle of chain, bone, and scales.

Jack's body shook, hands gripping Cerb's spurs. Around him, Nyana's arms squeezed as she screamed. Yet it was only thanks to the screaming woman that Jack knew what to do. It had been a long journey from the Mountains of Twelve. Nearly three moon rings with very little rest. But Jack had made the most of his time with Nyana. First, he'd used some Sentheye to open her mind and establish telepathy. This incredibly smart move allowed them to communicate without shouting back and forth. After all, Jack had many questions about the Great Wall of Osonian, and Nyana had all the answers.

For example, Jack now knew the wall was full of corridors to allow the elves to navigate up and down the wall. They left small slits open as shooting lanes for the archers. And on the back side, they had constructed great platforms at varying heights. These held the trebuchets, which were trough-fed using a combination of counterweights and trolls. Once the boulders were raised up to the stone platforms, the work fell to the trolls. Apparently, these trolls were some strong bastards whose job was to place the tarred boulders onto the trebuchets. No. Jack had not been idle on his journey back. He had asked every question he could think to ask about the wall, the elves, the slave dragons, the trolls, and the city in the massive tree.

Knowing exactly where to place his Sentheye-filled dragon fire, Jack struggled to form words: *N… o… w, Cerb!*

Cerb released a torrent of black fire from his center mouth, dense as the darkness between two stars. The blast exploded a swath of stone like an axe through a wall of Jell-O. Rubble rained down, revealing the inner working of the wall, but even better, dozens of elves spilled out from their inner posts and into the open air, plummeting to their deaths.

The damage created a serious gash in the wall, but it didn't pass completely through. Jack laughed, knowing he still had ten more enslaved elder dragons to draw from.

Jack! What have you done? Zerri asked accusingly. *You killed three elders you were supposed to be saving!*

Jack ignored the dragon queen. *Cerb! Swing around. I'm going to draw from four this time!*

Cerb roared with laughter. *Hold on, Taker!*

58

Behind the Wall

God Stones – Moon Ring 6
Osonian

Breanne ran into her brother's arms, hugging him. "I thought you… Damn you, Paul Gregory Moore, you scared me half to death!" She wanted to cry in her big brother's arms and slap the shit out of him at the same time.

"Then it was true? The goddess, Rán, she came to you in the Craw?" Stone asked.

"She did, and without her, there would have been no way I could have made it out."

"We must move now!" Key urged.

"She's right. Everyone inside!" Garrett ordered, leading Lenny, Breanne, and her brother through the door. The others followed close on their heels.

Once through the door, Breanne saw a dökkálfar body on the stairs as she passed. "Is he… dead?"

"I hope not," Paul answered with a grim look. "I tried to hold back."

Staying behind the building, Garrett and Lenny crept forward, peeking around the corner.

"Oh my god," Garrett said, pulling himself back.

"What is it?" she asked.

"You got to see for yourself," Lenny said, eyes wide in amazement.

Breanne maneuvered to the edge of the building, while behind her more and more men and women piled through the door, running down the stairs to gather below. The area would not hold some one thousand people – they would have to get out from behind this building.

Garrett motioned her toward the edge.

Breanne eased forward and peeked out. What she saw stole her breath. A great wall, tall as... as god she didn't know what. Tall as some buildings in downtown Chicago. But it wasn't the size of the wall that stole her breath. After all, she had seen it from across the battlefield the day they'd come through the portal. No. It was the mechanical operation taking place as she watched.

The wall itself pitched out toward the battlefield at an angle. The angle of the wall combined with the way it sat wedged between the mountains reminded Breanne of the Hoover Dam. Elves were appearing and disappearing from openings in the wall. The openings connected to large stone platforms built at various heights, each holding large trebuchets. A massive counterweight system lifted baskets up to the platforms where she saw giants – no, not giants. Trolls? Were those things the troll creatures Key had spoken about?

Their legs were thick as tree trunks, and their arms were disproportionately large, as were their heads. They had no hair, and their skin was a sickly, jaundice yellow, and slick like a frog's. The massive beasts were lifting the boulders from the baskets and loading them onto the trebuchets. Next to the trebuchets stood vats, with fires lit beneath them. The troll things dipped oversized mops into the steaming vats, slopping black goo onto the boulders before lighting them on fire. Quickly, elves ran forward, releasing the mechanisms. Breanne's wide eyes followed the burning boulders as they sailed high above the wall until the black smoke, already filling the sky from shot after shot, swallowed them.

Someone shouted, drawing Breanne's attention back to the ground. She leaned out a bit more to see several dragons being led by dökkálfar, like giant pets on leashes, into the openings at the base of the wall. Behind them, hundreds of elves lined up in formation – row after row of armor-clad elves, numbering in the hundreds, maybe in the thousands. Behind them was a whole cavalry of horse-like creatures, with riders holding long poles similar to a lance but much longer. One woman in gleaming armor held a sword high as she sat atop one of the horse things, shouting orders.

"I think that's Saria," Garrett whispered over her shoulder.

"I thought she would be on her way back through the Shadow Forest with orders to kill us by now," Breanne said.

"Let me see!" Lenny said, switching spots with Garrett to peek out over Breanne's shoulder. "Yeah, well shit, that's her alright. This might be an even worse idea than I thought."

Breanne leaned out a little more, wanting desperately to see the tree. She'd only seen some of it the day they had entered Karelia, but now she could get an unobstructed look.

As she leaned out, the tree came into view. It was farther away than she expected, across a bay of still water. But a path of land led across to the tree. It was unbelievable. Larger than any tree could ever be. It stretched up and up into the sky, tall as a mountain and impossibly wide. From its branches, small cities hung from vines thick as redwoods. Quickly, she counted. "One, two, three, four... seven cities in all." She could even see small trees growing in the city closest to her.

The Last Gift

What held the ground the cities were built upon in the sky like that? And the light... there was light coming from inside the tree's canopy, illuminating everything below in a dim wash of soft yellow. Around the base of its massive trunk, a strange-shaped stone building rose from the ground in a terraced formation a full quarter way up the trunk.

Breanne couldn't pull herself away, and as she stared, she noticed something large falling from the tree. The objects, two at first, then three more, twirled and swayed. Then she realized what she was seeing – they were leaves. They must have been as big as a plane for her to see them from here. After a moment, she understood something else. The tree was sad. No. Sad wasn't the right word. It looked... not sad, but sick. It must have lost over half its leaves. And the branches – they were sagging. Now she noticed something else was really wrong. The seven cities weren't level; they were tilted.

A voice shouted in dökkálfar, "You there!"

Breanne gasped and jerked herself back behind the wall, but it was too late. The soldier had been looking right at her. And even though he was speaking dökkálfar, she understood the language and the soldier's next words: "Stop in the name of King Loravaris."

Others were shouting now. Hooves galloped toward them.

The space behind the building was nearly full, with half their own soldiers safely inside as others still pushed their way in.

We must do something! They're coming! Breanne shouted in mind speak.

It's time to transform, Lenny! Garrett said.

I know what you mean when you say that, but we need to come up with something cooler in the future, Lenny said.

Garrett shrugged.

Lenny smiled apologetically at Tell, and then he was

suddenly a foot taller, over seven feet now, with pointed ears and deep purple skin. His eyes changed too, taking on the classic swooshing S shape of the elves, though less pronounced.

The crowd of human soldiers gasped, taking several steps back.

"More secrets, my queen? I thought we were past secrets?" Key asked, looking quite displeased.

"Last one. Promise," Breanne said.

"Somehow I doubt that," Key said, her brows creasing as she glanced at her daughter.

Tell looked at the ground.

"Daughter, you knew? And you too kept this from me?" Key asked.

"My queen thought it best," she said, giving Breanne an apologetic look.

Breanne didn't offer anything else, instead turning to follow Garrett, Lenny, and the other sages, who were already rounding the corner of the building accompanied by Governess and Kilug. Over her shoulder, Breanne shouted back to Key and Stone, "Let us handle this. You guys just get our army inside and get that door secured."

When Breanne rounded the corner, six riders were approaching with swords drawn.

"Halt!" one elf shouted.

They halted.

Oh, man, you guys, they look really pissed! David said.

Give me the order and I will root their beasts to the Earth, young lord, Governess offered.

Not yet. Remember, we want to help them, not fight them, Garrett said.

"You there!" An elf with a strong jaw and chiseled features pointed accusingly. He was looking at Lenny. "I thought you a dökkálfar... but you're... what on Karelia are you?"

"He looks like he's part us and part something else," another elf said in a husky voice.

"That's impossible. The gods would never allow it," said another.

Husky Voice narrowed his eyes. "No. This must be the one General Saria told the king about. Word is spreading through the guard."

"Lie down on the ground, scum," Strong Jaw said.

One elf circled his horse thing around, flanking them. "Well, well, well. Now, what do we have here? Not just a few humans. They're traveling with a dwarf."

"We won't be lying down, and if you want to live, I suggest you go get your general and let her know I am here," Lenny said.

"And who are you?" Strong Jaw asked.

"I am Lennard Wade Loravaris, son of Syldan Loravaris, grandson of King Vulmon Loravaris! Now go get your general, or I will see you beheaded!" Lenny shouted up at Strong Jaw.

The elf's eyes went wide. He opened his mouth to speak, then shut it, finding no words. "Stay with them," Strong Jaw said. Eyes still locked on Lenny, he bent forward and spoke to his horse thing. "Quickly, take me to Saria."

"Yes, my lord," the horse thing answered in a feminine voice before turning and bolting off in the opposite direction.

Or I will see you beheaded? Really, Len? Pete asked in mind speak.

Too much? Lenny asked.

Maybe a bit, Garrett agreed.

Well, it worked.

That it did, kid, Paul said.

Sudden commotion broke out high on the wall as elves shouted. Far above, dragon fire spilled over in a great plume of blinding orange.

The dragons being led to the wall were gone now. They must have been sent through and into the battle.

"We don't like your ilk here in our city, human," one elf said, then spat at the ground near Garrett. "When Saria gets here, we will see who loses their head. Spreading lies about our prince is punishable by death."

Behind them, more and more of the army shuffled out from behind the building.

"What is this?" the husky-voiced elf asked.

"There's more of them! Go over there and see how many!"

"One of the king's personal escape routes is behind that building. It must have been breached."

Two riders took off toward the back of the building, leaving three to guard Breanne and the others.

Across the field of cobblestone, Saria turned her attention to the approaching guard as he pointed back toward them. She looked over, then shouted something to her men. Her horse thing charged toward them with a dozen more guards in tow.

Well, here we go, Breanne said.

Yeah, Lenny said nervously.

Hey, Len. Maybe don't threaten to have her beheaded, okay? David said.

Saria slid her beast to a stop in front of them, its massive hooves scraping across the stone. The horse thing looked as annoyed as Saria. "What is the meaning of this?" she asked.

"I told you I would come. Now, where is my grandfather? Where is King Loravaris?"

"Lower me," Saria ordered.

The great beast lowered itself onto its knees. The armor-clad woman dismounted and marched toward Lenny.

"What did I say I would do the next time I saw you?" she asked. But before Lenny could speak, she continued, "I said I would kill you, your friends, and all the women of Sky! Now lower your voice," Saria said with a warning look. Her hand rested on the hilt of her sword, but she didn't draw it.

Breanne watched as Garrett reached over his head, finding the hilt of his own sword, preparing to draw it.

Lenny held up a hand and sheathed his blade. "Wait, Garrett. Saria, we haven't come to fight with you. Where is the king?"

Saria's jaw tightened and Breanne was sure she was going to draw her sword.

"I want to see my grandfather, Saria. Did you keep your word to me? Did you give him Coach's diary?" He glanced back, motioning. "We've brought an entire army with us to join you in this fight!"

Saria looked past them toward the crowd, still spilling forth from behind the building.

Stone and Key were giving orders, lining up their men and women in formation.

"I see you have. Just as the king said you would. Honestly, I thought him mad. I thought his dreams fever charged. And the seer accompanies you," she said, locking eyes on Breanne. "You're the one he met when he stepped through the portal. He claims you saved his life. He claims you played a vital role in killing Apep?"

Breanne nodded, remembering in vivid detail the moment she'd grabbed the dagger, driving it into Apep's back and twisting. In her mind, she still heard the bones crunching, felt them churn through the handle of the knife. "Yes," she said, but there was no pride in her response.

Saria nodded too. "I remember you from the Shadow

Forest. Such a small creature to kill such a powerful foe, and now look at you. You wear a crown."

Breanne had forgotten about the tiara she'd donned atop her braids the night they'd named her queen.

"She is Queen Breezemore of Sky," Garrett announced, letting go of the pommel and lowering his hand.

"Indeed, and by order of the king, you, queen seer, are protected," Saria said.

Near the center of the great wall, dökkálfar screamed warnings as they pointed toward the sky and fled the area.

Breanne looked up in time to see a brown-and-black dragon appear from the blackened sky in a freefall, a large iron spike piercing its chest, the point coming out of its back. When it struck the ground, Breanne felt the vibrations through her boots and up her legs.

Saria looked back, clearly feeling the urgency in her absence.

"My grandfather, Saria," said Lenny. "I demand to see him."

"Is it true?" Strong Jaw asked. "Is he really the son of Prince Syldan?"

Saria bit her lower lip and turned to the elf. "He is."

Looks of shock and murmurs raced through the group of elves.

"Silence," Saria ordered. Looking back at Lenny, she said, "You cannot see your grandfather, Lenny Loravaris."

"But I demand—"

"King Loravaris is dead."

59

The Golden Staff

God Stones – Moon Ring 6
Osonian

"Oh, Lenny, I'm so sorry," Garrett said, placing a hand on his best friend's shoulder.

"What do you mean, dead? How?" Lenny asked.

Saria's eyes welled with tears, and Garrett knew she wasn't lying. "Our king was severely wounded trying to get back to the wall the day you arrived."

"When you and I first met, you knew! You knew, and you didn't tell me?"

"No. I only found out when I returned. I was on a mission in the Shadow Forest when the attack came."

"When did he die?" Lenny asked.

"This very moon ring, just before the suns came."

Lenny rubbed a hand across his face. "So close."

"He read Syldan's diary, Lenny," Saria said, "and he gave me orders."

Saria drew her sword.

Garrett drew his. *Get ready!* he called out to the sages in mind speak.

Paul stepped forward.

Pete focused as Governess began a quiet chant.

David spun his staff, and Kilug lifted his war hammer off his shoulder.

Garrett focused too, prepared to grab time and give his friends the minutes they needed to take out the nearly twenty soldiers on horseback.

Behind Saria, her soldiers drew their weapons – pointing lances, brandishing swords, and pulling back bowstrings.

"Hold!" Saria ordered. "Lennard Loravaris, step forward," the general said, her sword suddenly held in a way that looked less threatening.

Lenny took a cautious step forward.

Careful, Len, Garrett warned.

"The sword I carry into battle today is not my own. This blade, forged in the fires of Thunder Keep, belongs to the King of Osonian." Saria raised her voice to a near shout. "Our king died this very morning. His heir, Prince Syldan Loravaris, was murdered by his own brother! A brother whom our own king beheaded and whose name is forbidden to ever be spoken, by order of the king, from this day forward." Saria's words carried with them a warning.

"Dökkálfar who can hear me now, let them hear. The king himself predicted his grandson would arrive on this day with an army in tow, along with a seer, and the descendant of a god."

Garrett shared another look with Bre, her expression telling him he'd heard that right.

"Is the descendant with you?"

Lenny looked at Garrett. "He is my best friend."

All eyes followed Lenny's and fell upon Garrett.

Saria drew in a breath. "Very well. Kneel, Prince."

The Last Gift

Lenny blinked.

The tall elvish woman nodded and lifted her chin. "Kneel, Prince Lennard Wade Loravaris!"

Lenny looked at Garrett with eyes so big they seemed like they might pop right out of his head. *Is this really happening?* Lenny asked in mind speak.

Garrett smiled and nodded.

Lenny glanced at the others, all of them urging him forward with excited looks.

He looked back to Saria and knelt.

Extending the sword forward, she reached to touch the tip to Lenny's shoulder.

From behind her, an elf lunged forward, his own sword raised high as he swung.

Garrett gasped, reaching for time, but he couldn't grab it. He wasn't ready! In his excitement, he'd stupidly let his guard down.

Saria lifted the blade from Lenny's shoulder and spun, stabbing behind her as the soldier charged. The blade ran the elf through to the hilt. Saria ripped the blade free, spun again, and separated the elf's head from his shoulders.

She looked up at the others, her face arrested in a grim warning. "You do not have to like your king's decision, but you will abide by it. Any who dare interfere with our late king's dying order will suffer a fate far worse than I allowed Adamar," she said, pointing as she knelt down next to Strong Jaw's headless corpse.

I told that dick I would see him beheaded! Lenny said in mind speak.

Behind them, a thousand humans packed in, overflowing from the space around the side of the building all the way to where they stood now. Breanne was looking back uneasily.

Garrett followed her gaze up the stairs as the final few

were piling through the hidden door. *David, can you please make sure that door gets closed and locked?*

I'm on it, Garrett, David said as he disappeared back through the crowd.

Dozens of other soldiers were galloping up now, crowding their horse creatures in around the others.

Saria wiped both sides of the bloody blade on the now-headless Adamar's sleeve, stood, and turned back to Lenny, once again touching the tip of the blade to his shoulder. "Lennard Wade Loravaris, son of Prince Syldan Loravaris and heir to the throne of Osonian. Do you acknowledge your birth name and your birthright, before the highest servant of Osonian, the general of the dökkálfar army, Saria Liavaris the Night Slayer?"

"I do!" Lenny shouted.

"Do you swear before Goddess Ereshkigal and all the dökkálfar of Osonian to rule with the dökkálfar's best interests in mind and to always protect your people?"

"I swear to rule with all people's best interest in mind!" Lenny answered.

Saria frowned slightly at that, but she lifted the blade from his shoulder and held it out horizontally. "You kneel before me a prince, but by birth and promise you are a prince no more! Rise, King Loravaris! Take your sword and lead your people!"

Lenny stood and lifted the sword from Saria's hand, weighed it in his own, and then spun it dramatically, whipping it back and forth.

Show off! Garrett said.

All the soldiers watching dismounted their beasts and bowed to their new king.

Saria smiled wickedly. "Get the king his armor. We've dragons to slay!"

"Wait!" Lenny said, drawing his other sword.

Saria looked at the blade. "Shadow Blade! I thought you lost."

"I believe this belongs to you," Lenny said, tossing the elf woman the sword.

Saria snatched it out of the air, nodded sharply, and smiled.

Behind Garrett and the others, a man screamed.

Garrett spun to find a giant standing inside the door. It was huge, dressed in black armor that looked like bones, and around its neck hung a necklace of tennis shoes. In one hand it held a massive axe; with the other it grabbed a screaming man and lifted him in the air. The monster's mouth stretched open to reveal a mouth full of teeth Garrett could see from eighty yards away. The giant pulled the flailing man to its mouth and bit his shoulder off.

The man's arm fell to the ground.

The giant roared like a wild beast and tossed the man down the stairs as if it were tossing a cat by the tail. The man flailed his one remaining arm and bounced hard down the stone stairs. Behind him, two more giants ducked low and stepped through the door.

"The giants have discovered the king's passage! We must secure that door!" Saria shouted.

The giant with the shoe necklace chewed the contents of his mouth as he took two steps down the stairs, finding his next victim.

Everyone was fleeing the area, pushing toward Garrett and the others like a mob rushing the stage at a Prince concert. Except for one idiot, who stood frozen in fear at the foot of the stairs.

Is that David? Breanne shouted in mind speak.

Oh, god, David! Get out of there! Garrett shouted.

He and Lenny bolted into the oncoming crowd with the others on their heels. But they were way too far away. *We won't get to him in time!* Garrett shouted. Dammit, why did he have to send David to close the door? Why David?

A loud roar emanated from beyond the wall. It was a dragon's roar but deeper, louder – unlike anything Garrett had ever heard.

The crowd froze suddenly, unsure whether to keep running or turn back.

The ground beneath them shook as the sound of exploding stone smothered everything else. The wall trembled. One platform collapsed, dropping a troll along with a trebuchet onto the cobbles below.

Hundreds of soldiers shuffled back, their weapons raised as if expecting something to come completely through the wall.

"This is not good!" Saria said.

"Ya think?" Lenny replied.

Garrett looked from the wall to the tennis shoe giant, whose attention had also been pulled toward the wall.

Take the opening, David! Lenny shouted.

Run, David! Gabi yelled.

But David didn't run. He stood there on the stairs, already short and made shorter by the stairs, as he looked up at the giant. *Go back! Go back or meet your end!* David shouted.

Lenny stopped short. *Whaaat in the Reese's Peanut Butter fu—*

The giant bent forward and belted out another angry roar, bloody spittle and bits of flesh falling out of its still-full mouth.

The monster swiped its massive hand downward at David.

There was no time for David to retreat now. But David wasn't retreating. Instead, he ducked down low, letting the massive fist pass overhead. The boy sprang back up and ran forward, thrusting the staff upward as if holding a spear, the tip poking the giant in the belly.

A flash of yellow light radiated up the staff and out the tip as it sank deep into the giant's gut. Golden force exploded in the giant's midsection, lifting the monster off the ground and sending it airborne into the two behind it.

David slid backward, stumbling down the steps, but somehow stayed on his feet.

The tennis shoe giant lay limp across the other two as they struggled to get out from underneath the bigger giant.

Garrett was almost there now, with Lenny right on his heels.

The two giants pushed the tennis shoe guy's limp body over and crawled to their feet. One lifted tennis shoe guy's axe from the ground and reared back, fixing his strange eyes on David.

David appeared disoriented, staggering forward toward the giant.

Garrett ran past David, stepping onto the bottom step and leaping upward in a twist.

The giant chopped down as if aiming to split wood.

The giant's axe blade swooshed by Garrett's face as he swung the dragon slayer, severing both the giant's hands at the wrist.

Lenny jerked David back as the axe came down and stuck fast, wedging itself in the cobbles, both of the giant's six-fingered hands still attached.

Garrett landed in front of the giant, jumped again, and ran his blade deep into the monster's chest. The monster frowned in confusion, falling forward.

Garrett jerked his sword back and sidestepped.

The giant tipped slowly forward like a felled tree, dead before he hit the ground.

"I got the other one," Lenny shouted, running up the

stairs, his new sword in hand, but the giant turned and ran back out the door. "Oh, come on!"

"Close it quick! Before he comes back with more," Garrett said, running up the rest of the stairs. Both Lenny and Garrett grabbed the door and heaved. Outside, a giant shouted and others ran forward.

"We're not going to make it!" Lenny shouted.

Another set of hands slapped against the door. "Yes! We! Are!" Paul grunted, as the door swung forward so fast Garrett nearly fell to his knees.

Giants crashed into the door from the other side – how many, Garrett couldn't say.

"Lock it! I got the door!" Paul shouted as his whole body flexed and rippled with muscle.

Lenny and Garrett scrambled for the bolts, quickly sliding them into place.

The three of them stood gasping. Dull thumps sounded from the other side, as giants beat on the stone-covered door, but they might as well have been beating on the mountain itself.

Kilug and David appeared on the stairs, running toward them.

"David, that was amazing!" Garrett said.

"It's the staff! I knew it would work! I just had to believe in it is all!"

Kilug ran toward the door. "Aye, fine job! Now, all of yous, out of the way!" the dwarf said, pushing past them to examine the door with a squinted eye. "Ha, just as me thought! This 'ere's dwarven-work! There ain't no giant on the planet breaking through! Dat ye can be sure!"

Lenny put a hand on David's shoulder. "David, what you did had nothing to do with that staff, you little mustached, staff-wielding monk, you! I say we get you a robe and shave your head. What do you say? I think monks can have mustaches – we'll call it a monkstache!"

"I'm telling you guys, it's the staff! It's a magical item. C'mon, Garrett, tell him. This was Turek's staff, for crap's sake!"

Garrett shook his head. "I'm with Lenny on this one, pal." Garrett smiled, but his smile was replaced with a frown when another roar sounded from beyond the wall. This one was even louder than before.

Again, the ground shook and the sound of fracturing stone popped, echoing out into the bay. Then came the shouts. Far away from them, at the opposite end of the wall, a portion of the stone wall glowed bright red, like molten iron.

"Come on!" Garrett shouted, jumping from the stairs and pushing his way back through the crowd of men and women.

As they reached Breanne, Saria, and the others, the roar built again, shaking the cobbles beneath their feet.

"No! Back! Get back!" Saria shouted, but no one could hear her.

When the stone could glow no brighter, the far section of the great wall burst inward, showering the far flank of the elven army in molten stone.

"This can't be! It's impossible. The wall is impenetrable," said Saria.

"Aye, what of the stories me grandpa tells of yous having elvish wizards?" Kilug asked.

Saria nodded gravely, her focus trained on the wall as she moved back toward her horse thing. "Yes. 'Had' would be more accurate. The head of our dragon master guild, Teklorth, was our only remaining master mage, but he went missing in the first battle. Rumor has it he was killed by a human with red eyes and a three-headed dragon. But even without Teklorth, breaching the wall should be impossible! We should have over a dozen dragon masters on that wall and more in the field!"

Clearly, Saria was wrong, for Garrett didn't need to be a seer to know what came next.

A dragon head appeared through the new opening, then another, and still another.

Garrett's stomach turned and his heart smashed against his chest as if it were trying to escape. On the dragon's back sat a familiar boy in a black leather jacket.

"Jack," Garrett breathed.

60

No Way Out

God Stones – Moon Ring 6
The Creators' Mountain, Karelia

"Well, well, well, sister. It seems you have been keeping quite the secret." Turek smiled, looking at Rán.

Sentheye flushed pink through Rán's face. "He is an amazing creation, Turek."

"Set aside your mundane infatuation, sister!" Ereshkigal snapped. Turning to Turek, she wagged a finger. "King Vulmon died this very morning after announcing your abomination heir to the throne of Osonian! How can this be? How could King Vulmon do such a thing? He must have gone mad as he neared death! Now this creature has been named king by that harlot, Saria, and my magnificent wall has been destroyed! There is nothing standing in between your psychopathic creation, Jack, and the father tree!"

"Calm yourself, sister. We need but think a thought and we will be there, poised to put an end to this," Aurgelmir said.

Typhon turned. "Brother. You, too, are full of surprises. How did you get the nephilbock to abandon their war on Osonian?"

"Oh, they've not abandoned their desire to take the kingdom, but they understand who they serve and who they do not." Aurgelmir narrowed his eyes at Typhon. "I've also given these Earth-born creatures instructions. No harm shall befall Metsavana."

"Is it so simple, brother? Is your trust so easily gained? Creatures you did not even create!" Rán said.

Aurgelmir shook his head. "No, sister. I do not trust these abominations, and it is because of what they are that I am forced to take further precautions. I assure you they will not be an issue."

"One of them just killed a human in a single bite!"

"Perhaps I should clarify. They will not be an issue for Metsavana. How they fill their stomachs is no concern of mine."

"That may be, but your Jack is a concern for all of us!" Druesha said, pointing a finger at Turek.

"As are your dragons, Typhon!" Durin said.

They were right. They were all right – and Turek knew it. But there was something happening here. He could feel it in his bones – well, his metaphorical bones anyway.

"Look at them," Turek said, peering into the circle. "This fight is not lost to anyone on any side. We must be ready, but we must hold."

"What?" snapped Ereshkigal. "Hold for what?"

"We are all represented by our favorites. Surely that can't be a coincidence. And who truly believed all our favorites would come together beyond the wall in the way they have?"

"Represented? Everyone is most certainly not represented. I am not!" Druesha said. Turning to the others, she pointed, "Rán is not! And the dwarves are not present."

The Last Gift

"Actually, I am quite represented," Rán said. "The bay behind the wall holds three of my most powerful children, two brothers and a sister to Hafgufa, the sea kraken of Earth. I spoke with them, and they are quite eager to serve. Quite thirsty for revenge. And no matter which direction the dragons attack from, Metsavana is surrounded by water." She smiled wickedly.

"Are you creating flying kraki these days, Rán?"

"Flight? Of course not! I know my place is in the water, brother. Why would you ask me such a thing?"

"You know dragons fly, don't you?" Typhon asked.

"Oh sarcasm, brother, how witty. Of course, but this Jack wasn't smart enough to lead them over the wall, or to circle and attack from the ocean. Instead, he takes the wall. Seems foolish to me. So, perhaps he will be foolish enough to try engaging my kraki too."

"Fine! But what about me? What about Durin?" Druesha asked.

Turek smiled. "Kilug, the dwarf, represents Durin."

"One dwarf?" Durin protested.

"Ah, but I hear dwarves are mighty indeed. And you, sister, have a most magnificent creation in Governess Larrea. You haven't seen her full abilities, but I have, and I assure you she is quite the champion indeed."

Druesha scoffed, but Turek ignored her. "So, you see. We are all in good company."

"Then spin the knife and one of us can go now!" Ereshkigal urged as she watched the circle, wide-eyed.

Turek picked the knife up and sheathed it. "No. We are done with this. Now we watch, and if we need to go, we—"

"Look! Your Jack is through the wall!" Ereshkigal gasped, pointing into the circle. "Oh, Great Mother! What is he doing?"

"Turek! Is this what you were waiting for – all this death? Look at them!" Durin said.

A sob broke from Rán. "Paul! Oh please don't let him die."

Turek felt like a knife had been stuck in his gut. He'd misjudged. Jack was killing them all! He'd been wrong all along. This creature was too powerful. *Great Mother, what are you trying to show me?*

"Turek!" Typhon shouted. "They are lost! It is time for us to salvage this. Forget everything else. We must save Metsavana."

Great Mother, they were right; they had to go, and go now! Turek stood, his head nodding. "Yes. To the surface then."

As all of them had done thousands of times before, they closed their eyes. It was as simple as taking a breath. Turek simply imagined where he wanted to materialize, and when he opened them… nothing. He was standing in the same place, unmoved. Confused expressions stared back at him. Eyes closed and opened.

"Great Mother, what's happening?" Druesha said.

"I can't transport!" Typhon said.

Panic seized Turek. He spun and took three running steps. Taking flight, he soared like a bird across the Great Hall to the white corridor where he'd ascended from the surface, arriving here only a handful of moon rings prior. The others followed close behind him. But when Turek reached the wall, there was no opening – only stone. The corridor was gone.

"Impossible!"

"This way," Typhon shouted, spinning toward the balcony where sat the creators' seven thrones. "We will jump and float to the surface!"

The Last Gift

Ereshkigal gasped. There was no balcony, only more stone – an entire wall of it.

"What is this madness?" Durin asked.

"We are the creators. Focus! Create an opening. Create a door, or tunnel, or new balcony!" Aurgelmir shouted.

They stopped and stood still, all of them focusing on the task of creating a way out.

Nothing worked.

"Who is doing this? I want to know which of you are responsible!" Typhon shouted.

"And to what end?" Rán asked.

"And how?" Durin said. "Yes. Who and how?"

All eyes fell to Turek.

"You think this my doing?"

"Of course it's you! Who else?" Ereshkigal accused. "You and your games. How? How are you doing this, Turek? What secrets have you learned while you were away? Is this what you wanted all along? To trap us here and watch these abominations destroy Metsavana – destroy us?"

Turek dropped his hands to his sides and walked away from them. Back to the circle. Back to the show. He glanced back over his shoulder. "You are welcome to think as you please, but I've no interest in being destroyed. I've no interest in seeing you, my loved ones, destroyed. Nor am I interested in seeing all we've worked for destroyed. I assure you, Ereshkigal, I've nothing to do with this."

The others walked toward him, each now suspicious of the other. But Turek knew better. This had to be the owl, and what could the owl be but the Great Mother herself? There was no other explanation.

Together they stood and stared through the circle, the window to their fate. The most powerful beings in the universe were now prisoners in their own creation. Turek sat first, legs crossed. "We should keep trying, but I don't think we are going anywhere until this ends."

"Without us to stop Jack Nightshade and his fire breathers, we are all doomed," Ereshkigal said.

Turek glanced at the other sullen faces as they nodded in agreement, as if there was nothing to do but simply wait to die. But Turek would not wait. In this, there must be a purpose – a lesson. Perhaps the lesson was faith. No, Turek would not give up. Instead, he would watch, and he would hope, and most of all, he would pray to the Great Mother.

61

Lead from the Front

God Stones – Moon Ring 6
Osonian

Breanne's eyes rolled back as a vision took her. But this vision was strange. In this vision, she didn't see anything. Nothing at all. Only white light. Then, a woman spoke to her in a familiar voice. The voice of the owl. "You will need to tell him what he is, Breanne Moore."

"Tell who?" she asked.

"He won't believe in himself enough. But he will believe in you. You're the one who must stand in front of him. You must lead him. Show him, Breanne Moore. If you fail in this, all my children die."

"But I don't understand," she said.

"From the front, Breanne Moore. Lead him from the front and show him, or all is lost."

As the white light cleared, dragons filled her vision. Not one or two, but hundreds. Where was everyone? She looked back over her shoulder to find Garrett was standing behind her – naked. No. No, not naked, just shirtless. His runes...

they were burning in his skin. His lips were moving! What was he saying? Her name! He was shouting her name.

Breanne! someone shouted, grabbing her hand, but it wasn't Garrett.

Breanne's vision cleared. She was back.

What? What is it?

Gabi pointed.

A massive three-headed dragon stood half in and half out of the hole in the wall. Atop sat Jack and someone else, a woman maybe, but it was hard to tell from here. Gabi tugged at her hand again.

Across the cobblestone field of soldiers, the dragon loomed, its big heads swinging from side to side as if searching. Then, with a breath of fire, dozens of dökkálfar erupted in flame. Elves screamed and burned; some tried to run away from the flame consuming them.

"My army!" Saria shouted, jumping onto her horse thing. "Forward!" she commanded.

The horse thing bolted.

We have to stop Jack before he kills them all! Garrett said.

The other elves turned their horses to follow.

"Halt!" Lenny commanded. "You guys get off your horses. We need them."

The dökkálfar closest to Lenny turned, his lip curling into a sneer.

"You saw what happened to your friend," Lenny ordered again, pointing at the headless dökkálfar Saria had killed. "Now give me your horse," he said firmly, waving a hand toward the beast, which clearly was not called a horse.

That's right, Breanne thought. *You know damn well what he's asking for.*

The dökkálfar tipped his head slightly and dismounted. The others followed suit.

The Last Gift

The sages quickly mounted their steeds. Breanne with Garrett, Gabi with David, Governess with Pete, Lenny with Tell, and Paul locked forearms with Kilug, lifting the dwarf onto the animal.

Across the field, Cerberus swung his two outer heads from side to side, smashing them into the walls. Stone exploded, widening the hole. The hole was already big enough to pass through. Why waste their time and energy? *What's he doing?* she asked in mind speak.

I bet he's widening the opening for his dragons, Pete said.

No. This is just Jack showing off. He's making sure all who see know just how powerful he is, Garrett said.

Paul turned back to Stone and Key. "You need to take the army straight down shore to that land bridge," he pointed. "It leads to Osonian and the big tree. Get them across the water quickly."

"I'm not blind. I know where it leads. What I don't understand is why we would come all this way to flee now?" Key asked, frowning.

"Not fleeing, just repositioning. We need to get on the other side of the water."

Key and Stone looked at each other and then back at Paul. "To what end?"

"To what end, indeed?" Stone echoed. "Dragons can simply fly across."

"Paul, what's going on?" Breanne asked, adjusting herself into the saddle.

"Rán told me we need to head for the tree if the wall didn't hold," Paul urged.

"If my brother says to pull them back, then pull them back!" Breanne ordered.

Garrett nodded. "You heard her, Stone. Get these people across!"

"Anyone know how to make this thing go?" Pete asked.

"I kicked it with my heel, and it growled at me and told me if I value my life, I shouldn't do that."

"This *thing* is called a hursue, and why would you kick it?" Tell asked.

"To make it go, obviously."

"That is very curious. Is it your way to kick others when you want them to move?"

Pete frowned. "What… I mean, but it's a… No."

"Why would you not simply ask it?" Tell asked, shaking her head.

Ahead, Saria had nearly crossed the field.

Lenny nodded, raising his voice. "Hursue, take us to where the wall collapsed."

"My name is Olusa, my lord," Lenny's hursue said.

"Sorry, Olusa, please hurry," Lenny pleaded.

"Near the strange dragon, my lord?" Olusa neighed disapprovingly.

"Yes! As fast as you can run!" Lenny ordered.

"Lenny, wait. You may not want—" Tell started, but it was too late.

"Very well, my lord." Olusa bolted forward, prompting the other hursue to respond in kind.

David shouted a terrified scream while Gabi giggled in mind speak, her laughter filling Breanne's mind. Meanwhile, Breanne's head snapped back, the sudden jolt nearly throwing her from the saddle.

They crossed the span of a mile quickly, soldiers making way as Lenny shouted, "Move, by order of the king." It grabbed the elves' attention as they parted or dove out of the way.

Finally, they reached the front line. The army had given the dragon and his riders a wide berth, but Breanne knew they were still too close – they were all too close.

The Last Gift

"Jack!" Garrett shouted as he led his hursue and the other sages out beyond the retreating edge of the army.

Lenny stayed at his side, the other sages all close behind.

"You must be mad!" Saria said, but she urged her hursue forward alongside them.

"Order the army back to the bridge!" Lenny shouted.

Saria pulled a face, opening her mouth to protest, but as she did, Cerberus roared from one head that had disappeared inside the broken wall.

Flames must have followed because the corridor inside the wall filled with dragon fire. All the way down the wall, screams rose in pitch as the elves inside burned.

Cerberus withdrew its head, fixing all six of its red eyes on Garrett and the others.

"Damn that foul creature! Damn it to the underworld!" Saria spat at the ground and shouted back over her shoulder. "Fall back to the land bridge!"

Metal shuffled on stone as the soldiers backpedaled.

Across the distance of only fifty yards, Jack slid off his dragon's back, as did the girl riding with him. She was a dökkálfar, Breanne realized.

Jack sneered, walking slowly forward, but his companion stayed behind.

He's talking to the girl! Gabi said.

What's he saying? David asked.

Then suddenly Breanne could hear Jack speaking.

Stay with Cerb. I'll be back! he told the girl, who then ran forward and hugged him.

Breanne blinked. *What the...*

I will be fine. Now go, Nyana! It's time to settle the score.

Jack spun back toward them, lifted a hand, and pointed toward Garrett. "No more running—"

A female voice bellowed in mind speak, cutting Jack off as a dark shadow filled the hole behind Cerberus.

Zerri! Gabi shouted.

Jack turned his head, narrowing his eyes toward the hole.

A female dragon hissed, *You killed them! You killed the ones you swore to save!*

Jack's lip curled as his red eyes glowed inhumanly bright. *So what? I traded the lives of a handful of dragons to kill all the dragon masters and destroy the wall! Besides, we have more dragons between my hordes and your Karelian army than we'll ever need!*

I warned you of this, Jack Nightshade. I warned you of your betrayal and what it would cost you! You killed eighteen of my elders! Zerri snapped, stepping from the shadow of the wall into the light.

Gabi gasped in mind speak, *Zerri? But how?*

Zerri looked nothing like the little grey dragon that had saved Gabi's life back on Earth. This dragon was three or four times larger, with black scales that sparkled under the Karelian suns as if dusted in glitter. Each black scale was tipped in red, as if it had been hand-dipped in blood. She wore a crown shaped to fit a dragon's head, and in the center of the crown sat fixed a God Stone, opaque and swirling with Sentheye. Breanne hadn't seen anything more terrifyingly beautiful in all her life.

Are you sure that's Zerri? Breanne asked.

Positive, Gabi said, not taking her eyes off the dragon as she slid off her hursue.

Gabi! What are you doing?

She's the Queen of Queens now, Gabi answered, sounding almost happy for her as she walked forward.

Cerberus spun, turning on Zerri, his three heads hissing.

Zerri, order your dragons through the hole now! Jack commanded.

Zerri snarled, *No. You have erred greatly, Jack Nightshade. Our lives are not yours to spend. My army is mine to command, and they will not cross through the wall to serve your whims.*

Jack laughed. *You think I need you or your army? I guess it's you who messed up! It was my power that made you what you are!*

I am what I would have become in time.

"Hey, Garrett!" Jack shouted, obviously having no idea they had heard everything he'd said in mind speak. "You ready? Throw your best punch, 'cause I'm throwing mine right now!"

What's he talking about? Lenny asked.

The vision flashed through Breanne's mind again along with the words from her vision. *You must lead from the front!* She didn't know what it meant. Without understanding the what, how could she understand the when? She ran forward to stand next to Garrett, hoping to see some sign of what to do next.

Black Sentheye, thick as old car oil, shot from Jack's splayed fingers, hitting Zerri.

"No," Gabi cried, running toward the dragon.

Gabi, wait! Breanne tried.

The dragon queen hissed and roared, but Jack poured it on. A red glow filled the stream of black Sentheye, pulling the life from Zerri back toward Jack.

Zerri fell onto her side, kicking at the air.

62

Stand Witness

God Stones – Moon Ring 6
Osonian

Garrett grabbed Jack in time, slowing him and with him the magic he was using. But Garrett's hold didn't reach far enough to trap Cerberus, who stood behind the bully.

The chaos was too much – all the noise and his nerves – and Jack, with those red eyes and weird scales around his brow. When had that happened, anyway? The many distractions made Garrett's time hold shaky at best. He couldn't focus… couldn't think… couldn't…

Breanne appeared at his side. "I'm here, Garrett. I'm with you," she said aloud. "Take a breath. You're okay."

Hearing her voice calmed him, just like it had that night in the tunnel when he first fought Jack. Garrett took a breath. Centering his focus, he tightened his grip on time and on Jack while remaining acutely aware of everything around him. Behind him, he clearly heard the armies of humans and elves shouting, heard the fear in their shaking voices, discerned their footsteps running along the land bridge. He could feel the eyes of those waiting for their turn to cross boring into him. Deeper, his focus narrowed, and he heard the water in the bay stirring unnaturally. Inside the wall, he heard stone popping and crackling from the dragon fire breathed only a moment ago. From beyond the wall, he heard more dragons descending toward the hole, landing on the battlefield, screeching and growling. In his peripheral vision, he saw Gabi running toward the fallen dragon queen.

Gabi turned her attention to Jack, shoving her hands forward. *I said no!* she screamed.

Both Jack and Gabi flew backward as if struck by an invisible force. The wave of power radiated outward, washing over Garrett. The pulse forced him to lose his hold on time, but Jack was no longer casting. He, too, was lying flat on his back.

David ran forward, shouting, "Gabi, oh man, are you alright?" He knelt, shaking the girl. "Wake up, Gabi!"

Jack sat up. *Jack's horde! Cerberus the Mighty and Taker have made a way. Now get your asses in here!* he shouted in mind speak.

Pete and Governess ran toward the hole, which Garrett thought was a bad idea, but there was no time for him to worry about the others. He had to trust they knew what they were doing. Garrett's focus had to be one hundred percent on Jack.

"You think this means anything, Garrett?" Jack shouted, raising his hands again.

Cerberus roared and stepped forward to straddle Jack between his two front legs.

Behind them, the first dragon through the hole was smaller and brown. Before it cleared the opening, the sounds of bones breaking echoed off the walls. The small dragon collapsed and went still.

Pete wobbled like he might drop to one knee but quickly recovered, steadying himself.

Another dragon scrambled over the one Pete had killed, but before it cleared the wall, the cobbles erupted as thorn-covered trees burst from the ground, blocking its way. The dragon roared in pain as the long thorns found their way into its underbelly. Enraged, the dragon spit fire into the trees.

Governess continued to chant as new trees burst upward, replacing the burnt ones. But Garrett knew dragon fire would not be held at bay by trees, and Governess could not keep this up for long.

In front of him and Breanne, Cerberus's neck glowed bright red.

"Breanne, look out!" Garrett shouted and shoved her hard to the side as the flames building in Cerberus's throat released from his center head. The dragon flame came full on, dousing Garrett with a force that made him stagger backward.

The warmth of fire consumed Garrett like it had before, but this time he welcomed it. Even more, he begged for it all, pulling it in, willing it to be drawn into him and only him. He would not allow flame or heat to touch those around him, especially Bre, and like a chimney drawing all the smoke from a fire, the flame obeyed.

The runes on Garrett's arms and chest burned. It was uncomfortable yet reassuring, for he understood this discomfort was his protection and the only way he could protect the others.

Garrett had survived Cerberus's dragon breath, but Jack was already attacking. Only it wasn't Garrett he went after.

"I'll kill everyone you love! Just like you killed Danny! Starting with her!" Jack pointed.

The Last Gift

Breanne, having just climbed back to her feet, bent forward and coughed vomit onto the stone cobbles.

"No!" Garrett shouted, reacting almost instantly to slow time.

Burn the rest of them, Cerb! Jack ordered as he slowed.

Cerberus roared, building to fire once more.

A female voice hissed into Garrett's mind. *You betrayed the gift my mother bestowed upon you, Jack Nightshade!*

Zerri hit Cerberus in the side in a clash of scales, talons, and bone. The two dragons rolled away, slamming into a rock face where the great wall met the mountainside.

Garrett held on to Jack, and Jack held on to Breanne, draining her life into his, albeit slowly.

Garrett pleaded, *Help her, David! Please! Hurry!*

The rest of the sages, plus Governess, Kilug, and Tell, were all at the hole in the wall, fighting to prevent the flood of dragons from pouring in.

What sounded to Garrett like commands were being shouted from a platform on the wall.

A troll jumped from the platform as another troll leaned over the side and lifted a boulder. Seeing the thing this close, Garrett realized they were even bigger than he'd thought. The one still on the platform dropped the boulder to the one on the ground, who hefted the boulder and ran toward the hole, spun in a circle, and chucked the boulder like a shotput into the smoldering opening. It turned and ran back for another boulder. They were trying to seal the hole!

I'm here! David said, drawing Garrett's attention back to Breanne. David was already glowing golden and pouring it into Breanne.

I'm here too! Just tell me what to do! Paul said, having come running back when he heard Garrett call David for help.

I can't... can't hold Jack forever! Garrett said. Jack was no longer the annoying bully from Petersburg. That much was clear. The power coming from the kid was incredible. Garrett knew he was about to lose him – and to lose his hold meant Breanne might die.

You have no idea what I am, Garrett. You have no idea of my power.

Somehow, being caught in time was not slowing Jack's ability to speak with his mind.

I know you can hear me, you coward! Jack's head slowly turned, the makings of a smile creeping ever so slowly onto his face.

Paul doubled over and puked. Behind Jack, Lenny, Tell, and Pete fell to their knees. The troll gagged, hands going to its throat. Governess grabbed her head and cried out as her human form slipped. The tree woman lost color and rooted to the ground.

A dragon pushed a boulder aside, snatched the troll in its jaws, and yanked it back off its feet, into the wall's opening. Another dragon appeared, barely visible in the shadows of the hole.

The troll shrieked as the dragons fed.

Garrett was lost. He couldn't stop this. He couldn't save them all. What good was slowing time if it were simply to watch his friends' lives be sucked away in slow motion?

To Garrett's right, near the mountain wall, Cerberus shouted in a deep growl, "You are queen of nothing!" He was on top of Zerri now, jaws snapping and biting. She was losing. There was no one left to help. The armies were retreating! His friends were dying!

Jack. I… he started.

Go on. Say it. Beg for their lives… coward!

Jack was shaking now. He was drawing too much power and he couldn't hold on to it, but caught in slowed time, he couldn't release it either.

The Last Gift

Let go of them... Let go and use it on me! Just let them live!

You have to suffer! You have to feel... what I feel! You have to know what it's like to lose everything! Jack said.

David's glow spread from Breanne, to Paul, to Lenny, and then Pete. It spread to the dwarf and then to Tell. The glow even passed through Governess too, but it seemed to have no effect on her.

That's good, David! You're keeping them alive! But when David didn't answer, Garrett turned to find his friend shaking like Jack, only he was changing too. He looked like all the blood had drained from his face. His eyes were sunken and black, his lips cracked, and he appeared to have lost several dozen pounds in mere moments. David looked sick... like... Oh, no. David was dying, and still, he poured out the golden glow.

Jack! I'm sorry! Garrett shouted into the boy's mind.

You're... what? You're... sorry? You think that matters?

You hate me, Jack! And I get it. I killed Danny. I didn't mean to, but I did it. You think killing them will bring him back? It won't! And I know you, Jack! You're not a monster! Pete and David were your friends!

Shut up! You don't know me! You don't... you don't know what... what I've... done!

You are going to die, Jack! I won't let go of you until you kill yourself with all that power you've sucked in! Unless you let them go!

Jack's strained face changed, and Garrett caught it. Something he had missed.

You don't get it! I'm already... dead, the boy said.

What?

You heard me. When... when you let go... I'm dead. I can... can feel it. I've taken too much. He laughed, but there was no humor in it, only irony. *Taker... has taken too much.*

Stop drawing the lives out of them, Jack! Stop, and maybe we can fix this.

Jack shook his head in slow motion. *Even now, even after what I've done, you would help me? You expect... expect me to believe that?*

I will! Just tell me how. What do you want, Jack? What can I do?

David fell to his knees, his glow fading away.

I want Danny back, and I want you to pay!

Garrett shook his head, pleading. *I am paying, Jack. Every day, I think about Danny. But killing these people won't change it.*

Killing you and everyone you care about is all I wanted... at first, but then... I made Cerb, and we got all this power. I wanted more... I wanted them to write songs about me... you know? Now I don't know... I think... I think I want... Jack paused, his face contorting, wrenching in the agony of holding too much power. *I think she might have loved me.*

Jack's eyes, ears, and nose were bleeding now.

Jack, you can do one good thing. One last good thing, and I promise, they will write a song about you – a good song!

I don't think I care about the songs anymore, Garrett.

For the first time, the look on Jack's face wasn't one of murderous hate. He almost looked like someone else.

Please, Jack!

And you know what else? I don't think I care about you anymore either. Jack dropped his hands to his sides, letting go of the others, but everything he'd drawn in built up inside him like a pressure cooker with the needle pegged in the red.

The only thing keeping Jack from whatever the power overload had in store for him was Garrett's hold on time.

Krakens... ancient trees... elder dragons. I've taken all

their power... killed... them all... and it's your sages... their power... that's too... too much! Garrett, will you do... something for me?

Garrett nodded, feeling his time-hold strain.

Will you make sure... Nyana isn't punished? I think... well, maybe I could have loved her too. I think I could have really felt it... you know?

I promise she won't be harmed. Garrett strained with all he had not to slip as tears ran down his face.

Jack nodded. *Let me go, Garrett.*

Wait, Jack. Call... off... the horde! Garrett begged.

Jack's... horde...

Garrett's hold on time slipped.

Cut short, Jack gasped, his face contorting horrifically as his mouth stretched open in an unnatural yawn, a pained scream escaping his throat.

Garrett met the boy's bulging red eyes.

Jack punched an unclosed fist of bent fingers into the air. His other hand raked claw-like down his cheek and neck.

Behind Jack, Cerberus let out something between a roar and a scream.

In that moment, Garrett wished he could save Jack. Not because he felt sorry for him. Not because some last little piece of regret in the kid could somehow erase all the horrors of what he had done. It was quite the opposite. Jack had done too much, hurt too many – Pete's mom being one of them. Being allowed to die here and now, rather than being forced to live with what he'd done felt wrong. It wasn't fair – like in some strange way, Jack was winning. But this was outside Garrett's control. Within his control was the ability to stand witness. He could stay his eyes, and for all those Jack had hurt, he could watch.

Determined, Garrett held eye contact as convulsions

seized Jack. It looked as though the boy was having a grand mal seizure while standing upright.

"Mmmmaaaaaaahhhhh!" Jack's inhuman red eyes widened with fear, then burst in their sockets a split second before the rest of his body exploded.

63

Purple Rain

God Stones – Moon Ring 6
Osonian

The sky swirled with purple snow as fat flakes melted against Breanne's cheeks. She pushed herself off the stone and wiped her mouth across the sleeve of her grey hoodie. As suddenly as her stomach had wrenched with agony, it untwisted, the pain subsiding. She took another breath and swallowed. Someone screamed. *Oh, no! Garrett!*

She reeled around in time to realize the scream wasn't Garrett's. It was Jack. His whole body was shaking and then… he burst apart. The space Jack had occupied was suddenly a cloud of red mist and purple snow.

Garrett's hands dropped to his sides, and he collapsed to his knees.

She ran to him. *Garrett!*

I'm… I'm okay, he said, waving off her concern with an exhausted hand motion. *Guys! Are you all okay? David?*

A woman screamed. It was the elf woman who had been riding on Cerberus with Jack, and she was running straight at them. She was tall and pretty, with long hair that flowed behind her as she ran. She wore what looked like rags for clothes, but what caught Bre's attention was a satchel tucked under her arm, secured with a strap slung across her shoulder.

Breanne couldn't be sure, but it looked as though the woman was about to attack Garrett for killing Jack. She could have anything in that bag, a knife or some other weapon.

Breanne pulled her pistol and took aim.

Wait! Garrett said, waving his hands. Switching from mind speak, he shouted in dökkálfar, "It's okay! You're okay! We won't hurt you."

The woman collapsed beside the mess that had been Jack and cried.

C'mon, we need to check on the others, Breanne said.

Bre? Gabi cried.

Gabi? Gabi, are you okay?

I'm okay, but Zerri! Oh, Zerri! Please don't be dead!

Breanne scanned the area. Near the mountain wall, Cerberus lay lifelessly across Zerri. The dragon queen showed no signs of movement either. Beneath the dragon, a pool of blood spread, filling the cracks between the stone cobbles.

Gabi was running toward the trapped dragon.

We've got to help her! Breanne said, as her brother's voice entered her mind.

Sages, sound off! Is everyone okay?

Breanne's mind filled with moans and chatter as the other sages climbed to their feet.

I feel like I got punched in the balls and the stomach at the same time, Lenny said. *David, you good?*

My head. It feels like it's split open, and my brains are falling out, David said.

Not a big loss, David, Lenny mocked.

The Last Gift

Screw you, Len! You know I saved your ass, and you still got jo—

Guys, um, we have a problem... a lot of them! Pete said.

Breanne looked ahead toward the hole in the wall and found Pete and Governess, who also looked mostly recovered, staring at a medium-sized brown dragon.

Um, I thought you were the smart one, Pete! So why aren't you running? Lenny said.

Right! Pete said, grabbing Governess by the hand and turning to run.

Three more dragons appeared from the hole: two grey ones and a larger greenish-brown one. The brown one set its sights on Pete and roared. Fire followed.

No! Pete! Garrett cried, reaching out a hand. *Too far. They're too far.*

Six more dragons appeared from the hole, and more were piling in behind them.

The others ran toward Breanne and Garrett.

Go! We got to get across the land bridge! Paul shouted.

Breanne couldn't understand what crossing the bridge was going to do to save them. Flying over water was easy for a dragon.

Before the fire engulfed Pete, Governess transformed into a four-legged animal reminiscent of a cheetah, but with additional long arms that reached out and pulled Pete on top of her. She darted to the side with inhuman speed, narrowly dodging the stream of dragon fire.

Standing next to Cerberus, Gabi was still trying to wake up Zerri.

We got to move to the bridge! Paul ordered.

Lenny and Tell passed them, followed by Governess and Pete.

Come on, Gabi! We got to go! she shouted, as she and Garrett backpedaled toward the land bridge.

I think she might be dead, Bre! Gabi said, choked with emotion and clearly unaware that dozens of dragons were flooding into Osonian.

David, get out of there! Garrett shouted.

More dragons piled in.

"What have you done with Taker?" a dragon shouted, though Breanne couldn't say which one.

One dragon far to her right noticed Cerberus and the queen lying in a heap. Like with Jack, when the dragon spoke in mind speak, they all heard it.

What is this? What has happened to our Queen of Queens and Cerberus the Mighty?

A dragon noticed David staggering away and darted in to bite him.

Kilug appeared, dropping his big axe from over his shoulder onto the dragon's neck. "No ye don't, ye overgrown lizard!" The dragon's head toppled.

Another hissed, snapping its jaws at Kilug, but the dwarf ran forward between its legs, axe slicing through one of the dragon's front legs at the joint.

David turned and let out a screech as another dragon lunged in. He swung his staff, connecting it with the side of the dragon's head in a golden burst of power.

The dragon dropped like a wet towel.

Run, David – dammit! Garrett shouted.

More dragons gathered in front of the hole in the great wall – forty, then fifty, and they just kept coming and coming.

They have killed the Mighty Cerberus and the Queen of Queens!

Avenge our Taker and Cerberus the Mighty!

Avenge the Queen of Queens!

Take the city!

Eat them all!

Breanne stood next to Garrett, motioning to David and Kilug. "Hurry!"

As the two finally reached them, Garrett shouted, "Nyana, run to us!"

The woman stood and ran, the mysterious satchel bouncing off her hip.

Breanne looked for Gabi, who was still talking to Zerri, trying to wake her up. The bulk of the two dead dragons hid her from the invading horde for now, but if she didn't get out of there, they would discover her soon enough.

You guys! What are you waiting for? We need to cross, Lenny shouted.

Stone and Key appeared next to them.

"My queen! The armies are safely across. We must go!"

Garrett drew his sword.

"Garrett, what are you doing?" Pete asked.

"We can't leave Gabi. They'll find her."

"We can't fight all of them! Our best chance is for her to hide and for us to cross! If we don't end up dead, we'll come back for her!" Paul urged.

Garrett shook his head. "Paul, those dragons will fly over and kill everyone! Key, Stone, and Saria – order the armies to retreat into the city. Maybe the stone buildings can offer them some protection. Governess, can you dart in and grab Gabi while I distract them by killing as many as I can?"

Governess bowed her head, her auburn locks falling into her face. "If this is your wish, my lord, but I am afraid you will not make it back."

"I... I will. Just get her back and I will join you after... now hurry."

It was a lie, and Breanne knew it was a lie. She knew it one hundred percent. No. He wouldn't be back. He was going to sacrifice himself.

The vision had told Breanne to lead him from the front.

They were missing something! Something important. She'd had one brief image of Garrett during the vision. He wasn't wearing his sweater or shirt. The lines on his skin were burning bright red, radiating the color of dragon eyes.

The dragons advanced, spreading out and crossing the field of cobbles. They were almost to the land bridge, almost close enough to breathe fire.

Yes! Take the city!

Kill them all and burn it to ash!

Today we feast!

Garrett raised his sword and started forward.

Breanne stepped in front of him, blocking his path. Spinning, she turned her back to the horde of dragons.

"What are you doing, Bre?"

"This isn't the way, Garrett."

"Then what?"

"Take off your sweater."

"What?"

"You trust me?"

Garrett handed her his sword and pulled off his sweater. The lines on his arms were glowing red.

"Your shirt too," she said.

Garrett frowned, but he obeyed, removing his shirt.

"My gods! He's a dragon master, but how?" Saria asked.

"What do you mean, how?" Lenny asked. "You had lots of them. Isn't that how you controlled the dragons?"

"Yes, but we create the conditions. A dragon must bleed onto an elf and then douse the blood-covered elf in fire. Only then do the runes form, and only after much training can a dragon master control a dragon. For this to happen as a natural occurrence would be incredibly unlikely, and to a human... I've never heard of such a thing."

"Well, it happened," Lenny said plainly.

"Bre, you better move," Garrett said, grabbing his sword.

Something Saria had just said clicked with Breanne. Control. "Garrett, look at me."

"Move, Bre!"

"Look me in my eyes," Breanne said.

"This is crazy!" he said, taking his eyes away from the hundreds of dragons creeping forward to cross the final yards.

"Just do it! Save me, Garrett," Breanne said, taking a step backward, then another. "Don't slow time. Forget that part of you and use the runes. I believe in you, Garrett!" She stepped back again.

"Breanne, stop!"

She walked back another step and then another as she watched everyone's eyes widen.

From behind Garrett, Paul ran forward.

Pete focused his eyes.

Governess said a word in the gods' language.

Key pulled back her atlatl.

None of them believed what she believed. None of them believed he could save her, but none knew what she knew.

Behind her, a dragon hissed. The smell of its foul breath washed over her neck.

"Sis! Please!" Paul shouted.

The dragon's roar drowned out all their shouts and screams. None of them could save her now. None of them could kill all the dragons. She knew what came next.

Garrett's next words filled her mind, *Bre, please!* he begged in mind speak, running forward.

In mind speak she answered, *Control them. Make them stop. I believe in you with my whole heart! With my life!*

Light blossomed from behind her, casting her shadow on the stone. Garrett and the others' faces were set aglow in the light of blossoming fire.

All around her, the purple snow turned to purple rain.

64

Mercy

God Stones – Moon Ring 6
Osonian

Breanne became a dark shadow in front of Garrett until all he could see was her silhouette. Behind her, bright fire filled the throat of the leading dragon. But the roar was not a single roar. The roar quickly became a chorus. Dozens of mouths stretched open as fire ignited through the ranks.

Twice before, Garrett had tried to save Breanne and failed. He'd failed in the temple to save her from Apep, and he'd failed to save her from Pando back in Utah. In fact, she had saved him. Garrett didn't feel like he understood anything, but he understood this: Breanne Moore could not die. He would give his life one hundred times over if he could, but she could not die.

No. Not her. Not Bre! He shouted the command into the mind of the dragons. Not into the mind of one, but of all. *You will not breathe fire! You will not burn her!*

The red lines on Garrett's arms, chest, and back burned like never before, his own body radiating electric red until

The Last Gift

the runes themselves lifted from his body and projected into the air in front of him like a 3-D hologram.

Slowly, the glowing dragon throats faded to cool embers as hundreds of toothy mouths closed. The mass of dragons filling the paved field stood quietly now, staring at Garrett.

Garrett ran forward and grabbed Breanne's trembling body, hugging her. "I thought I lost you. I thought you were…" Tears spilled down his face.

"I knew you wouldn't let me be lost." Breanne smiled, but she looked like she might puke.

"I love you, Breanne."

"I love you too," she managed.

"Please don't ever do that again!"

"Well… Sometimes a girl's got to do what a girl's got to do," she said, glancing back to give the horde of dragons an uneasy look.

Garrett glanced back at the other way, first to the others and then across the land bridge. Thousands of humans and elves stood on the shore of Osonian, just as still as the dragons. "Apparently, my orders to take cover in the city didn't mean a lot."

Behind the armies, the father tree towered high above everything, like a massive mountain. It too was silent, as if waiting to see what came next.

Saria and the others approached cautiously. "Impossible. Even Syldan could control only three at once, and he was our greatest dragon master. You control not one or three, but all of them," she said in a trembling voice.

"That's my boy!" Lenny said, slapping his shoulder.

"They are yours to command. You can order them to do anything. You are their master now," Saria said.

Garrett took Breanne's hand and squeezed it.

Saria turned to face him squarely. "Did you hear me?

You're their master. You have an entire army of dragons enslaved to you. They can do your will if you order it so."

"No," Garrett said evenly. "They won't be my slaves or anyone else's."

"Then order them to destroy each other!"

Garrett looked at the dragons. In the surrounding air, the runes glowed brightly. *Breanne, do you see the dragon runes floating in the air?* he asked her in mind speak.

I don't see anything floating. Just the ones on your skin. They... they look like they are burning. Are you okay?

I'm fine, he answered. Then looking up at the army of dragons, he shouted as loud as he could, his voice carrying across the cobblestone and echoing off the great wall and mountainside, "Dragons! Hear me now! Go home. Go home and do not come back here!"

The dragons looked around as if suddenly lost and confused as to their purpose for being in Osonian at all.

Finally, one spoke into Garrett's mind, *We must leave this place.*

What followed was a flood of chatter from the horde.

Yes, we should return to the Mountains of Twelve!

We must name a new Queen of Queens.

Who cares about a queen? We need food.

I am hungry, and there is food in the Mountains of Twelve!

Yes! Plenty of fish!

So many!

There is nothing for us here!

We should never have come back to this awful place!

The dragon in front of Garrett flapped his wings, lifting from the ground. He flew straight up in the air, higher and higher. Others followed, wings pumping. Dozens rose and then dozens more. Wind stirred the snowy ground, gusting across Garrett's chest and arms, reminding him he was shirtless. The floating runes only he could see faded away and, as the dragons vanished over the wall, his skin cooled.

"You showed them mercy in freeing them," Saria said, her face a frown.

"But?" Garrett asked knowingly.

"But you realize that with an army like that under your control, you could rule Karelia? No one would dare oppose you."

Garrett shook his head. "Saria, just because you can, doesn't mean you should."

"I don't understand. What does that mean?" Saria asked.

"We'll get her there," Lenny said, smiling.

Across the field, Cerberus moved.

"Garrett look!" David said.

"Balls," Lenny said.

"Where's Gabi?" Breanne asked.

They ran across the stone field again, reaching Cerberus as the giant dragon flopped over, his wings slapping limply against the flat stones.

He looks pretty dead to me, Pete said.

Next to him, the Queen of Queens rose to her feet, her crown slightly askew.

"Zerri!" Breanne said. "And look! There's Gabi." She pointed at the girl, who now stood directly in front of the queen.

"Aye! Do we fight the foul beast?" Kilug asked, lifting his axe.

"Wait," Breanne said.

Gabi's voice filled Bre's mind. *I missed you, Zerri. I missed you, and I'm sorry.*

Zerri lowered her head and hissed into their minds, *You killed my mother. You used me. And worst of all, you lied to me!*

I know, Gabi said, putting out a hand to tell Breanne and

Garrett not to come any closer. *I did, and I don't care what you do to me! But I love you, Zerri! I love you, and that's the truth too!*

Panic swelled in Breanne as her heartbeat throbbed in her ears. *Please. Please, oh god, please.*

Zerri stared at Gabi for a long moment that felt like a hundred years. *I missed you too, Little Lion.*

Gabi ran forward and pressed her cheek against Zerri's, throwing her little arms around the dragon's chin.

Breanne let out a relieved laugh. "Thank god."

The Queen of Queens shuffled forward, one wing bent back all wrong, blood dripping from her belly, and scales missing where Cerberus had bitten into her. Reaching Garrett, she spoke aloud, "Garrett Turek, you too saved me. For when you killed Jack, Cerberus died. I would not have defeated him. For this I thank you."

Garrett nodded.

Zerri seemed to study Garrett. "The runes on your body were gifted to you in death by a powerful two-headed dragon. They bear their name, Sylanth. You are, as my mother explained to me, dragon marked. This gift is, however, finite in its power. Today, you used a great deal of power to control the horde. Even now, I see the runes in your skin have faded. To what extent this gift remains, I cannot say, but for at least a moment, you had the power to destroy all dragons of this world. Yet you used your power to save not only the creatures of Osonian but the dragons too. For this, I am forever in your debt."

"Thank you for explaining this to me, Queen Zerri," Garrett said.

Zerri bowed her head slightly, turning her attention back to Gabi. "Not only did Garrett save me, but you stopped Jack from poisoning me with Sentheye. Gabi the Lion, with my whole heart, I forgive you. From this day forward, I and

The Last Gift

all in my queendom are friends to you and humans, so long as you and yours are friends to the dragon."

Zerri looked at Saria next. "However, I will be curious to see if the elves seek forgiveness or war. I suppose only time will tell."

"Peace and forgiveness if I have anything to say about it, and I guess since I'm the king I get plenty of say." Lenny smiled up at Zerri.

"Guys, speaking of time, I hate to break up this little reunion, but every inch of my gut is telling me we need to cross that land bridge, and I mean now," Paul said.

"Paul, what's the big deal? They're gone! We're safe, bro! We won!" Lenny said, slapping the big guy on the shoulder.

Saria nodded. "Come. I want to show you the city – your city, King Lennard – and I'm sure your people will be excited to meet you."

They turned their backs to the great wall and walked toward the great Osonian and its father tree.

Lenny smiled. "Yeah? Cool, but my first order of business is to open this place up to everyone. Like it should be."

Saria shook her head. "Grand. I will have a full-time task ensuring you aren't assassinated."

Lenny smiled an ornery smile and looked up at the black-and-red-scaled dragon queen. "Zerri, please come with us and see the city that will be as much yours to visit as anyone else's."

Zerri nodded. "Yes. I should quite enjoy seeing the great gifting tree up close."

As they hurried back toward the land bridge, Garrett walked next to Breanne with her hand in his. Stone walked to his left while Key walked next to Bre.

"My queen, may I walk with you? We've much to discuss," Key said.

"I too would like a word," Stone said.

"You? What business have you with the queen?" Key asked.

Breanne smiled. "It's okay. I can talk to you both. Now who's going first?"

Stone nodded his head. "Please, proceed, Lady Key. My concerns can wait."

Silence.

Breanne turned. "Lady Key, what—"

Key fell forward, sprawling onto the ground, a long bone handle protruding from her back.

Behind them, a great horn blew.

65

Now Is Our Moment!

God Stones – Moon Ring 6
Osonian

Helreginn seethed with red anger. First his son, now his greatest warrior of the High Guard, Zebrog, lost to this war. No more asking others to lead. He was the king, and he would lead the battle through the wall. He would be first to kill, and if death were to find him, he would happily be first to die.

"Father, the dragons are fleeing!" said a nephilbock who looked like a smaller version of Gato. The king's twenty-first child, Wolog, was only half the warrior his brother had been.

"You will address me as king, or you will join your brother!" Helreginn answered, pointing his Shard Mountain steel at the young warrior's throat. He looked up, peering out from the edge of the forest. Forced to abandon the useless attempt to break through the door in the mountain wall, the king had led his army back to the edge of the battlefield. Once the dragons had broken through the wall, he'd known it wouldn't be long.

But this was unexpected. Why had the dragons fled? It wasn't possible they could have already killed and eaten the entire army of elves! There were humans inside too, hundreds of them! He'd seen them through the door before Zebrog fell. Even if they had eaten everyone, they wouldn't have left so soon. They would have stayed to let their full bellies settle and to take rest. No, they must have left for some other reason. But it was of no matter. More glory for him. More food for his army!

"Nephilbock! Now is our moment! Today we take the city and claim our kingdom! Follow your king! Through the wall!" Helreginn shouted.

The nephilbock banged their weapons off their chest plates. "Through the wall!"

King Helreginn ran forward, leading his army along the front of the great wall.

Arrows rained down and grunts of pain spread through the warriors behind him as arrows pricked the skin of his people like porcupine needles.

Glancing up into the swirling snow and black dots of arrowheads, the king grimaced. *I will see you all eaten alive for this.* A boulder banged down, not an arm's span away from him. Still, Helreginn pushed on.

Somehow unscathed, the king reached the hole in the wall. A hand grabbed his shoulder. "My king, please, let me go first!" a warrior in High Guard kraken bone armor pleaded.

This warrior was not one of his sons. "No, Mubor. Whatever risk lies beyond this threshold is for me to weigh. Stay close, but I will lead."

"My king, at least have the great wolves at your side," the concerned warrior pleaded.

"Yes. Obos! Toas! Come!" Despite protesting yips from

The Last Gift

pups too small to keep pace, the great wolves shot forward, darting from in between the ranks of nephilbock.

Flanked on either side by wolf fangs bared to bite, the king's lip curled to reveal his own gnarled yellow teeth. "Now, let us finish this!" Helreginn snarled and entered the hole. When he emerged on the other side, he saw the dead dragon. It was the three-headed dragon the false god had ridden upon, and it was dead. Scanning the area, he quickly spotted a group hurrying toward a land bridge, which led to a city of stone structures built around the trunk of the largest tree he'd ever seen – a tree so large it must be its own world. Helreginn smiled. Soon the city, the tree, and all its inhabitants would be his.

King Helreginn drew a long, bone-handled knife from his waistband, took aim, and threw. The knife swished through the air, burying itself into its target. "Sound the horn!" Helreginn shouted. "Obos! Toas! Attack!"

66

The Irony of His Fate

God Stones – Moon Ring 6
Osonian

"Key!" Breanne gasped, grabbing the woman under the arms and lifting to her feet.

"My... my... Tell!" Key shouted.

Everyone, run to the bridge! Paul shouted in mind speak.

They piled onto the land bridge and ran. Zerri in front led the way, bleeding badly and unable to fly with her broken wing.

Breanne looked back to find two massive wolves running toward them at breakneck speed. They were black as panthers but the size of Clydesdales. Behind them, the nephilbock charged.

Key moaned, "I... I can't... Tell... Tell!"

"We have to move!" Breanne urged.

Stone was there, wrapping his own arm under Key's. "Lady Key, you must move and move now!"

Breanne! You have to go! Garrett shouted.

I know, but Key is hurt bad!

The Last Gift

Suddenly Tell was there at her side too. "Oh, dear gods! Mother!" She knelt and pulled on her mother.

Key grabbed her daughter and pulled her close as she collapsed on the bridge.

In front of Breanne, a wolf leapt. She drew the nine and fired, missing three times before she finally connected. But one bullet would wouldn't stop an animal like this. It was like shooting a grizzly with a BB gun.

The wolf froze in the air. A second wolf leapt, and it too froze.

"Lenny!" Garrett shouted.

"My pleasure!" Lenny said, running past Bre, sword drawn. He leapt from the ground, meeting the wolf in the air as he swung the elvish blade in a high arc.

Garrett must have let go of time because the wolf sped back up as Lenny's sword sliced through its neck.

Time slowed again and the other wolf froze, but not Lenny. The boy spun, cartwheel flipped, and drove his sword into the other wolf's chest just as Garrett let go of time again. Both beasts dropped lifeless onto the bridge.

Beyond the bridge, a nephilbock roared with rage.

"We have to move!" Paul shouted.

"Tell. Listen... listen to me!" Key said, blood trickling from the corner of her mouth. "The queen is yours to advise. She will need... need you in the days to come. Make... me proud... as I know you will."

"No. No, Mother, please! David! David, hurry!" Tell begged.

"No... child. Not this time. Now... run!" She exhaled the last word as her eyes fixed in death.

"No!" Tell screamed. She jumped to her feet and wrenched back her atlatl. "I hate you!" she shouted, and threw the spear with a fierceness Breanne had never seen.

The spear flew true.

The lead nephilbock twisted, the spear missing his head by inches only to sink deep into the narrow eye of a much younger nephilbock behind him. The nephilbock crumpled to the ground.

The old nephilbock looked back, then forward. He raised his sword and shouted, "Eat them all!"

Tell collapsed in a heap of tears.

Breanne grabbed one arm, the elven girl Garrett called Nyana grabbed the other, and together they dragged the screaming girl away.

Stealing a glance back, Breanne saw Garrett and Lenny walking backward, swords raised against a hundred giants running onto the bridge.

It's too far! We're not going to make it! Garrett called out in mind speak to all who could hear.

Paul's voice, all will and desperation, filled her mind. *Just get across! We have an entire army on the other side! We can fight them as they funnel off the bridge!*

But Breanne knew Garrett was right. It was too far. The distance across was still more than a football field away. Ahead, she could see the soldiers forming ranks, readying themselves for the battle to come. Others waved their hands, urging them on, shouting words too far away to be heard.

Metal cracked against metal.

Breanne let go of Tell and spun back.

The old giant had swung his sword and was swinging again. Garrett blocked the strike as another nephilbock stepped alongside and swung an axe. Lenny ducked and rolled.

"This is it! We have to fight!" Breanne shouted, drawing her Toledo sword and running back toward her friends.

In her peripheral vision, she saw something shoot from the water. At first, her mind didn't understand what it was seeing, but then the bay erupted in a boil as dozens of tentacles torpedoed from the water. Oh god no! Not another monster! Not now!

"Holy shit balls!" Lenny shouted, falling back onto his ass as a thick black tentacle shot past him.

A tentacle wrapped the old nephilbock around the waist. Another grabbed the one next to him around the throat, jerking them both off the bridge and high into the air. Tentacles were everywhere, coming from both sides of the bridge, tangling the giants and lifting them, dragging them, sometimes throwing them.

～

Helreginn fought the sea demon as she ripped him from the land bridge. How could he have been so foolish? How could he not have known what would wait for him in the oceans of Karelia? The sea goddess and mother of Hafgufa had found out what he had done.

And so it was, a fate sealed before he ever left the center of the Earth. Helreginn had killed the daughter of Hafgufa, made a throne of her skull and armor of her bones. Later, Helreginn had come to the surface of Earth and taken part in the slaying of Hafgufa herself when the sea demon had surfaced to avenge her daughter's death. And now, on another world far from Earth, he'd pay his debt to the sea goddess. This was the irony of his fate. *I'm coming, Gato! I'm coming, Zebrog. Soon I will stand alongside you on the battlefields of Valhalla. I'm coming!*

67

The Lowest Class

God Stones – Moon Ring 6
Osonian

High above, Breanne watched as the old giant chopped at the tentacle with his sword, but another tentacle darted in and snatched the sword away. Tentacles wrapped around the old giant's legs, arms, neck, and waist, pulling like a pack of hungry wolves fighting over a piece of meat. And when the old nephilbock had stretched out until he could stretch no more, they pulled harder still, and the giant pulled apart.

Breanne turned her face away.

"Guys, we are so screwed!" David cried out.

"No. No, we aren't! Just don't attack the tentacles. As long as we don't attack, they aren't here for us," Paul said knowingly.

"This is Rán, isn't it?" Breanne asked.

Paul jogged up to her, his face a big smile. "Roger that!" he said, taking Tell and lifting her into his arms. "Let's move!"

They ran down the rest of the bridge as the kraken fed on the nephilbock, not allowing a single giant to pass.

When Breanne and the others stepped off the bridge, the crowd of humans and elves erupted in cheers. The crowd parted, giving a wide berth to Zerri and allowing the sages and their companions through. Together, they made their way toward the city.

Breanne gave a last glance back. Across the bay, several hundred giants filled the stone field behind the wall. Many stood along the shore, chopping at the kraken tentacles as they lashed out from the bay. It was as if the giants were building up their nerve to charge into the water. Farther back, across the stone field, those elves still alive to defend the wall were surely lost now as the giants invaded the wall itself.

As more nephilbock poured into the cobblestone field, Breanne knew that outside the wall, thousands more waited to enter. She wondered how long it would be before they simply charged into the bay and attacked the krakens head on. Thousands of giants against what she believed were three or maybe four individual kraken. The nephilbock would take heavy casualties and for those that made it, the Osonian army would be there to meet them. Still, the thought caused shivers to run down her spine. They could come. Would come. The only question was when.

They passed between stark white buildings of carved stone that reminded Breanne of the city of Cloud, only these structures were affixed not to a mountain but around the trunk of the massive tree. Fully under the canopy now, she looked up to see the underside of cities hanging high above. From beneath them, a mass of roots and dirt tapered down to points like ice cream cones. She had no idea what held them together. "Saria? What's with the cities that hang from the tree?"

"Ah, those are Osonian's Aerie of Seven. Originally, each of the gods' favorites had a place here, but my people won the wars of old and took all the cities. Then we built the great wall."

"How do you get up there?" she asked.

Saria smiled. "There are many ways, both inside the bark of the tree and via counterweights used to take up larger loads. Please, this way," she said, standing to the side and pointing down a set of twisting steps. Until this point, they had been climbing; now it seemed they would descend.

As Tell passed, she paused, swallowing down emotion. "It seems to me your greed is killing the tree."

Saria's smile changed to a sneer. "I understand that your mother was just killed, but you would be wise—"

"Do not speak to me of wisdom, elf! And do not speak of my mother!"

Saria drew her dagger.

"Stop!" Breanne said, stepping between them. "We're not enemies! Not anymore! The enemy is out there." She pointed back the way they had come. "On the other side of that bay, thousands upon thousands of giants are trying to figure out how to get to this side and eat us alive! So hear me when I say this stops now." Breanne turned. "Lenny, tell her."

"Bre's right, Saria. It's time for both of you to bury this. We have much bigger problems."

Saria bowed slightly. "As you wish… my king."

"Fine," Tell said, stomping past him.

"Wow, Len, you travel halfway across the universe and still find a way to piss off the opposite sex," Pete jabbed.

"Well, I haven't managed to get backhanded across the face yet, so I guess I'm still doing better than you."

"Touché," Pete conceded.

"Saria, Tell isn't wrong, is she? I mean, the part about the tree dying?" Garrett asked.

Saria shook her head. "No," she admitted. "We've known for some time Metsavana has been sick."

"Not enough Ice Ember to sustain him?" Bre asked.

"At first, maybe, but he no longer bestows gifts and hasn't for many moon cycles. His leaves are steadily falling, his bark is discolored, and his branches are drooping," Saria said.

"He is sick, Saria. Metsavana's roots have dried out. I've seen this myself. He doesn't gift because he can't! I suspect he draws the Sentheye through his roots. Without the ability to draw on the Sentheye, he can't give gifts," Tell said, her tone sharp.

"How could you know this? How could you have seen his roots? Are you a seer?" Saria asked.

"Oh, are you surprised a human could know something you don't?" Tell snapped.

"Tell, please," Lenny pleaded.

Tell crossed her arms. "No. I'm no seer. And I am not at liberty to speak of the secrets that have kept my people alive and safe from elves. It is enough to say I have witnessed the retraction of Metsavana's roots firsthand."

The stairs narrowed again. Zerri's wings scraped along the walls. Any narrower and she was going to get stuck.

"Our only hope in saving those waiting back on Earth is if Metsavana helps us," Garrett said worriedly.

"I do not believe the tree will help you for any amount of Ice Ember, but you are welcome to try. We are almost there," Saria said. "How much have you brought with you? Though I feel it is unlikely, perhaps if the amount is substantial enough, the father tree will give you the gift you seek."

"We don't have any," Garrett said.

"What? Then how will you ask for a gift?"

"Oh, I have a little! I found two small fragments before we found the big piece!" Pete said, reaching into his pocket.

"Here, you can have it!" he said, dropping them into Garrett's open palm.

"Thanks, Pete," Garrett said, clearly trying to hide his disappointment.

"Maybe there's another way," Nyana said. It was the first time she'd spoken since they crossed the bridge.

"Yes. I have been meaning to ask, why was this peasant accompanying the human and the three-headed dragon? And why on Karelia are you with us now? You should be seized, stretched on a rack, or beheaded." Saria looked at the girl with disgust.

"She's with us because I want her to be," Garrett said firmly.

Saria pulled a face. "She is the lowest class of the dökkálfar, fit only for fetching or cleaning."

Nyana cowered into herself. Her face twisted in fear, and for a second Breanne thought she was going to bolt. "It's okay, Nyana."

"Did I mention we are abolishing the class system, effective now?" Lenny said.

A horror-stricken Saria looked over at Lenny.

"You will get used to it, babe. We're going to make a lot of changes around here."

"What is a babe? Are you calling me new? Suggesting I am dimwitted?" Saria asked.

"What? No! It's a compliment. Never mind," Lenny said.

"Oh, your backhand is coming, Len. It's coming," Pete said, smiling.

Finally, they stepped off the last step onto a bone-white herringbone travertine courtyard. The courtyard itself was dotted with sculptures, fountains, and fire pits. Across the yard was an area of exposed trunk stretching from one side of the courtyard to the other before disappearing behind stone structures that melded seamlessly into the tree.

The Last Gift

"This way," Saria said, leading them across the deserted courtyard.

When they approached the wall of the tree, Breanne could see the visages of seven gods carved into the face of the tree, one for every favorite. Dragon, dwarf, tree, mermaid, human, dökkálfar, and nephilbock. In the center of the carvings was a shallow opening, only about the size of a shoebox. The grain of the wood seemed to curve around the opening, as if the trunk had grown that way naturally.

They gathered around the opening in the tree.

"So this is it?" Garrett asked.

"This is the offering portal," Saria said. "Place your gift inside and make a wish."

Garrett looked down at the two small slivers of Ice Ember.

"Wait. Nyana, you said there might be another way. What did you mean?" he asked.

"You're asking the peasant? She would never be allowed to—"

"Saria! Knock it off," Lenny said. "It's okay, Nyana, tell us, what did you mean?"

The girl nodded slowly, her face pulled back as if waiting to be struck. "I... I think you should offer him these," she said, lifting the strap of the satchel over her head and handing it to Garrett.

Garrett frowned curiously, taking the satchel. He opened it and peered inside, but Breanne didn't need to see inside to know what he'd found. The glow of otherworldly light washed over Garrett's face in a color her mind couldn't comprehend. Yet this was a familiar color that she'd first seen at the bottom of the money pit on Oak Island.

Garrett's eyes went wide.

68

The Wish

God Stones – Moon Ring 6
Osonian

Garrett gasped and closed the bag. "You have to be kidding me."

"Well done, Nyana," Zerri said. "When we left the Mountains of Twelve, Jack refused to leave the God Stones behind. He insisted on carrying them with him."

"Could this work?" Garrett asked.

Saria's brows pinched together in thought. "I don't know. No one has ever offered anything other than Ice Ember. Certainly no one would dare offer their God Stone – for how could one wish for something more powerful than a God Stone? I strongly recommend you consider this action carefully."

"With these, I could open the portal home," Garrett said.

"You would need to know how to assemble them into the Sound Eye, and for that you would need Ogliosh or one of his nephilbock with the remembered knowledge," Zerri said.

"But we still wouldn't have the item for my people to remain unbound," Governess said.

"Unless we could give Pando a God Stone," Pete said.

"Negative," Paul said. "Even if you could assemble the Sound Eye, open the portal, somehow disassemble the stones—"

"Disassembly is easy enough – that I could show you," Zerri said.

"Okay," Paul continued, "but we would still have to cross back here before the portal closed."

"And none of this solves the other problem," Tell said.

"Other problem?" Garrett asked.

Breanne took his hand in hers. "The tree, Garrett. This solution doesn't save Metsavana."

Everyone stared at him, thinking, trying to solve what felt like an impossible puzzle. They had a bag of God Stones, six to be exact, and he needed all seven to open the portal, which meant Zerri would also have to be willing to let him borrow the one in her crown. But even then, he had no way of assembling them and no way of knowing if this would satisfy Pando and still allow them to get back. He certainly couldn't give her all of them, so he would have to disassemble them and then get back with the remaining six. How would that work? Once the stones were disassembled, the portal would close – which meant they couldn't be on Earth's side of the portal with the stones disassembled.

"Garrett?" Breanne said quietly.

He looked up, meeting her eyes.

Everyone was still staring expectantly. Waiting for an answer they expected him to have. They had followed him across worlds, fought armies of monsters, risked everything to be here right now, and he didn't know what to do. And where in the hell was Turek in all this? Garrett turned his back to them and looked at the dying tree. *Where are you, Turek?*

Garrett didn't have a solution, but he had a feeling. Metsavana needed help. Of course, James, his mother, Bre's dad, Ed, and all the humans still alive on Earth needed help too. But the decision before him wasn't whether he should save the father tree or Earth. The decision was whether to risk saving neither to save them all.

Garrett looked back at the others, nodded, and stepped forward, approaching the offering portal.

"Garrett? What are you doing?" Breanne asked.

"The right thing... I hope." He looked down at his fist and opened his palm to reveal two small slivers of Ice Ember. He dropped the small bits into the bag. This was everything he had. He stepped forward and tried to place the bag in the cubby hole, but it wouldn't fit. Damn!

Zerri cleared her dragon throat, and it came out sounding like a growl. "Perhaps you should... Well, perhaps... Perhaps I should..."

"It's okay, Zerri. Your stone wouldn't fit anyway. Heck, I'm not even sure I can get all of these in here at once," Garrett said, as he positioned the stones through the bag, making sure each God Stone was stacked atop the other. Following his instinct, he pushed the bag against the cubby. It still wouldn't go, but if he turned it just so... there! The bag slid into the hole without an inch of room to spare.

Garrett drew in a deep breath. *Please, Metsavana, this is all I have.* Kneeling on one knee, he placed both hands on the tree, bowed his head, and made a wish.

The portal glowed brightly. Garrett shielded his eyes as if trying to look into the sun.

The tree shook. The ground shook. It was like he'd triggered an earthquake. "Is this normal?" Garrett asked, standing and backing away from the bright cubby hole. What had he done? Was the whole thing going to fall over?

"This is definitely not normal," Saria said, her expression fixed in concern.

The light faded as, around them, seven shapes appeared in the courtyard, masked in a veil of mist. Somehow, Garrett knew what he was looking at – Sentheye. Wind whipped the Sentheye into a swirl and it dissipated. Garrett stared then, his eyes not believing what he saw.

He was looking at the seven creators as each solidified, taking the form of their favorites. His wish had been granted.

Behind him, Metsavana grew still once more.

Saria dropped to her knees, bowing her head at the feet of Ereshkigal, a stunningly beautiful elf.

Next to her floated a mermaid.

"Rán!" Paul said, running to her.

She smiled, throwing her arms around his neck. "My love," she said.

Next to her was a familiar dwarf, Durin. "Kilug, me lad. Ye boys done well," he said, a smile buried somewhere under the thickest beard ever grown.

Next to him stood something shaped like a tree but made of jewels, gold, and silver.

"Druesha," Governess announced, kneeling before the tree.

A quite frightening-looking nephilbock stood next to her, smiling. His parted lips revealed a mouth overstuffed with shark teeth.

Next to the giant stood a dragon with a hundred heads. But it was only about fifteen feet tall, as if it had shrunk itself to the space, which made its heads, especially, look almost laughably small.

Beside the dragon stood an old man in a white robe. "My

wish! You came!" Garrett smiled, feeling the emotion choking his throat.

Turek smiled a child's grin. "I never doubted you, my boy."

"We still don't have a way to get back to Earth. And we don't have a magic item for Pando to keep her unbound," Garrett said.

"Oh, I don't know about that," Turek said, giving Garrett a slight wink.

One of Typhon's dragon heads spoke. "Zerri, I am quite pleased with you. You of all the favorites kept your God Stone. If ever there was a winner of the game, it is I. It is my favorite that kept her God Stone. It is my favorites who now hold the power. I am very pleased indeed."

Sudden arguing broke out among the creators.

"Garrett, what's happening?" Breanne asked.

"I… I don't know!"

"Typhon!" Zerri shouted, and all the creators fell suddenly silent.

"Yes, my child," Typhon said proudly.

"You seem to be confused."

"Confused? In what way, child?"

"I don't have a God Stone," Zerri said.

The dragon's heads cocked to the side like a hundred curious pups. "Yet it sits plainly atop your head for all to see."

"True. It sits atop my head, but it is not my God Stone. You see, I was already going to give this to Garrett before he placed the other stones into Metsavana, but alas, it would not fit. It would not fit because Metsavana knew this stone was needed for another great purpose."

"What are you talking about? What great purpose?" Typhon asked with great annoyance.

"I now understand why I was hesitant. I understand the overwhelming feeling to hold fast just a little longer. But that feeling is gone, and what I am supposed to do is clear. This God Stone belongs to Garrett Turek."

Garrett looked at Bre as she mouthed the word, "What?"

Garrett felt his jaw hit the floor.

"Come forward, Garrett Turek, and claim your God Stone."

Garrett stepped forward but froze when Typhon's heads shouted all at once. "This is preposterous! Why would you do this? Why would you give away the last God Stone to… to a human?"

Around the courtyard, humans and elves alike pushed for the stairs or cowered down on their hands and knees in fear of the god's wrath.

Zerri, however, continued unafraid. "This is no mere human, Typhon. This is my friend, and he saved my life. But more, he showed mercy to my dragons – your dragons! He could have simply forced them to destroy themselves, wiping your entire creation from the planet! In return for his mercy, he has asked for nothing." Zerri paused, but her expression said there was more she wanted to say, and so she did. "But you care about only one thing, and it isn't me. It's winning this game of yours. Well, this is no game for us, Typhon. I lost my mother. Gabi lost her parents. No. This is no game to us."

Typhon seemed to swell, looking suddenly bigger, twice as big as before. All his heads sneered and all bared teeth.

Zerri ignored him, seemingly unconcerned, as she looked upon Garrett with a dragon's smile. "This is the last gift I have to offer you, my friend. Please take it." Zerri forced her broken wing to move as she lowered herself with a painful hiss and bowed her head.

Despite the menacing creator looking as though he might breathe flame from every one of his sinister mouths, Garrett swallowed thickly and stepped forward, reaching for the crown.

He wondered how in the heck he was supposed to manage lifting such a large crown. It was as big around as a garbage can lid and must have weighed as much as a car tire. Hesitantly, he took hold of the massive crown with both hands, lifting it from the dragon's head. To his surprise, it weighed almost nothing. As Garrett lowered the giant crown, he gasped. It was shrinking right before his eyes. Slowly, his hands drew together as the crown resized to fit the head of the one who now held it.

"Whoa," Pete breathed.

"Thank you, Zerri," Garrett said, feeling the power of the God Stone radiating through the crown and into his hands.

Typhon settled back onto his haunches. "You may think this wise now, but when this dragon marked casts you in chains, do not look to me to save you, Queen of Queens."

"I'll take my chances," Zerri said.

Typhon's two hundred eyes bore into Zerri. The courtyard was momentarily silent as the creator seemed to contemplate something. "Very well," he said and spoke a word of power.

Zerri's missing scales grew anew. Her twisted wing straightened and healed, and she was once more made whole.

"Thank you, Lord Typhon," Zerri said.

"Despite my displeasure in your most recent action, I couldn't very well sit here and watch one of my own suffer. Especially after she faced a three-headed abomination and avenged the murders of our elder dragons."

Zerri bowed.

Turek smiled. "I think there may be some hope for you after all, brother."

Behind Garrett, a great creak sounded from the father tree, reminiscent of a moan. He looked up at the drooping branches high above. The cities of seven leveled out. Above them, massive blossoms bloomed pink and red flowers.

Leaves even bigger than the ones they had ridden on the Climbing River budded and grew to full size right before their eyes.

"Look!" Governess pointed. Garrett spun to find the formerly dry and diseased bark of the great tree flushing rich with a blue-green hue.

"Well, it seems you have returned Metsavana to his former glory," Druesha said.

"Indeed," Turek said, smiling. "Now, let's get you back to Earth and keep that promise you made."

"So it isn't too late?" Breanne asked.

"If you are asking whether you have made the deadline set forth by Pando, the answer is no, you have not."

Garrett's stomach turned, and when he looked at Breanne her eyes filled and threatened to spill.

"I knew it! I saw it in my dreams… horrible things," Breanne said, tears running down her cheeks. "What I saw… it really happened."

"Now hold on. All may not be lost. You are late, this is true, but whether you spent another year or five or fifty really does not matter as long as we open the portal, and you keep your word."

"I don't understand. What does that mean?" Pete asked.

The sound of a metal rake dragging through gravel pulled their attention to the imposing nephilbock creator as he cleared his throat. "What it means is that we can open the portal just after it last closed."

Garrett's face drew up as he tried to puzzle it out.

"You're saying we can go back to the very moment we left?" David asked.

Turek's eyes twinkled. "Just after, yes."

Could it be that simple? Garrett wasn't sure how James had been faring when he left or how many Keepers he'd already lost, but this meant they still had a chance to save them all!

Turek turned to the other creators. "Who's up for a road trip?"

"What be a road trip?" Kilug asked.

Rán frowned. "The journey requires no roads, brother."

Turek sighed. "Who wants to go to Earth?"

Saria cleared her throat and stood looking at Ereshkigal. "I am sorry, goddess, but there are thousands of nephilbock outside the wall, likely plotting their attack. I must stay and defend this city. She turned to Lenny. "As the King of Osonian, you should stay here and aid in its defense."

Ereshkigal pulled a face, twisting her beauty into something hateful. "Yes. King Lenny. You should know, Lennard Wade, I do not approve of your existence. However, I will allow it. As I have concluded, the dökkálfar will not accept you, and this problem will take care of itself soon enough."

"Well, you know, you're pretty until you talk. Then it's all ugliness. That's okay, Resh. I'll enjoy how pissed off it makes you when I prove you wrong."

"Resh? Well, I never—"

"And you never will with that attitude, lady," Lenny said, cutting off the elvish creator.

Turek laughed. "Do not fear, Lennard Wade. I not only believe in your existence, but I welcome it with open arms!"

"Okay, but the nephilbock?" Saria reminded them.

The giant cleared his throat again. "You needn't worry about the nephilbock, little one. Ogliosh has arrived in full force with all the might of Karelia's nephilbock."

"Aurgy?" Turek turned to his brother. "You were busy indeed when you won the spin. But tell me, are you going to wipe them out just for being mixed with humans? I thought we were progressing past this."

"No, Turek. I have given specific instructions to Ogliosh.

The Last Gift

He will give the Earth-born nephilbock a choice – leave these lands or die."

Garrett watched as Turek's face shifted to concern.

"Oh, do not look upon me like that, brother. You must understand, they are angry, vengeful, and now kingless. If left unchecked, they will destroy this city and, with it, Metsavana."

Garrett had seen plenty of these things up close with their shark teeth. A shiver ran down his spine as he remembered the one David killed with the tennis shoes still holding feet in them. Let the big giants kill the little ones for all he cared as long as they left this place and never came back.

Turek nodded. "I understand. Now, if we are all happy, may we depart?"

Garrett squeezed Breanne's hand. Were they really about to see their parents?

"Ed and Pops! Hooah! Let's do this!" Paul said, still holding Rán's hand.

"Gather close to me," Turek said, then spoke the words of power.

Directly in front of them, a portal opened like a window to another world.

A window to Earth.

69

Road Trip

Saturday, May 7 – God Stones Day 31
Rural Chiapas State, Mexico

Breanne felt Garrett's excitement as his hand squeezed hers. She wanted to be excited too, but none of them had shared her nightmares. None of them had seen what she had. Garrett hadn't watched Elaine carry Apep's head around as she talked to it. Paul hadn't seen what their father looked like after six months of being held prisoner on the pyramid. And none of them had heard the strange bird tell James he was about to die horribly.

As Breanne prepared to step through the portal, a big part of her feared what they would find on the other side. What point in time would they arrive? What had happened to her dad... to Ed? If they...if they were dead, she wouldn't be able to bear it.

Garrett stepped forward, pulling her along. She felt her hand sweat in his as her heart thumped in her ears. They were really doing this. They were going back to Earth.

When Breanne stepped from the cool Osonian courtyard

into the dry Mexican heat, she found the temple roof empty. She immediately began scanning the area, knowing exactly what she was looking for. The others piled through behind them. All the sages, Kilug, Governess, and the creators gathered on the empty rooftop. "Not empty," she breathed as she found what she was looking for.

"What's that?" Garrett asked.

"Look! Apep's head," she whispered, observing that it wasn't rotted. It looked… fresh. The rest of Apep lay crumpled only a couple yards away. As she glanced about, there were other signs too. From beyond the southern part of the roof, smoke rose. "El Tule," she said, pointing at the smoke. She knew if she looked over the side she would find the broken tree smoldering right where it had fallen the night they had opened the portal to Karelia – this very night.

The sound of feet slapping stone came from the stairwell.

Everyone turned to look as the man Breanne recognized as James from her dream emerged in a run. This version of James had no limp, no scab-covered knuckles, and no frailness about him. He slid to a stop, his eyes going wider and wider as he looked from the portal to the creators, and finally to Garrett.

"It's okay, James. Don't be frightened," Garrett said, letting go of Breanne's hand and holding up both of his own palms out. "Easy, bro. It's okay."

James's eyes darted to Turek.

The old man in the robe smiled. "It has been a long time, James Paul."

James stepped forward. "You came back! I… I…"

"I know, James. I know. You have Garrett and his friends to thank for this. I've very little to do with it. Oh, pardon me for a moment." Turek turned to the nephilbock creator. "Brother Aurgy, would you kindly see to it that the nephilbock sleeping on the stairs don't wake up just yet?" He pointed over the west side of the temple.

"Brother?" James said, pulling a face.

The enormous giant took three strides to the west side of the roof and spoke in the language of the gods.

"Garrett!" Elaine exclaimed, appearing from the stairs. The last time Breanne had seen the woman was in her dream, months from now. In the dream, Garrett's mom had completely lost it. She'd looked frail and close to death. But not this Elaine. This woman may have been travel-worn and exhausted, but she was healthy and vibrant – and she was sane. Breanne's eyes didn't linger on Garrett's mom for long as she was followed closely by…

"Daddy!" Breanne shouted, running toward her father. She couldn't believe it! It was really him! He was alive and he was okay! He was thin, but not as thin as she'd seen in her vision.

"Pops!" Paul shouted, darting forward.

"Baby girl! Son!" he shouted, his voice breaking as he reached for them with outstretched arms.

Breanne threw her arms around her dad, tears spilling down her own face. "Oh, Daddy, I thought… I was worried you… oh, you've lost so much weight!"

"Now, now, I'm fine. Travel has been rough on your old man, but I'm here… by god, I'm here! We've James to thank for that."

Garrett let go of his mother and hugged James. "Thank you for getting them here safe, James."

"Yes. Thank you," Paul said, nodding toward James.

For the briefest moment James seemed to go somewhere else, as if reflecting back on how far they'd traveled or perhaps what dangers they'd faced. "I don't know how you guys did it, Garrett, but you're here and you brought Turek and these other – what? – gods back with you. You were only gone for a moment! I don't understand."

"Let's just say for us it was a lot longer."

James nodded along, but Breanne could see confusion in the man's face. "When you spoke to me a few moments ago, I—"

"Spoke to you?" Garrett asked, sharing a confused look with Breanne.

"Sorry, maybe it was a lot longer for you, but for me it was only a moment. You said, you were sorry and told me to keep them safe."

Garrett nodded. "That's right. We tried to wait, but Apep had other plans."

"I see, and now you hold a strange crown with a single God Stone embedded within it."

"It's a long story, but one I will be happy to tell you all about when we get back home."

"Home. I would like that," James said, forcing a smile.

"What is it, James?" Garrett asked.

James shifted uncomfortably. "For a moment, I doubted you. And I doubted Turek. When I saw the portal close, I felt sick. I had this awful feeling. I thought… I… Garrett, I hate to think what would have happened to these people if you hadn't come back. I just hate to think of the horror we might have faced."

Breanne smiled as she wiped her eyes on the sleeve of her grey hoodie. But behind the smile, a nightmare she wouldn't wish upon anyone flashed through her mind with precision clarity. She wished she could forget the horror of what would have been, but she knew she could not. Instead, she pushed the awful thoughts to the back of her mind as she took Garrett's hand in hers. "Garrett wasn't going to let anything keep us from getting back here."

Garrett grinned at her. "None of us could have done it

alone. It took all of us to get here, but we're here and only death could have kept us away."

"I believe you — one hundred percent, little brother." James looked at him again. "You're so different from the kid I knew back in Petersburg."

Her dad stepped back, appraising her anew.

"Daddy? What?"

"Yes. James is right. I see it too. My little girl. You're a woman."

"Dad!" Breanne said, embarrassed.

Garrett smiled.

"And you, my son. There is something different about you too!" her father said, grabbing Paul by the shoulders and giving them a squeeze.

Keepers were arriving on the roof now. A doe-eyed girl who couldn't have been much older than Breanne appeared next. She had fiery red hair and a freckled face. She froze in fear, not able to comprehend what she was seeing — no doubt trying to understand why a dragon, a nephilbock, and other strange creatures were here simply chatting with them.

James raised his hands. "It's alright, Annie! Everyone, listen to me. I know this seems strange, but we are among friends! We are with the gods! Rejoice, for Garrett has returned with Turek, and the portal is open!"

More feet clapped against the stone as six fully armed soldiers appeared from the stairwell, handguns sweeping this way and that as they emerged.

"DeKeyser, shield wall on my count," a familiar man with a salt-and-pepper beard shouted.

"Shawn? It's okay, Shawn! There's no threat here." Garrett said, stepping forward. "You're among friends."

The Ultra Six kept their guns trained on the dragon and the giant, unease and confusion twisting their faces.

"Jenna?"

The Last Gift

"Impossible. I can't read them. Their mojo is... well, it's overwhelming," the woman breathed.

Shawn stepped forward, his eyes sharp, finger still on the trigger of his nine mil. "Did you do it, kid? Did you save the world?"

Garrett and Breanne looked at each other. "I sure hope so."

Shawn nodded. "And all these... these things are with you?"

"Uh-huh," Garrett said, a grin stretching across his face.

Shawn holstered his weapon and nodded to the others.

The others relaxed a little and holstered their weapons too.

"I thought you had to get back to the States and report to the president?" Garrett asked.

"Yeah, well that was the plan until we saw... well, what looked like one hell of a lightning show followed by... what I'm guessing was a portal to another world," Shawn said, looking past the creators into the Osonian courtyard. "Looks smaller than it did earlier." The rugged soldier pushed at a wad of tobacco with his tongue. "Just what the hell is happening here, kid?"

"Yeah. That's a long st—"

Below, the forest emitted a deafening creak. Breanne turned, squinting into the darkness to see. Light from the portal found its way to the forest below. The vast valley, once scorched by dragon fire and void of all vegetation, was now filled with a forest of trees from all different parts of the continent.

The creaking, Breanne realized, was a parting of the forest. A path formed between the trees, and along it walked a woman too tall to be human or giant. Breanne knew what she was looking at, but Garrett confirmed it.

"Pando."

70

So Long

Saturday, May 7 – God Stones Day 31
Rural Chiapas State, Mexico

Garrett peered down from atop the tallest pyramid in Mexico, maybe the tallest in the world. Below, Pando walked up the stairs. When she reached the temple, she simply grew up the fifty-foot wall. Her neck extended, pushing her face out to hover a few feet above the temple roof. Pando's head shifted into a snake's nest of woody roots, all knotted and balled up as they moved within each other. A new shape formed, and suddenly the human, Nefertiti-like version of Pando appeared, standing on the roof. Her long gown trailed back to the now-headless structure that stood next to the temple wall. The visual made it appear the trailing gown was spilling up out of the larger headless structure's neck and onto the roof.

Keepers gasped, backing away from the tree queen.

A small man, oil-slicked and covered in ants, appeared from the stairwell, followed by a tall Indigenous American woman.

Breanne leaned close, whispering in Garrett's ear. "It's Jurupa and that little man, I... I saw him in my dream. Pando called him the 'Devil's Garden.'"

Garrett remembered the too-tall woman, but what was with the little wet guy? "Why does he look like he's covered in Vaseline... and are those ants?"

"Yeah, and I think it's some kind of acid."

Pando's neck creaked as her head twisted to fix eyes on Governess. "Governess Larrea. I see you have ensured the return of the descendant. This pleases me. But how, pray tell, have you achieved this so quickly? And who are these creatures you are keeping company with? A nephilbock? A dragon? A...

Druesha, in tree form, glided forward. Her emerald trunk seemed to glow from within as her golden leaves rattled musically, like a hundred wind chimes. Light from the portal filtered through her majestic foliage, casting golden rays onto the stone roof.

"Druesha!" Pando said, bowing low.

"Yes, daughter. It is I."

"Then these must be—"

"Yes. We are all here."

Jurupa and the little ant-covered man followed their queen's lead and bowed.

"To what do I owe this honor?" Pando asked.

"The honor is mine. Too long have I ignored the creations I placed on this world. I am here to ask you, daughter, do you wish to come with me? Do you wish to come home to Karelia?"

Pando's face crinkled as a wave of wood grain radiated through her skin. "No. Earth is my home. And these trees are my forest." Her attention turned to the greying old man, her smile falling. "What I wish is for Turek to explain himself. What I wish is for this so-called god to testify in front of all of you as to why he allowed his creations to break their word and destroy us by the thousands!" Her voice rose with each word.

Turek stepped forward. "Pando. I am sorry you and yours suffered. I am sorry I never came back to you. Time is a tricky thing for one not bound by it. For you, this was an unfathomable period. For me, these last few hundred years were only a blink. I am here now, and my descendant is here to keep the promise he made."

Garrett stepped forward and held out the crown.

Pando looked down. "A God Stone?" she asked.

Garrett nodded. "Actually, it's the dragons' God Stone."

Pando looked at Zerri. "Who are you, dragon?"

"I am the daughter of Azazel. I am the Queen of Queens."

"And you give this stone willingly? You, the daughter of one who ordered the death of so many of mine?" Pando asked.

"I give it to Garrett willingly. What he does with it is no concern of mine," she said evenly.

"I see." Pando took the crown in her hands and placed it upon her head. The crown twisted, bent, and reshaped to fit her.

"Daughter," Druesha said, "if you choose to stay here, you will be free to roam this planet, but I ask you to strive for harmony with the humans. It is time to forgive."

"Do you believe the humans will strive for peace with us?" Pando asked, her voice even.

Pete pushed forward from the crowd, holding Governess's hand in his own. "They will. We will make sure of it," Pete said.

"Pete? What are you saying?" Garrett asked.

"I... I'm saying Governess and I are..." He looked at her.

Governess nodded, giving Pete the reassurance to say whatever he was going to say.

"We're staying here, Garrett."

"Pete, you don't have to do that! You can both come with us," Garrett tried, his stomach knotting as a lump formed in his throat.

"Garrett, I know, and I'm sorry, but peace will take work and understanding. Together, Governess and I can help drive the change that needs to happen. And… well, I love her."

"You are a human. What you are saying is an impossibility!" Pando snapped.

"I love Peter Ashwood as well, my queen," Governess said.

Pando's eyes flashed. "Love… a human?"

Jurupa's face twisted in disgust. "Sister! What has happened to you? Has the human done something to you?"

Governess looked at Pete. "Oh, yes. He most certainly has."

Pando glanced toward the short, greasy man. "This is blasphemy and punishable by death!"

"Hold, Duroia Hirsuta," Druesha warned, turning her attention back to Pando.

The small tree creature bowed and stepped back.

"You scold her for loving a human, yet you appear before me in a human woman's form," Druesha said. There was no anger in her words, only the simple truth. "Do you not like the form I created you in?"

"No… I mean, yes, of course. I… I only appear this way to show the humans they are no longer in control."

"That is a very strange way to show this, daughter."

Turek cleared his throat, his eyes darting from Druesha back to Pete and Governess.

Druesha's canopy nodded. "Pando, I have learned that love is a strange thing indeed. It seems it sees no race, no color, and, well, no species. Love has proven time and time again to refuse to obey any rules we impose."

"You are gods. Can you not control this?" Pando asked.

Turek lifted his voice. "It's time you all know the truth."

Garrett looked around the temple roof as the attention of every creature present hung on Turek's next words.

"Turek, what are you doing?" Ereshkigal asked.

"Telling them, Eresh." Then, lifting his voice once again, he said, "We are not gods. We are creators. It is true we created all of you. But we, too, were created. We call the one who created us the Great Mother. Consequently, we cannot control love as we did not create it, nor did we create hate, fear, or happiness. These things came from the Great Mother. So you see, Queen Pando, love follows no rules."

But Garrett noticed Turek was no longer looking at Pando or Druesha. Instead, his stare was fixed on Ereshkigal.

Silence fell as a purple gust of snow blew through the portal, melting as it crossed the threshold.

Pando creaked, and her body twisted to face Governess. "Love between a tree and a man may be possible, but a physical bond simply is not. Will your love be enough? A human's life is such a momentary thing. Perhaps you can sustain this infatuation until the human dies. Only a tiny blink in time to a tree."

Garrett saw Pete's face fall.

But Governess was quick to respond. "I will love him for as long as I can despite any obstacles you point out. And further, my queen, our love shall be the bond that brings humans and trees to a place of harmony. This shall be our life's work, for I have learned the power of friendship," she said, looking at Garrett, Breanne, and the other sages. "I promise you, my queen, it is a bond worth having."

"Thank you, Larrea." Pete's smile had returned, but it

The Last Gift

seemed forced now, and Garrett could see Pando's words had really shaken him.

Turek and the other gods nodded, and Garrett had a suspicion something was happening. Some internal mind speak he couldn't hear.

Turek approached. "Governess? I would like to give you a gift."

Governess frowned apprehensively.

"It's alright, dear, you've nothing to fear." Turek placed his hand upon Governess's shoulder. "There, how do you feel?"

"You did something to me. What did you do?"

"I suspect you and Peter will have many, many children."

Governess's eyes went wider than would have been possible had she been a human.

Turek laughed at the cartoonish facial expression. "I can take it back. If you would like me to?"

"No!" Governess answered quickly. "No. I want nothing more!"

Jurupa huffed, turning her back to Governess and the others and disappearing back down the stairs the way she had come.

Governess gave Pete a consoling smile. "It is alright, Peter Ashwood. In time, my sister will see. Everyone will see."

"Peter, come forward," Druesha said.

Pete stepped forward. Druesha placed a branch upon Pete's shoulder. "Oh, this is tricky. Help me, brother," she said.

Turek placed a hand on the opposite side of Pete's shoulder. "Ah, yes, maybe just a little more here."

They stepped back. Pete looked around, then looked at his hands. "What is it? What did you guys do?" Pete asked.

Turek grinned. "You shall see in time, Peter."

"Oh, come on!" Pete pleaded.

Druesha laughed, rattling her golden leaves. "I will give you a clue. You'll have some five thousand years to practice the new gifts we've given you."

"Yes, plenty of time to make the world a better place – together." Turek grinned.

Pete blinked. "Five thousand?"

"Give or take," Turek said.

"This is against everything you taught us!" Pando said.

"Pando, the descendant has paid the debt. It's time to forgive and move toward tomorrow. Can you do that?" Druesha asked.

Pando nodded slowly. "Yes. The boy has kept the promise." She looked at Governess. "If the humans want peace and treat us with the respect we deserve, then peace is what they shall have."

"Splendid," Turek said.

Pando creaked again, her body twisting to look upon Breanne, Paul, and their dad, who stood huddled to Garrett's right.

"Moores, you will be happy to see your Ed Moore is unharmed."

Ed appeared from the stairwell. "Pops!" the musclebound man shouted, running toward them from across the roof. The family embraced, all smiles and tears, as they hugged and laughed. Garrett's own emotions found his eyes blurring.

Turek cleared his throat. "Now, I think it's time we depart. James, if you would please direct the Keepers through the portal. Let's get you all home."

Garrett, Lenny, David, and the others crowded around Pete.

"Are you sure you want to stay here, bro?" Lenny asked.

"I am sure," Pete said. "Look, guys, you have all been good friends to me and I am going to miss you like hell, but

I have to stay. It is... I do not know, a sort of feeling deep in my gut telling me if I do not stay, Earth may not have a chance."

Shawn from the Ultra Six stepped forward. "Pardon me, folks. I'm still not sure exactly what on Earth has got us to this point, but I got enough of the gist to know you two are the key to the future of the human race," the soldier said, addressing Pete and Governess. "I'd like to offer our services in helping to get you in front of the president of the United States. With us backing you, he will listen."

Pete looked at Governess, who smiled and nodded. "Yeah," he said. "Yeah, we would sure appreciate that, Shawn."

Garrett tried to fight back the tears by blinking them away, while David didn't fight them at all. Crying openly, he grabbed Pete in a bear hug, laying his head on the boy's shoulder, and squeezing. "I'm going to miss you so much, Pete!"

"I know," Pete said, hugging him back, his own eyes watering.

Garrett couldn't stand it anymore, piling on and then feeling Lenny's long arms wrap around his back and squeeze.

Choked for words, Garrett struggled to find the right ones. "See you later" wasn't in the cards. Finally, he managed, "You take care of yourself, Pete."

Green light crackled through Pete's eyes. "I will, Garrett Turek, and you do the same."

"Lord Garrett Turek, I will personally see to it that Peter Ashwood is in good care," Governess said.

Smiling at the two, he said, "I know you will. And thank you for everything you've done, Gov. I never thought I'd say this, but I'll miss you too."

"As will I. Take care, my lord," Governess said.

Breanne stepped forward and gave Pete a hug, then

turned to Governess and, for the second time since they'd met, wrapped her arms around the shorter woman.

This time, however, Governess returned the embrace, and the two hugged.

"Farewell, Breanne Moore."

"So long, Governess," she said, wiping her cheek.

Garrett took Breanne's hand, and together they walked toward the portal.

Garrett glanced back one last time to see Pete standing hand in hand with Governess, a huge smile plastered across his face. The couple were flanked by the Ultra Six and Pando. Pete nodded and smiled.

Garrett nodded back and stepped through the portal.

71

Reunited

God Stones – Moon Ring 6
Osonian

Breanne, the sages, and the Keepers sat in the massive courtyard under the canopy of Metsavana. A cluster of purple clouds had moved on, allowing the new arrivals to witness the suns as they began their journey back toward each other. Soon they would embrace in forbidden love, a precursor to ebon night. But for now, the sky was on full display, with all seven moons smiling upon the unlikely crowd. The large space was full of Osonians as they came and went, eager to get a glimpse of the creators. Eager, too, for a glimpse of their new king.

Long tables were quickly erected, and a feast to rival any Breanne had seen was spread out. Strange meats, fruits, and vegetables crowded the tables. Wine and beer filled cups as elves and humans alike ate, laughed, and sang. Food and song, it seemed, were a universal language. And while the language barrier prevented the Earth-born humans from conversing with the people of Sky, neither could speak with the elves. This was a problem to be sure, but one that was quickly remedied when David agreed to part with the Eyra of Tunga, allowing it to be passed around.

Breanne sat at a table covered in a golden cloth with ornate embroidery barely visible between the trays of meats and vegetables, some of which looked familiar, some of which looked completely foreign. Next to her, Breanne's father was introducing her and her brothers to Emily, who was preparing to visit a hursue stable. The woman with the long black hair and knee-high boots seemed excited to see the horse-like creatures.

"I hear they can even talk!" she said.

Breanne smiled. "They can. I heard it myself when I got to ride one earlier."

"Oh, I can't wait!" she laughed.

Breanne's dad explained how the woman had owned a large horse ranch back in Petersburg, and the God Stones had opened a special ability for her to heal animals, similar to how David could heal people. The woman hugged Breanne then and smiled fondly at her father. Breanne caught something in the exchange. It was subtle, but she knew her dad, and she knew that smile. Did he *like* like her? She blinked, realizing she'd stopped following the conversation.

"Those hursue can run faster than any horse I've ever seen," Paul was saying.

"Fast indeed," Rán said, as she floated next to Paul. "They are Durin's creations. My brother has created many four-legged creatures. He truly has mastered the art of land speed. Typhon created an animal called the pegasus that looks quite like the hursue, but each has a set of beautiful, feathered wings. Much rarer, the pegasus," she said matter-of-factly. "Now Durin would tell you Typhon simply stole the design from him and added wings, while Typhon would insist just adding wings would not simply give a creature like the hursue the ability to fly. I say the truth is somewhere in the middle."

As fascinated as she was to learn that pegasuses existed, Breanne decided to capitalize on the distraction of Rán's explanation. "Dad?" she whispered.

"Yes?" he whispered back in a curious tone.

"Is she married?"

Her father lifted an eyebrow. "Emily? Well, no. She was, but she is recently widowed."

"Uh-huh," Breanne said.

"Don't you give me that look. I am far away from being ready for anything like that. But it was a long journey, and she has been a good friend. We've both suffered much loss."

"Uh-huh," Breanne repeated, turning her attention back to the courtyard.

As bellies filled, the Keepers strayed from the tables, gathering and taking inventory of the few belongings they had carried with them. Others dozed near the fires, unable to fight their exhaustion, while still others couldn't get enough of song and dance.

Word soon came that King Ogliosh and his army had chased away the Earth-born nephilbock and then vanished into the southern forest, leaving the battlefield in front of the wall clear for all to come and go safely.

It must have been around this time the party truly began. As the language barrier dissolved, Keepers, people of Sky, and Osonians alike gathered around the fire pits to sing and tell stories of their adventures.

The people of Sky explained what the Keepers could expect on their upcoming travels to Cloud. Of course, no one would come or go today – not until they were sure that giants, whether Karelian or Earth-born, were no longer in the vicinity. Breanne hoped she would never see Ogliosh, or any other giant, ever again. After a couple of days' rest, the humans would make their way back through the Shadow Forest to their new home, the city of Cloud. Until then Breanne hoped to get some rest and of course time to explore the ancient city of Osonian.

Stone approached Garrett, who was sitting on Breanne's other side. "My lord, I feel my skill as a stone bender will be better served working with stone rather than leading armies. If you will allow it, I wish to remain here to assist with the repairs at the wall."

Garrett placed what looked kind of like a chicken leg onto his plate and nodded. "We have Tell, Paul, and Ed to advise and lead the armies. I agree. Please, stay and help Lenny and the others with the wall modifications."

There was a conversation Breanne needed to have with Garrett. She had been named Queen of Cloud, and she didn't know what that title meant for the future of the men and women of Cloud or her role in helping bring them together. She wasn't sure what Garrett wanted, but she only hoped he realized how much work lay before them from a cultural and government perspective. Not only would they have to deal with the issues of societal unrest between men and women, but now they were also introducing another thousand Keepers from Earth who would no doubt have completely different ideas about how society should be structured.

She wished she could talk to Key. But Key was gone, and it hurt her heart, but more, she knew Tell would struggle. She'd lost her mom, and Breanne knew the days to come would be hard. Tell would need her.

Breanne also wondered: What did Turek want? Did he have a plan? Did it even include her? She felt doubt seeping in… she felt like an imposter. A queen? Her? Who was she kidding? Still, if he hadn't had some plan, why would he have whispered her name on the wind? Had he just been using her to unite the women with the men? She watched him now, walking among the Keepers and the people of Sky. The creator made his rounds – all smiles, standing here and there. One moment he was by a fire pit, hands gesturing as he laughed. The next he was weaving in between fountains and statues of what must have been important elves from the past. Turek seemed to enjoy himself as he visited, telling stories, and laughing with childlike pleasure. She smiled too, watching the joy and happiness spread through the crowd.

Breanne decided answers to her questions would have to wait. Right now, she wanted the moment to stretch out – to stretch out and never end. She was with her family, her friends, and her people.

Typhon, standing alone on one side of the courtyard, seemed more than ready to leave. Most did what they could to avoid going near the scary-looking dragon with a hundred heads.

Then the great dragon stepped forward and cleared his throats. "Brothers and sisters, it is time for us to depart," he announced. Then, addressing all present, he said, "Creations of Karelia, the time of the God Stones is over, and thus the balance we longed to create among our creations is no more. I wish you all the best on your quest for balance and peace. But be warned, by your very nature, you are different. You have different desires... different needs. I am skeptical you will make it long without war, but I look forward to the show. Queen of Queens Zerri, I do not approve of you or your relationship with this human. Do not expect help from me when your weakness for humans costs you everything."

Zerri seemed to stand straighter then, giving Typhon a formal nod that Breanne read as "challenge accepted."

"Well, that was a buzzkill," Lenny said.

"Typhon, please... a moment before you go?" Rán asked.

"Do you not mean before we go?" Typhon asked in his grizzly bear voice.

Breanne frowned, wondering what was happening. The mermaid, who hadn't left her brother's side since first she appeared, floated forward into the center of the courtyard. "Brother Turek, if you could join me."

Turek, looking pleasantly curious as he broke from the crowd of humans, joined Rán in the center of the courtyard.

Around them, the Keepers and Karelians fell silent. Elves froze in place, giving the two their full attention.

Breanne looked over at her brother, Paul. "What's happening?"

"I... I'm not sure," Paul answered, his brows knitted in confusion.

"Turek, do you remember when you said that we should all live at least one life as our creations and that you had lived many? You told us of making love, of having children, of growing old."

"Indeed, sister Rán," Turek said, smiling. His eyes seemed to twinkle knowingly.

But Breanne didn't know, and as she looked around at Garrett and the others, it was clear no one else knew where this was going either.

"I want to do the same thing."

The other creators looked at each other in surprise.

Turek only nodded. "But not as one of your creations?" he asked.

"No, Turek. Not as one of mine."

"Sister Rán!" Ereshkigal gasped.

"Oh, shut up, Eresh," Rán said.

Breanne couldn't help but smile as she struggled to stifle a giggle. She liked this Rán.

"Will you allow me to live as one of yours, brother?"

"Of course, but does he desire you in the same way?"

The Last Gift

Rán looked back at Paul.

"Paul, what's going on here?" her father asked.

Paul stood up. "I love her, Pops. I love her," he said, louder this time.

Breanne looked at her father and Ed, making no effort to suppress the giggle this time.

Ed stood up and clapped, and then everyone started clapping. Even the elves who'd seemed to segregate themselves to one area of the courtyard applauded.

Paul walked forward, and when he reached the floating mermaid, he kissed her softly on the lips. "I love you."

"Well, that's good enough for me," Turek said. "Please, sister, allow me to help." He took Rán's hand in his own. "But be warned, my dear Rán, while you are immortal, your body will not be. You will feel pain and joy. You will feel energized and tired. You will sleep and you will eat, and—"

"And I will love," Rán cut in, smiling up at Paul.

"This is what you want?" Turek asked.

"Are you sure, Rán?" Paul asked.

"Oh, yes, I have never been more certain. Will you have me forever?"

Paul didn't hesitate. "Yes. Yes, I will."

"Then it is done." Turek's own hand changed into white light, while Rán changed into something else. At first, Breanne had to shield her eyes against the brightness of swirling color, of light strange yet familiar.

Next to her, Garrett was able to put a word to it as he whispered, "Sentheye."

The mermaid's shape transformed and Rán settled to the cobblestones, standing on bare feet she hadn't had only a moment ago. As the light faded, what remained was a woman in white silk that hugged her perfect frame. Her milky white skin was different now, as if kissed with just the right amount of sun. Her cheeks showed a hint of rose while her long silken black hair remained unchanged. So too were her eyes unchanged, as they sparked crystal blue.

From the center of the circle, Turek said, "I give you Rán, the human."

The courtyard, balconies, and stairs erupted in applause.

Breanne felt Garrett's hand slip into her own and squeeze.

"Look at them. They're beautiful," Garrett said.

Breanne smiled.

Typhon did not smile.

As if to show support in her own strange way, Zerri lay down on her belly. Gabi ran up her tail and sat upon her back.

Gabi? What are you doing? Breanne called in mind speak.

We're going to stretch our wings! The little girl giggled.

"Outrageous! This entire world is out of control," Typhon said, directing his glare upon Turek. "Brother Turek, you left this world as an outcast and return as an infection! You, a virus on our world! A disease destined to spread. All who can hear, be warned! The only cure for a plague is annihilation!" And with those words, Typhon was gone.

The crowd erupted in gasps, followed by urgent chatter.

Turek raised his hands. "Not to worry, good creatures of Karelia. My brother just needs time – time for you all to prove him wrong!"

Zerri flapped her wings, and Gabi shouted and laughed. Then up they soared, high above Osonian, vanishing around Metsavana's monolithic canopy.

The crowd of humans and elves quieted, and a slow clap built into another round of applause.

Breanne started to say, *Be careful, Gabi!* But she stopped herself, then blushed, realizing she would sound like her own mother.

Garrett smiled. "Gabi will make a good ambassador between humans and dragons."

Breanne turned in her chair to face him. "Garrett... I... I need to talk to you. I wasn't going to do this now, but I need to understand the plan."

"The plan?" Garrett asked as the applause died down.

"The plan for us – for them," she said, motioning to the people. "They are coming from different places, and you heard Typhon. He doesn't believe we can maintain peace among the species and to be honest, I'm not so sure we can even sustain peace among ourselves – not without a lot of work."

"I see," Garrett said, meeting her eyes. "So what are you asking me?"

From behind them, a woman cleared her throat. "I'm sorry, I didn't mean to eavesdrop," Elaine said, sitting down next to Garrett. "I think what she is saying is that you, Garrett, as the leader of the humans, have much work ahead of you."

And there it was. Exactly what she'd feared. Elaine expected Garrett to lead. His people expected it. And she was sure the men of Cloud would expect it too. Still, she felt her heart sink. She didn't know why, but something didn't feel right about this. She shook her head. Was she really expecting she would lead? Would she even be allowed to lead alongside him? "Just tell me how I can help," she managed, feeling her heart sink even deeper into the pit of her stomach.

"Mom, I—"

"I'm sure Garrett will appreciate your support as he takes on this most difficult challenge of leading—"

"Mom!" Garrett interrupted.

Elaine drew back. "What did I say?"

"Sorry, I didn't mean to yell, but... Listen, I did what I

did these last several weeks because you, James, and Phillip told me I had to. I never wanted this! I begged you not to make me do this alone. Instead, you sent me into a temple to face Apep, a giant, and a two-headed dragon! And need I remind you, I died!"

Breanne scanned the courtyard, which had fallen silent at Garrett's raised voice.

"Garrett, it's okay," Breanne said.

"No, it isn't. Everyone, can I have your attention?" Garrett said, sliding his chair back and standing. He held out his hand.

Breanne took it and stood, her brows bunched in confusion. "Garrett, what are you doing?"

He led her to the area Rán and Turek had just occupied. Turek stepped to the side.

"Everyone," Garrett began, "we need to get something cleared up. Breanne Moore was named as the chosen one to lead the people of Cloud." He motioned to Turek. "Turek himself named her on the wind for all to hear. This was proven when Breanne Moore passed the test of prophecy given by the late great Lady Key. After which, Lady Key herself named Breanne Moore as Queen Breezemore, the true queen of Sky! So hear me now! Let Turek himself witness! No matter if you are man or woman, Earth-born or Karelian, our future will be decided under the rule of Queen Breezemore!"

Breanne's eyes teared up. She had no idea what to say. So she said nothing and instead threw her arms around Garrett and hugged him with all she had.

As the two suns Ellis and Soul finished their journey across the sky, just beginning to join, Osonian erupted in applause for the third time.

Turek cleared his throat and motioned with his hands for silence. "It is true. I spoke your name on the wind, for what I knew had to be done, only you could do." Turek reached out, offering her his open hand. "Step forward, daughter."

Breanne swallowed, her mouth going suddenly dry as she placed her hand in the creator's.

"May I?" Turek asked, motioning at the simple crown upon her head. She'd forgotten she was wearing it.

Turek held the simple crown in his palms and closed his eyes. Sentheye, bright and white and good, flowed from Turek's fingers into the crown. Fine lines of silver, gold, and ember swirled around each other, twisting and braiding into ornate designs ending in small vertical spears of crystal.

The glow faded.

Turek smiled and placed the new crown upon Breanne's head. "There now. A special crown fit for the true queen of Sky," he said, and gave Breanne a wink. Then, turning to the crowd, Turek lifted his voice. "Should this crown find its way onto the head of any other than the true queen of Sky, sickness and death shall follow." Turek let that hang heavily in the air for a moment, his head scanning the crowd. "Good. Now that things are as they should be, I give you your queen!"

Again, Osonian erupted in applause.

Standing next to the old man, Breanne smiled and waved, as she searched the crowd. Her brothers were clapping, and her father was crying. She motioned them forward, and they rushed into the circle, all hugs and laughs. Lenny and Tell were there too, crying, hugging, and laughing through the tears.

Tell smiled. "My mother would be so proud of you, Bre. I only wish she'd been able to see Turek for herself. To know she was right all along."

Breanne smiled curiously. "To know she was right?"

Tell's eyes glistened. "She is so beautiful."

Breanne's frown deepened as she followed Tell's gaze over to the old man.

"Turek reminds me so much of my grandmother," Tell said, a tear rolling down her cheek.

Breanne gasped. Turek's attention found her then, and their eyes met. The creator's own eyes seemed to twinkle, and he gave her a knowing wink. Breanne put a hand over her mouth and laughed in wonder. *We see what we need to see,* she thought in amazement.

"Excuse me, Breanne," Elaine said, pulling her attention from Turek.

Those around her fell silent.

"I just wanted to say that I'm sorry about earlier. I... I didn't know. Please forgive me and know that I... I'm so proud of you. I'm so proud of all of you!" she said, tears running freely down her cheeks.

Breanne embraced her with a hug, and it was warm and good. They stayed there in the moment laughing and crying, hearts happy and full of joy, until a golden glow caught her eye from across the courtyard. As she turned, she found a crowd gathering around David, who'd just healed a man's arm. Judging from the man's bloody sleeve, it had been some sort of flesh wound. The small crowd cheered, drawing the attention of others.

James passed through the crowd, assisting a man who couldn't have been much older than her own father. Holding James's arm and leaning heavily on a cane, the man slowly shuffled forward.

"Come on, you guys, Let's go see our boy in action," Lenny said, as others lined up to see if they could get a turn with the healer.

As they reached the center of the small circle, David stood, wobbling momentarily but bringing it quickly under control.

The Last Gift

"David, can you help Mr. Bradbury? We think he slipped a disc back in Arkansas."

"In Arkansas?" David asked.

"Yeah. Trust me, you don't want to know," James said.

Mr. Bradbury grunted. "That's a memory I could sure do… do without."

David nodded, placing a hand on the bent man's lower back. "I'll sure do my best, James!" The golden glow swallowed David's hand, spilling into the man's lower back.

A curious frown spread across the man's face as he slowly stretched upright, as if waiting to feel the agony of his efforts. "I can't believe it! I… I don't feel anything!" Mr. Bradbury tossed his walking stick into the crowd and danced a jig.

The crowd laughed and cheered.

As more wounded were making their way up from the shore, an elf walked into the circle, still clad in blood-splashed armor from the battle. The tall warrior bowed and asked, speaking dökkálfar, "I have badly wounded soldiers in the infirmary. Will you come there and heal them?"

In perfect dökkálfar, David said, "I'm sorry, but my gift won't work on elves."

The elf looked disgusted. "You come here and eat our food, gulp down our drink, but you won't share your gift! My soldiers are dying!"

"No, it isn't like that!" David tried.

The elf spit at the ground, turned, and marched away.

"I don't know why it won't work on your kind, but it just won't! It isn't my fault!" David shouted after him.

"It's okay, David. I'll explain it to them," Lenny said consolingly.

"How are you going to explain it when I don't even understand it, Len! Christ's sake, I healed a rat back in Petersburg! I healed Kilug! But I couldn't heal Coach Dagrun, and I can't heal any other elves!"

"Perhaps I can explain," the kind voice of Turek chimed in.

Breanne turned to see him standing behind them.

"Did you know I did not create the rats of Earth?"

David frowned and shook his head.

Breanne exchanged a curious look with Garrett.

"No, indeed. You see, it was my brother Durin who created the rat. You may think them not his finest work, but they are impressive creatures. They can chew through just about anything. Did you know that?"

"Yeah, I saw a giant rat tear apart a nephilbock once! And I'm not talking about the Earth ones, I'm talking about a full-grown Karelian giant," David said with a shiver.

"Hmm. Yes, the pyramid in Petersburg. I remember. Forgive me, I digress," Turek said.

Durin appeared next to Turek, and Breanne wasn't sure if he'd come from the crowd or had just materialized.

"Telling stories about ole Durin, er ye?" the dwarf creator asked.

"Just bragging about your achievements with creation, brother."

"Durin, this is David." Turek motioned to the boy.

"Aye, I remember ye. The boyo with the golden touch."

"He can heal humans, rats, and dwarves, but not the dökkálfar," Turek said, raising a shaggy grey eyebrow at Durin.

"Hmm. Have ye tried to heal a nephilbock or a dragon?" Durin asked.

"No, sir. I haven't healed a giant or dragon. I stay good and far away from them if I can help it," David said.

"It wouldn't matter, brother. He couldn't heal them either," Turek said.

"Then why he be healing mine if he's one of yous?"

Turek laughed. "Come on, brother. I expected you to

solve this by now. When you first created dwarves, where did you create them?"

"Aye, yer not sayin' what me thinks yer sayin'?"

"You created your first version on Earth."

"But me took them all back to Karelia, Turek – I'm sure of it!"

"Not all, Durin." Turek laughed even harder now.

"Yous saying this one 'tis as much mine as yers?" Durin asked.

"I'm saying he has the lineage, miniscule as it might be. He has it!" Turek was bent now, hand on knees.

"I don't know what ye laughing fer!" Durin said with annoyance.

"It seems our creations have been breaking the rules since the beginning of creation itself!"

"I'll be damned! David's a dwarf!" Lenny shouted, joining in on the laughter.

Kilug stepped forward. "Brother!" he said, somewhere between a shout and a growl. He threw his massive arms around David's stomach and squeezed.

"Put… me… down," David said, dropping his staff on the ground.

Kilug dropped the boy, and David immediately reeled on Lenny. "Just you shut up, Len, or I swear you're getting all the elf jokes I've been saving up!"

"This explains why you're only as tall as my belly button, your dwarven dental drapes, and the fact you had a five o'clock shadow at the age of four," Lenny laughed.

"You didn't even know me when I was four!"

"I've seen pictures, you little fur baby!" Lenny shot back.

"You know what, Len? How about we talk about your ears!"

"Well, come on, kid, let's see what you got!"

Breanne giggled as the two began their familiar back-and-forth banter.

"David, I believe this is yours." Turek chuckled as he handed David the staff.

"Um, thank you!" David said nervously. "Mr. Turek, can I ask you something?"

"Of course, David."

"Can you tell me about this staff? Lenny said it was yours."

"Oh, well, let me see now. Yes. Yes, I believe I made that in the time of the Templars and passed it on to my dear friend John Brockridge."

"And it's made of some special wood, right?"

"Hmm, yes. I believe I made it of olive." Turek narrowed his eyes at the staff.

"Olive? Okay, but I didn't see any runes on it. Did you imbue it with Sentheye, or was it some other magic?" David asked.

"Imbue? Um, no, David. It is for all intents and purposes, well, just a stick. Granted, it is a fine staff, if I do say so myself, but it is only that."

"But I don't understand. I saw magic come from the staff three times now! It must have something inside of it." David's eyebrows knitted together. "It killed a nephilbock only this morning!"

"Yes, I saw. Do you know who that nephilbock was?"

David shook his head.

"He was Zebrog, the leader of the king's High Guard. Quite an adversary, that Zebrog. He has killed hundreds of humans. Did you happen to see his necklace of shoes?"

The thought of the giant with the tennis shoe necklace caused Breanne's skin to goose pimple.

"But… how did the staff do it?" asked David.

Breanne looked around, seeing the looks on the faces of

all of David's friends. They all knew the answer, but David still hadn't caught on.

Turek glanced around at the knowing expressions and knelt down, leveling his eyes with David's. "My boy, if only you had the faith in yourself that your friends have in you. I will tell you a secret."

David's eyes brightened, excitement filling him at the prospect of finally learning the truth.

"The magic did come from inside."

"I knew it!" David blurted.

Turek held up a hand. "But! It came not from inside the staff."

David frowned again.

Turek reached forward, his index finger poking out from the sleeve of his robe. He touched David's chest. "It came from inside you."

"Me? But... but how?" David asked.

"Your love for your friends. You see, when your love for your friends reaches beyond your own fear, you become a powerful mage, David. Indeed, you become a dangerous foe."

"Me?" David whispered.

"You," Turek whispered back with a mischievous smile.

Lenny threw his arm around David's shoulder. "I tried to tell you! I always knew you had it inside you! But I think Turek's got it wrong."

Turek raised a thick brow. "Oh?"

Lenny nodded. "Yep. It's probably all stored up inside that fur trap of yours! Better tell him never to shave that dead pelt off his face, Turek!"

"Dwarves do not cut their facial hair, elf!" Kilug said, crossing his thick arms.

Both Turek and Lenny busted out in renewed laughter, and Breanne couldn't help but smile. She scanned the crowd, watching the women and men interact with elves and each other, part of her filled with hope. Maybe they had a chance. Maybe, despite their differences and the past, they all had a chance after all.

A voice spoke to Breanne from her opposite side, and as she turned, she found Turek standing next to her. She frowned. The creator had just been standing by Durin and laughing with Lenny and David only a second ago.

"My good Queen Breezemore," the old man said, as if he were proud to speak her new name. "May I trouble you to borrow Garrett for a moment? I promise a brief absence and a speedy return."

"Of course." She smiled, feeling her face flush at the formality.

Garrett nodded, leaned in, and kissed Breanne on the forehead. "I'll be right back."

72

The Walk

God Stones – Moon Ring 6
Osonian

Garrett followed Turek out the back of the courtyard, opposite to the end they had entered. A stream to his left ran clear and deep, fed from a pool at the base of the tree. The crowd was still thick, with elves coming and going. From above, crimson petals danced on the breeze as they drifted downward like oversized feathers to land gently on the stone. A young elf – Garrett guessed him to be ten, but he'd no idea how this equated in elvish years – carried a woven basket, his eyes downcast as he collected the petals. The boy practically ran smack into him before he finally looked up with a gasp, eyes widening.

"It's alright," Garrett said.

The boy turned and bolted. Garrett wasn't sure if it was because he was human or if the boy knew who he was. Then again, maybe the boy knew who Turek was.

They walked on in silence, finally reaching the shore, where the stream spilled lazily into the open water. Iron-forged grating stretched the length of the stream, obviously put in place by the elves to keep the creatures of the ocean away from the father tree. Idly, Garrett envisioned Lenny ordering it removed from the stream and Saria rolling her eyes.

Beyond the shore, water stretched on as far as his eyes could see. They were on a different side than where they had crossed, near the bay, and Garrett realized they were staring out into the open ocean.

Turek stopped and turned back to face Garrett. "Garrett, I want you to know I'm very proud of you," he began.

Garrett felt his face flush with warmth. Not knowing what to say, he managed only a nod and muttered, "Thank you."

"I don't know if you fully understand what was at risk, but if you hadn't stopped Jack… If any harm would have come to Metsavana… Well, it could have meant the end of life on Karelia. For instance, your willingness to sacrifice yourself to get Jack to release the others, and then once Breanne helped you believe…" Turek shook his head, as if momentarily lost for words. "Garrett, your decision to show mercy to the dragons rather than destroy them is, frankly – well, it's the single reason Typhon is tolerating any of this. It's why he hasn't killed Zerri and probably Gabi too. But my brother also understands it is you and your sages who saved us all, my boy."

"Saved you all? I'm… I'm sorry I… I only did what felt right. And I don't really understand all this," he said, building his nerve to ask what he really wanted to ask. The question that had been playing at his mind since Typhon had said what he said.

"What's troubling you?" Turek asked.

Garrett drew in a deep breath. "Before Zerri gave me her God Stone, I heard Typhon say he'd won the game. I think his exact words were something like, 'Because my chosen are the only ones who still have a God Stone, I have surely won the game.'" Garrett met Turek's eyes. "Was all this a game?" he asked, the question having more bite than he meant for it to.

"Oh, dear boy, this was far more than a game. True, there were rules, mostly about interference, but it was to prove… well…"

"It's okay. I don't think I need to know all that. But I need to know this was something more than a game creators play."

Turek smiled apologetically. "It was more. So much more."

"Did you?" Garrett asked.

"Did I?"

"Did you prove whatever it was you were trying to prove?"

"My, you are an intuitive lad," Turek said, shaking his head. "I'm afraid the honest answer is yes… and no."

"The prophecy said that I had to right an ancient wrong. Did I do that?"

"Your questions are indeed difficult. But yes, Garrett. Yes, I think you must have."

"But didn't you make up the prophecy?"

Turek winced. "That too is complicated."

"Okay," Garrett said, smiling apologetically, although he didn't know why he should feel apologetic. "So what happens now? Are you going to leave us?"

"Ah, good question. I have much business to attend to with the work of creation, but I will be checking in."

Garrett nodded, bent, and picked up a small stone. He chucked it, skipping it six times across the glassy water.

"Garrett, may I ask you a question?"

"Well, sure," Garrett said, straightening.

"What is it you want?"

"Huh?"

"What do you want? Obviously, it isn't to be an emperor or a king."

"I got everything I want. The people on Earth are safe. Pete will see to that. We got the Keepers here. I got my mom and James. I got my friends."

"And you got the girl," Turek interjected.

"I was getting to that part! You save the best for last, you know." Garrett grinned, then said, "And she's not just any girl. I got the queen of the human race."

Turek laughed. "Indeed, you did!"

Garrett's face flushed warm again. This time, he'd embarrassed himself.

"Let me put it another way," said Turek. "What are you worried about now?"

"Well heck, I was so busy feeling relieved I haven't thought about it."

"I think maybe you have. You leave this place on the morrow, Garrett. It will take you a few moon rings to get back, even with the more direct route through the forest to the Mazewood."

Garrett nodded.

"Lenny won't be going with you."

Garrett's face fell.

"Even if you both had two of the fastest hursue, it would take you the better part of a moon cycle to meet in the middle. I'm afraid a busy king won't be able to make the journey often."

Garrett hadn't figured out the specifics, but the thought had been there in the back of his mind. Lenny was his best friend in the whole universe. For several years, he had lived just across the alley. The two ran cross-country, took martial arts, and did everything else together. There hadn't been a day in Garrett's memory that he and Lenny hadn't spent time together in all the years he'd known him. His stomach knotted, his throat clenched, and he'd be damned if he wasn't about to cry right here on the spot. Embarrassed, he turned away, wiping his eyes on his sweater.

"Don't be ashamed of your love for your best friend. On Earth, it was commonplace for kids to be friends, grow up, move away, or just grow apart. People fall in love and start families. One day, you look around and realize you haven't talked to your best friend in years. Now, because of the task laid upon you and your sages, the outcome will require distance. Look at Pete and the decision he made to leave all of you for what he believed was right. Now, in a smaller sense, you are being asked to do the same with Lenny. And since it will not be convenient for you to see each other, the likely scenario is that you will grow apart."

Truth or not, Garrett didn't want to hear this. He didn't want to lose Petersburg, his home, his dad, his school, Pete, and now Lenny too. Not Lenny too! But unfair as it was, he knew it was the truth. All of it. The women, men, and children waiting back in Cloud needed them, and he and Bre had to get the Keepers and the soldiers home.

"But..." Turek said, letting the word hang in the air.

Garrett looked up, desperation filling his eyes.

"I can help you. I will help you." He smiled.

Garrett didn't understand, but it didn't matter. Help. He needed help. Desperately, he needed help. Relief filled him, and he blurted, "Thank you!"

"This is the least I can do. Hold out your hand," he said mischievously.

Garrett did so.

Turek placed his own hand lightly over the top of Garrett's. Warmth filled Garrett's palm as the old man's hand transformed into a burst of pure Sentheye.

Garrett tried to watch, but the brightness became too strange to look upon. It hurt not just his eyes, but his mind. Turning his head, he slammed his lids down tight, squeezing them for all they were worth. When he finally opened them again, the light was gone and sitting atop his open hand was the old, wrinkled hand of Turek.

"You remember the rune coin David has? The one that gives the ability to know a language after only a few words are spoken?"

"Sure, the Eyra of Tunga," Garrett said.

"That's right. Did you know Ereshkigal made it?"

"No… I didn't know that."

"It's true. She gave it to a king long ago and long forgotten. She would say it was created to help bridge the gap and bring peace, but unfortunately, this is not how the elves used it. Instead, they used it to learn the secrets of their enemies. But again, I digress, as that is another story for another time." He pulled back his hand to reveal a palm-sized medallion crisscrossed in a cradle of silver wire. Like the Eyra of Tunga, this too had runes engraved upon it. But rather than being made of metal, this medallion looked like it was made of some type of precious stone. It was like Ice Ember, except that it was an opaque turquoise in color. A sort of cloudiness filled it, as if he were looking into a crystal ball.

Garrett lifted the medallion to find a silver chain pooled beneath it.

"May I?" Turek asked.

Garrett nodded, not taking his eyes off the strange gift.

Turek lifted the medallion by the chain and draped it over Garrett's head. "Perfect!"

"I am about to teach you a word from the language of the creators. If you are standing in the courtyard of Cloud and speak it twice in a row, you will arrive in the courtyard beneath the father tree. If you are standing in the courtyard of Osonian and speak the word twice, you will appear in the courtyard of Cloud. This item will take you nowhere else. You need not worry about protecting the word – the item will only work if you speak the word. If anyone else speaks the word, it will not work. This medallion will transport up to seven, including yourself. You need only hold hands."

Turek spoke the word once.

Garrett repeated the word once.

"Good," the old man said.

"Turek, thank you so much! This means more than you could know," Garrett said, his face stretched in a smile.

Turek nodded. "Garrett, one more thing. You may not want to hear this, but in time I think you will see I am right."

Now Garrett's own brows bunched with curiosity. "What is it?"

Turek's childlike expression vanished and his face became serious, making him look the ancient being he was. "Darkness has not been snuffed out, my dear boy. For us to have light, there must be darkness. Its ember burns even now and eventually it will grow to flame."

Garrett nodded along, but he'd no idea where this was going.

"You don't desire to be a king, nor an emperor. Fine. I know you think you're not a leader, either. But those who follow you would say otherwise, Garrett Turek. And when darkness rises again – and it will rise, for it must rise – you will be called to serve. I needn't ask you if you will answer the call because I know you will. It is in your very nature to do so – to protect those you love and to protect those who can't protect themselves."

Garrett shook his head, his face filled with worry.

"Don't look so grave. I only tell you this now so that you may brace for the inevitable. You have time, and you have those you love." Turek smiled, his youthful expression returning.

"Turek? Can I tell you something?"

"Of course."

"What you said earlier about not completely proving what you hoped to. I don't think that's over for you yet. I... I think you've still got a chance."

"Oh? What makes you say that?" Turek asked, his wild eyebrows bunching up like two caterpillars preparing to wrestle.

"I just got a feeling," Garrett said.

Turek smiled curiously. "Thank you, Garrett. Now, best get back to your friends. They will want to hear all about this new item you have."

Garrett smiled at that. "You bet they will! David's going to freak out! Hey, what about you?"

"I'll be along in a few minutes."

"Okay," Garrett said, throwing his arms around the old man.

Turek laughed and gave Garrett a hug that was much firmer than an old man ought to be able to give.

Garrett didn't walk back. He ran, excited to join Bre, Lenny, David, and all the rest! But as he hit the stairs, he hesitated, stealing a last glance back at Turek. The old man's expression seemed sad. *Whatever you're looking for, Turek, I sure hope you find it,* Garrett thought.

As for Garrett, his heart was heavy too, but for different reasons. For his heart was weighed down with love, happiness, and the promise of tomorrow in a new world with the girl he loved. He had a sky full of sunshine, his friends both new and old, and a world full of magic waiting to be explored.

From the direction of the courtyard, Garrett swore he heard a guitar playing and people singing. Was that Lenny?

The Last Gift

Where did Lenny get a guitar? As he drew closer, the voice became clearer. "Purple rain, purple rai-ya-ain!" It was Lenny alright, and he was playing "Purple Rain." The smile fixed stupidly on Garrett's face was so big it hurt as he dashed up the stairs toward those he loved and whatever tomorrow held.

Epilogue: Turek

God Stones – Moon Ring 6
Beneath the Father Tree, Karelia

Turek watched as Garrett climbed the stairs. Just seeing the boy so completely happy should have filled his heart... should have. Yet still questions remained unanswered. What was the ancient wrong that Garrett and his sages had to right? Was it that all races should be free to love as they chose? Was it returning his humans back to Karelia? Perhaps it was making amends with Pando and the trees of the Earth. Surely saving Metsavana from imminent death and thus saving themselves was righting an ancient wrong? After all, the father tree was as old as they were.

A curious sound pulled Turek from his thoughts.

"Hoo! Hoo! Hoo hoooooo!"

He glanced back in the direction Garrett had gone. There on a stone wall sat a familiar bird. Turek's eyes widened, but before he could react, the owl turned its Sentheye-filled eyes away from him. Then, with a flap of its wings, it glided down toward the water.

The Last Gift

Hurriedly, Turek followed the strange owl, practically running to keep up, but this time it didn't seem to be trying to lose him. No. This time, he felt like it wanted him to follow.

The owl reached the water's edge and landed on a stone, where it watched him with unblinking eyes as he approached. Turek rushed forward, excitement filling him. When he was nearly within reach of the bird, it flapped its sparkling wings again, this time flying out over the water, where it turned back toward him and froze perfectly still – very unlike an ordinary bird.

Twenty yards out over the water, the owl folded its wings and hovered there, a man's height above the water. Impossible for an owl – impossible for any bird. Water was no barrier to Turek. Frowning curiously, he stepped onto the bay's smooth glass-like surface. Beneath his feet the water rippled; the hem of his robe became wet, but he did not sink.

Turek stepped forward again, prepared to cross the bay or the entire world if it were required. But as his foot touched down again, the world around him changed. Turek gasped. He was no longer standing on the water. In fact, as he looked about, he realized he was no longer standing on Karelia. He came to this conclusion not because he knew every inch of Karelia – he most assuredly did not. Even areas of the planet that he did remember had likely changed since last he'd seen them. No, he knew this was not Karelia due to what he saw, not what he failed to see.

Turek was now standing atop an all-too-familiar temple positioned atop a pyramid – a pyramid in Mexico. Across from him, the bejeweled owl sat atop the Sound Eye altar, sparkling in the moonlight. How was he here? When was he here? He glanced around at the strange scene.

The *how* he didn't understand at all. He'd seen no portal. But the *when*... well, the clues were all round him. The burning tree, the decapitated head of Apep, and sleeping giants told him he was experiencing the time just after Garrett and his sages had entered Karelia. Soon, James and the others would burst from the forest to find the portal closed. Then it would open again, and he and all the other creators would be there. He was in the moment in between. How was he here? More importantly, why?

The owl spoke. "You have many questions, my child."

Turek gasped and fell to the floor, pressing his forehead against the cool stone. "Great Mother! I knew it was you! I knew it had to be you!"

"Stand, Turek. Children should not bow to their mother," the owl said, transforming into a being of Sentheye and taking on the shape of a human. Turek stood on shaky legs. "Let me see you as I created you," she said. With her words, his human form fell away, revealing him in his true form. "Yes." She smiled approvingly. "Now come forward."

Turek felt himself being drawn to her. Her arms wrapped around him in an embrace.

Warmth washed over him, through him, and he wept. "I knew..." he started, but choked on the words.

"Do you know why I have brought you here – to this very place?" she asked.

Turek looked around, having momentarily forgotten where they were. He shook his head. "No. I've no idea."

"Have you not been asking yourself what the great wrong was?"

"I... I have. Yes. In the beginning, I made the prophecy to see if you would show me... if you would give me a sign." His words seemed silly now, standing before the Great Mother. "I mean... yes, of course."

She smiled, and it made Turek smile even wider. "Child, we are in the place in time where your children will soon realize Garrett has left them behind. In the place before you,

The Last Gift

young Garrett, and his sages will open the portal once more and save James, his Keepers, the Moores, and the others."

Turek nodded, having already realized this.

"You see, time is not a linear thing, but you already know this. What you don't know is time is not a circle either. It doesn't spin like a web or twirl in a spiral. Time is shaped like the planets, like the stars, like the universe itself. Time is a sphere. Inside the sphere, time follows rules. For example, a portal can only be opened to a specific dimension as far back as the last time it was opened.

"But then how—"

"How indeed? Let me try and explain. If one can move in and out of the sphere that is the universe, then choosing a place in time is truly limitless. Understand?"

Turek heard the words, but they made little sense. "I don't understand."

She nodded consolingly. "It is a hard concept to grasp."

Below them, people were shouting and running up the pyramid stairs.

"I brought you here to witness what would have happened should your sages have failed to open the portal back to Earth. I brought you here to understand. Brace yourself, child."

They stood silently as time flashed forward. And in only moments, Turek watched as six months passed. He watched as every Keeper died. He watched as Elaine lost her mind before she too died, along with Charles Moore, his son Ed, and finally James Paul. As Turek continued to watch, he wept uncontrollably. More time passed... months more. Pando rooted to the ground, as did all the trees. Meanwhile, an uncaring Earth continued to spin. "They all died horribly," he breathed.

"Oh, yes, and not just them, but all your remaining humans – billions. That is, until the portal opened again."

"Then this was the ancient wrong?" Turek asked, his heart aching.

She nodded. "It was, but so were all those other things you were thinking of. Saving the father tree. Bringing harmony and unity among the races of Karelia. Well, just look at Gabi and Zerri! I truly expected the girl to be eaten! There is still some work to do among the other favorites, but it is a truly magnificent start." Her eyes brightened then, and she smiled. "Breanne, now in a position to lead humans into a future free of discrimination. The others finding their own purpose too. Lenny and David!" She gave a childlike giggle. "Oh, Turek, they are so good!"

Then she became serious once more. "Jack and Garrett both found their true purpose, even though it cost one his own life. Still, in the end they both showed they were very much your children. One poisoned with darkness, the other overflowing with light."

Her smile widened again. "And you! Oh, you I am most proud of! Showing your brethren there is more to life than sitting inside a mountain creating. Showing them they too need to live and enjoy their creations. Just look at Rán!" She laughed again. "What a surprise! Oh, and I am truly sorry for that business of locking you all inside the mountain, but it had to be done. I feared your brethren would intervene, and I wasn't having it. You had brought them too far to throw it away." She clapped her Sentheye hands. "But you taught them, Turek! You taught them to keep their faith, and in the end you showed them the Great Mother is out there watching! Whether they learned it to be truth is still a mystery only to be discovered by the passage of time."

"But you are here, and you made it all work out. You have always been here!" Turek said. "And this is what you wanted me to understand? That you have always been here?"

"Turek," she said, smiling, "you are the only one of my

seven children who has always known the secret to creation. The others create, but you understand creation."

Turek didn't know what to say.

"You understand life isn't yours to rule. You have done your part and set them on the right path, but your brothers and sisters still have much to learn about letting go of their creations. But not you, my child! You know! And this brings me to my purpose and the purpose for revealing myself to you now."

Turek felt Sentheye surging through him, reminding him of the time he'd spent as a human. The times when excitement would cause his heart to rack against his chest.

"What I want you to understand is this. I have been watching you for some time. Yes, I manipulated your prophecy. Yes, it was I who visited in the dreams of your chosen. It was I, forever in the background, offering small encouragements, pushing here and nudging there. Oh, nothing too obvious or blatant."

"But why?" he asked.

Her face became stern, perhaps even angry. "When your brethren turned their backs on you, forcing you to flee Karelia, they were wrong. You don't know how close I came to punishing them for what they'd done to you. Not just you, but Ellis, Soul, and their child – guilty of nothing but love! Still, I refrained, deciding instead to observe. When your humans multiplied on Earth so quickly, well, it was plain to see you needed help. But I admit that wasn't my only motive for interfering. I knew how much you wanted the Great Mother to be real, just as I did... just as I still do," she said.

Turek blinked. The air sucked from him, hope suddenly ripped away, like a rug being yanked from beneath him. He couldn't have heard that right. "What? What did you just say? As you still do?"

She nodded, her smile widening. "It has always been you

who understood, and it is you... you of the seven I feel are ready to join me on my quest."

"Your quest?" he asked, panic rising inside him.

She nodded excitedly. "My quest to find the Great Mother, of course. Like you, I have been looking for the Great Mother my entire existence. The key to finding her is to find the beginning of time – or perhaps the end, but admittedly, I've yet to find either," she said, a look of puzzlement crossing her face.

Turek suddenly felt sick, like a nephilbock had punched him in the stomach. "But I thought—"

"I know what you thought," she interrupted. "And technically, I am your mother. After all, I created you and the others, but I am not the one who clapped her hands together when there was nothing and created everything."

Turek dropped to his knees, then sat back on his heels, his mind reeling.

"Do not be upset, Turek. I can show you the universe as you have never seen it. You cannot possibly imagine how vast this universe truly is. To be honest, I'm still not sure. I can teach you how to travel through time in ways you can't even understand. Sometimes, in ways I don't even understand. That's why I need you, my child. What I don't know, we will learn together. Join me on this adventure, and together we will find her!" she said, offering him a hand.

"What of Karelia? What of my brethren?" he managed.

"You have shown them the way. I think they will be fine without you."

All of this, and she wasn't the Great Mother. Turek's mind spun. He'd been so sure, but none of what he'd seen, either here or back on Earth, was the Great Mother. Now what? He could go with her. He could go and truly seek the Great Mother. Turek looked at her.

"Yes, Turek. Come with me," she pleaded.

The Last Gift

"What is your name?" Turek asked.

Looking slightly embarrassed, the being of light said, "I spent so long alone, if ever I knew, I've long forgotten."

"Are you the only one the Great Mother created in all the universe?"

"I don't know. There could be more of us out there. Perhaps we will find out? Turek, what would you like to call me?" she asked earnestly.

Turek looked up at the sky full of stars. "I think I would like to call you Tara."

"Ah, yes. It means star in some ancient human language, does it not?"

Turek nodded.

"I like that," she said, smiling.

"Tara, do you remember the dream where you spoke to Garrett and he asked you if you were god and you said no? Then he asked, 'Who is god,' and you answered—"

"I answered she is the mother. The one who clapped her hands when there was nothing and then there was everything. Yes. I remember," Tara said.

Turek nodded sagely. "After that, Garrett saw some of his loved ones who had died. His father, Phillip, and his teacher, Mr. Brockridge. You made him see them? You brought the dead to his dream?"

She looked curious. "No. I saw nothing of others. Did you see them, or did he tell you about them?" Tara asked.

"It doesn't matter. Tell me, Mother Tara, where do we go when we die? And where do our creations go?" Turek asked.

"Mmmm. Perhaps when we find the Great Mother of the universe, we can ask her."

Turek stood silent for a moment. "You didn't bring Garrett back from the dead on the riverbank, did you?"

"No. Even I can't bring someone back from the dead."

"Can you go back in time and change the outcome?" he asked.

She cocked her head curiously. "No. I have tried. This example I showed you wasn't time being changed. It was simply two alternate timelines. I couldn't change how either transpired by going back."

"Yet, you were here and able to manipulate events with, as you said, slight nudges."

"It is complicated. Those things I did in real time or for the first time. I could not now go back and change those things."

Suddenly Turek wasn't so sure this being of Sentheye had as much figured out as she thought. But this lack of knowledge presented Turek with a revelation. "Tara, what image were you created in?"

"What a strange question. I was a spherical creature, a ball of light. But soon I found this shape" – she held out her arms – "which is more practical. I was pleased so many of my own children elected to create in much the same image."

"I see. A spherical creature in your true form," Turek repeated, nodding slowly.

"You're not coming with me, are you?" Tara asked.

Turek shook his head, a bright smile lighting his face. "I want to go home to be with my creations, my brothers, and my sisters."

"But don't you want to find her?"

Turek shook his head. "I don't need to look for the Great Mother anymore, Tara."

Tara's colors flashed through her body of light in shock. "You're giving up? I didn't expect this of you, child."

"No. I'm not giving up," Turek said assuredly, and he suddenly felt very, very good. "I've already found her."

Tara shook her head. "Oh, dear child, I've already told you. I'm not her. This isn't some trick or test."

The Last Gift

"No. I know it isn't a trick. And I know you're not her. But don't you see? The Great Mother can't be found. She isn't hiding in some corner of the universe." Turek laughed, and he couldn't stop. The longer he laughed, the harder his laugh came until he was roaring with laughter.

"I don't understand," Tara said, her face a mix of confusion and delight.

"The answer has been... been in front of me this whole time!" Turek gasped, trying to speak between bursts of laughter. "The Great Mother didn't clap her hands when there was nothing and create everything. She was the clap itself! She is all around us. She is everything. She is everywhere. The Great Mother *is* the universe!"

Tara shook her head. "No. No, that can't be right."

"Oh, Tara. It is absolutely right. All this time, I thought we were created in the image of the Great Mother – arms and legs, a torso, and a head. But you created us in the image you found practical. Not your true image! And what is the universe but spheres, planets and stars, dimensions? And what are we at the microlevel? What is Sentheye at its most basic structure? Spheres, Tara! Spheres of power too small for most to see! We are all created in her image. You said time is a sphere! I say the Great Mother *is* time! We are all the shape of the universe – and maybe, just maybe – we are all the Great Mother after all!"

Tara's face washed in white Sentheye like a human face draining of color, her shaking head telling Turek she didn't understand, and her words confirming it. "You're speaking gibberish, child. The Great Mother is real! She is out there, and if you come with me, I will show you."

"Yes! She is real indeed. Oh, I am sorry, Tara, but I already see her," he said. For the first time in a long time, he was happy with his place in the universe. He knew what the

Great Mother wanted. He knew his purpose. "Tara, will you take me home, please?"

Tara's shoulders sagged, and she forced a smile, but there was no joy in it. "Are you certain?"

"Never have I been more sure of anything," Turek said, unable to suppress his own smile, so full and true and glad.

"As you wish, child. Step toward me and you will be home."

Turek lifted his foot… then paused. "Will you come back with me? I know the others will want to see you – to know you. Come and be with us!"

Tara's smile fell away. "No, child. I am happy you feel content. However, there are still many secrets of this universe yet to be discovered. The greatest of all is finding god. So, you see, the search for the Great Mother must continue."

Turek nodded. He couldn't blame her. She would need to come to her own conclusions in her own time. "Thank you for this time, Mother Tara. I hope to see you again."

Warm colors swirled within the mother creator, and her smile brightened. "As do I."

Turek stepped forward and, when his foot touched down, he was standing on the shoreline. In front of him, Metsavana stood tall and proud, whole cities hanging from its massive branches. In the distance, music played and people laughed. He imagined their arms intertwined, spinning and dancing. Oh, how he wanted to dance!

Turek was finally home and for the first time, maybe ever, his heart was full.

Acknowledgments

As always, I want to thank my dear wife. Once again you allowed me the time I need to create my crazy stories, and for this I thank you and appreciate you.

Mom — even today, many years after your untimely departure from this world, you still inspire me in my life and my work. I miss you.

I want to thank my editing team, specifically Kristen Tate at the Blue Garret. We did it! We finished a whole series! As always, you made editing fun and I learned even more through the process. As bittersweet as this is, I am already looking forward to our next project!

A special thanks to the readers who took the time to not only read my work but also review it. Reviews are incredibly important to authors and I appreciate each and every one. It's like warm apple pie with just a little bit of ice cream on top… only better.

Finally, I want to thank my friends and colleagues who read the early drafts, for the conversations on the long Saturday trail runs and over lunch at work. Thank you for getting excited with me.

Otto Schafer, April 2023

About the Author

Otto Schafer grew up exploring the small historic town in central Illinois featured in the God Stones series. If you visit Petersburg, Illinois you may find locations familiar from the books. You may even discover, as Otto did, that history has left behind cleverly hidden traces of magic, whispered secrets, and untold treasures.

Otto and his loving wife reside in a quiet log cabin tucked away in the woods. When Otto isn't writing you can often find him running the forest trails near his home, deep in a tangle of thoughts he'll need to rush home to put on paper.

Sign Up to Read More

Garrett and Breanne's adventure has concluded, but this author still has many more stories to tell. If you want to start a new adventure with me, please sign up here and I will be sure to keep you abreast of how the next story is progressing. Just click here to sign up or go to my website: www.ottoschafer.com.

If you enjoyed this book, I'd love to hear from you and hope that you could take some time to post a review on Amazon. Your feedback and support will help this author continue to create future works for your enjoyment. I want you, the reader, to know that your review is very important and so, if you'd like to leave a review, just go to my author page on Amazon. I wish you all the best and thanks again.

Check out my website and blog here: www.ottoschafer.com

Connect with me on social:

Instagram – www.instagram.com/ottoschaferwriter

Facebook – www.facebook.com/ottoschaferauthor

TikTok – www.tiktok.com/@ottoschaferauthor

Made in the USA
Monee, IL
14 April 2025

15605258R00381